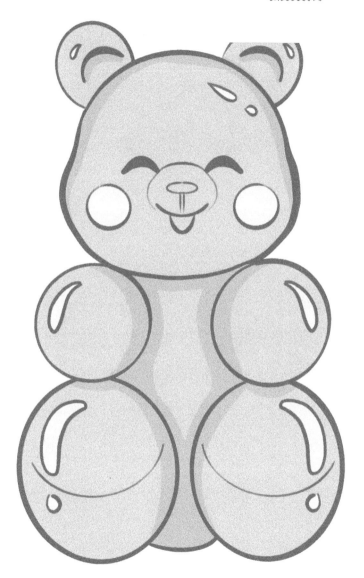

Pinky Promise

Rebecca Rennick

For everyone who's burnt out from heart wrenching fantasies & dark emotionally charged novels. Take a breather.

Part of

The Gummy Bear Orgy Series

Sweet but naughty Rom-com's

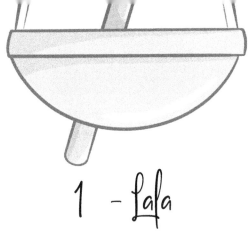

1 – Lala

Turn his frown upside down

I'm kissing a strange man in the middle of the street. Granted, he's a very attractive stranger, but a stranger nonetheless. I just couldn't help myself. He looked so grumpy and frowny, and I just wanted to turn his frown upside down. Maybe make his day just a little bit better. I mean, really. Who would be upset if a girl with pink hair sexually molested them in the middle of the afternoon while walking down the street minding their own business? Ok. I can see how that could sound bad, but it isn't. I swear. Let me rewind a bit and you'll see.

I had decided to try the brunch spot Fawn had suggested the other day at Pilates class, Bella Italia. She claims it's the best place in town for gnocchi—my favorite. So, of course, I had to test her claim. It's a personal goal of mine to try every restaurant, or food, my friends tell me is "the best". If not to prove them wrong, then to enjoy the deliciousness that is food. As a traveling nomad, being a foodie is kind of a requirement. There's no way I could travel the continental United States without trying the local cuisine, now is there? Ok, granted gnocchi is not really a local dish but it is made locally and bragged about by locals. Therefore, local cuisine.

Earlier Paloma ran into me (literally) while on her morning run and decided to tag along. Being five years younger than me, she has far more energy to burn on the reg running her standard two miles every other morning. Most mornings I prefer to wake slowly, shuffle around, and wait for my chai tea to brew before making my chai tea latte. I feed Fred, my ferret, his breakfast, and pick out my pink outfit for the day. Sweating and running are not my forte.

I met Paloma and her twin sister, Pilar, through their social media account. Each of us have a love for all things color, specifically; Paloma loves blue, Pilar loves yellow, and of course, I love pink. Looking at the two of them side by side, it's like if you drew the same exact picture but one is cyber punk in every shade of blue imaginable and the other is sweet floral cottage core in buttery yellows. We had connected and become online friends, and even met up now and then at conventions or renaissance fairs. When they'd told me they were parked in a tiny house village in Pittsburgh—and I didn't feel like spending another southern summer in Savannah, Georgia—I decided to drive on up here. It's nice coming to a city and already knowing people. Made it easier to acclimate. Not to mention they already knew great places to go for fresh produce, shopping, and hair maintenance. Keeping your hair in pristine pink condition is no easy task. Most of the time I do it myself to one, keep the cost down, and two, so I don't have to worry about some new person messing it up. But every now and then, you just want to go to a professional and let them handle the mess you've made.

Today Pilar is busy, so it's just me and Paloma sitting at the cutest outdoor table like we're at an Italian bistro in the Piazza de Spagna. Lounging under yellow and white striped umbrellas, on buttercream yellow riviera dining chairs. Pilar would have loved it.

Pinky Promise

If Pittsburgh doesn't work out, maybe I'll take my nomad life-style overseas to Italy. I'm sure there's some way to get Tallulah, my remodeled pink school bus—aka a Skoolie—to Europe. There are boats that do things like that, right? I suppose I'll have to register it there and get a European driver's license. Perhaps I'll just get a new vehicle for my European adventures. Like a van. That would make it easier to navigate those ancient narrow roads.

Oh, and I can't forget Fred. He'll have to be up to date with all his shots before we leave, because there's no way I'm going without him. Fred, my albino ferret, well, he was albino, now he's pink. I give him a beet juice bath every so often to give him his glossy pink coat. Anyway, he goes everywhere with me. He has since I rescued him from a shelter I volunteered at for a few weeks one summer five years ago in Montana. Who knew they were more popular than hamsters in big sky country? Not me, until that summer.

Fawn was right, this place is adorable. I may have to come here more often. The street it sits on is large enough that there's a steady stream of cars but not so busy that I'm worried to jay walk for fear of going splat. There are other restaurants and independently owned stores lining the sidewalk. Fawn told me this neighborhood has been on the up and up for the past couple of years. Bringing in developers, small business owners, and young families. From what I can tell, it's a pretty nice place.

One store is a rather enticing roller skate shop called Wheel-ies, that I very much plan on visiting there as soon as we're done enjoying our brunch. Well, lunch, really. We'd planned on it being brunch, but Paloma took a little too long primping after her run. Therefore, it's more of a lunch than a brunch.

Paloma's cobalt hair, expertly curled in soft beach waves that look effortless, but in reality take forever, drifts on the light breeze, pulling my attention back to my friend.

"I don't know what I should get. Everything sounds delicious. What are you getting?"

"The gnocchi, of course. I was told it was the best in town, and I need to find out if it's true."

She hums in thoughtful pondering while still perusing the menu. "I think I'll try the caprese pizza."

Good choice. One can never go wrong with caprese anything.

Food decided, I set down my menu and watch the people walking by. It's one of my favorite pastimes. People watching, guessing where they're heading and why. When you move around as often as I do, you get to see a vast array of different types of people.

Today being Saturday, there's a plethora of all kinds wandering the streets. Mothers pushing strollers in matching leggings and tops that you know have never seen the inside of a gym, men in khaki shorts chatting animatedly and checking out said M.I.L.F.'s as they walk by, and overly stylish teenagers typing away on their phones, carrying bags filled with their frivolous purchases.

I would have given anything to be a teenager in a city like this instead of the backwater country bumpkin town I grew up in. Not that it's a bad place. Just a little...detached from modern society. The corner store that's been there since the dawn of the dinosaurs didn't get a credit card terminal installed until my senior year of high school. The owner, Mrs. Witherston, had been using old school carbon paper copies until her grandson ordered, installed, and trained her on how to use the credit card terminal. We were all extremely grateful.

I can only imagine what people walking by think of *us*. We must look like two life-size human Crayola crayons. Me, the cotton candy pink, and Paloma the denim blue. We make quite a pair. If we could find a few other girls with granny smith apple green, mango tango, and purple mountains majesty hair, we could have almost a whole box.

We order our food with the friendly server, then I return to enjoying the spring sunshine. It's warm on my skin. Even though it's already April, it's not nearly as hot as down south. The breeze is cooling and fresh against my cheek, just enough for a sweater when the sun goes down.

"So, what are your plans for the rest of the day? Any markets on your schedule?" Paloma runs her fingers through her cobalt hair and turns her face to the sun. She looks like a sea goddess that belongs out in the water, not on land in the middle of a concrete jungle.

"Not today. Only every second Saturday. But tomorrow I have the Squirrel Hill Farmers Market in the morning." I've been setting up Lala Boba at the Squirrel Hill market for just over a month now, and it's been a decent steady gig, but I need more. One day a week just isn't cutting it.

"What about that convention you said you applied for?" Paloma clinks the ice in her glass, smoothing the condensation off the sides.

"Haven't heard back yet. It's not until July. But I should be hearing from them soon." Even if I do get it, it's only a one weekend event, a whole three months from now. Which doesn't help me or my bank account today.

"I'm sure you will. It's anime weebs. They all love Boba."

"That we do." I chuckle as the server appears with our meals. Placing a clean white plate with perfect fluffy looking gnocchi drizzled in pesto and roasted tomatoes in front of me and a crispy thin caprese pizza in front of Paloma. Who promptly takes out her phone and snaps a quick photo before placing her napkin in her lap and picking up a slice. Is that what followers want to see nowadays? What I'm eating for lunch? I'm not the best at maintaining my social media. It's sporadic at best.

"Finally. I'm starving."

"That's what happens when you run so much."

"There is nothing wrong with how much I run," she garbles around a mouthful of cheese bread and tomatoes.

"Says you."

We say little as we dive into our meals. I go in hard and shovel a spoonful of gnocchi into my mouth and *oh my Italian lover heaven.* I'm pretty sure a NSFW moan slips between my lips when I bite into the potatoey goodness. Reluctantly, I have to agree that Fawn was right. It is the best gnocchi I've had in town... so far. She's never going to let me forget she was right.

Speak of the devil, my phone chimes in my pocket with a text. It's Fawn, and like some sort of psychic she knows I've eaten the gnocchi and now wants to gloat.

Fawn: *So...how is it?*

Lala: *You already know the answer to that.*

Fawn: *True, but I like to hear how right I am.*

Lala: *Fine, you were right. It's fucking delicious. Pretty sure it just had sex with my mouth.*

Fawn: *Told ya.*

Fawn: *We still on for next weekend?*

Lala: *Absolutely.*

Fawn: *I think I know of a few more places you could set up your booth at. I just need to find all the addresses.*

Lala: *Sounds perfect. I can use any leads you have.*

Fawn: *No problem, honey. Happy to help.*

Lala: *Thank you soooooooo much. You're awesome! *star eyes emoji**

Fawn: *Of course. You still going on Thursday for Pilates? *smiley emoji**

Lala: *Absolutely. I have to do something to burn off all the gnocchi I'm going to eat this week *muscle flexing bicep emoji**

Fawn: *You're welcome. *winky kissy face emoji**

Fawn was the first local friend I made in Pittsburgh when I moved here three months ago. As soon as I arrived, I started scouring Groupon for places to work out on the cheap. Anything really—yoga, Zumba, tai-chi. I didn't care, as long as it was cheap. Pilates offered a free first class and fifty percent off your first month. Ding-ding-ding. Thank you, Groupon, we have a winner.

It was in my second class—the first one I actually paid for—that I met Fawn. She was all long legs and glorious caramel hair with her matching leggings and sports bra top. She sat down on the reformer right next to mine, complimented me on all my pink, and BAM! Instant friends.

We meet up once a week for Pilates on Thursday afternoons with smoothies after. Last week we were discussing our favorite foods, and she mentioned Bella Italia, which is how I ended up here today.

"Who was that?" Paloma asks around another mouth full of pizza.

"Just Fawn, flaunting how right she was about the gnocchi."

"Well, you did sound like you had a foodgasm when you bit into it. You can tell her the caprese pizza is also amazing here. Five stars, would recommend." Another slice goes into her mouth as she hums in delight.

The sun is warm, the breeze is light, my stomach is full and happy, and the world is bathed in pink through my sunglasses. Including the man who just walked out of the apartment complex across the street.

Dressed in charcoal gray sweats and a matching t-shirt, the man fills them out like it's his life goal to look sexy as hell in workout clothes. The sweats cling to his ass in a way I thought only possible in wet dreams. Sexy sweatpants man is frowning down at his phone as he shifts a small duffle bag hanging off his shoulder. The displeased look on his face only partially diverts from his attractiveness level. He barely takes a moment to glance at his surroundings. Either he has amazing peripherals, or he walks this path regularly. He's not walking quickly though, his steps slow to a stop in front of the coffee shop a few doors down from where he came, his gaze pondering entry.

"Well, hellooo hottie." Paloma comments. I don't have to ask who she's referring to because it was obvious the moment he stepped outside. A handsome man in gray sweatpants and a growing frown on his beautiful face is hard to miss.

"Agreed. Except for that epic frown and radiating grumpiness. He looks like he could use a hug."

"Or a good fuck. He looks...backed up."

My laugh emanates between us as Paloma joins in. "You're not wrong."

We could all use a good fuck every now and again. I know I could. It's been a while since my last romp in the sack with a man. That's what vibrators are for, after all, and my collection is extensive. Girl's gotta have options. I'm not always in the mood for the same old thing.

"So why don't you go over there and give him something to smile about?" Paloma wriggles her eyebrows suggestively at me.

"Excuse me?" I say, sliding my pink heart-shaped sunglasses down my nose and glaring at her over the top.

"You know how you're always spreading smiles and making people happy everywhere you go? Well, there's a needy subject right there if I ever saw one." With one hand, she gestures to the still grumbling sexy sweatpants guy whose attention goes from his phone to the coffee shop and back to his phone.

Again, not wrong. But I don't know this guy. He's just a stranger on the street. That could be his normal face. He could actually be super happy right now, and I wouldn't know it. "Should I just walk up to him and hug him? How do I know he doesn't have a weapon or know Krav Maga? Maybe he'll body slam me."

"One can only hope to be body slammed by a man like that," she says, longingly checking him out up and down.

"I don't know, Paloma. This is different than making jokes and dancing in the rain with someone I already know. What if he doesn't like being touched? What if he's a germaphobe and freaks out when I approach and start touching him?"

We both ponder in silence momentarily. Paloma speaks first. "Ok, how about this? You go over there and give that guy something to turn his frown upside down, and I'll..." She pauses for dramatic effect. "Come to the farmer's market tomorrow and stream live and blast your boba tea booth all over my socials to get people to come out and buy one."

Shit. She's got me. She knows I'll do just about anything to promote my business. I push it on my own socials but hers are far larger than mine, spanning in the multiple hundreds of thousands rather than my measly one hundred and two thousand. Ok, so that's not a horrible following to have, but still we all know half of those are bots. Since her and her identical twin, Pilar, post twin shit all the time, and are hot and funny to boot, it just naturally garners real followers. They call themselves PilPal, and it's so twintastic it's sickening. But it could bring more people to the booth...

Reaching out her hand she extends her pinky, wiggling it at me suggestively, knowing my weakness. *Damn it.* My pinky itches to reach out and link with hers. It twitches in my lap, and I give in and link it with hers.

"Ok, fine. You win. I'll go make that guy's day... I hope."

Paloma remains sitting and pulls out her phone, no doubt planning to record whatever ridiculousness is about to ensue. With me set loose on this poor guy I'm sure it'll be worth the watch. I quickly skip across the street, hands in my back jean shorts pockets feigning casual nonchalance, on an intersecting course with Grumpy McSweatpants. Who has decided he doesn't want coffee and has again resumed his walk down the street.

We collide in the front of some sort of artisan pickle store. Literally. I don't give him a chance to bob and weave or avoid me. I'm on a mission and I will complete it. His very happiness depends on it. My steps are brisk, and he doesn't see me coming till I'm on him.

On my way over I realized Paloma was right. He needs more than a hug, but since I'm not going to rape the man on the sidewalk, I figure a kiss would be the next best thing. Assuming he's straight. Jeez, I hope he's straight *and* unmarried. Luckily, my brain is functioning enough to check the ring finger on his left hand holding the phone that he's scowling at now. It's bare. Score one for Lala paying attention for once.

I don't think. I just do. Throwing myself at the stranger, who is even more attractive up close, a strange shiver runs through me, almost halting me in my tracks. But I don't let it. I don't let his brooding handsomeness and thick tempting black hair distract me, even though it's practically begging me to run my fingers through it and pull. His moss green eyes flash up at me right before impact. Shock and, surprise-surprise, irritation flashes in them. Probably angry I'm slowing him down on his journey to... the gym? Where else could he be going in sweats?

His lips are full and pouting, which only makes them more kissable. Smooth, clean skin brushes my cheek. He shaved this morning. I like a little stubble on a man, but there's nothing like running your lips over a smoothly shaved jawline. He, of course, does not respond to my embrace. Standing stone still, one hand frozen holding his phone, while the other, I realize, is loosely clasped at my waist. A natural reaction, I suppose, when having a body thrust at you. But his lips do not react naturally. They're still and uncooperative, slightly parted in surprise, allowing me to press fully into them but nothing more.

Since closing my eyes would seem inappropriate for a surprise kiss, I'm staring straight into his, and they are gorgeous. Of course they are. Men like him don't have flaws like thick thighs or a disproportionate ass to body ratio and are definitely not vertically challenged. No, he has perfectly lush thick lashes, a strong jawline that could make granite jealous, and shoulders worthy of a woman's legs wrapped around them.

His unresponsiveness doesn't alter the way I feel. Which is more than I should when kissing a stranger. Unlatching my arms from around his neck and my lips from his, I slide back down his body, because of course he's tall compared to my five-foot four stature. My hands slide down his chest, which much to my delight and dismay is rock hard. Oh, how I would love to linger and find out how much more of him matches that hardness. But alas, I said I would not ravish him, and by joe, I'm sticking to that.

Patting his chest, I look up into his furrowed brow, give him as much of a coy smile as I can muster, and in what I'm hoping is a sexy sweet voice, say, "Have a nice day."

See. Not crazy. Just trying to make a grumpy gus's day better. It was all in the name of happiness—and maybe a little self-satisfaction. I'm not actually sure I made him any happier, but I'm certainly smiling more. It's hard to read his expression as I saunter away and quickly cross the street back to a slack jawed, bug-eyed Paloma. Who was recording the whole thing... great.

2 - Henry

My sexual needs are being met just fine

What the hell was that?

The pink blur of soft curves and lips is gone before I even have time to contemplate what just happened. I'm left standing stunned and irritated and oddly... tingly. The heat of her body is already fading from her abrupt embrace and retreat.

Did that really just happen?

That woman just threw herself at me and mauled my mouth. That was certainly not on my schedule today. Only moments ago, I had decided I didn't want a coffee before going to meet Eddie at the gym. I wasn't prepared for... her. I don't know that I could ever have been prepared for that. Whatever *that* was.

It takes me a whole ten seconds to shake off the encounter, which is long enough for the woman to be back across the street, walking away with another woman with bright blue hair. From here, the only detail I can make out is her shapely ass covered in denim shorts. I wasn't paying close enough attention when she approached. All I recall are her bright aquamarine eyes, and of course, the pink. So much pink. Her hair, and who knows what else. It seemed to permeate around her in a fuzzy pink haze.

I hate pink.

Shaking off the odd *encounter*, I continue on my way. Whatever that was doesn't deserve the time in my day it would require to figure out. I have other things to do than try to understand the whims of a woman. Such as this escrow I've been trying to close on a building downtown that just won't end. The current owner keeps haggling with us at every step, wanting more and more with every passing day. He's not going to get it, though. If he won't accept our current offer, we're moving on to more aggressive tactics. I want this property. It's a good investment, but I won't overpay. Might have to implement some strategic negotiating that they will definitely not like.

Returning my attention to my phone and not the pink woman, I finish and send off the email to my assistant regarding the offer. Nothing will be done about it till Monday, because apparently people like their weekends off from work. Weekends seem like a waste to me. So much more could get done if people didn't insist on taking those days off.

By the time I slip my phone into my pocket, I've reached The Left Hook, the boxing gym near my condo. As soon as it opened six months ago, Eddie and I started working out here. The only place I'll commute to is my office. I like everywhere else to be in close proximity to my home. When I moved here two years ago, after buying the building I now reside in, I had to commute for everything. Dry cleaning, the gym, coffee, groceries. Thank the internet for Postmates.

There were a few stores here, yes, just none of which were up to my standards. Most of this area was old warehouses and vacant storefronts. There was a run-down VHS repair shop that really should have closed its doors decades ago. I mean really, who still owns a VHS player? There was also a sandwich shop that hadn't passed a health inspection in two years.

Once I helped push this neighborhood along, new businesses started opening on a regular basis, filling it with locally grown produce, hipster coffee shops, specialty stores, and a few renowned restaurants, similar to the Strip District. That was the original inspiration, after all. I wanted to duplicate the trendy neighborhood, but do it better. So far, I think my plan is right on track. Living in the area just means I'm right in the middle of it all to make sure it moves forward as planned.

Once people started hearing about the rejuvenated area of town, they began moving into the renovated condos and stylish lofts. Thanks to a few strategically run commercials, radio ads, and social media blasts. Now this area is growing, booming, and becoming what I knew it could be. It just needed a little direction. I may not own all the buildings and be able to decide exactly who leases them, but I know enough people to keep my finger in the water tracking the temperature.

The boxing gym, however, was a pleasant surprise. I wasn't sure it was something I would like, but after my first visit, I found it rather cathartic. Beating the shit out of another person without them pressing charges is a great way to exert agitation and release tension.

Entering the gym, I'm greeted with the smell of sweat and bleach. The sleek black boxing ring sits center stage surrounded by punching bags, weight benches and sparring mats. Instantly, a sense of calm washes over me, the strain of last week's work sliding off my shoulders.

I find my best friend, Eddie, and my brother-in-law, Leo, waiting for me near the receptionist's desk. They're both dressed similar to me, Eddie in basketball shorts and shirt, Leo in tear away pants. Leo only joins us on the rare occasion he decides to unglue himself from my sister long enough on the weekend to do more than have a quick cup of coffee. They're both busy with work during the week and rarely leave each other on the weekends if they can avoid it. That's how my sister ended up in her current pregnant state.

Her desire for marriage and family has always contrasted from my own. There are definitely no wedding bells or baby showers in my future... other than my sisters.

"Henry, you're late." Eddie reaches out a hand to shake in greeting and I accept it.

"Got distracted on the way here."

"You? Distracted? Impossible." Leo keeps pace beside me as we make our way to a line of punching bags to warm up.

"I was accosted by a woman." Shrugging my bag off my shoulder, I drop it onto a bench against the wall. Removing my phone from my pocket, I slide it inside.

"Excuse me?" Eddie stops me with a hand on my arm as I pull my fast wrap training gloves out of my bag.

"Accosted how?" comes Leo's surprised concern etched into his pretty-boy face, a blond lock of his abnormally silky hair falling across his furrowed brow.

"Some woman with pink hair flung herself at me and kissed me, then told me to have a nice day and walked away." I don't mention the slightly enticing ass I watched sway as she walked away. Turning, I slip my fingers into the glove and wrap the band around my knuckles and wrist, done with the conversation and attempting to begin my work out. The pink-haired assailant already made me late. She doesn't need to be any further cause of distraction.

"Hold on." Eddie's hand stops me again before I can take another step toward the bag. Groaning, I narrow my eyes at him. He ignores my subtle protest and keeps talking. "You can't just say something like that and not elaborate."

Eddie's a good guy. I met him my second year at Columbia, discovered we both hail from PA, and have a great dislike for keg stands. For the rest of our college career, we were roommates and study partners, working our way through frat parties and midterms alike. His family isn't as publicly known as mine, but still has a hefty bank account that would impress even the Kardashians. With a degree in business and the personality of a Labrador, he's done well for himself helping run his family's construction company. He's a smart businessman and a good friend. Unfortunately, his opinion on relationships is vastly different from my own. He's what you would call a hopeless romantic, with his classically handsome features and what I've heard women describe as dreamy brown eyes. He's had his share of possible Misses vying for his attention. Any mention of women in any capacity beyond familial grabs his attention. Which is why a stranger making out with me in the middle of the street is a giant blip on his love radar. He no doubt already believes she's my soul mate.

Why are the majority of my male friends more in love with love than most women? I suppose it's a better alternative than how my brother views women and love. As playthings and nothing more than an indulgence to pass the time.

"What is there to elaborate on? That's the whole story. Girl ran up to me, kissed me, then ran off. The end. Can I get to hitting the bag now? I'd like to work out some frustrations."

Eddie chortles under his breath. "Sexual frustrations, no doubt."

I still hear him. "Not even. My sexual needs are being met just fine."

"Not by a woman. It's been how many months since I've seen you go out with a woman?"

"I've rarely gotten more pleasure from a woman than I have my own hand. I don't see the point in dealing with the annoying hassle of making arrangements with a woman and ultimately disappointing her when she realizes I mean it when I say I don't do relationships."

Eddie and Leo stand scowling at me. I don't know why. They already knew this about me. My lack of desire for a relationship is nothing new. I'm just stating the facts.

Eddie is the first to shake it off. "That's just sad. Anyway..." He draws out the word like it can magically erase what I just said. "What did she look like? Was she hot?"

"How should I know? All I saw was pink hair and aqua eyes." That may be all I saw, but I also felt the skin around her midsection when her barely-there shirt rode up. Her skin was smooth and warm. But that fact has no premise in this conversation or at all—ever.

"That's it? That's all we get?" For some reason, Leo is more invested in this than he should be. He's not as annoying as Eddie when it comes to my romantic relationships, but being married to my sister, I'm constantly getting berated from every angle. They all want me to find that "special someone." That one girl that will make me change my ways and decide marriage is what I want, after all. If I were them, I wouldn't hold my breath.

"Why do you care? It's not like I'm going to ever see her again."

"You don't know that. She was in your neighborhood. Maybe she's a new tenant in one of the apartment complexes." Leo's optimism at the possibility of me seeing this woman again is highly unwarranted. As if this momentary encounter was kismet, and by some cosmic magic, we will find each other again when we least expect it.

He really should get out more and interact with people other than my sister. Her happily ever after belief in love is tainting his view of reality.

"I doubt it." I attempt to return to my workout, succeeding in getting a few rounds in finally.

"So that's it? Something interesting actually happens to you that has nothing to do with work and you just brush it off."

"Yes."

At my obvious lack of interest in this conversation, they both drop it, thank fuck. Because I really don't want to talk about the pink-haired girl anymore. She's in the past.

Moving on.

Leo puts on his own training gloves and stands on the opposite side of the bag, holding it still while I jab and punch. Hitting the sand filled leather instantly releases the tension from my shoulders that has built up over the past week. My swings hold a little more power in them than normal. Sweat trickles down my neck within minutes.

"You're still coming over next week, right?" Leo asks in between my jabs.

"Of course, your wife won't let me miss our monthly obligation. Samson's not trying to worm his way out of it again, is he?"

"Not if he values his life."

We both know my sister would literally disown him and never speak to my younger brother Samson ever again if he were to miss one of her mandatory family dinners. Well, sibling dinners. Our parents aren't exactly the hugs and kisses Sunday brunch type. Especially after the divorce. Malcom Bardot and Lucielle Cartwright have barely spoken directly to one another since I was twelve, a good eighteen years ago. Using their assistants, schoolteachers, nannies and rudely worded expletive text messages as their preferred form of communication instead.

Samson and I made sure our sweet, heart of gold sister stayed that way. Seeing only the good side of our parents and lives. Ensuring she turned out way less cynical and disdainful towards life than the rest of us. That doesn't mean she didn't know things weren't normal or right. None of us are close to them. Even though I work with my father at his real estate firm, we are strictly business associates, nothing more.

My father owns the top real estate firm in the city, Bardot Real Estate & Management. My mother owns Diamond Star Real Estate, second in the state only to dad's. She was less than pleased when I chose to work for Father right out of college. His firm specializes in large apartment and condo complexes, business centers, and commercial real estate, as well as managing some of said properties. Mother, on the other hand, went the residential route. Selling multi-million-dollar penthouses and townhomes.

I don't really fit into the smile and nod and bake fake cookies to sell a client on buying a home. I'm much better at terse negotiations and precise contracts. I'm not there to coddle and woo a worrisome couple picking their forever home. I'm there to make money and help others do the same.

We finish at the gym an hour later, dripping with sweat, my muscles burning. Leo leaves with a skip in his step, heading home to his wife. Eddie is off to get ready for his date tonight. No doubt he's already picking out flowers and color schemes for their wedding. I don't have the heart to tell him anyone he meets on Tinder is not likely to be the future Mrs. Edward Saint James. More like the future ex-Mrs. Saint James, along with half his money.

If it comes down to it, I'll make sure that doesn't happen. I won't stop my friends from getting married if they're truly in love, but if I smell a gold-digging liar, that bitch is history. Even if it breaks poor naïve Eddie's heart temporarily.

Stepping off my private elevator into my penthouse, I head straight for the shower. Walking briskly across polished concrete floors and past an expertly mounted one-of-a-kind watercolor, the only color in my entire place, then through the wide double doors to the one and only bedroom.

My style is modern minimalism with sleek lines and very little color. The only color other than black, gray, and white in my wardrobe is navy blue. Once, a woman told me all the color I needed in the world resided in my eyes. I blocked her number the next day. I have also hated my vibrant green eyes ever since, wishing they were bland brown. That would be more suited to me.

As they say, eyes are the window to the soul and mine lacks the vivacity that is the verdant green of my eyes. It may not be completely black and soiled. I do still *have* feelings. It's just not as bright and shiny as the desperately optimistic would like it to be.

There has been plenty to dampen my soul and kill all delusions of happily ever afters. Reality is not as forgiving as fiction. Having a child does not always make things better. Staying in a loveless marriage does not always work itself out in the end. Pretending does not turn into truth with pure will power.

I may not believe in love, but that doesn't mean I shit on other peoples. When my sister announced she was getting married, I congratulated her and bought her a full ten place setting of real silverware. She loves entertaining.

After a shower and protein-heavy late lunch, I sit in my ergonomic desk chair and turn on my computer, scrolling through new listings and sales, checking the flow of the market, what has gained and what has lost. Returning emails and opening my paper mail. Cleaning and organizing my life, so when Monday morning hits, all my ducks will be in a row and the week set and ready for me.

3 - Lala

Meet any nice boys?

For most people, Sundays are a day of rest and relaxation. A time to chill out and lay back, take it easy. Walk around your house in your underwear and eat whatever the fuck you want. For others, it's a day to wake up early and make their way down to the local farmer's market for fresh produce and locally made honey and cheese.

Now historically, I've been a firm member of the former club. Sleep in and slink about in oversized cardigans and leggings while binging some new docuseries on Netflix. However, owning your own business really makes you reorganize your life. I am not part of the "up at five a.m. on a Sunday" crowd, if only out of necessity. Driving to the market and setting everything up before people start to show between seven thirty and eight takes carefully orchestrated practice. Especially when I only have one employee... well helper. I pay her a little cash under the table to help me at the market. Not nearly enough to involve the I.R.S. Fuck, I hate taxes.

Do you have any idea what kind of a headache I deal with every April owning a traveling beverage company? Trust me, you don't want to.

We've been set up at the Squirrel Hill Farmer's Market for four hours, and it's been a slow Sunday. And I mean irritatingly, hair pullingly, bang your head against a wall kind of slow. So much so, I had to pull out my kindle from my messenger bag just to keep occupied.

I've sold a grand total of ten Boba's today. *Ten.* Even with Paloma *and* Pilar stopping by to stream their farmer's market adventure featuring Lala Boba, the world's best boba—according to them.

This is so not good. That number of sales won't even cover the cost of the gas to drive here, let alone the measly hourly wage I pay Shay, and the market's fee to even be here in the first place.

I am so screwed if this keeps up. I wonder if Paloma and Pilar know of anyone in the black market I could sell a kidney to. Probably not the best idea, though. People go missing far too often when they get involved in the dark web. Best to keep to the regular net.

Maybe I could do product endorsements and become one of those online ambassadors like the twins do so often. They get free shit all the time and can work whenever they want.

Maybe I'm in the wrong business.

I need more work, like last week. Why is it so hard to get a spot at a market or fair these days? It's like everyone is set in stone and there's no wiggle room to add any more. I'm trying to stay positive and to keep upbeat and optimistic, but it's hard.

Ha-ha. That's what she said.

Anyway, self-cracking up aside, I put on my serious face and internally refocus. If I put positive vibes out into the universe, I'll get them in return. At least, that's what I'm hoping when I plaster on a smile that doesn't quite reach my eyes.

Shay has taken up residence on a full box of cups, scrolling through her phone while I've parked my ass on the cooler holding the backup stock of tea, milk and lemonade. Which of course there was absolutely no need for this morning. Apparently, I was extremely optimistic last night when preparing everything.

Shay had answered my post looking for a part-time weekend helper with a flexible schedule and able to lift twenty-five-pound boxes. Unloading and loading all this shit isn't easy and I'm not exactly She-Hulk here. There were a few others to respond, but Shay stood out. A kindred spirit. We hit it off after my first question. What's your favorite color? Her answer was neon orange, like a traffic cone. So much better than the boring answers of blue and black.

With a short pixie cut and her orange painted lips, that by the way ninety-nine percent of everyone in existence can't pull off and she does effortlessly complimenting her tawny brown skin and golden hazel eyes, she fit right in with my all pink boba booth. Although she switches up her lipstick to varying shades of pink so as not to clash. Today's shade is Candy Yum Yum.

I fully intend to purchase it as soon as I can afford anything beyond the food necessary to survive.

I'm in the middle of a rather steamy scene in my monster romance book (who knew tentacles could be such a turn on?) when my phone rings from my back pocket. The caller ID reads "Ma".

Great. Just fucking great. And of course, it's a Facetime call. Now she can see my epic failure first-hand.

Maybe I should just ignore it.

No, that'll only make her call more.

Standing, I position myself so all she can see is the line of trees behind me and not the empty booth in front of me. I click the green answer button and hope and pray she doesn't ask to see the setup.

"Hi, Ma."

"Hi, sugar-pie. How's everythin' goin'?"

Damnit. Right out of the gate. Sucker punch me to the gut, why don't ya? Ouch.

Mom's smile is bright and cheerful, and unlike most ladies over sixty, she refuses to cut her hair into the traditional "old-lady-do" as she calls it. Instead, her hair, which is closer to white than blond these days, is braided neatly in one long tail that rests over one shoulder. Her thickly sweet Kentucky accent rings out clearly through my phone.

It makes me miss home a tiny bit. And I mean microscopic. But it does warm me a little on the inside to hear the accent every time she calls. Mine was practiced and worn out a long time ago *on purpose.* I always wanted to sound like the girls on TV, so I mimicked and taught myself to speak like them. Not sure if it helped or hurt me, but no way to change it now. There are still a few words I can't say without the twang, like farm, barn, yarn. Basically, anything with an a-r in it. And there's no way around saying y'all in casual conversation. It's just not gonna happen.

"Um... great just taking a little break before we wrap everything up for the day." I lie and hope she can't see it in my face. I smile extra big, just in case.

"Oh, good. I was hopin' to have a minute to chat at'cha. I wanted to tell ya all about our week. We went to a place called Sea World. They have whales there. Can'ya believe that?"

Mom and Dad moved to Florida when they retired and sold the ranch back in Kentucky. Mom would have stayed there till she died, but thankfully Dad was ready to retire somewhere near the ocean and away from the buckets of animal manure. And after I made it abundantly clear I was NOT taking over the family business, they found someone to buy the property and animals.

As most retirees do, they flocked to Florida, buying a cute little three-bedroom bungalow in one of the many Villages scattered throughout the state. Mom was insistent they had to be inland to avoid the hurricanes and tropical storms that hit the coastlines regularly. The extra rooms—they claim—are for when I come to stay... with my nonexistent husband and children.

Over the past couple of years, they've been going out to explore the state, and all it offers. Apparently, this week was Sea World, and now she's telling me all about their dolphin encounter where she got to kiss the cutest fish in the sea. *Adorable.* She promptly shows me the printed souvenir picture she has framed on their shelf of adventures.

I never would have thought Mom would agree to moving to a new state after living her entire life in Kentucky, let alone do all the new things she has done since moving.

I zone out most of her story. I know what Sea World is, and Disney World and Universal Studios. I can't live in a remodeled pink school bus called Tallulah, traveling the countryside without stopping at in least one of those.

"That sounds great, Ma."

"Well nuff 'bout us. How was your week? Meet any nice boys?"

Any nice boys? I swear she still thinks I'm sixteen and hanging out at the bowling alley on weekends to meet "nice boys". For a moment, the sexy grumpy sweatpants man from yesterday flashes in my mind. I wonder if he's a *nice boy*. I couldn't tell through the scowl. He was definitely a hot boy—man. So not a boy. He was all man under those sweats, and what I felt under that t-shirt. Yowza. He could give a girl a heat stroke.

Internally fanning myself, I shake off the mental image of what I think Mr. Grumpasouraus would look like shirtless and refocus my attention back on my mother.

"No, Mom, I did not meet any new nice boys." My answer is a little too sarcastic but she asks this every time we talk. It's getting old.

"Oh, shame. I'm not gettin' any younger here. I'd like to have grandchildren before I die."

She's exaggerating. Although I was their miracle baby, seeing as she got pregnant with me at forty, she's only sixty-seven. Nowhere near dying, and I hate it when she says that. It makes my heart hurt thinking of my parents dying.

"Stop saying stuff like that. You know I hate it when you talk about dying."

"I know, honey. Don't you worry your pretty pink head. I'm not goin' nowhere, and neither is yer daddy."

"Good." We're both silent for a moment, and then I see it a split second before she starts to speak again.

"So, no chance of a weddin' and a little one anytime soon?"

"Ugh! No, Ma. I promise if I decide to get married, *or pregnant*, you'll be the first to know."

"I better be."

"Is Dad there? Can he please come talk to me like a normal person?"

"I'm right here, little Lala." Dad's very red face comes into view, and I can't help but startle at the sight. It's a stark contrast from his graying hair, which, to his delight, is still plenty thick. The full beard he used to sport back in Kentucky is now a short, neat goatee, but still ever present.

"Woah, Dad. What happened?"

"Forgot sunscreen on our little adventure this week. Florida sun ain't no joke, honey-pie. But don't you worry none. I stocked up with plenty of SPF fifty, so when you visit you won't have to look like an overripe tomata."

"Thanks, Dad. You know I won't be visiting for a while, right? I've only been here a few months. I'm still setting up recurring markets and special events. I won't be able to come down for some time."

"Where are you again?" Mom interjects, turning the phone so only half of her face and half of dad's show on my screen now. They look like Two-Face smooshed together on the screen. One sky blue eye from dad, and one aquamarine eye from mom. I take after her more than Dad physically, but personality wise me and Dad are kindred spirits.

"Pittsburgh... Pennsylvania."

Dad squishes his face closer to Mom's. It's funny to watch them face wrestle over screen time. Don't they know they can just hold the phone farther away and I'd be able to see them both fully?

"You should go see a Steelers game while you're there."

"A what game?"

"Steelers. Football," he says, annunciating loudly.

"Ick. No thanks. I'm sure I'll find plenty of other things to entertain myself without having to subject my poor soul to four torturous hours of watching men in shiny spandex grunt, throw a ball, and slap each other on the ass."

"You know it's more than that. Don't be a sass," he says with a mock scowl on his face that instantly shifts into a laughing smile.

"Yeah, yeah. I know." How could I not? I lived in a small town in the south. The most exciting entertainment we had was football. "I'm still not going to go to a game willingly."

"Your loss."

Checking the time at the top of my phone, I realize the market will be closing in fifteen minutes. "Hey, I gotta go, guys. I'll talk to you again next week?"

"Of course, honey. Love you. Be safe."

"Will do. Love you, too."

"Bye, sugar-pie," Dad yells into the phone from off screen right before Mom hangs up.

I slip the phone back into my pocket and release a long breath. That went Ok. At least they didn't ask about my finances this time. It's easy to deflect questions about men and babies, not so much my bank balance.

"Your parents are so adorable." Shay stands from her makeshift seat and starts to pack everything away.

"That's one word for them. I prefer nagging, overbearing, or intrusive." I smile so she knows I only half mean it.

"I would love to have parents who cared for me that much. My parents couldn't care less about my love life or future grandbabies. Hell, I don't think they even want them. They barely wanted their own children."

"Oh… um, I'm sorry." I stumble through my words, suddenly feeling stupid complaining about my overly-loving parents. They may be overbearing at times, but it's only because they care so much. I'm lucky to have parents who love me and simply want to be part of my life.

Shay shrugs while stacking cups and reusable straws into the box she was previously using as a seat. "It's ok. Me and my siblings are used to it. We're very self-sufficient."

We continue packing away pitchers, napkins, sliced and whole lemons, pink sugar packets, cream, ice, containers of bobas, cups, lids and straws and all the other things needed to make my Boba teas. This includes all my marketing materials, business cards, flyers with my logo and menu on the back. Complete with pastel pink psychedelic bubble font spelling out Lala Boba, my company's name. And of course, everything is pink.

It's always good to have a strong logo and design. Easily recognizable from a distance, memorable and well made. If only more people would have been here today to use all my cute products.

Shay grunts as she lifts another box onto the collapsible dolly I use to cart everything back and forth to my Jeep. Which, yes, if you must know, is also pink.

"Didn't you mention wanting to get a trailer or something instead of carting all this around all the time?"

"Yes. That would be the dream. A tiny trailer with a cute retro set up inside, with a fridge and ice cooler and blenders. Painted pink and white on the outside with a cute little striped awning over the pickup window. Huh." I sigh wistfully at the dream. "Alas, if I keep having Sundays like this one, that'll never happen."

"You have the goal, though. Just keep that in mind, and one day you'll get there. Your bobas are delicious. You just have to get in at the right place, make a few networking connections. You'll see. I bet you by this time next year, you'll have that tiny pink trailer of your dreams." She smiles, whole heartedly believing that to be truth. I smile back, nodding noncommittally. It's enough to assuage her, and she wheels a stack of boxes off to my Jeep.

Little does she know, that's been the dream for the past six years. Ever since I set out on this little adventure of mine after college. I can't seem to stay in one place long enough to plant the kind of roots needed to generate the funds for my tiny trailer. Nor the kind of roots my parents would love for me to have.

Stay in one place, meet a nice boy, settle down, and have a litter of kids. It's not that I don't want any of those things. I just... can't seem to find them. I can't seem to find the right place or person that makes me want to.

When I first started this journey in my pink bus, I wanted to see the country, meet new people, and learn new things about places I'd never been. At first, it was to escape the trappings of small-town life. Then it morphed into soul searching. Somehow, somewhere, I think I got lost while getting lost. Now... I don't really know where I belong or where I should go.

Pinky Promise

At twenty-seven, I know it's time to decide what I should be doing with my life. Keep moving every other year to a new city with new people and new places? Or do as my mother wants. Find a man and settle down? *Can I though?* I've been running from stagnancy for so many years, I don't know what standing still feels like anymore.

Maybe Pittsburgh will have the answers. I can only hope.

4 - Henry

Cost, eleven thousand and worth every penny

It's Wednesday by the time I've managed to persuade the seller of the business complex to agree to my offer. This acquisition will pad our portfolio quite nicely. Owning and managing a building with dozens of firms and corporations right in the heart of the business district is going to generate income for years for Bardot Real Estate & Management.

The papers still need to be finalized, and I sit in my corner office polishing off the numbers before passing them on to my assistant to send over to the title company for underwriting to start the dolling process of waiting for other people to do their job.

Low descending light filters in through the floor to ceiling windows that line two walls of my office. It's neatly and professionally furnished in dark charcoal grays and off white. Calming neutral colors and silvers help to make my office open and inviting without being too casual and comfortable. This is a place of business, after all. I do not need nor want people to linger in my office for very long.

Thomas, my assistant for the past couple years, enters with a brown paper coffee cup in one hand, and a clear cup filled with some sort of milky green substance with black dots swirling around in the bottom in the other. He hands me the plain, nondescript coffee cup, which I know holds a dark roast coffee with just a splash of half and half. I still don't know what the other one is.

"What in the world are you drinking?" I ask as he practically chugs the concoction through a straw far too large for anything other than commercial size spit wads.

"Boba."

"Come again?"

"Boba tea."

"Never heard of it."

"Not surprising."

"What does that mean?" I raise an eyebrow in challenge, as if that will stop him from being bluntly honest. It's a quality I thought would annoy me, but is rather refreshing from all the fake placating going on in the world.

"It means that although you can morph a run-down vacant warehouse district into the next hot new place to live and work in town, once you decide on something, you do not change your mind. Like your coffee, for example. You've been drinking the same exact thing every single day since I started working for you two years ago." Thomas sits down gracefully in the seat across from my desk and "sips" on his whatever tea. Straightening his tie with a smoothing hand down the front, he pops open the button on his suit jacket.

This is what first caught my attention when Thomas interviewed with me, his impeccable taste in suits. Not nearly as custom or expensive as mine, but still well-tailored and pressed. He wore a three-piece classic navy-blue Burberry suit with a properly accented double Windsor knot tie. First impressions are everything in this business. If a seller or buyer thinks you don't have the money to back up an offer or insight to the industry, they may take their business elsewhere.

I, myself, am always immaculately dressed in a custom-tailored Tom Ford, Armani, Brioni or Givenchy suit. Today, it's a Brioni in slate gray virgin wool. Cost, eleven thousand and worth every penny.

"What's your point?" I ask tersely.

"My point is that maybe if you tried something new every now and then, you would know what Boba tea is."

Watching him drink the strange liquid, I don't think trying new things includes ingesting something so questionable. "Thanks. I'll pass."

"For your information, even though you didn't ask, it's a tea that originated in Taiwan. It's made with a blend of tea, milk or cream, sometimes fruit, and Boba tapioca balls. And it's delicious." His face sours and he winces. "Well, this one not so much. I think the boba has expired or sat out in the sun too long."

"Then why are you drinking it?"

"Because my boyfriend brought it for me, and it would be rude not to." Begrudgingly, he takes another drink.

"He's not here now. You don't have to drink it. Just dump it."

"That's not the point."

"What is then?" I'm thoroughly confused. For some reason, I'm now invested in his damn boba tea story. I've stopped typing my emails and am leaning my forearms on my desk, waiting for his reply.

"It was a thoughtful gift. He took time out of his day to get it for me and bring it here, and I'm going to drink it, damn it. Even if it makes me vomit."

Now I'm cringing. "Well, just don't vomit in my office." He stands, re-buttoning his jacket with one hand, readying to leave my office. "Don't forget the Peterson documents. These need to get to the title company today for underwriting." I hand him the thick stack of paperwork. With all the paper we deal with in real estate, we must be killing thousands of trees every hour. Why can't this all be digital like the rest of the modern world?

Thomas mock solutes and takes the papers. "Aye, aye, captain."

"Also, have we heard back on the Schmidt deal? Have they made a decision?"

"Yes, Mr. Schmidt has agreed to the terms and will be ready to sign next week. You're going to make what… five million in commission on that deal?"

"Five point six."

"Shit."

"Shit indeed. Stick with me, kid, and someday you'll make that much too."

"Seriously?"

I call him kid, but he's twenty-four to my thirty. We're not really that far apart in age, but sometimes I feel like a dinosaur in this business. I've been working here since I was sixteen. Started as a grunt, getting coffee and transporting documents between departments, working to earn my status as head of new acquisitions. Father wouldn't allow me to be handed everything. He said if I can't work hard to get it, I don't deserve it. As soon as I graduated and got my realtors license, I proved my worth with my first deal. A mediocre midrange mall that I managed to sell for a cool twenty-five million.

Not bad for a few months' work at twenty-two. That was where I got the money for the down payment on my first investment. Nothing too grand, just a little complex, with a dozen units averaging around twelve hundred square feet each. I did a little remodeling and polishing, and now those rentals make me a passive income of three hundred thousand a month after expenses.

I have a team of building managers that work directly for me, and I check in at least once a month at each of the properties I own. Although I don't have to worry about the day to day, I like to be kept in the loop of what is happening on my properties.

If I wanted, I wouldn't have to work a day in my life ever again. But then what would I do with my time? I like working. I like aggressive negotiating and dealing. I'm good at it.

"Sure. As long as you work for it," I tell Thomas. He knows my position on work ethics and understands the value of hard work.

"Noted. Oh, before I go, Debra wanted to know if you'll have a plus one for the annual Charity Gala? This year it's supporting local public-school teachers. Help pay for extra curriculars and supplies they might not be able to afford otherwise."

"No."

"Are you sure? Might be nice to have a pretty lady on your arm for the night. Debra said this is the last day to make additions to the guest list, so it's now or never." Thomas wiggles his eyebrows at me suggestively, like the idea of being able to fuck a woman that night will convince me I need a date. For a brief second, a blur of pink hair and aqua eyes fills my mind. Followed closely by a succulent, swaying ass.

It must be getting late, because my mind is slipping. I pick up my coffee to help clear the obvious delusion from my mind.

"Then never it is."

"Oh, come on, boss. Really? Stag again? Doesn't it ever get boring going to all these events alone?" His arms drop to his sides so dramatically, he almost spills his disgusting tea on my floor.

"No. There are plenty of other people attending I can socialize with, and none of them will nag me to stay longer or take tequila shots. If I want female company, I have other avenues of doing so."

I return my attention to my emails after a hefty swallow of coffee to help clear the cobwebs away.

"Please do not tell me you go down to some seedy rent by the hour hooker hotel."

"Not at all. I go to the presidential suite in the five-star luxury hotel we own, with a very expensive call girl from a very discreet service," I reply in a flat tone.

Thomas chuckles, I don't. "You're not serious... are you?"

I simply shift my gaze from my computer screen to him and back again. I'm dead serious, but he can assume whatever he pleases.

"Right. Ok. Well, got it. No plus one." He gives a finger gun point and backs out of my office, returning to his smaller one directly next to mine.

Closely following Thomas's exit, another form fills my doorway. My father, Malcom Bardot, stands one hand in his front pants pocket, the other scrolling through something on his cell phone. Knowing my father, it's either nudes one of his "girls" sent him or details for our most recent sale. Fifty-fifty chance, either way.

My father is not an ugly man. Pushing seventy, he looks to be only in his late fifties. Money can help in that way. He's had a little work done, but nothing drastically obvious. Most of it can be attributed to the Bardot family genetics. Our height and broad shoulders hail from his side of the family. His hair is a dark mix of salt and pepper, which he gets trimmed every three weeks. Now-a-days, he sports a neatly kempt beard a few shades lighter than his hair. If I had to compare him to someone, I'd say he's close to Sean Connery before he went bald, and without the charming accent. The charming, disarming smile he carries in spades, however. Samson inherited that from him.

Being such a handsome older gentleman with plenty of money to spread around, he manages to snare the younger ladies who care more about the size of his wallet than the size of anything else.

"Henry. I heard you've finally locked in the Peterson complex. Nice work." He slides his phone into his jacket pocket and takes a seat across from me in one of the two black leather chairs.

"Thank you. It took some persuading, but they finally agreed to a number I'm comfortable with."

"Glad to hear it. We should have a drink to celebrate." He has a drink to celebrate just about everything. No matter the time of day or occasion, there's nothing unworthy of a tumbler of amber liquid. These days, my father is more women and booze than actual work. It's a miracle he manages to maintain himself during office hours. Must be all the years of tolerance built up.

"You know I don't keep liquor in my office." Anymore. I used to, until I realized it was only adding to his excuses to drink. Now I only keep a Keurig in the corner for clients. I don't drink that dirt water, but it's enough to placate thirsty clients.

"Oh right, right. You're no fun. I forgot."

He didn't forget.

"Was there something else I could do for you, Father? I do have other work to attend to."

"You always have work to attend to. Don't you ever take a break and just let loose?"

"No."

"You could really benefit from a vacation. Perhaps you should take a few weeks off. Go somewhere tropical, where clothing is optional. I met this sweet little piece of ass named Sonya, that would be great company for you on such a trip. I can send you her info if you're interested."

Interested in one of my father's empty-headed, money-leeching booty calls? No, thank you.

38

"I'm good."

"Suit yourself, but you're missing out. Sonya takes the clothing optional suggestion seriously."

"No doubt." I roll my eyes and tap a finger on my keyboard, signaling I would like this conversation to end sooner rather than later.

"Anyway, I was hoping you could suggest something for me to get for your sister. For the baby. I don't want to come off as a stingy grandpa, but your mother and nannies took care of buying whatever you kids needed. And I figured since she didn't appreciate my gift of a good divorce attorney for her wedding present, I should try another avenue this time."

He wasn't the only one with a good divorce attorney lined up. Mine was just kept quietly on retainer for the first year of their marriage, until I realized it was sticking.

"How should I know? Just order the most expensive thing off her registry. And actually sign a physical card. Don't have it printed like your Christmas cards if you care so much." Perhaps I let a little too much of my personal disdain for his attempts at being part of our family seep out. I have no idea why he cares about his soon to be grandchild. Probably for posterity.

"I just figured you see her more often than I do and might have some insight."

"Not in the slightest. I'll be using her registry as well."

"Ok, then. Guess I'll get out of your hair and have that celebratory drink for both of us."

You do that.

Normally I can interact with my father in a very civil manner. We aren't friends or pals, and haven't been family in years, other than in name and blood. The day he retires and signs over Bardot Realty to me will be the day I have a real celebratory drink at work. Considering his age, it should be within the next five years.

As soon as he's gone, I return my full attention to my work at hand. Sending a memo to Thomas to pick something off my sister's baby registry. She hasn't scheduled a baby shower yet, but might as well get it now and have it ready. I also make a personal note to pick out a card personally.

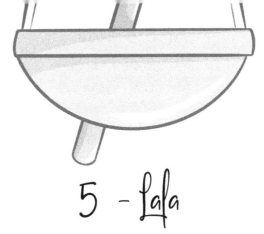

5 - Lala

You're not texting and driving, are you?

Current checking account balance: six hundred and forty-two dollars.

Rent for the space I park Tallulah due next week: four hundred dollars.

Amount I made at last week's farmer's market (after expenses): fifteen dollars.

Number of prospective future gigs: one—if I ever hear from the anime con people. Otherwise, zero.

I need to find more places to sell my Boba, and fast. My savings have been depleted, and it's the eleventh hour. Thankfully, I'm headed over to Fawn's place tonight.

> **_Lala:_** *On my way. Should be there in ten, if traffic stays light.*
>
> **_Fawn:_** *No worries. Leo is just putting the wellington in the oven now.*
>
> **_Lala:_** *Great... and how many places did you think of for me to look into?*

Fawn: At least a dozen. Maybe a few more.

Fawn: I even remembered the craft fair coming up. It's huge, and there's always a ton of people that go.

Lala: That's fantastic. I really need to find more large events with a big turn over.

Fawn: You doin' ok? Do you need money? You know you can always ask me if you need a loan or something. Me and Leo are always happy to help.

Lala: No, no I'm fine. Just need to schedule a more regular circuit is all. Haven't been able to get the right ones locked in.

Fawn: Ok. You'll tell me if you're in trouble, right?

Lala: Of course.

Fawn: Good.

Fawn: You're not texting and driving, are you?

Lala: No. I'm using voice to text through the sync in my car. Don't worry.

Fawn: Ok, then. See you soon.

6 - Henry

Nice and bland and boring, per usual

What is it about Saturday that turns people into someone completely different? My sister, who during the work week is a hardass attorney with a heart of gold, fighting for the little guy, dressed in sleek and stylish power suits, always an espresso in one hand and a take no bullshit attitude. But on the weekends, she's Suzie homemaker. Wearing long flowing dresses and a frilly apron while whirling through the kitchen like Martha freaking Stewart with the place settings to match.

Most people in her profession work all weekend, but not my sister. Oh no, she banned work on weekends in her house years ago. After watching our parents work non-stop, and how it affected our family, she was determined to not let that happen to her. As have I. My approach is slightly different, however. Even before she got married to Leo, it was a rule. No shop talk on Saturday or Sunday.

I personally never agreed with her understanding of what ruined our parents' marriage. It wasn't their jobs. They were great at their jobs, making millions, and gaining prestige and assets. The issue was they decided to get married and have children. They mixed family life with business. They should have just focused on one or the other. Once they separated and allocated us to our nannies, they prospered professionally. Without others to hinder their progress, they became moguls in their fields.

We all would have been better off if they had not tried to be family people *and* business professionals. You can't run a multi-million-dollar real estate firm and raise three kids properly. Which is why I will never marry or have children. I will not subjugate them to the childhood I had. I'm happy with my work and everything it affords me.

Trying to avoid whatever bug my sister has contracted, just in case it's contagious, I linger in the living room with Samson, who's behind their wet bar, topping off his old-fashioned with an orange peel.

"You want one? I can make another."

"No. Far too sweet. I'll take a vodka soda."

"Of course, you will. Nice and bland and boring, per usual." If I cared, I would roll my eyes. But I don't. Instead, I lean one elbow on the bar and wait.

Samson pulls the bottle of vodka and soda water from behind the bar and begins to make my drink. He's twenty-five and all about the flavor of life. Parties, girls, cars, yachts, sometimes drugs, and anything that sounds fun to him. Which, unfortunately, is usually everything. His motto is try everything once, and if you don't like it the first time, try it again just to make sure. There have been a few incidents, thanks to his style of living. One even involved a Sheikh and a member of his harem. Don't ask, but just know Samson is never allowed back in Palestine under penalty of death.

"You know, it wouldn't kill you to try something new every once

44

in a while." Funny considering how his trip to Palestine turned out.

Why is everyone telling me that lately? First Thomas and now Samson.

"It might, depending on what the new thing is. For instance, if I decided I wanted to try being a drug mule for the cartel. But in transit, the balloon filled with rock cocaine I have shoved up my ass bursts, and I overdose, writhing on the floor and biting off my tongue. It could very well kill me."

Samson has paused his movements in pouring my drink to stare at me, one eyebrow raised in disbelief. "That seems a little dramatic."

"And yet completely plausible. Hence the tried-and-true vodka soda." Waving one hand at the half-poured drink on the bar, I gesture for him to continue. He finishes the drink and slides it to me with one finger, slightly disgusted and offended by my choice. Not only in libation, but in life, I'm sure.

Sipping his drink, Samson narrows his eyes at me in a way I don't really understand. "Speaking of new things. Leo told me you had an interesting encounter this week."

"Interesting encounter?"

"With some random girl with pink hair."

"Oh yeah, *that*."

"Yeah, *that*." When I don't reply, but simply sip on my drink, he groans. "Oh, come on. Just a little bit of gossip wouldn't hurt. Tell me more about this pink-haired mystery girl."

"There's nothing to tell because I don't know anything else. She was short, pink, and a little aggressive with her kissing. I haven't seen or thought of her since." Not entirely true, but I blame that fleeting thought on Wednesday on my lack of coffee. "Besides, I'm thirty. I don't do gossip."

"Please. Everyone gossips. Even at the ripe old age of thirty. You used to be way more fun than this. When did you become such a stick in the mud?"

"Right about the time you got arrested for streaking through the mayor's daughter's wedding."

"Hey, I was eighteen, and that was hilarious."

"Not for the poor flower girl. I'm pretty sure you scarred her for life."

"Ok, I didn't mean to do that. *That*, I feel bad about. And that I never get to hook up with horny, drunk, hot bridesmaids."

"Not to mention, we never get invited to prestigious weddings anymore." Not that I'm complaining. In reality, he probably did me a service. Not having to fend off gold digging bridesmaids, or to explain why I didn't want to ask that girl I fucked once to attend a wedding with me as my date, is an issue I've never had thanks to him.

Should I thank him? Probably. Am I going to? Never. That would be giving him way too much power in our relationship. I am the oldest, and he the youngest. I have power and he does not. And that's the way I like it.

Luckily, or unluckily, I'm not sure yet, Leo joins us from the adjoining kitchen and dining area, holding a glass of wine in one hand.

My sister and brother-in-law's house is a well-maintained Tudor style home from the early twentieth century. When they moved in, they wanted to keep a lot of the original "charm", as they called it. Only updating important things like the wiring and appliances. Keeping the polished hardwood floors, built-ins, and a few stained-glass windows intact. Originally, it was a lot of space at just over four thousand square feet, and five bedrooms, for only two people. Apparently, that's not going to be an issue for long because they both plan on filling it with children. Unlike my one-bedroom penthouse, which has no extra room for anyone. Perfect.

"Were you able to get any more information on his mystery woman?" Leo asks Samson. Taking a sip from his wine, he joins us at the bar, both him and my brother eyeing me for answers. Samson's eyes are a few shades darker green than mine, and Leo's are a bright, happy baby blue.

"Not a thing. Not even a vague description."

"Damn it."

They're both oddly disappointed at my lack of interest in this mystery woman. "Is there any particular reason you two are so gung-ho about this woman?"

Both sip their drinks and Samson clears his throat before answering. "We just thought maybe this encounter might have stirred something in you. That maybe she sparked an interest, or jump-started your emotions."

I frown at my little brother grumbling. "I have emotions."

"Just not happy ones. I don't think I've seen you smile in years. You need to smile. You might die at forty of a dead heart if you don't."

"I have a perfect heart, and it's beating just fine. I'm probably healthier than you are. When was the last time you ate anything healthier than a protein shake?"

"Just because I like to indulge in the finer things in life doesn't mean I'm unhealthy. I won't eat anything below a four-star rating."

My brother may be a womanizing, splurging party boy, but he has a point. It's not like he's eating at McDonald's or Denny's on a regular basis, or at all, for that matter. He may indulge, but at least it's high-quality indulging. And he basically spends half his time in his home gym. He is definitely not out of shape physically.

The doorbell rings, interrupting our little argument, and both Samson and I turn to look towards it.

"Are we expecting another guest?" Usually, it's just the four of us, so I have no idea who could possibly be here.

"Yeah. Fawn decided to invite her friend from her Pilates class. Something about helping her find work. I'm not sure. I haven't met her yet. According to my wife, she's an 'absolute sweetheart, and we're going to love her'. So be nice, will you?"

I frown. I don't like unexpected guests. Especially ones I don't know who need help finding work. Sounds like a freeloader to me.

"Pilates, you say? So that means she's bendy. I like bendy. How old is she?" Exiting from behind the wet bar, Samson unsnaps the top button of his gray Henley, standing straight to his full height instead of slouching like he was just moments ago. We're the same height, but you wouldn't know it with how he's always lounging and slouching everywhere he goes. Now he's all smiles and attentive politeness, with a sprinkling of obvious sexual interest. He hasn't even met this woman yet, and he's already thinking of ways to get in her pants.

"Don't even think about it Samson. She's Fawn's friend, and we did *not* invite her over for you to hit and quit. Understood?"

"Yeah, yeah sure. Got it. Don't worry. I'll play nice."

"You better," Fawn says, gliding in effortlessly to answer the door, her husband close on her heels. They are the picture of perfect hosts. Samson makes his way closer to the door, but stays back a few paces, waiting to see this new mystery woman and flirt with her relentlessly until she either gives in and sleeps with him or outright shuts him down. It's always one or the other with Samson and women. I don't think my brother is capable of having any kind of relationship other than sexual or outright loathing with a woman.

Fawn wipes her hands on her white ruffle apron and opens the door to her friend. I hear a sweet female voice coming from the other side of the small group. I can't see her yet as I have not moved from my perch, leaning against the bar, drink still in hand.

It's only once Fawn and Leo part and begin to introduce the new arrival to my brother and me that I see her. And her pink hair.

"You!" My rather loud and abrupt declaration startles the smile right off her pretty pink lips as she catches sight of me.

"You," she gasps, mimicking my one-word shock of recognition.

"You two know each other?" Fawn asks, stepping up beside the pink-haired woman, pointing back and forth between our mirrored shocked glares.

"No, not really. We kind of... bumped into one another the other day," says Pink Hair, her cheeks staining a shade that almost matches her hair, and her strawberry patterned dress, and her shoes. That's a lot of fucking pink. Including her sweet, pink skin, miles of it are visible across her collarbone, the swell of the peak-a-boo cleavage, and her toned arms.

Focus, Henry. We are not here to gawk. That's Samson's job. We're mad. Remember? The kissing assault. Be angry, not horny. You're a grown man, so act it.

"I wouldn't exactly call it 'bumping into one another' when the point of contact was our mouths." Ok, not so adult of me to put it that way, but whatever.

"Wait, what?" Fawn looks absolutely appalled.

"Hold on. Pink hair, blue eyes." *Aquamarine eyes.* "This is the pink-haired kissing assailant that mauled you, isn't it?" Samson makes the connection about two whole seconds before Leo does.

"No shit," he breathes out, his mouth remaining open in shock, inspecting pink-hair a little more closely now.

Pointing an accusing finger at me, Fawn asks Pink Hair, "This is the sexy sweatpants guy you kissed?"

My eyebrows shoot up into my hairline. "Sexy sweatpants guy?" I shake my head and refocus on my sister. "Wait, why are you surprised? How could you not make this connection before now?

Didn't you maybe think a pink-haired girl in my neighborhood, where you attend your Pilates classes, might have been the same person that assaulted me?"

"I did not assault you," Pink Hair squeaks out, clearly offended. I don't care.

"Technically, according to the law, you actually did sexually assault him," Fawn agrees begrudgingly.

"Whose side are you on, Fawn?" Pink Hair whisper shouts at my sister. Fawn doesn't answer her and turns to me instead.

"I didn't know you were the sweatpants guy because I only heard the story from Lala."

"Lala?" That's the most ridiculous name I've ever heard. Of course, someone who wears all pink would be named *Lala*.

"It's short for Micaela."

"No, it's not," I argue.

"Yes, it is," she argues right back, placing her tiny fists on her generous hips. "I think I know my own name."

"Okay, okay. Let's just all take a breath and relax." Raising his hands in a placating motion, Leo gestures for us all to be quiet and calm. "I never had a chance to tell Fawn the story of the kissing pink-haired bandit, and she never told me Lala had pink hair. So, neither of us made the connection."

We're all silent after Leo's short but clear explanation. Micaela's cheeks are still a rosy flush as she glances up at me from beneath thick lashes, and something weird and warm happens in my chest. Then lower.

I don't like it.

Narrowing my eyes on the little pink intruder, I'm in the middle of trying to discern the feeling, when the host of all hosts intervenes in our silent standoff. Fawn, the best, and currently worst sister ever, smiles graciously. "Ok, well, now that we have that out of the way. Lala and I have some things to attend to, and perhaps one of you boys could get her a drink?"

"I got it," Samson instantly offers with a huge shit-eating grin. "What'll you have, Lala?"

"Wine is fine. Anything red or rosé. Just not white."

"You got it. I'll find you. You two just do what you need to do." With a suspiciously friendly demeanor, Samson returns behind the wet bar to find and open a bottle of wine.

I do nothing but scowl as I watch the pair leave. Once again, my day is thrown far off kilter with the appearance of this pink woman.

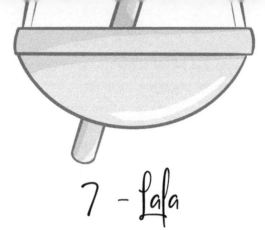

7 - Lala

Introducing Master Cranky Pants McFrowny

Mister Grumpy Sexy Sweatpants is here.

He's Fawn's brother.

And he's just as hot in a crisp tailored suit and pressed button down as he is in sweatpants. I'm pretty sure my entire body is flushed bright pink right now. Seeing him, hearing the deep gravelly voice that goes along with that face and body, and holy hell. *Am I turned on? I am, aren't I?* This is not good. I need to focus. I came here to get info on events and markets for my boba booth, not to ogle Fawn's incredibly hot, sexy brother.

"So, your brother… he's the guy I sneak attack kissed on the street. What a coinkydink, huh?"

"Yeah. What are the odds of that happening?"

"Not sure, but there's probably a lot of zeros involved."

Fawn leads me into the kitchen where the most heavenly aroma greets us, and I cannot wait to find out how that smell tastes. Her home is warm and inviting, filled with colonial style furniture that has been immaculately restored to its former glory, paired with modern flourishes and rich color. Their kitchen has been renovated to fit the space, but not in that gouache way where everything is ninety-degree angles and sterile hospital white. It's all rich, dark woods and cozy greens. Perhaps I should consider using a few deeper tones in my home to make it a little warmer. Balance all the bright soft pinks.

We sit at a smooth granite island where Fawn has set up her laptop and has a folder of papers neatly stacked next to it.

For the next ten minutes, we go over the list Fawn made. She has even printed out a map of the city, marking each location for me. She's the best. I really should not be getting all hot and bothered by her brother. That's completely inappropriate. Although, I suppose I flew right by inappropriate, waving at it as I passed right into possible felony by kissing him on the street without permission.

He didn't look very happy to see me again. I guess my plan on making his day better didn't work. From the looks of his indifferent and cold expression, I'd say that feat may be nay unachievable.

For some reason, that makes me want to try harder.

Everyone should enjoy the joy that is life. Being so grumptastic all the time is no fun at all. I wonder if he even knows how to have fun. I doubt it. He probably steals candy from small children and pops balloons tied to unattended strollers. He probably likes kale and granola. Gag.

Maybe I could help him with that while I'm here. Show him a little sunny disposition. Perhaps it'll rub off on him. Who am I kidding? That's like assuming a cactus is a good cuddle partner.

Fawn's much nicer and smilier brother brings me a glass of rosé, introducing himself to me as Samson, the "attractive and friendly one". His words, not mine. I agree, he is definitely the friendly one, but it's a toss-up on which brother would be considered the attractive one.

Fawn is lean, with legs for days, mahogany brown hair that always falls in perfect waves around her shoulders, and eyes a brilliant hazel. Her brother Samson is tall, just like his brother, Sir Frowns-a-Lot, his hair a few shades lighter. More on the chestnut brown scale than outright black. His eyes are a darker shade of green, like the pine needles in the redwood forest of California, where I once attended a wedding with an Elvis impersonator as the DJ. But his smile definitely sets him apart from his brother, who I notice, stays in the living room and does not introduce himself.

I don't see him again until it's time to sit down to eat. He sits directly across from me, in direct scowling line of sight. Samson takes the seat next to mine, making polite small talk, grinning and casually brushing against my arm. Asking how I met Fawn, how long I've been practicing Pilates, if I do any other physical activities, and if I have a boyfriend. They're harmless questions on their own, but I feel like he's trying to catalog something in his mind, and I'm not quite sure what it is.

His brother, I learn, is named Henry, and not because he introduces himself, but because Samson keeps trying to engage him in conversation, which he's masterfully ignoring.

Introducing Master Cranky Pants McFrowny. The Earl of Boredom, who breaks all proprieties by being overly sexy in athletic wear.

Seriously, does this man never smile? He hasn't even so much as quirked a lip, smirked, chuckled, chortled, or grinned. Is it possible his facial muscles have atrophied and have forgotten how to move upwards? Perhaps he needs a refresher course.

Henry seems to not care for our polite dinner conversation. Too good to input his opinion on the new doughnut shop that just opened, and if their oddly phallic themed doughnuts are clever or disgusting. Merely grunting and nodding if needed, not contributing one little iota. This will not do.

"So, Henry. I wanted to apologize for… the incident last weekend. You see, my friend and I thought you looked in need of a good hug. Well, actually, she thought you needed something a little more *satisfying* than a hug. But she suggested I give you a hug anyway, to try and make your frown turn upside down. You just looked so… bummed, and we wanted to try and make your day a little brighter."

Henry watches me from across the table, saying nothing. No expression crosses his face. Not even a raised eyebrow or tilt of the head. Nope. I get nothing. Nada. Zip. Zilch. Just a flat, dead face watching me ramble on. This is going to be harder than I thought.

"So, anyway, on my way across the street it did look like you could use something a little stronger than a hug, and I just kinda went with my gut and… well, you know what happened. As does everyone else at this table, apparently."

"Did it work?" Samson asks, staring at his brother who places a precisely cut piece of meat into his mouth and chews before replying.

"Did what work?"

"Did she turn your frown upside down? I know if I had received a kiss on the street from such a pretty girl, I would have been smiling." Samson turns to face me, said smile plastered on his face.

"No. No, it did not." Henry states firmly.

"Well, that's a shame. I wonder what it would take to make you smile." I ponder out loud.

"Keep wondering."

"Ok, so who's ready for dessert?" Fawn once again breaks our banter, smoothing out the tension wrinkles in the air. She's pretty good at that. Probably from being such a great attorney. She's going to be an awesome mom.

Fawn and her husband Leo serve dessert and refill our drinks. I hadn't met Leo before now. He never came to Pilates, and they're always so engrossed in one another over the weekends, it just never lined up right. Fawn showed me pictures of him, of course, but he is far cuter in person than those photos. With beachy blonde highlighted hair and dreamy baby blues on a physique that says I can hold you up against a wall and not break a sweat. Not to mention he's extremely sweet, thoughtful, loving and smart. I can see how she fell for him so hard and wants to hoard him all to herself. I would too, if he were mine.

The two met one afternoon in a coffee shop. A total meet cute story. Girl orders coffee, boy bumps into girl, spilling coffee on himself, then orders girl a new coffee. Girl and boy spend multiple hours drinking coffee and talking, then end up going out the very next day. I've never had a meet cute. It would be nice to have it happen once in my life. Even if the relationship didn't end well, a cute story to tell would be fun.

As the conversation between us flows once again, without much input from Henry, we move onto the subject of my work and boba booth.

"Wait, boba tea?" asks Henry, the first time he's willingly entered a conversation all evening.

"Yes. I sell it at farmers markets, conventions, fairs. All kinds of events."

"You mean that weird concoction with the balls in it?" Is it weird I want to hear him say *balls* again? Totally isn't, right? That's completely normal.

"Yes."

"And people actually like it?"

"Yes." I don't like how he's moved on from no expression to one of disgust when discussing the subject matter of my business. This is my livelihood here, and he's just sneering at it like it's a smudge of dog shit on his five-hundred-dollar loafers. I cross my arms over my chest and sit up straight and tall. Well, as tall as I can in a room full of people pushing six feet tall. "People actually love it. There's quite a demand for it. It's healthy, tasty, fun, and makes people smile."

"Why does a drink need to make people smile?" Henry asks haughtily.

"Why shouldn't it? Isn't the point of living? To enjoy life?"

"Not in my opinion." he mumbles, sipping on his clear drink that is no doubt something boring and bland with no taste.

"And what is it you do, Henry? I bet it's something that requires a lot of paperwork." I sip my drink in a manner I hope conveys his level of disinterest. I have no idea what he does, but anyone who wears a suit on the weekends, even at Fawn's with her no work on weekends policy, must be some sort of paper pusher.

"I'm in real estate."

"Oh, so you sell houses?" Still has a lot of paper, but also a social aspect to it I didn't expect him to possess.

"No. I'm a commercial real estate agent and manager. I buy skyscrapers and office complexes, and the company I work at either sells them or manages them."

Oh, well, that makes more sense.

He barely contains the condescending eye roll I can tell he desperately wants to set free. I'm agitating him... and I like it.

"What company would that be? Would I know it?" I ask, as if the names of local Realty companies is something I just know off hand. I don't. But he doesn't need to know that.

"Not likely, but I work at Bardot Real Estate & Management."

"He works with our father." Fawn stage whispers to me. "He owns the company. Our mother owns Diamond Star Real Estate, and she was not happy when Henry chose to work with Father over her."

"So, why isn't it Bardot & Son Real Estate?"

"We're not that kind of family." is all Henry says before returning to his dessert of homemade rhubarb pie. I devoured mine in five bites, while he takes his delicate time eating bites small enough not to fall off the fork and land on his crisp white shirt.

Fawn makes an air sucking sound of revelation, diverting my attention from my argument with Hot Harrumphing Henry. "Oh my gosh, I just had a thought."

"What?" I ask.

Turning her triumphant attention to her brother, she asks, "Henry, isn't your company having a conference soon? Where there will be lots of attendees from all departments?"

"Yeah. What about it?" Henry squints at Fawn, trying to read between the lines of whatever she's eventually getting to.

"Well, don't you guys usually have food and drink vendors there?" Fawn raises a brow at him, gesturing with her eyes to admit she's right. It's a look I bet she uses in the courtroom a lot when she has a witness on the stand that doesn't realize she knows about their hidden stash of illegal furbies.

"Perhaps." he agrees hesitantly. "Why?"

"Well seeing as Lala here happens to be a drink vendor in need of an event to sell at, and not to mention the networking opportunities something such as this would afford her, perhaps you might consider having her set up at your conference."

Henry is dumbfounded into silence. From the look on his face, he does not like her suggestion. I was hopeful when she started talking. Now—not so much. I can see the rejection sitting on the tip of his tongue, waiting for him to just let it fly right off and stab me in the throat.

"I don't think that's—"

"Why don't you check out her booth first? See first-hand what she's capable of before rejecting the idea completely." Fawn says, cutting him off before he can finish his killing blow.

His lips pinch together in a thin line as he and his sister have a stare down. His face is tight with agitation, hers is open, smiling, and unrelenting. The rest of the table waits with bated breath for his response. Both Leo and Samson watch with big anime eyes, engrossed in the sibling spat, as if this sort of thing occurs more often than not.

"I suppose that would be the professional thing to do." he grits out between clenched teeth.

"Great, it's settled then. Tomorrow, you'll go to the Squirrel Hill farmer's market to check out Lala Boba before you decide she, and her product, are amazing and hire her for the conference." Fawn claps her hands as if the matter is all but decided. I still have doubts he will actually show up and follow through with his word. So, I do the one thing I know will ease my tensions.

Stretching out my right hand across the table, pinky extended, I demand from him the one unbreakable oath. "Pinky promise?"

Those soft moss green eyes shoot to mine. "Pinky what?"

"Promise."

"Like a five-year-old?"

"Are you five?"

"No, I'm thirty."

"Then like a thirty-year-old."

Taking in my serious face, Henry cocks his head. Interested perhaps? "Why?"

"Because I find people more inclined to keep their word when forced to engage in an act that creates a contract, or promise, but without all the paperwork. Pinky promise you will come tomorrow and judge for yourself if my boba tea business is worthy of your conference, before saying no."

All eyes watch me, him, and my pinky, still waiting. Pink nail polish glinting in the warm light. He seems to be pondering my offer seriously now. I don't know what part of that speech snagged him, and I don't care. Because he's about to accept. I can feel it.

"Fine." With long, dexterous fingers, he reaches out his pinky, interlocking it with mine. Solidifying our pinky promise.

"Now, if you break it, I can hunt you down and seek ultimate revenge."

"And what would that look like?" Samson asks from my side. His voice surprises me. I'd all but forgotten there were other people in the room while I had my little pinky promise standoff with Henry.

Taking in a steadying breath, I withdraw my hand to my lap, where my pinky feels warm from being locked with Henry's. I turn to face Samson, his dashing features somehow minimized under his brothers. "I think it would have a lot to do with pink dye and all his white shirts."

"Speaking of pink, we have an announcement." Fawn threads her fingers through her husband's and looks at him with the utmost love and adoration. He nods for her to go ahead, and she turns to face the rest of the table. "We're having a girl."

The entire table, minus Henry—so really just me and Samson—erupt with gleeful congratulations and praise for her future baby girl. Henry may not have erupted with elation at her announcement, but he does eventually offer his congratulations. As a matter of fact, he looks constipated when he finally does reach out to shake Leo's hand, and nothing more.

"Oh, my goodness! A little girl. Do you have any names picked out yet?" I ask. I love babies, and not to be biased, but little girls are my favorite. I know they can decide on any color for the nursery, but I'm partial to pink. Obviously.

"We have a few, but haven't settled on one yet. I think we'll know when she's born. We both feel it's best to wait and decide then."

For the next twenty minutes, at least, we all talk about nursery themes. Fawn is thinking classic France with an Eifel Tower mural. Leo wants a jungle theme with tigers and elephants.

Samson and I input our name suggestions, a few of which Fawn makes note of in her phone. Henry, of course, says little if nothing at all. He does give his sister a reassuring glance that he's not a complete douche. It seems enough for her, so I suppose it's enough for me.

The rest of the evening is far less eventful than dessert was. But I leave Fawn's, not only with a list of potential regular gigs, but also with the hopeful optimism of one rather big event that could lead to exactly what I need to get my tiny trailer.

8 – Henry

I don't need to try cocaine to know I don't like it

I can't believe I'm here right now. And all because of a stupid pinky promise. *Who does that past the age of six?* I shouldn't be wandering around this hipster farmer's market, trying to find Lala, the pink-haired kissing assailant.

What a waste of my Sunday.

Sundays are my day to prep for the coming week. I should be at home, at my computer, confirming appointments, double checking the status on my active escrows, and checking my stock market portfolio. Not being asked if I want to taste test beet pickled eggs. Gross. They're like pink alien eggs bobbing around in the giant jar on the counter. Not only do they look gross, but that can't be good sitting out in the sun all morning.

It's almost nine a.m. when I spot the pink tent with bubble letters spelling out Lala Boba nestled between artisan kettle corn and vegan cupcakes. It's easy to spot Micaela. I can't bring myself to call her Lala. It's far too childish. Even amongst all the other pink, her hair and matching pink logo shirt stand out as she moves about, making drinks for the small line she has in front of her booth.

Her movements are natural and practiced, while her smile is genuine and bright, lighting up her face and making her not so unpleasant to watch. Deciding to take the opportunity to watch her in action, I find a seat on a discrete bench under a nearby tree. Sitting at just the right angle, I can watch her movements and not be spotted.

If I'm going to legitimately consider having her business at our upcoming conference, I need to ensure her ability to handle the demands. Ten minutes pass and she continues her effortless movements and smiles. Customers seem satisfied, walking away smiling as they drink their tea. These teas aren't the same horrid color as Thomas's was. Some are opaque pink, others transparent light green. I didn't know there were multiple types and flavors of this boba tea. The balls in the bottom of their drinks aren't black like Thomas's either. Instead they're a bright pink. *Is she even making proper bobas?* How the hell should I know? I didn't even know what a boba was until last week.

Another half hour passes as I watch her in her element. There's another girl working the booth with her, just as vibrant with her pink lipstick that pops against her russet skin and short caramel hair. Her logo t-shirt white instead of pink. The two women move in tandem, alternating between making drinks and taking payments.

After about an hour, there's a lull in her line, leaving it empty and giving the two women a moment's respite, where they sit and drink from water bottles. Micaela's smile still firmly in place. I have a feeling she smiles a lot. My own lips twitch downward in disapproval.

I figure this is as good a time as any to make my presence known. Rising from the bench, I make my way to her booth, which remains customer free. Micaela doesn't notice me when she makes her way outside her booth, a cup in hand filled with a dark pink drink. Squatting, she fiddles with the tablecloth hanging over the front of her booth.

I watch her as she cocks her head side to side then nods in approval, standing before turning to finally face me. Since she turned directly to me, I thought she knew I was standing here. But when she jumps, lets out a high-pitched squawk, and flings her hands into the air, I realize she had no idea. Her outburst of surprise and subsequent arm flinging results in her dark pink drink flying right into the face of her coworker. It drips off her chin and streams rivers of pink liquid down the front of her shirt.

Micaela has little time to process my presence as she turns and rounds the table into the booth, apologizing profusely to the other girl and trying to help her wipe the drink from her person. They succeed at only removing it from her face, not her hair or her shirt.

"I'm going to go try and wash this off in the bathroom. I'll be right back." She half-heartedly smiles at me as she passes, holding her shirt away from her skin as she goes.

"Sorry again, Shay, it really was an accident." Micaela calls after her. Then she turns her burning glare on me. "What the hell was that?"

"What was what?"

"Why didn't you say something? Announce yourself, cough awkwardly? Anything but creep up on me assassin's creed style and scare the living bejesus out of me."

"I didn't creep up on you. I walked up, out in the open, at a normal pace." I offer, slightly offended she thought I cared enough to creep up on her. "So, this is your booth?"

"Obviously. What gave it away? Was it my name in giant letters or all the pink?"

"Actually, it was the nauseatingly bright smile you've had plastered on your face for the past hour."

Said smile is nowhere to be seen at this moment, as she's taken to gawking at me with an open mouth and furrowed brow. "You've been watching me for an hour, and that's not considered creeping?"

"No, because I wasn't watching you. I was investigating your business. How many customers you have, how many sales you make, customer satisfaction upon tasting your product. As well as professionalism and appearance, of course."

"Of course. Makes perfect sense." she drawls.

"It should."

For a long moment, we just stare at each other. I find that silence makes most people uncomfortable. I personally find silence a much-preferred alternative to idle chit chat about nothing. As I knew she would, Micaela is the one to break the silence.

"So, what conclusion have you come to on my business?" she asks, shrugging her hands at her sides, obviously irritated with me. Good. I'm irritated at her for making my promise to be here and waste my morning.

"It's cohesive. The logo fits the aesthetic of the product, customers seem to walk away smiling more than not." Leaning back, I inspect her prices, neatly scrawled on a standing sandwich chalkboard. "Your price point is accurate for the product. At least, according to the cursory research I did last night."

"So... does that mean you'll sign me on for your conference?" Her megawatt smile returns to her face with open hopefulness at my possible confirmation of her request, a tiny dimple appearing in her right cheek. She's about to be very disappointed.

"Not likely."

"What? Why?" she shrieks, the dimple disappearing as quickly as it appeared.

"I just don't think your pink concoctions are appropriate for a corporate function such as this."

Bright aquamarine eyes stare at me in blatant disbelief, her smile faltering but not fading completely. I have to hand it to her, she recovers quickly. It takes her only thirty seconds to process and formulate a new plan to convince me to change my mind. Before she can get one word out, Shay, her helper, returns with damp hair and an even damper shirt. It appears she was unable to remove all the pink goo.

"So, good news and bad news. Which do you want first?" she asks Micaela.

"Bad."

"My shirt is soaking wet, and the strawberry isn't coming out. I need to go home and shower all the sugar out of my hair."

"Then what's the good news?" Micaela asks, again hopeful but apprehensive.

"I found you a replacement to take my place and help you finish out the rest of the day." Shay says with a mischievous grin.

"Who?"

"Him."

"Him who?" Micaela looks around for this mystery man Shay has offered up as a sacrifice.

"Him." Shay says again, this time turning her gaze on me and pointing.

"Me? I don't remember agreeing to such a thing." I argue.

"Sure you did. The moment you scared the shit out of Lala, forcing her to throw her pink paradise in my face."

Pink what? I have no idea what this crazy person is talking about, and I most certainly will *not* be working in this Pepto-Bismol nightmare.

"I don't think Henry wants to help out. Even if it *is* his fault." I turn my scowl on Micaela, sharing my dissatisfaction with them both.

"Sure, he does. Look at his relaxed posture, casual attire, and continued interest in you."

"Excuse me, but I do not have a continued interest in Micaela. I never had a starting interest in her. I didn't even want to be here today." I remove my hands from my jeans pockets, where they were "causally" tucked, and cross my arms over my chest, taking a more closed off stance. Realizing I'm standing flush with the front of her booth, I also take a healthy step back.

There. Now let her think I'm anything but UN-interested.

"Too late, tall, dark, and brooding. You're helping Lala, and that's that." Shay declares.

"No, I'm not."

"Yes, you are." she sing-songs.

"No, he's not." Micaela interjects.

"Yes, he is."

When both Micaela and I attempt to continue arguing, Shay raises her index finger at us and makes a weird 'ahk' noise in the back of her throat, cutting us off every time we try to speak. And now, I'm behind the pink table, standing next to Micaela, who huffs out a frustrated breath. Clearing her throat and tightening her ponytail, she slips on that effortless smile as a new customer approaches.

It's official. I have no fucking idea what I'm doing. When I tried to make one of her "pink paradise" drinks, I nearly sprayed the entire table with the mix when I didn't securely tighten the lid on the blender. Then, I spilled an entire half carton of half and half on the ground, and once Micaela and I both turned at the same time and smacked into one another front to front. I may have, although I will deny it under oath, momentarily groped her breasts. They were, to my dismay, both perky and supple. I hadn't given any consideration to her tits until that point. Now I can't *not* give them consideration. They fill and stretch her t-shirt perfectly and... *why am I staring at her tits? And now, I'm staring at her ass. Great.* I need to get the hell out of here.

Due to my ineptitude at blending drinks, I have been regulated to cashier. All Micaela's boba drinks have their own special button on her tablet app, and if there are any customizations needed, Micaela asks while mixing, pouring, and blending orders. She's not nearly as busy as she was earlier when I was watching from my bench. The bench I so fervently wish I had never left to walk over here.

Once I'm far away from the ingredients, we manage to finish out the morning without any further catastrophes. As the market begins to die down an hour later, I'm more than ready to remove myself from this pink jail.

"I suppose I should thank you for your help. At least for the help that didn't involve spilling my supplies everywhere. You didn't have to stay, and you did." Micaela turns her sweet smile up at me, that dimple I barely noticed before appears on her right cheek again. It's cute.

"You're welcome." I murmur, running my hand through my hair, unsure why hearing her thank me makes me feel... something inside. Because, of course, she's right. I didn't have to stay, but I did. *Why did I stay?* Not even I know the answer to that question.

"I suppose you'll want to get going now." Her fingers fidget with a stack of cups, lining them up and readjusting them, even though they weren't askew, before she removes them completely and places them in a box under the table. "I should start packing up anyway. Without Shay, it'll take me longer than usual." She huffs out a breath as she surveys her organized chaos. Most likely contemplating what to pack up first.

When she starts putting things away, the part of me that was raised by a strict nanny when I was twelve hears her scolding, *"Be polite and courteous to women. Always assist when needed and physically able. There's no need to be obstinate when one can be civil and respectful."* With an exhale of exasperation, I relent to my childhood nanny's inner reprimand.

"You pack up all the small things, leave the larger heavier items to me. Where's your car parked?"

Micaela's movements halt and she looks up at me, clear confusion written across her too-sweet face. "You want to help me pack up."

"It seems so."

"Well, don't sound so excited about it."

"Trust me I'm not."

A half smirk pulls at one corner of her lips. "Well, in that case, please excuse me while I make myself a celebratory boba before we put everything away." Picking up a cup, she starts to assemble something before turning to me with the other corner of her mouth hitching up into a full smile. "How about I make you one too? As a thank you."

"No, thanks."

"Why not?" Her bright smile pulls into a pouty frown. This woman can go from a hundred to zero and back again faster than the speed of light. It's exhausting.

"I don't like boba tea." I state plainly.

"Have you ever *had* a boba tea?" she asks.

"No."

"Then how do you know you don't like it, if you don't try it?"

"I don't need to try cocaine to know I don't like it."

"Sure, you do."

"I'm sorry?" I stop dead in my tracks, the sandwich board in one hand, a gallon of milk in the other. "Have you tried cocaine?"

"Of course. How else would I know if I liked it or not?" she says, completely serious as she stacks cups, lids, and straws in the box at her feet. Bending over, she gives me an unwarranted profile view of her ass in rolled denim shorts. Revealing a tattoo that, for some reason, I cannot peel my eyes away from. Two pink ribbon bows with crescent moons at their center are inked right under each full, rounded butt cheek. "But I prefer crystal meth. So much more exciting, don't you think?"

Straightening, she blocks my view of her inappropriately desirable ass. Why is someone so insufferable so oddly appealing? At least to my body. Everything that comes out of her mouth is nothing if not eye roll inducing. *Wait, did she just say crystal meth?*

Her laugh is musical and open as she takes in my frozen stance and open shock. "Relax, Henry. I'm joking. You need to learn to loosen up and spot sarcasm when you hear it." With the practiced fluid motions I've seen her using all day, she now has two cups and begins to mix chopped strawberries and red syrup with skim milk and way too much sugar in the blender with ice.

"What are you making with so much sugar?"

"Pink paradise. You'll love it."

"I don't eat that much sugar. Haven't you ever heard the phrase, 'my body is a temple'?"

"Oh, I've heard it. But my body is not a temple. It's an amusement park. Filled with popcorn, corn dogs, neon lights, and loud music. With creepy clowns and fun houses and roller coasters that make you scream with joy and vomit afterwards."

"You are one strange pink covered lady, Micaela."

"Please, call me Lala. No one has called me Micaela since my high school history teacher, who never used nicknames and put miss or mister before everyone's name, like we were in turn of the nineteenth century England."

"It's your name. Why wouldn't I call you that?"

"Because I prefer Lala."

"Well, I prefer Micaela. Calling you Lala makes me feel like I'm talking to a kindergartener." Her irritated sigh of annoyance signals my victory.

"Whatever. Here, try this and I won't correct you every time you call me Micaela." She hands me the same pink drink she spilled on Shay earlier. I eyeball it, then her. "Go on, it won't kill you."

"So you say." Reluctantly, I sip through the enormous pink straw, and one of those silly little bobas shoots right into my mouth. On reflex, I bite down and it explodes, popping juice and sweetening the already sweet milkshake-like drink. The flavor is regrettably— good. *Damn it.*

"I thought these were supposed to have tea in them?"

"Some do, some don't." she replies, shrugging one pink clad shoulder. "Well? What do you think?"

I suppose it would be wrong of me to lie, but that doesn't mean I have to compliment it either. "It's not disgusting."

"That's it? Well, I suppose it's better than nothing."

When she turns her back, I ingest a hearty gulp of the drink before sitting it down on the table and returning to my duties of stacking and carrying boxes. All in all, it takes roughly thirty minutes to load everything into the back of her pink Jeep. I make a hasty retreat as soon as it's finished, giving her no finite answer on attending the conference.

9 – Henry

It's not a spank bank photo

awn manages to go an entire two days before contacting me to ask me why I didn't tell Micaela she could be a vendor at the company conference. I'm in the middle of my work afternoon when her demanding texts ping on my phone.

> **Fawn:** *Why won't you let Lala sell her boba at your conference?*
>
> **Henry:** *Because it's not professional enough.*
>
> **Fawn:** *That's a stupid reason. If you don't give me a legitimate reason, I'm going to go to Dad.*
>
> **Henry:** *Go ahead, he's going to give you the same answer.*
>
> **Fawn:** *This is ridiculous. Boba is great, Lala is great. I don't see the problem here.*

Of course, she wouldn't see the problem. She's not me. She gets the normal side of Micaela while I get the absurdly peppy Micaela who's determined to make me *smile*. Not to mention those damn pink bows and her ass keep popping into my head at the most inopportune times.

I decide to turn my aggravation onto my sister just as my brother walks in. I set aside my phone momentarily to question my brother's sudden and unscheduled appearance.

"Hey, bro." Samson drops himself into the chair across from my desk and promptly leans back, placing his pristine white Versace Greca sneakers on my desk.

Nudging the toes of his sneakers, I try to push them off, but they don't budge. "Samson. What are you doing here?"

"Was in the neighborhood. Thought I would stop by and say hi to my big bro. Oh, and the old man, I guess. Not that he would notice either way."

He's not wrong. Dad stopped paying attention to us pretty much the moment he hired someone else to do it for him. Only checking in at the end of semesters to make sure our grades were acceptable and none of us had sired illegitimate spawn, or in Fawn's case, become impregnated in a way that would taint our family reputation. Once we were all out of college and fending for ourselves, him and Mom pretty much became ghosts. No holiday dinners or family vacations. Just a printed Christmas card that said the same thing to everyone on their mailing list. I'm pretty sure most years, they didn't even know a card went out, leaving it to their overworked, and most likely depressed, personal or executive assistants.

Which makes my father's presence in my office last week asking about baby gifts that much more out of place.

"Have you gone to see him yet?"

"Yeah. He was unavailable, and his newest assistant, who by the way, looks like she could be a freshman in college, said she would 'let him know I stopped by'." Samson uses air quotes around my father's most-likely-under-twenty-one-years-old-assistant's words.

"And now you're here."

"And now I'm here."

We sit in silence, Samson relaxing more into his seat. I stare at him expectantly and he just stares right back.

"Well, if that's all you came to say, then you can leave now. I have work to get back to."

Just then, my phone pings with another text from Fawn. I glance at the screen since my phone is still sitting face up on my desk.

Fawn: _Hello? I'm not done yelling at you yet. Pay attention to me!_

"Who's that?" Samson asks.

"Fawn. She's trying to convince me to let Micaela be a vendor at the conference."

"Who the hell is Micaela?"

"The pink girl that kissed me and then showed up at Fawn's family dinner."

"Oh, you mean Lala." Samson's eyes grow wider and brighter, much more interested in my day now than he was when he first walked in. "You should let her attend. That way, I can see her again and work my charm on her. She's hot."

"That's not why Fawn brought her over, and you know how she hates it when you seduce and bed her friends."

"Bed her friends? Who the hell talks like that? You know you can just say fucks, right? I want to FUCK her friends."

"You're disgusting and have a much too expensive education to speak like that."

"Like what? Just because I went to Columbia doesn't mean I can't say fuck. Besides, I know you say it too. I've heard you use it plenty." he admonishes.

It's not that I'm opposed to using the term fuck or fucks, but I am in my office in the middle of a workday, and I must retain some sense of professionalism. Even if my brother does not, dressed in his Prada jeans and Tom Ford white button down with the sleeves rolled to the elbows. Untucked. Slacker.

I suppose he doesn't have to try harder than that when he makes his money playing the stock market. A long time ago Samson realized he didn't like working for a living, and he especially didn't like doing what others told him. So, he decided to just make his money directly for himself. Using his Ivy League education to buy and sell and profit. As a result, he's left with a lot of free time to fuck around, as he would put it.

Ignoring my brother and his lack of work ethic, I respond to my sister before she starts calling nonstop until I answer her. She does not like to be ignored, or told no.

> **Henry:** *This conference is going to be filled with professional realtors, bankers and agents wearing gray and black designer suits who make more in one month than she does in five years. She's too pink, too bright, and too peppy. It's not a good match.*
>
> **Fawn:** *That's a load of horseshit. Just because they have poor fashion sense and too much money doesn't mean they don't enjoy sweet treats.*
>
> **Henry:** *You're not going to leave me alone until I say she can go, are you?*
>
> **Fawn:** *Nope.*
>
> **Henry:** *The answer's still no.*
>
> **Fawn:** *We'll see about that.*
>
> **Henry:** *What does that mean?*

Three little bubbles appear, then disappear. A moment later, a picture appears, and I curse under my breath. It's a photo of Micaela from behind, in skintight workout leggings. Fuck me. Her ass looks spectacular. Even better than it did in the jean shorts. And her thighs... Jesus fucking Christ, what is my sister trying to do to me?

When I manage to unglue my eyes from her ass and discreetly readjust myself, I notice Micaela is looking over her shoulder and winking at the camera. I have to compose myself before responding.

__Henry:__ Is that supposed to mean something?
__Fawn:__ No. Just thought you'd like to see what you're missing.
__Henry:__ That makes no sense.
__Fawn:__ Looks like we both aren't making any sense today. Why don't you just stew on that and get back to me.
__Henry:__ How about I don't.
__Fawn:__ But you will.

She's right. I do stew on it. Far longer than I should. Long enough for me to forget Samson sitting in my black leather guest chair.

"What did she say that has your rapt attention?" Removing his shoes from my desk, he leans over, trying to see my screen. I don't move fast enough, and he catches sight of the photo. "Who the hell is that?"

Before I can hide my phone or exit out of the text thread, Samson has rounded my desk and snatched my phone from me, taking a few large steps away so I can't reach out and take it back.

"It's no one. Give me back my phone." I say, hand extended, now standing as well. We're posed like a pair of teenagers playing keep away in the schoolyard.

"Oh shit, this is Lala. Why is Fawn sending you spank bank photos of Lala's ass?" he asks, eyes still glued to the phone.

"It's not a spank bank photo. I have no idea why she sent it. Somehow, she thinks it's going to convince me to hire Micaela." Leaning against my desk, I cross my arms over my chest, waiting for him to finish his immature snooping.

"It sure as fuck is convincing me, and I didn't even need to be convinced." Samson's fingers skim over the phone screen before he hands it back to me. Glancing down, I see he's forwarded the picture to himself.

"Seriously, Samson?"

"Oh, most seriously. It may not be spank bank material for you, dear celibate brother, but it sure as hell is for me." He winks, and I scoff, returning my phone to my pocket.

"Again, you're disgusting. Can I get back to work now?" I return to my seat behind my desk and sit.

"Sure. I got a lot more than I came for today."

"Goodbye, Samson."

"Later." He waves over his shoulder as he saunters out of my office, his other hand in his pocket and a wicked grin on his lips.

I try for the rest of the day not to look at the "spank bank" photo, as Samson so crudely put it. I slip only once. This pint-sized, pink-haired woman seems to have gained my attention, and I need to stop. NOW. So, I do. Focusing on what's important. Work.

10 – Lala

Barf Twins Do Not Serve

Fawn looks like she's literally holding in her gag of up-chuck, leaning over, almost putting her head between her knees. At least as best as she can with her baby belly in the way. So, I do what any friend would do. I try to think of something to distract her.

"Don't think about it. Think about the nursery. All the cute, girly things you're going to buy her. What colors you want to paint the walls. Which rocking chair you want to buy. Trust me, you want a glider with a footrest. Most comfortable chair ever."

She's looking a little less green around the gills, and I know I'm feeling less vomity now. Thank goodness.

"Ok, Ok. I think it's working." Taking in a few deep, steadying breaths, Fawn finally sits upright again. "That was a close one. You can't do that to me. Everything is on a hair trigger these days. I cry, and fart, and pee all the freaking time." she whimpers, taking a cleansing drink of her smoothie.

"I had a friend in Texas who was pregnant, and she had every symptom in the book. Poor girl. But her baby came out beautifully, and all that unpleasantness was forgotten the moment she set eyes on him."

I wasn't there to witness their first moments, but I did visit a few days later, and she was positively radiant. A sharp sting lances my heart. A quick but painful longing I haven't experienced before, even when holding my friend's newborn son. There was no stab of jealousy or pining for something I didn't have. My biological clock must be going off or something. At some point the alarm was set, and now it's ringing like a damn cathedral bell, alerting me to my need for a baby.

Why is it always a desire to procreate and make more tiny humans? Why can't it be something less stressful and inexpensive? Like a root canal. There are plenty of people on this planet. You would think mother nature would turn off our alarm clocks that fill us with hormones and unexplained urges that push us to be mothers. I don't know that I'm ready to be a mother. I may not even be ready to be a wife or spouse. Mother nature really needs to get her priorities straight.

Fawn, unaware of my derailed train of thought, now stares at me thoughtfully.

"About my brother," she starts carefully. "he's been a little... stagnant the past couple years. Well, actually more than a couple. And none of us have been able to shake him free of it. Except you."

"Me?"

"Yeah. There's something about you that gets under his skin."

"That we can agree on. He doesn't seem to like me very much."

"I don't think that's it." Fawn says thoughtfully, tipping her head to one side and inspecting me while drinking her smoothie and rubbing her growing baby bump. At twenty-one weeks, she's showing quite nicely now, and her skintight leggings and top only accentuate her perfect mommy body.

"Well, it sure as hell isn't the warm and fuzzies he feels for me."

"Hmmm," she hums as if that's a real answer. "Maybe you could spend a little time with him? Get him to come out of his self-inflicted shell of all work and no play makes Henry a dull boy."

"I don't know if that's a good idea," I say, pulling one leg under me and settling into the cushioned bench seat.

"Sure, it is. You'll see. Plus, it will give you more opportunities to convince him you should be at the conference. Trust me, he just needs a little push. You'll be at that conference."

Across the shop, a bell chimes when a couple enters, easy smiles on their faces, their fingers intertwined. For a moment, I'm distracted by the couple. I've always wanted someone to be my other half. A man who knows me inside and out, to laugh at my jokes, and put up with all my pink things. A man who won't make me feel suffocated by seeding my roots. One who won't make me feel squished and smothered and entombed in one city for the rest of my ever-loving life unable to leave. *I'm not hyperventilating. Are you hyperventilating? Breathe, just breathe, Lala.*

All I want is a man who will make me finally want to put down roots and stay still without going into cardiac arrest. Where being with him for more than a bit of fun won't send me into a downward spiral of cabin fever, forcing me to move cities—and sometimes states—away.

Sadly, no man has yet to tempt me to do such a thing. I've always felt smothered, unable to breath whenever they spoke about moving in together or meeting the parents. All I could see was that small town and the lackluster life of confinement it promised.

Shaking myself from the morose memories, I refocus on Fawn and her idea of me helping Henry. Henry, the grumpy, annoyingly hot and well-dressed man whose lips I can't seem to forget kissing.

I wonder if he thinks about my lips.

Rubbing her stomach, Fawn leans, stretching out her back. "Ooh. That was a big one, my goodness." Shifting her hand around to feel better, a glow appears on her face that I love seeing in pregnant women. That glossy eyed look of awe and love and joy. "Here. Feel."

Reaching around, she grabs my hand and places it on her belly, guiding it to where the baby is kicking. A small but strong bump comes from inside my friend, pressing against my hand. It's amazing, though it kind of reminds me of Aliens. I smile, holding in my chuckle at my own inner thoughts of the baby ripping through my friend like an alien.

"You are going to be a great mom, I can tell."

"Thank you," she says, tears obviously welling in her eyes. Pregnancy hormones make her far more susceptible to crying these days. She cried just the other day when she saw a Pomeranian dog wearing a dress.

"Now, don't try to distract me. I'm not letting you leave without making a plan to get you and Henry together. We will convince him one way or another."

"I wasn't the one distracting you. You're the one who has a small alien kicking at your insides and wanted me to feel it."

"Oh, ha ha, very funny."

"I thought so." We both laugh, but I can tell she's not done yet.

Distracting myself with my smoothie, I swivel the straw and focus on my cup, waiting for Fawn to say what it is she's really planning. I don't have to wait long.

"I have an idea."

"Of course, you do." I lament.

"Of course, I do, and it's a great one." she confirms. "My brother works far too much. And that's coming from an attorney, who works twelve-hour days. I think you should take him out, make him do something fun. Something he wouldn't ever think to do himself. And basically, in general, be your amazing, wonderful self."

I eye her suspiciously. "This sounds an awful lot like a set up for a date."

"What? No, not a date. Just two people going out to do something enjoyable together."

"Also known as a date."

"Call it what you will, I don't care. Either way, I still think you are the one who can get him to agree."

"I still don't know why you think that."

"Let's just call it a sister's intuition."

Huffing out a breath, I watch her, trying to decide if this is a bad idea or not. Considering I still need to convince him to have me at the conference, and I'm personally determined to see him smile, it doesn't sound like a completely horrible idea.

As she knew I would, I relent and sigh, giving in once again to Fawn's flawless argument. Now I need to figure out the best place to take Henry, the unsmiling grouch-o man, to make him smile and convince him I am a professional businesswoman. If only I knew what a professional businesswoman would do. I feel Fawn is like a unicorn in the world of boss bitches. She's too upbeat and nice to be considered one of *them*. So, I can't use her as an example.

Besides, she told me to be myself, NOT a stuffy, boring, corporate stick-up-her-ass "lady". I'll just have to settle for convincing Henry I can handle whatever his fancy shmancy conference can throw at me.

The air is warmer outside the smoothie shop, the bright spring sunshine almost heated enough to consider it summer. Fawn left to return home and I decided, with nowhere else to go, I would stroll through the street and shops.

After my abrupt kiss with Henry, I never had the chance to peruse any of the stores, being far too embarrassed to stay in the vicinity for fear I would run into him again. Which is also why, up until now, I hadn't taken the opportunity after Pilates to do so. I didn't want to risk a confrontation with the mystery sweatpants guy in case he decided to press charges. Now that I know who he is, and know he's not likely to send me to jail for sexual assault, I feel safe walking down the street. Heading straight for the roller skate shop I saw that day.

It's extremely unlikely I'll buy anything since my bank account is emptier than a brothel with floor to ceiling windows and bright halogen lighting. That doesn't mean I can't daydream over which pair I would order if I had the funds.

The walk might do me some good. Help clear my head of a certain sexy realtor.

It's not working.

His frowning face the entire time he helped in my booth plays on repeat in my head. I am going to get him to smile if it's the last thing I do. Fawn seems to think I'm capable of it for some reason only known to her.

Passing a store that sells only linen clothes, I stop in front of a charming bookstore called Turn the Page. A display of their newest release is in the window. A fantasy retelling of Peter Pan. Just one more thing to add to my list of "to purchase after getting paid" list. I make a mental note of its title and keep moving.

Walking another half a block, I stop and sit on a bench in front of a small park area, a newspaper fluttering in the breeze on its painted wooden slats. There's a young girl walking at least four dogs, being pulled in just as many directions and a man playing with a toddler on the jungle gym. Other than that, the green space is empty and shadowed in the cover of the lush trees. The smell of fresh cut grass and something floral wafts on the breeze.

It's moments like these that make me appreciate my ability to experience them. Most people fill their days with tedious work and too much time staring at their cell phones. Their time is consumed with the hustle and bustle of making more money to pay for more things that don't ever lead to their true happiness.

Remodeling the bus into a Skoolie and living in it may have been inspired by my need to travel and see the world beyond the city limits of Farmington, but in doing so, I learned something else. Financial freedom. Sure, I require money to pay for food, gas, and rent for wherever I park my bus. Add up those numbers and compare them to someone with a three hundred-thousand-dollar mortgage and utilities to match, there's no competition which I would choose.

Freedom from restraint and debt confinement was an unforeseen benefit to my lifestyle. There are, however, downfalls to being a nomad.

Firstly, being unable to visit my parents and family whenever I want. No Sunday brunches or large birthday parties. I try to make it down to Florida for Thanksgiving or Christmas, but I can't always manage it. Along with that comes the lack of close friends. Sure, I meet all kinds of people like Paloma and Pilar and Fawn, but the twins are like me. They move around. Pittsburgh isn't their forever home any more than it is mine. And with all that I love Fawn and what she's done for me, I doubt she wants to be my emergency contact. Not to mention, once the baby arrives, she'll have even less time for socialities. I fully expect our Thursday Pilates classes to cease.

Then there's the loneliness that creeps in. Humans are social creatures, having private quiet time is appreciated, but sharing a space with someone else, having someone else along for the ride, would make a tremendous difference.

These days, my insides are at war with one another. One side wants to press on, keep going, and find the next adventure. The other just wants to stop moving, share space with someone for more than a few months. Find love.

Can it be possible to please both sides? I doubt a truce will ever be signed by my ever-warring subconscious. Which only means that one day, I'll have to decide which side wins. The lonely nomad, free of chains and anchors, or the stationary romantic, who deep down agrees with her mother.

While pondering my existential crisis, I pick up the newspaper and casually flip through its smudged pages. This must be a Sunday edition because in the back are ads and coupons. One grabs my attention and I fold it up carefully and slip it in my messenger bag.

Feeling the need for a distraction, I return to my walk, getting tangled in the leashes of the dog walker on my way to the sidewalk.

"Oh, my goodness. I'm so sorry. These little rascals are just a handful today."

Her "little rascals" consist of a Great Dane, German Shepherd, Dalmatian, standard poodle, and a collie, the only one even slightly little.

"It's not a problem. I love dogs." I offer her a smile and give the Great Dane trying to lick my face a firm scratch behind the ear.

"Wow. I love your hair. Wish I could dye my hair a fun color."

"Why don't you?"

"Work." she says with an eye roll that suggests she's tried before and was shut down.

"I didn't know dog walking had a dress code."

"Oh, this is only one of my jobs. I have two others, and the secretary position at the tax practice doesn't consider purple hair professional attire."

"Lame."

"Tell me about it." She shrugs, and the dogs take that moment to decide they wish to chase a squirrel. She yells her goodbye as she is pulled along on their chase.

Another block down the street, and I finally reach the skate shop I was looking for. A literal rainbow of wheels is arranged in the front window in the shape of a wheel. The store's name is painted in white, flowing script on the windows center. My eyes linger on the sparkly pink wheels, then drop to the bottom right corner where a small block letter sign is propped up.

Help Wanted.

Hmm. It wouldn't be the first time I took a part time job in a city when markets and events were limited. Maybe they'll have an employee discount and let me wear skates in the store while working.

That thought alone, of skating to work and at work propels me inside the store.

11 – Henry

I want to be that blueberry boy

There are two things in life I truly despise. One is bank holidays. Two is surprises. Number two just walked onto my floor and is currently making small talk with my assistant. Her and her two friends stand out like flashing neon lights in the middle of a moonless night during a black out. Micaela's pink hair is now flanked by one vibrant cobalt blue—I'm assuming the girl she was with the day she kissed me—and one soft yellow-blonde.

Does she not have friends with normal colored hair?

Micaela's aquamarine eyes lock onto me across the floor of desks and computer monitors, a sly smile spreading slowly across her lips. I have a feeling I'm not going to like the reason on the other side of that grin.

Standing at the entrance to my office, files in hand, I watch in horror as her two friends, twins now that I look at their faces, circle Thomas and engage him in conversation. Turning his attention to them and angling his body away from Micaela, allowing her to back away slowly and make a b-line straight for me.

For a moment, I'm torn between retreating to my office and locking the door behind me, and finding out the reason for the sudden appearance of the Crayola bunch in my office. Knowing my sister had something to do with this, I stand my ground, ready to reject her and call security to remove them from my building. This girl is nothing but a distraction and I'm working.

Crossing my arms and assuming a no-nonsense stance, I settle my face into a flat, couldn't-give-a-shit expression that I hope conveys my appreciation for her invasion of my office.

As she saunters across the floor, heads turn to watch her, like fish watching an innocent seal swimming towards a shark. Eyes shift from her to me in uncensored horror and disbelief. My employees know where my priorities lie and my level of tolerance for disobedience. This ranks at a nine on my irritation meter. But when Micaela rounds a bank of desks and is headed straight for me, that nine drops to a four, and is replaced with my arousal meter, clocking in at a hard eight and a half. Honestly, I haven't been aroused by anyone in a long while, and I didn't think it was still possible to be... stunned like I've become.

What, pray tell, could possibly flip my switch so fast, you ask? Well, I'll tell you. That would be Micaela, the pink temptress herself, dressed in painted-on, pink tie dye athletic shorts and a soft pink crop top that delicately slides off one shoulder. Her hair is curled in a way I haven't seen it before, making large, soft waves that frame her face, and I swear I see glitter shimmering on her cheeks.

Those delectable hips and well-defined thighs sway as she keeps her seductive pace towards me. A few of the employees tilt their heads to get a better view of her ass as she passes, and for some reason that makes me want to fire them all. I can feel the skin on my knuckles stretching as I fist my hands. My biceps flex and stretch against my Tom Ford suit jacket, almost to the point I might pop a seam.

It takes her an inordinate amount of time to cross the floor and stop herself right in front of me. I was right, there is pink and silver glitter dusted across the apples of her cheeks. This girl—this woman—somehow manages to take something so juvenile and innocent, and make it look absolutely illicit. I have the sudden urge to lick that glitter right off her skin. Probably not the healthiest thought in any way, but I still want to do it all the same.

"Hello," says the pink she-devil, staring up at me with false innocence we both know she doesn't possess.

"What do you want?"

"Me? Oh, nothing much." Lies. She wants something, otherwise she wouldn't have bothered with the whole charade taking place in my lobby. I glance over to see Thomas has realized he lost one as he catches sight of me and Micaela. Poor guy looks like someone just ran over his dog.

"I know you want something, Micaela, and I'm pretty sure my sister has something to do with it, so just spit it out."

"Is that what you tell all the girls? Just spit it out? Seems… messy, and you don't look like a guy that does… *messy.*"

What in the actual fuck is happening right now? I am turned on, pissed off, and suddenly want to be messy with this woman. Fucking hell.

"No, I don't do messy. So. Spit. It. Out. Micaela." I don't mean for my voice to deepen, or for it to rumble in my chest and reverberate down through my body, but it does. I feel every word in my veins, and if the shiver I see dance across her skin is any inclination, she does too.

"I… thought perhaps I could steal you away for the afternoon." Her voice is small and unsure. Apparently my words affected her more than I meant them to.

She's so short compared to me, barely reaching my collar bone. With all that pink rosiness, she reminds me of Strawberry Shortcake. But in an X-rated way. I'm sure there's a porn site out there with Strawberry Shortcake getting rammed by that blueberry boy. Right now, I want to be that blueberry boy and taste the sweetness of her shortcake.

Fuck me. I'm screwed. This is so not going the way it's supposed to. She is not supposed to be able to sway me with big glittering eyes under thick lashes giving me "I wanna fuck you" vibes. She's not here for that. She's here to get a spot at the conference. Plain and simple.

Get your fucking head out of the gutter man, and focus.

"If you're here to persuade me about the conference, you can forget it. I have other things to do today." I turn to make my way back into my office and am stopped by a small, but strong hand on my elbow. Looking over my shoulder, I can see she's not deterred one bit.

"I'm not here for that at all. I'm here because you still look like you need your frown turned upside down. And I'd like to be the one to do it." She plasters on a sickly-sweet smile to top it all off.

Rotating, I face her fully again, shifting the file under my arm and sliding my hands into my pockets. I take my time running my eyes up and down her body, taking in the shorts I want to remove with my teeth so I can leave bite marks on those thighs beneath them. My gaze lingers on the swell of her breasts and exposed shoulder before returning to hers. She seems to be holding her breath as I scrutinize her.

"And what makes you think you'll be the one to make me smile, Shortcake?"

For a moment, she thinks while exhaling slowly, the color in her cheeks rising. I like that I can fluster her. She flusters me, so it seems

Pinky Promise

only fair I can do it in return.

"I guess you'll just have to come with me and find out. Won't you?"

Oh, I'd like to come with you alright. Shaking away the intrusive thought, I steady my heart rate with controlled, even breathing. There's something about the mischievous glint in her eyes that has me wanting to go with her. To find out what it is she thinks would make me smile. I don't even know what it would take to make me smile anymore. Perhaps I want to.

"And if I say yes?" I don't know what in all the holy hell possesses me to ask the question, but I do. Micaela's face lights up, and she bounces on her toes, clapping her hands together in triumph. "I haven't agreed, yet."

"Oh, you will. Because when you say yes, I promise to give you an experience I guarantee you've never had before." If she only knew how much I would like to test that theory.

"Alright, you have my attention. Tell me more."

"Nope. That's all you get. You have to agree to come with me, and then you'll find out."

"Hmm." I squint down at her as if my will alone can force the explanation from her lips. It won't. She's far too stubborn.

"Pleeeeaaaasssse." With a popped bottom lip, she pouts and begs. Damn, I'd like to see that look on her face while she begs for me to give her something more than my smile.

I don't like the way this woman throws me out of whack, distracts, and pulls me in with her unintentional desire. It's unnerving how easy she can spin my head around and force me to do what she wants. First the kiss I was not prepared for, then the dinner and farmer's market, and let's not forget that fucking picture Fawn sent me. Now this. Leaving the office in the middle of a workday to goof off, doing God knows what. And yet, I can feel my resolve wilting,

91

an acceptance of her challenge forming on my lips.

"Fine. Only because I want to prove you wrong."

"Yeeesssss!" Her honest enthusiasm is cute. A weird tick tickles my cheek, almost as if it wants to curl up at her joy. That can't be right. My frown deepens, but it doesn't dissuade the bouncing shortcake in front of me. Her bouncing is even more distracting than her interrupting my office with all her color. Reaching out one hand, I place it on her shoulder to stop the tormenting bouncing.

"You are not going to regret this."

"I already do."

I regret it even more half an hour later when Micaela pulls her obnoxious pink Jeep into the parking lot of a place called The Bounce Palace. It looks like a ten-year-old's birthday party, but on steroids. Through the massive windows I can see straight through into the ninth circle of hell she's brought me to.

Giant trampolines cover the floors and walls of half the space. Squared out and lined with colorful red and blue padded areas, a dozen people linger, jumping one after the other on the trampolines like overgrown children. On the other half of the death trap are various padded obstacle course structures, and a few other areas I can't see clearly.

There's no way I'm going in there with her. I did not sign up for this. I thought she would take me to the zoo, bowling, or a traveling carnival. I should have known better. That would have been too normal for Micaela.

Now her sinful shorts make sense.

Why did she let me come here in my suit? Even if I were to participate, I'm not risking my Tom Ford for this.

"Please do not tell me this is where you are taking me." Rolling my head to the side to watch her, I see she is more than ecstatic about our destination.

"Of course, it is silly. Come on. No one can say no to trampolines!"

"I can say no to trampolines. Watch. NO. See, easy. Now let's leave."

"Uh-uh," she tisks, reaching into her back seat and hands me a shopping bag. Looking inside, I pull out the clothing. Black basketball shorts and a plain white tee.

"You have got to be kidding me."

"Nope. You, sir, are going to wear those clothes, and you are going to bounce with me and we're going to have fun. And maybe, if you're lucky, you'll even smile."

Micaela jumps out of the car before I have a chance to argue. Rounding to my side and throwing the door open, she pulls me out with a strength I did not see coming. To avoid face planting in the parking lot, I firmly plant both of my feet on the ground beneath me.

"Let's go, Mr. Grumpapotomus. We're gonna turn that frown upside down. Even if I have to do it literally." She's already halfway to the entrance, completely ignoring my refusal. It's not a bad view watching her walk away from me. Her ass entices me to follow, and I do, like a God damn puppy dog.

Micaela pays our twenty-dollar entry fee with cash and a coupon for a two-for-one on your first visit. We have to sign a liability waiver, which I read through thoroughly, receiving more than one exacerbated sigh and groan from Micaela as she waits for me to finish.

"Do you always read all the fine print?"

"Yes. Don't you? You really should. For all intents and purposes, that's a binding legal contract. You should treat it as such. Always read the fine print. Never sign something you haven't read and don't understand."

"Why? They all say the same thing anyway. Don't sue us if you hurt yourself being a dumb fuck and not following the rules. Pretty basic stuff." Her happy go lucky attitude on casual binding contracts irks me. No one should sign their name so carelessly. It makes me want to sit her down and go through the do's and don'ts of adulting.

"Come on, grumpy cat. Let's get you changed and bouncing."

Ten minutes later, I'm in the shorts and shirt Micaela bought me, which feel like sandpaper against my skin, standing on the precipice of my doom.

12 - Henry

Corn n' cow festival like it's the Macy's Thanksgiving Day Parade

The first time I bounce on the trampoline, it's mild and I barely go six inches in the air. The third time I bounce, Micaela is giggling nonstop and decides she wants me to go higher, launching me two feet in the air. I'm not prepared and fall on my ass, growling at her like the grouchy old man I am. A gaggle of teenagers laugh and stare. I feel like an incompetent fool. Micaela doesn't care and bounces away like a frog, landing gracefully on the stable padded frame.

"Why a trampoline park? Couldn't we go somewhere a little less dangerous?"

"Trampolines aren't dangerous. You're such a worry wart." *I am not a worry wart. I just simply like to be in control of my own bodily movements.* Trampolines don't exactly allow for that. "I dunno. I just saw the coupon in the newspaper, and the idea made me happy. I thought it could do the same for you. Letting go of the tight grip you have on everything and just allow the chips to land where they may."

"I don't like the idea of letting go."

"I can see that." Her eyes shift to my fisted hands. I try to relax my grip, unclenching my fingers and stretching them out

"Do you often take guys to places like this?"

She ponders me while deftly stepping back onto a trampoline to bounce casually, effortlessly, mockingly... seductively. She doesn't put much effort into the bounce, barely reaching just to my eye level. But her breasts still bob with her movement, and it takes considerable effort for me to watch her face and not her tits.

"I've gone to a few arcades, mini golf, indoor skydiving, paintball, wine and paint nights, rock walls, Velcro walls—"

"Velcro walls?"

"Yeah, where you wear jumpsuits with Velcro on it and jump on a wall with the other side of the Velcro so you stick to it. It's awesome." My head bobs up and down, following her movements as she continues to bounce while listing all the strange places she's been on dates to.

"And you went to all of these places with guys? Different guys? On dates?"

"Not all different guys, but yeah. I hate boring dates where you just stare at each other across a table pushing food around on your plates trying to think of something to talk about only to relapse into conversation about the weather. How lame is that? I want to do and experience something new. To learn about the person naturally without feeling like I'm on a game show with a buzzer in my hand just waiting for someone to yell 'You are the weakest link, goodbye' and drop me through a trapdoor in the floor." Micaela barely breaths during her long-winded speech. Somehow, speaking in these long-unhinged trains of thought is normal to her. I can barely follow along.

"Well, that's definitely not how I feel when having dinner with a woman."

"Of course, *you* wouldn't. You look like the kind of guy who likes playing twenty questions. You probably have them all listed in your phone before you go out, and if she doesn't answer one the way you like, there is no second date. You're not trying to get to know her on a personal level." Finally, she stops bouncing and lands on the padded area next to me, thank goodness. I don't know if I can handle a whole afternoon watching her bounce. "You're trying to interview for a position. Looking for qualifications and references. You have to know her blood type, menstrual cycle, and medical history. Not what her favorite flower is, or why she wears so much pink."

With one swift arm sweep, she gestures to herself to demonstrate my lack of interest in her as a person. Apparently, she missed the part where I've been checking her out since she walked into my office and demanded I leave with her.

"You just want to know my business plan and gross profit for the year to decide if I'm worthy. Not if I'm an honest, reliable person."

She has me there. Not once did I question why she wears so much pink, or why she sells boba, or anything really. I don't even know her last name.

"What's your last name?" My question visibly stuns her, but she still answers.

"Hart."

"Micaela Hart." I test out her full name, rolling it around on my tongue and letting it settle into my taste buds. I imagine she tastes fucking delicious. "Ok. So, why do you wear so much pink, Micaela Hart?"

"Ooooh, so now you want to get to know me? Now that I've pointed it out. Typical man."

"What's wrong with that?" I ask, following her as she makes her way to the side of the room where there's trampolines on the walls.

"I'll tell you when you get back on a trampoline and bounce with me." Her grin is all evil glory, knowing now that I want to know, I'll do it to get the answer out of her.

Relenting, I step onto the trampoline next to hers and lightly bend and flex my knees to get me moving. Not allowing my feet to leave the flexing material, I still move in an up and down motion that seems to placate her.

"I come from a very small town in the middle of nowhere Kentucky."

"Kentucky? I don't hear an accent." I don't mean to interrupt, but she in no way sounds like a native Kentucky girl.

"I got rid of it a long time ago. So, in my small farming town of Farmington, everyone knows everyone, as they do. Everything revolves around the farming season and livestock. As such, my world was a wash of dirt brown, camo green, and denim blue. When I was about seven years old, my mom took me into Mayfield, the nearest city to ours, to buy a dress for the Corn n' Cow Festival."

I have to bite my cheek to keep a bark of laughter from bursting out of my mouth. I haven't wanted to laugh in ages, but hearing her talk about attending a Corn n' Cow festival like it's the Macy's Thanksgiving Day parade is just so ludicrous the reaction is almost involuntary. Micaela continues with her story, none the wiser to my almost mental break.

"Mom took me to this store in town and said I could pick any dress I wanted. It took me a whole two seconds to spot the pink princess dress on the mannequin and point it out. It was so bright and colorful and happy. The complete opposite of all the dull, drab colors my life was engulfed in. I wore that dress all day. Even went to bed in it. Everyone complimented me and smiled when I passed. It was like I was a walking ray of sunshine, and people couldn't help but be happy when they saw me."

She stops jumping and stands in the center of her trampoline, which sinks slightly under her weight. Fingers twirl the ends of her hair, and her eyes are downcast in fond remembrance. The small smile that tugs at the corner of her lips is different from the others I've seen so far. This woman has so many varying smiles, I'm starting a catalog of them to keep track.

There's her mischievous smile when she knows she's going to get what she wants, even if the other person has no clue yet. Then there's her laughing smile when something truly makes her happy, even if it's something as simple as bouncing on a trampoline. There's also her tight, polite smile she dons when she is anything but pleased, but can't stop herself from smiling. There's her casual, easy smile when serving customers at her booth, making her appear like she's right where she's supposed to be. And now, there's this one. A far-off fuzziness to her eyes, and a sweetness to her features that has nothing to do with anyone else but her and her memories.

Micaela has a literal rolodex of smiles categorized and saved. I don't even have one. I couldn't even muster one for my sister when she announced that soon I'll have a niece. All I could think about was how big a mistake she's making, bringing children into the mix of their busy lives. They'll never have time for her, and she'll be neglected and alone. Just like I was.

Her smile shifts again, now to a comfortable, relaxed grin. "So, after that, I started wearing pink as often as possible. There were always smiles, and if there weren't... well, by that time I didn't care anymore about just making others happy. It made me happy." She pauses for a moment before tilting her head to inspect me with a quizzical look. "Why don't you like pink?"

"Who says I don't like pink?"

"Ok, well, why don't you like color?"

"Why would you think I don't like color?"

"Because every time I've seen you, you're wearing grays, blacks, and whites. Nothing in your office has any color or personality. You can tell a lot about a person based on their choice of color."

"And what does my color say about me?" She scrunches up her face and looks to the ceiling, recalling whatever it is that she thinks my colors are.

"You definitely put off an 'I only eat vanilla ice cream, have no family photos on my wall, drive in silence, have sex in the dark with no cuddling, and a six-figure bank account vibe'."

"Eight," I correct, off-handedly.

"What?"

"I have an eight-figure bank account," she scoffs and makes an ooh face, raising her eyebrows in mock surprise.

Our conversation is interrupted by the sounds of bickering laughter coming from the teenagers cackling nearby. I scowl in their general direction, but Micaela sees it and grabs my hand, pulling me into her trampoline. Flexing her knees, she begins to jump again, slowly letting me match her pace.

"Ignore those guys. Just bounce with me."

I do. For about two minutes, then she tires of my slow, controlled movements and again switches to her own, so she can jump high and hoot with laughter.

"Come on, sour puss. Jump higher, like this. You can do it."

Watching her enjoy herself so much, I figure perhaps there is something to this bouncing around like a child thing, and give it a go. The first bounce is small, but I catch air, and with every following leap, I get a little higher. By the fifth, I'm pushing a couple feet off the mat, and stupidly I look down. Big mistake. Midair, I lose control of my movements and when I come down, I land on my ass, then my side, then my face. Micaela's giggle is sweet and friendly, whereas the teenager's is not. I roll to my back to see frothy pink hovering over me. It's a sight I don't mind at all.

I wonder if she would be up for a little romp in the sack. Would that be unprofessional of me? Probably, but I don't really care. It's not like I'm going to marry this woman, or even date her. I always lay my cards out face up for all to see when getting involved with a woman. No relationship, no future, my work always comes first, and I will push her to the side if she gets in my way.

From the few interactions I've had thus far with Micaela, I'm not quite sure where she lands on the relationship scale. Casual sex, casual dates, friends only, friends with benefits, serious girlfriend, wife material? She's a free spirit, alright, but if that mindset translates to her sexual relationships, I'm still not sure.

"You, ok?" She's wearing a new smile now. One that says, I'm trying not to laugh at your expense, but I can't help myself. "Anything broken?" she asks, biting on her lip to keep in her amusement.

At the sound of the peanut gallery behind me, I glare over my shoulder as I sit up and see the obnoxious frat bros and their female companions chortling. I hear words like, old man, loser, wannabe, and boomer. *Boomer?* I am thirty, not sixty, and I look fucking fantastic, if I do say so myself. And if the leisurely eye fuck the girls with them are giving me is any indication, they say so too.

The teens still watch as I stand and ungracefully make my way to Micaela's side on the stable and unmoving platform. If those kids only knew my net worth and last name, they wouldn't be laughing so openly and mocking me.

Then it hits me who I am and what I'm capable of.

"I'll be right back. Need to... pee." I don't need to pee, but I tell

Micaela I do because it's the only way she'll let me leave her side. I start towards the restrooms, but make a hard right to the front desk. The twenty-something kid behind it sees me coming and his I'm-working-and-have-to-be-polite-to-all-the-customers smile falls into place. He stands straighter to greet me.

"How can I help you, sir?"

"I'd like to speak with your manager."

I return to Micaela and the trampolines after having a few words with the manager, and I feel a little better now that I've remembered who I am.

"Ok, so I want you to launch me now. I think with our size difference I could get pretty high."

I let her instruct me on how to properly "launch" her on the trampoline before attempting it a few times. The third time she bounces higher than my head. Her laughter and smile are easy and bright and something in me lightens watching her.

This girl doesn't need anything more in life to be happy than to bounce around on woven polypropylene. No fancy clothes, diamond jewelry, expensive cars, or three Michelin star restaurants where the portions are smaller than easy bake oven cakes. It makes me stop and think.

What in my life gives me even a fraction of the joy she has right now? My job? My generous bank account? The numerous galas and conferences I attend every year?

Alone.

When she comes down from her giant moon bouncing, Micaela drags me over to an area where the obstacle course looking contraptions are. There's a spinning triple armed device, an area with two elevated small platforms, and a pit filled with giant foam blocks.

"Which one do you want to do first?"

"First? I don't want to do any of them."

"Sure, you do. Once you try it, you'll enjoy it. Trust me." For some reason, I do. Micaela spins on her heels, apparently looking for something or someone, just now realizing the lack of people and constant buzz of voices that was here when we first entered.

"Where is everybody?"

"Gone."

"What do you mean gone? Where did they all go?"

"I don't know and I don't care, as long as it isn't here," I state flatly, looking over the three options of torture she wants me to choose from.

"Did you do something?" Her deflated tone has me focusing my attention on her and her frown. I don't like her frowning. It looks foreign on her face.

"I paid the manager to rent out the entire space for the rest of the day. Told him to quietly direct everyone else to leave... immediately."

"Why would you do that?"

She doesn't look as happy as I thought she would when I originally coerced the manager with my black American Express Card.

"I didn't like the way people watched us. It was unnerving. If you're going to make me do this foolishness, I'm not going to do it with an audience of pimple-faced, spoiled teenagers."

"So, you thought; I'll just throw around money and ruin everyone else's day, instead?"

"I didn't ruin the manager's, or the owner's day. They made out better than they would have on the dozen or so customers they had to escort out."

Micaela raises an are-you-serious brow at me. "Do you ever think about other people when you do things like that?"

"I thought about you." Both her eyebrows shoot up, and her

mouth gapes like a fish a few times before she looks away. Her face is hidden behind the hand she runs around the back of her neck then over her jaw. I'm pretty sure she's blushing. It's hard to tell through all the pink surrounding her.

I watch her carefully. She seemed angry that I rented out the space, and now she looks perplexed. *Welcome to the club, Shortcake.* Something in me wants to wipe the concern from her brow. Smooth out the crease with my thumb. What a strange thing to think.

"Come on, Shortcake, why don't you show me how this contraption works." I point at the spinning triple armed... thing. It seems to be enough to pull her from her revelry.

"It's to test your reflexes. You have to jump or duck to avoid the bars, or get taken out by them."

"Ok, seems easy enough."

And just like that, smiling Micaela is back, laughing, no doubt at my expense. "Sure it is, come on your grace. I'll go first so you can see how it's done."

Without hesitation, she leaps down onto the padded area. One of the giant arms spins towards her and she leaps up, easily avoiding it, then ducks under the next. Her movements are swift and agile. Needing to show her I'm not completely inept, I don't wait for her instruction and jump into the fray.

I really should have timed my jump better. The middle arm you can go under or over swings at me and, at my height, sucker punches me right in my junk, sending me roiling. I instantly grab my groin to protect it from further assault as the arm pushes me over. I end up on my side in the fetal position, red-faced and hyperventilating, waiting for the throbbing pain in my balls to subside.

Micaela appears in my limited view, sitting on her knees. I can see she's laughing so hard she's crying.

"Gee, thanks for your concern." I manage to grunt out.

"I can't... you... whack... right in the nuts." she sputters between bouts of laughter.

"That's it. I'm leaving." Pushing myself into a sitting position, I keep one hand protectively over my genitals, just in case the spinning arm decides to fly off and get me a second time.

"No. No. We can't leave yet." Tears stream down her glitter smeared face, and she wipes at them with little concern to where all that glitter is going.

"I'm pretty sure we can."

"No, we have to at least do the foam pit before we leave."

I give her my best stern glare that would normally force interns to wet themselves. It does nothing to Micaela. Her sweet, pouty bottom lip pops in mock despondency.

I want to suck on it.

"Micaela," I huff out her name on a long exhale, expelling my last bit of patience and frustration. And yes, this time it is a little bit of sexual frustration. Watching her bounce around in skintight clothes all afternoon has me regaling thoughts of my most unpleasant memories to keep from pitching a tent in my pants like a fourteen-year-old boy.

"Promise. One foam pit jump, then we can leave, if you really want to."

We engage in a stare off worthy of my sister, sitting on the padded and colorful floor of this ridiculous establishment. And I can't do it.

I can't say no.

"Fine. One jump." I hold up one finger, emphasizing I'm only giving in to one.

"Yes!" she exclaims and jumps up to rush over to the launching trampoline into the foam pit. "You first. Just jump onto the trampoline and bounce into the foam pit like a pool."

Groaning, I run my hand through my hair and rub down my face, hoping it will clear the pain I'm still feeling in my balls. It doesn't, but seeing her light up and watch me hopefully, has me moving my feet to the spot she's pointing to.

I leap, I bounce, I land on my back in the soft foam squares to the sound of her clapping and whooping. The pain from before drifts away on the song of her joy. Not ten seconds later, I see her pink clad body flying through the air—right at me.

"Geronimoooo!"

"Fuck." I manage to roll to one side, so she lands on the foam instead of my face.

Her impact jostles me and the pit contents till we roll together in the middle. Struggling to gain purchase, I realize getting out of this pit is like being a turtle on your back, trying to flip over. Micaela and I end up pressed up against each other. She continues to giggle as our legs tangle and arms wrap in places usually reserved for a more private setting. Micaela doesn't notice as she rolls right on top of me in her attempt to right herself.

We're pressed flush together, and with her barely-there outfit, and the flimsy material of mine, nothing is left to the imagination. All of her soft curves press against my eagerly growing hardness. We're in a bubble of privacy down here in the pit, where no one can see us, and I take the momentary reprieve from the outside world to just be. To allow Micaela and her essence to seep in through the cracks of my exterior like no one has in years.

She smells of sugar and sunshine, like freshly glazed donuts. To most people that might not be a turn on, but to someone like me, who eats healthy and rarely partakes in sugary sweet treats, her sweet scent is heaven. An indulgence in sin and pleasure. The urge to bite and lick and taste her comes over me again. Before I can act on the urge or decide better of it, she stills.

Her laugh dies out when she catches me watching her, my arms firmly around her waist, my fingers trailing up her spine, our faces inches apart. So close to each other, I can see the swirls of color in her irises. Dark sapphire and bright aqua swim together in a sea of realization. Her curved lips never dip, but her eyes do, to my lips. Then to her hands on my chest and back up, searching every inch of me. For what, I don't know.

One of her hands reaches up and brushes hair from my forehead, and I feel tingling everywhere. Every inch of her body that touches mine feels like pins and needles on my skin, alerting me that it likes what it feels. I also like what I see. The easy smile, the lack of apprehension. A strange flutter buzzes through my chest, and I feel a pull on one side of my mouth.

"Wow."

Micaela's breathy voice comes out a split second before she leans down and closes the distance between us. Pressing her perfect pink lips to the corner of my mouth, then right in the center. Covering my lips with hers for the briefest of moments, in a kiss no less surprising than the one in the street, but far more intimate. Soft and gentle, reverent even. I barely get a chance to reciprocate before she's pulling away. Her smile, gone.

"I'm sorry. That was... I shouldn't..." Her words trail off as she extricates herself from my embrace, rolling to the side of the pit.

So, that's how you get out.

"Micaela. Wait." I call after her, mimicking her roll and easy escape from this pit. I manage to catch her by the arm when I climb out of the foam.

"I'm sorry. I don't know what came over me." Her eyes turn up to mine, and my stupid heart catches in my throat at the distress there. "You just smiled, and I wasn't ready for it. It caught me by surprise."

"I didn't smile." Why is my first thought to deny a smile? I should be focusing on the fact that she just kissed me. *Again.*

"Yes, you did. It's been so long since you smiled, you don't even know what it feels like." Her smile is sad and small, but knowing something I can't fathom. "Come on. I'll take you back to your office. I think I've tortured you enough for one day."

She does just that, driving me back to my office, far quieter than she was on the ride there. Stealing glances out of the corner of her eye as I collect my neatly folded slacks and dress shirt, pulling my jacket from the hook in the back.

"Thank you. For coming with me today," she murmurs without making eye contact with me.

"Thank you for taking me."

With a nod, she rolls her lips between her teeth and diverts her attention out the front window. I slide out of the Jeep with a weird confusion clouding my mind.

Did I just have fun bouncing on trampolines?

I think I did.

That pull at the corner of my lips is back, and this time, I know I'm smirking as I watch her pink Jeep drive away.

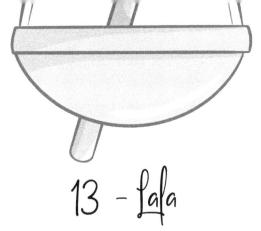

13 – Lala

Can demons possess ferrets?

Kill me now. Why do I keep kissing Henry? That's the second time I've thrown myself at him and he didn't respond. Although, I didn't really give him time to respond, I suppose. The kiss was so fleeting it almost doesn't even count. But how could I see that smirk and not kiss it? He didn't even know he was grinning at me. Even denied it after the fact. I guess I should feel lucky he didn't yell at me or outright push me away. But I also don't feel like it was completely unwelcomed either.

Ugh! Why do I have to be such a weirdo?

I bang my head against my steering wheel after parking in front of Tallulah. I just need to get my bearings before I get out. Deep breath in through the nose and out through the mouth. I have to do this three times before I'm stable enough to exit my Jeep and go inside my tiny Skoolie home.

Fred, my pale pink ferret, greets me by scurrying around in his cage, spinning in circles like I've been gone for years rather than hours. Entering, I unlatch his cage door and he climbs up my arm, burrowing under my hair at the back of my neck as he chatters away.

"Hey, Fred. Did you have a good day? I had a great day up until I shot myself in the foot being me again. I'm pretty sure I've scared him off thoroughly now." Fred doesn't reply. He can't, he's a ferret. If he did, I would be calling the roman catholic church to perform an exorcism.

Can demons possess ferrets? I don't see why not. They're a living creature just like a human. Can't really overpower much more than a mouse or small snake. Not ideal for taking over the world, so not a likely choice for demons.

Secure in my belief that Fred is *not* possessed by a demon, I make my way through my tiny home, wearing Fred like a scarf. Passing the couch on my right, the built-in desk on my left, and through the perfectly proportioned kitchen. Pink and white throughout, of course. White countertops, pink cabinets, pink upholstery, and gold hardware decorate my space. It's a happy, inviting atmosphere that always puts my nerves at ease.

To others it might be considered too bright, too girly, too monochromatic. I couldn't give a rat's ass what they think of it. They don't have to live in it. I do, and I love it. It has an art deco retro vibe, with all kinds of useful small house living hacks. Like jars with their lids screwed to the underside of the cabinets, holding pink sugar, loose leaf tea, pink salt (labeled so as not to be confused with the sugar), and some pink candy.

Fred and I collapse on my bed in the very back of the bus. It presses up against the sides and back wall surrounded by the original windows that came with the school bus. I installed a padded headrest covering two of the windows, and black-out roller blinds as well as sheer, gauzy, pale pink curtains. That way, I have complete control over the amount of light entering my bedroom.

The comforter is soft under my cheek as I plop face down on the cushy surface.

"Aaaahhhhh. Why do I keep kissing guys that don't want to be kissed?" I yell into the blanket. The pink fluffiness muffles my screams of mortification.

Henry probably thinks I'm some psycho who goes around kissing everyone, and won't hire me to be a vendor at his oh so precious conference now, for fear I might turn it into a kissing booth.

Mid self-deprecation, a knock echoes through my tiny house, followed by two very distinct voices. Voices that get louder as they enter my home without waiting for me to let them in.

Paloma and Pilar make their way inside and find me still face down, groaning on my bed.

"What happened?" Pilar asks. Both sisters sit on either side of me, the bed dipping under their added weight. Fred, the traitor that he is, scampers to one of them to get more attention that I'm not currently giving him.

"I kissed him." My admission is muffled by the blanket, but they hear it nonetheless.

"Again?" Paloma is rightly shocked. She was, after all, there to witness the first kiss.

"I didn't mean to," I say as I roll over onto my back, but I still can't bear to see their judgmental faces and drape one arm over my eyes. "I actually got him to smile. Ok, grin. Well, more of a smirk. But there was definite up-turnage in his lips. And he was... huh." I sigh at the memory of that one-sided upturn smirk. It was panty melting. No one pressed up against his hard body, that close to such a rare sight, would have been able to resist.

"He was so hot and yummy, and I don't know what came over me. I just leaned in and kissed him."

"And what did he do?" Paloma asks.

"Um, not much. It was a very brief kiss, and I didn't exactly lay there waiting."

"Lay there? Where were you that you were laying with him?"

I quickly regale my afternoon with hot Henry to the twins, and how we ended up in the foam pit, entangled together.

"What did he say after you kissed him?" Pilar asks, her soft, sweet voice just as buttery as the honey butter sun dress she wears.

"Well, not much. He denied smiling, then we left. He thanked me for taking him, and that was it." I hadn't really thought about it fully yet. I was too mortified to do anything else but drive him back to his office and say goodbye.

The first time I kissed him on the street, he was a nobody. Just a hot guy in sweatpants, walking down the street, frowning. The likelihood of me ever seeing him again was microscopic until Fawn introduced him as her brother and possible savior to my dwindling bank account. Now he's Henry Bardot, real estate mogul and millionaire with soft, oh so kissable lips.

Man, I really know how to pick'em, don't I?

"So, it's not a complete failure. You don't know. Maybe he enjoyed it, but you didn't give him time to make a move," Paloma offers, smoothing down my hair, trying to calm me.

"Maybe, I don't know. Do I want him to make a move?"

"Sure seems like it."

I groan again. I do. She's so right. I felt his semi through his basketball shorts, and I wanted to grind into him so bad it took physical effort not to. I bet he would be boring in bed. All that gray and beige. He's probably the methodical, silent type. Straight to missionary, and no play time or fun toys. *Le sigh.* What a shame. With the equipment he's packing, playing with him would be so much fun.

Groaning very unfemininely, I wrench myself into a sitting position. Fred crawls out of Pilar's lap and into mine, nuzzling and burrowing until he finds a comfortable position and settles. I stroke his fur mindlessly.

"So, what do I do about it?"

"Maybe next time you kiss him, wait to see if he kisses you back?" Pilar offers, unhelpfully. I am most definitely not initiating another kiss with Henry Bardot.

"Yeah, that's not gonna happen."

"Why not?" asks Paloma. "Don't you want to kiss him again?"

"Sure, I want to, but that doesn't mean *he* wants to. If there's going to be a third kiss, he's going to have to be the one to initiate it."

"When are you seeing him next?" Pilar asks.

"I have no idea. If he ever agrees to me attending his conference, maybe I'll see him then."

The way we left things, there's no way to know if that'll happen now either. Maybe I pushed him too far. I suppose I could ask Fawn to speak with him for me. She seems to be able to get through to him.

Alright, that's the plan. Beg Fawn to speak with Henry for me, and never speak to him again. At least until the conference... if he says yes.

"You could go to his office. We could run interference again if you need us to," suggests Paloma.

"Whatever you need Lala, we're here to help," comes Pilar's sweet supportive words of encouragement.

"Yeah, I don't think I should do that either. I'm just going to ask Fawn to talk to him. She was wrong when she said she thinks I'm something special. There is no getting through to Henry Bardot." I sigh, mourning the loss of something that never was. "I gotta pee."

Standing, I hand off Fred to the twins and make my way into

my small but functional bathroom. I've managed to peel off my shorts to relieve my bladder from its hard work of holding in pee while bouncing on commercial grade trampolines, when my phone, which I sat on the counter, chimes with a text. It's from an unknown number. I swipe open my phone, curious to know who's texting me that isn't saved in my phone.

Unknown: _I'll let you attend the conference on one condition._

I don't mean to scream, but I do, and in seconds the twins are banging on the bathroom door.

"Lala! What is it?"

"What's wrong?"

"Are you ok?"

From inside the bathroom, I can't completely tell who's saying what. "I'm fine. I just got a text, and I think it's from Henry."

"What?" comes the chorus of their tandem twin voices. I pull up my annoyingly stubborn spandex shorts, almost dropping my phone into my composting toilet at the same time. Completely forgetting my screaming bladder and my need to pee. Cursing, I finally manage to wrangle my shorts into submission and exit the bathroom.

"Look." I shove the phone towards the twins and wait for their mirrored looks of surprise.

"Oh, my goodness."

"How did he get your number?"

"I don't know. He's got like a bajillion dollars and owns property all over town. He probably has undercover spies that follow people around. I'm sure he could get my number if he wanted to."

"Or he asked his sister." Pilar bursts my little imaginary bubble with her boring logic.

"Yeah, that's more likely. So, what should I say?" Pilar hands me back my phone, and I stare at the words taunting me from the screen. He's obviously waiting for me to respond before telling me what this one thing is. Could it be a trap? Does he want something illicit from me? Even if he did, I'd be ok with that. Like I said, he has the equipment, so even if he is a bore in bed, I can work with what he's packing.

"Ask him what he wants, obviously. Then we'll decide if we have to chop off his balls or go shopping for a new outfit."

A new outfit? I don't have the funds for a new outfit. I barely had enough money to pay for the Bounce Palace. It was sheer luck that I found that coupon. Plus, I'm almost out of groceries. Soon, I'll be living off canned veggies and chicken. Ugh, I can't think about that right now.

Ok, focus, Lala. You have to sound cool, nonchalant. Like you're not the least bit hot and bothered by the very thought of Henry texting you.

Lala: *Who is this?*

Unknown: *You know who this is.*

Lala: *Perhaps you should clarify, just to make sure.*

Unknown: *It's Henry, Micaela, and you know that.*

Lala: *Ok, Henry. So, what is your one condition?*

Unknown: *Since you made me do something you wanted to do, you have to do something I want to do.*

Lala: *If it's watching paint dry, I'm busy that day washing my hair.*

Unknown: *Stop being such a smartass. It's not watching paint dry.*

Lala: *Then what is it?*

Unknown: *I'm not telling you, you'll just have to trust me.*

Lala: *Now why would I do that?*

Unknown: *Because you really want to attend the conference and promote your business.*

Fuck. He's right. But can I trust him? Yeah, he may be a grouch who is allergic to fun, but I don't feel like I'm in any danger with him. As a matter of fact, it's quite the opposite.

Lala: *Fine. When?*
Unknown: *Saturday. Be ready by 9am*
Lala: *That's too early. Make it 10*
Unknown: *Fine. 10. Be ready and dress normal.*
Lala: *I'm sorry, I don't know what normal is.*
Unknown: *Figures. Just dress casual.*
Lala: *Aye-aye, Captain!*

I save Henry's number in my phone and name it Mr. Grumpasaurus. I have no idea what he has in store for Saturday, but I can't wait to find out.

14 - Henry

Perhaps you should consider wearing less

It's seven a.m. on Saturday morning, and I'm already showered and dressed. It took me longer than I care to admit to pick out an outfit for today's "outing" with Micaela. After she dropped me off at my office, my head was still reeling from the afternoon, and that kiss. When I realized I still hadn't given her my answer to attending the conference, and we hadn't made any plans to see each other again, I had to do something. At least, to tell her she could attend the conference. Spending a few hours with her alone again is just an added bonus. Nothing more.

It's not a date.

Swear.

It's a business meeting.

My "business meeting" doesn't start for another three hours, and I'm already itching to get out the door. It feels like there are ants under my skin, tickling every hair follicle. It's unnerving. Any other time I had a date with a woman—even though that isn't what this is—I never felt anxious energy that made me vibrate with anticipation. There was no *need*. Not that I have a need for Micaela.

She's just attractive in a way that grabs my attention.

I'm physically attracted to her. That's all. If we had sex, this would all go away. Just like it does every time I get that particular itch. It's just an itch I need to scratch.

To calm my energy, I make myself a hearty breakfast; an omelet with diced onions, bell peppers, cheese, and fresh basil from the plant sitting on my windowsill. Along with two perfectly toasted pieces of multigrain bread. I sit and eat at a leisurely pace, trying to kill time.

Checking the Rolex on my left wrist, I see I've only managed to kill half an hour, so I make my way over to my computer to check emails. That always takes up a lot of time.

Micaela texted me her address and odd directions to her place. When I arrive at the address, the directions make more sense. She apparently lives in a tiny home. When she said to look for a pink bus, I thought she just had a RV parked in her driveway. No. The RV, or more accurately, the remodeled school bus—you know the kind with the flat front—IS her home. It sits in a row of cute and unique tiny homes that range from classic airstream trailers to miniature cottages and buses like Micaela's.

Her's isn't the only one painted a bright, distinct color. There's an ocean blue and pale-yellow double decker bus that looks like it swam over here from the U.K. parked right next door. A matching pair of eyes and azure and canary hair shift in the window, watching me. Where most people would duck out of sight when spotted, the twins just stand and stare. No doubt they knew I was coming today.

Ignoring the colorful twins, I return my attention to Micaela's pink bus. The name *Tallulah* is painted in bubbly font along its side. The pink monstrosity is paired with her pink Jeep at its side, along with a retractable pink and white striped awning and matching patio furniture. All of this is laid out in a picture-perfect setting on, you guessed it, pink Astro turf.

Why am I doing this again? Oh, that's right. This was my fucking idea. I should have just texted her that she could sell her damn pink boba at the conference, but no. I had to coerce her into a date that's not a date. Going somewhere I will enjoy. Since she lured me into going to that bounce house of death and discomfort, she will now have to endure my brand of "fun".

Serves her right.

Parking my Jag next to her Jeep I step out and only make it halfway to "Tallulah" when Micaela comes bounding out the door, a whirling mass of pink as she turns to lock her "home". She's replaced the folding bus door with a traditional one, complete with a round porthole window in it. The handle is one of those crystal looking knobs in a pale pink that matches her hair. Hair that is tied in two messy pigtails low behind her ears. Loose ringlets brush across her bare shoulders.

She's wearing a short skirt made up of layers of that sheer frilly shit they always make wedding dresses out of and a shirt that has about a trillion gathers along the entire neckline, which is pushed down to her biceps revealing completely bare shoulders and decolletage. The sleeves reach her elbows, and again are gathered, puffing them out into beach balls. The skirt is tight at her tapered waist, the shirt tucked in. Strappy sandals lace around her ankles and halfway up her calves. A heart shaped purse hangs from one shoulder.

The entire outfit is pink.

Every freaking stitch.

Some sort of sparkle detail on her skirt catches the morning sun as she twirls. It isn't until she turns around and practically skips over to me that I realize she isn't wearing a bra, hence the bare shoulders. Her breasts, still perky but free, move of their own accord in the rhythm of her step, practically hypnotizing me.

Her attire irritates and pleases me at the same time. I thought I told her to dress normal. This is NOT normal. Normal is what I'm wearing; dark wash jeans and a casual, untucked dove gray button down. I even went so far as to wear my black leather sneakers and roll my sleeves up a few times. You know, to appear casual, like I go on outings like this every weekend.

In case you're wondering, I don't.

My weekends are time for me to workout, catch up on emails, and research new properties. Not go gallivanting all over town on dates that aren't dates.

But what she's wearing will not allow us to go unnoticed in public. She's going to draw attention from everyone we pass. That was probably her plan.

Micaela approaches me, her casual, easy smile crossing her painted pink lips, never falling, even in the wake of my glower I know I'm wearing. Only the smallest quirk of the corner of her lips suggests she knows exactly what I'm thinking—and doesn't give a fuck.

"What in the fresh pink hell is this?" I ask as she finally stops her braless, entrancing frolic a foot in front of me.

"You must be a very unhappy man, Henry Bardot." One fist lands on her hip as she cocks her head up at me. If it weren't for all that gathering and elastic holding her neckline flush to her clavicle, I would have a great view down her shirt from this angle.

"Why is that?"

"Because pink is a happy color. Most people smile when they see it. But not you. I think it actually has the opposite effect on you."

"It's probably due to overexposure. You simply wear too much pink. Perhaps you should consider wearing less."

"Huh." She gasps in mock horror, clasping her free hand to her chest. "I shall never."

The brush of her arm over her chest causes her nipples to harden and point directly at me. Accusing me, daring me, tempting me. Instead of giving into their demands, I clear my throat and avert my gaze.

"We should get going. I doubt even if I made you change it would be any better."

Micaela just giggles, but follows me to my car, where I open the passenger door, and she slides in effortlessly. Her pink contrasts with all the black and silver inside, obviously out of place, and yet, looking right at home.

The drive to where I'm taking her won't take more than fifteen minutes, and we're about two minutes into it when Micaela reaches over and begins to fiddle with my radio.

"What are you doing?"

"Finding something to listen to."

"I like the silence."

"I like music."

"It's my car."

"And I'm your captive guest, so I should get to pick the music."

She flips through the channels faster than I can hear what is playing before settling on a classic rock station. Fleetwood Mac's *Say That You Love Me* bursts from my neglected speakers. The volume is turned up way past any decibel I've ever listened to it at. Micaela belts out the lyrics at the top of her lungs.

"Cause when the lovin' stops and the lights go down and there's not another livin' soul around, you woo me until till the sun comes up, and you saaaaayyy that you love me."

Her voice is slightly off key and she's a half second ahead of the music, as if she's so excited to get to the words, she can't wait to sing them. But she doesn't care. Not one little bit.

"Do you always do everything so loudly?" I ask, having to shout a little to be heard over the music.

"Probably." She shrugs and returns to her singing. It continues like this through three more songs by Journey, Earth Wind and Fire, and The Eagles. It's surprising someone her age knows so many classics. (Although, I don't know her exact age. I'm guessing she's in her late twenties if she's friends with my sister.) I thought she would listen to top forties Pop artists like Lizzo, and Katy Perry and I say as much.

"Oh, I listen to them too, but my favorites are the classics. It's basically all I listened to growing up. My aunt was the one who got me into them. She would blow into town unannounced and stir up all kinds of mayhem, making everything far more exciting. She was the one who inspired me to live in a bus and travel the country. Dad says she's a modern-day hippie who never really left the seventies."

Thankfully, we arrive at our destination before another song can begin, and I shut off the radio and pull into the parking lot of a large red brick building.

"A ketchup museum?" Micaela steps out of my Jag and stares up at the neon Heinz sign, complete with a classic glass bottle tipped upside down as if it's about to pour out right onto the side of the building.

"It's not just a ketchup museum. It's a local museum about everything Pittsburgh."

"But it says Heinz History Center," she argues. We walk to the front entrance, and I pay for two entry tickets.

"That's because it's named after Senator John Heinz, and although there is a section on the Heinz company, it functions as a branch of the Smithsonian, and houses multiple different museum branches within it. It's been here for over two hundred and fifty years. It's rich in history and extremely educational on local history specifically." I know a lot more about this specific museum, such as when it was first opened, it was used as a historical society and only allowed men that had lived in the region for more than fifty years, but slowly started allowing women and younger people in over time. It's also located in the Strip District, which was the inspiration for the enhancements and renovations in the neighborhood I now live in and partially own.

"Wow, so basically, anything I could want to know about Pittsburgh is in here."

"Sort of."

"Cool." Her eyes are bright and alert as we enter the first exhibit, *Mr. Rogers Neighborhood*. The exhibit is filled with sets and props from the original show.

"So, you're actually interested in stuff like this?" I hadn't thought she would particularly *enjoy* the museum, but maybe tolerate it for my benefit. Once again, I was wrong about her. She hides a lot of herself under all that pink.

"Of course. Why wouldn't I be?"

"It's not trampolines, indoor skydiving, or pink. I thought you might find it rather boring." We round Mr. Rogers's foyer set to find a collection of puppets in a glass case. Micaela stops and inspects them, bending over slightly to get a better look.

Does she even know who Mr. Rogers is?

"Just because it's educational doesn't mean I won't like it. And did you bring me somewhere boring on purpose to try and punish me for the Bounce Palace?" She remains partially bent over the case, but turns to look up at me accusingly, a hint of a grin trying to break her glare.

"Not at all..."

"I bet I could tell you two things about ketchup you didn't know before."

"What?" Micaela stands straight and crosses her arms over her chest, blissfully blocking my view of her nipples, which have been slowly hardening within the air-conditioned space.

I remain with my hands in my pockets, watching her watching me. "Are you trying to out fact me? You actually think you know something about Heinz that I don't?"

"Mmhmm." She nods and pinches her lips together, suppressing her smug grin.

I've been in this museum dozens of times and seen every exhibit about the Heinz company. I've lived here my whole life, and as an architect lover, have read almost all the history on all the important buildings in the city. If she thinks she knows something about it that I don't, I would love to hear it.

"Ok then, Shortcake, what do I get if I do know these two mysterious facts?"

"What, like a prize?"

"Sure, why not."

"Ok..." She taps her chin, pondering my prize. "Well, if you do know these two facts, I'll wear absolutely no pink for a week. But if you *don't* know them, you have to wear pink to work for a week."

"One day," I counter.

"Three days."

"One day."

"Two days. Final offer." She tightens her arms over her chest defiantly. Still not going to happen.

"One day," I state flatly. She eyes me and huffs. That's when I know I've won.

"Ok fine." Like at Fawn's house, she sticks her pinky out to me, but this time I know what she wants. "Pinky promise or it isn't real."

"That's not how it works," I argue, but reach out my finger to lock with hers for some unknown reason. Her tiny finger is soft and warm from being smooshed against her breasts, the nail painted a glittery pink that almost outshines her smile... almost.

"Yes, it is." Her smile is big and broad. It's her 'I've got you right where I want you' smile, and something about it warms my insides.

"Well, one thing is specifically Heinz, and the other is just about ketchup."

"Ok, then. Go for it, Shortcake."

"One," she starts, holding up her index finger as we resume our slow stroll through Mr. Rogers Neighborhood. "Heinz released a special edition millennial pink ketchup in 2019 to celebrate their one hundred and fiftieth anniversary. They set up special pink booths in a select few restaurants, where people could go to take photos and try the pink condiment. Some bottles were also sent to online social influencer accounts, and I was privy to receiving a few, thanks to my love of all things pink. I still have one sitting on my shelf at home."

While she speaks, we manage to walk through all of the Mr. Rogers exhibit, and are making our way to one of the other museums within the center. The sports museum.

"Ok, well, you've got me there. I didn't know that."

"Second," she continues, not caring that I just admitted she was right. "Ketchup can last up to two years past its expiration date when kept sealed in the pantry. And then, up to an additional one to two years past that once opened and refrigerated."

"Really? I had no idea."

"Yeah, apparently expirations dates are bogus. I think companies just put those on there so we think it is expired and buy more, even though we still have half a perfectly good bottle in the fridge."

We round a Steelers display that Micaela shows very little interest in. I'm not huge into sports either, but I partake in watching every now and again. Mainly to ensure I have some sort of conversational topic to fall back on if ever needed at an event. It came in especially handy at one fundraiser I went to that was hosted by the Steelers themselves. When you're introduced to the head coach of an NFL team, you want to be able to at least follow along in the conversation.

"You know, it probably has more to do with liability issues than anything else." She just rolls her eyes at me but continues walking.

We make our way through a few more museums until we finally arrive at the Heinz exhibit. Micaela is far more interested in the history of ketchup than the Clash of Empires: The British, French & Indian War, 1754-1763 or Meadowcroft Rockshelter and Historic Village. Personally, I find the shaping of our country a little more interesting than tomato-based condiments, but there's something about the red bottles that strikes her fancy.

We wander from a display case of Heinz themed jewelry to a giant ketchup bottle made of smaller ketchup bottles, and then to an entire wall depicting the history of Heinz through memorabilia, commercials, and advertisements. Micaela stops at one display of memorabilia, and I stop a few feet behind her. I've seen everything here already, so I allow her to view it at her own pace.

As I'm waiting for her, a tour group enters the exhibit lead by a woman wearing a Heinz History Center polo and a wired microphone connecting to a black box clipped to her slacks. I notice each person is wearing a headset so they can hear her. At first, I think the group is small, and by the sounds of it, they don't speak English.

Then I notice the people keep coming. There has to be at least two dozen of them, maybe more. They fill the space in a matter of a minute, pushing me to stand closer to Micaela.

She hasn't noticed the group, still intrigued by the displays, until I bump into her after one rather aloof middle-aged man wearing a fanny pack nearly sideswipes me. His eyes are everywhere but where he's walking. He doesn't even notice when I jump out of his way and almost take out Micaela.

I steady her with a hand to her waist to keep her from toppling over into the collection of plushy ketchup and mustard bottles.

"Sorry." Even though she's steadied, my hand lingers of its own accord, stroking the surprisingly soft material of her frilly skirt. "We seem to be overrun with oblivious tourists."

Bright aquamarine eyes shine up at me as we stand far too close for a "business meeting". Her chest rises and falls with quick, sharp breaths.

"That's ok." Her words are breathy and soft, and she smells like cotton candy. Again the urge to taste her surprises me. I bet whatever pink stuff she put on her lips that creates the sugary sweet aroma probably tastes like it too. Just one little bite is all it would take. A nibble on her plump bottom lip to find out.

Another irksome tourist bumps into me. This time, I'm a little more prepared and I barely sway toward Micaela. Our chests brush all the same, and her pupils dilate at the contact. So, she is attracted to me as well. Good to know. Now just to find out if she's a stage five clinger or open for something more casual.

I still haven't removed my hand from her waist as we stand and watch each other, waiting for the other to make the first move. To see who will break this strange bubble of silence and stillness we've unintentionally created. Our eyes are fixed and unwavering, not in challenge or protest, but in curious regard.

To me, watching her is like being part of national geographic, learning the abnormal habits of a wild animal, just waiting to see what she'll do next. She watches me like I'm a documentary on semicolons, too curious about something she never would have given a second thought about to not look away. Wanting to dissect and learn all that created me.

"Do you want to leave? Go somewhere less crowded?" I ask, breaking the silence first.

For a moment, she's quiet. Speechless even. Perhaps I should crowd her space more often if it shuts her up. But the momentary lapse passes, and she blinks away the haze of our stare. "No. I haven't seen all the Heinz stuff yet. It's the first exhibit I've really been interested in."

I nod and remove my hand, but stay close to block her from the bustling crowd scurrying about the space.

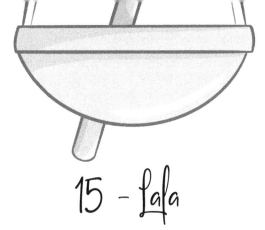

15 - Lala

Maybe one with less people and more dead things

When Henry picked me up today, I was a massive ball of nerves. Having no idea where he was taking me, although I had an inkling it would be somewhere drab, I had changed my outfit half a dozen times. I know he said be casual, but I couldn't be too casual. I am trying to impress him, after all. I want him to think I'm mature and professional… when I want to be. Settling on the off the shoulder ensemble, I was going for sundress level cute, but not in a five-year-old going to take Easter pictures kind of way. Perhaps I shouldn't have opted out of a bra because it seems to be distracting Henry.

It wasn't completely unintentional. Men are simple minded, horny creatures. Show a little skin and a smile, and they're putty in your hands. At least, that's what I was hoping for. It seems I have taken on the role of putty today, thanks to Henry's hands.

We've been wandering around the museum for a good hour, and are currently trying to see the rest of the Heinz display. A giant our group of rude and oblivious tourists keeps getting in our way. They bump into Henry or me, causing clumsy collisions that lead to touching and heart palpitations. Henry is far too attractive a man for me not to be affected by his touch and smell and height and his damn rolled up sleeves and forearms. I feel like when he gets dressed in the morning, the song, *'I'm Sexy and I Know It'* plays on repeat in his head as he stares at himself in the mirror. I know it would if I were him.

Leaving my bus this morning, I was completely prepared for a museum, but more like one of those boring ones with broken artifacts and mannequins posed in scenes like making a fire or building a hut. The Heinz History Center is actually entertaining. Dad will be thrilled when I tell him about the football history I learned about the Steelers. But the Heinz displays are the most interesting to me.

To see how something as simple and mundane as ketchup came to be and become a profitable home staple product is interesting. Some people like to know how governments were formed, how empires fell, and the types of deities ancient civilizations prayed to. Me, I like to see the importance and significance in everyday items and places. The things others take for granted. Decades of hard work and devotion have been put into making something as simple as ketchup. For us to be able to purchase it whenever we please at the grocery store, without thought or question. Its steady presence in our lives is near imperceptible. That is the history that intrigues me and draws me in to learn more.

That desire for knowledge has been interrupted by my desire for other knowledge. Like what cologne Henry wears that smells like sweaty man after sex, so I can go buy it and spray it on my bed whenever I masturbate. Seriously, it has to be made with testosterone or sex endorphins or something.

And other things like, does Henry have a girlfriend? Does he take all his business acquaintances on museum dates? Is this even a date?

There are a lot of things about Henry that baffle me. He continues to say how he hates pink and pretty much anything joyful in the world, but he went with me to the Bounce Palace and brought me here.

What's his game? Does he even have one?

Not that I mind being driven around by a hot guy that can pull off sweatpants *and* a three-piece suit. But there are a few things that need clarification.

As we skirt around a rather animated trio of tourists, who are gesturing in ways I'm not sure are appropriate for public viewing, I decide to plunge in and try to find out more about the grump guiding me by the small of my back.

"So," I begin so eloquently. "Do you bring all your dates to the museum? Or am I just lucky?"

"This isn't a date," he states flatly. Ok, then. Not a date. Kind of clears that up. Also, kind of a bummer.

"Ok. This isn't a date—"

"I don't do dates," he interrupts.

"Like ever?"

"Like never."

Henry doesn't seem like the kind of guy that has trouble getting a date. Maybe they all turn him down after one conversation. He isn't exactly the warm and fuzzy type. And the whole not smiling thing... is a turn off. Except for that one cornered smirk he gave me in the foam pit. If he were to fully smile, he would have a line of women, pantiless at his door begging for his attention.

I slide him a side eye, raising my eyebrows. There's no way he never dates. Even grumpy-gusses like him at least go on first dates or tinder booty calls. Right? He must comprehend my silent contemplation, because he huffs out a breath and continues.

"Dates lead to dating, which leads to girlfriends, which leads to marriage and children." He states all of this like it totally explains his lack of dates.

"And that's... bad?" I ask.

"Yes."

"Yes? Girlfriends and marriage and children are bad?" I clarify.

"Yes. They're a distraction, and cause grief and discontent, and I want nothing to do with it."

"Oooooh." I draw out the vowel, nodding in understanding. I get it now. "So, you're one of those guys that thinks families are a distraction, and have decided you're not even going to date so you can't be coaxed into a relationship that could lead to any of that, and to save yourself and them from the heartache and grief."

We stop walking and stand near the structure of ketchup bottles in the shape of one giant ketchup bottle. Soft jade eyes stare down at me and darken, his pupils dilating while trying to dig into my brain. We're silent as he contemplates his answer, the wheels of his mind turning and grinding. He's most likely assessing how much of himself he wants to reveal to me.

But I've figured him out.

If he never connects with a woman, he can't find himself in a place he believes he doesn't want to be. Maybe he doesn't. Maybe there's not enough happiness in his life to make him think a relationship could do more damage than good. Whatever it is guiding his behavior, I'm sure it's unpleasant and deeply rooted in his psyche.

I stare up at him as he decides how to answer. "Something like that," he says, his voice rough as he runs his hand through his thick black hair, which sits a little longer on the top. Every time I've seen him, it's been perfectly styled and quaffed. Now, watching him run his hand through it, messing it up to the point of delectable, I'm unable to look away. I watch as his dark strands pull between his fingers and fall back haphazardly.

There is need, and then there is *need* to touch something. Have you ever had the uncontrollable urge to poke, touch, push, or prod something you know you shouldn't, but want to anyways? Like big red buttons. That's how I feel about Henry's hair right now. And since I live my life under the motto "Why not?", I go ahead and give in. Brushing my fingers across his forehead, through the silky strands that fell out of place, I push them back along his hairline, and greedily run the tips of my fingers through... just a little. Lingering only momentarily, so he won't think I'm trying to seduce him.

I'm not. I swear.

There's just no way in hell anyone could resist that face, and that hair, and those forearms. It all culminated into madness, forcing me to subdue and give in. If only just a little.

Henry watches me, a little confused, a small crease forming on his brow. I get that I can be puzzling at times. His expression is nothing new to me. It's the same one everyone back home gave me when I decided I was going to buy the old school bus, paint it pink, and live in it. It's the same school bus I rode to high school in. The same one that drove us to field trips and summer camps. The same one I rode while getting laughed at for wearing pink every day. The same one where I plotted my escape.

Now Henry gives me *that* look, and it doesn't hurt or dissuade me. It just is. I remove my hand and loop it around my back to lace my fingers together in an attempt to keep from touching him again. Because just like the two times I kissed him, it doesn't appear my attention is appreciated.

"Let's just say I have first-hand experience seeing the effects of a failed relationship and marriage. It isn't what I want. It's not how I want to live, so I don't. I'm happy with what I am, and what I have. I don't want to be tied down and obligated to be something

I'm not. To bend to the will of another just because it's expected of me." He doesn't elaborate any further, and I can tell whatever it is he has experienced, he doesn't want to share. I can only guess it has to do with his parents. Not my place to prod, but we have more in common than he would expect.

"I can understand that." More than he knows. My reasons may not have stemmed from a bad example of marriage, and it's not even relationships or marriage I'm against. It's being trapped. Being obligated, as he says, to bend to the will of another. That's why I never got serious with any of my past boyfriends. That's why whenever they wanted to take me to holidays with their family, I would run away. Because I could. Making decisions for me and only me is easier. Being detached and free is better.

"When I really think about it, I'm kind of the same. I date, but it never gets serious. I never allow it to. Too permanent, too definitive. I like being free. Free to go where I want, to live where I want, and to leave when I want. Not being strapped down and leashed to one person or place. Being disconnected and un-entangled is... priceless."

The way Henry watches me is different than before. Contemplative and curious, but still frowning, possibly more than he has all day.

"Come on, big guy. Let's try another exhibit. Maybe one with less people and more dead things."

We stay for another hour, wandering through halls and displays, most of which are uninteresting, but there are a few I pay more attention to. Then Henry drives me back to my bus, and like the gentleman he is, walks me to my front door. It's been hours since he picked me up, so it's now lunch time, and I'm starving. It's only polite to invite him in for lunch. Right?

"Are you hungry? Would you like to come in for lunch?"

He stands outside my door, hands in pockets, eyeing my bus. Obviously wanting to say no. I can see it written all over his face. *Why no, I don't want to come into your sardine can house on wheels and eat whatever microwave meal you make for me.*

I want him to come in even more so I can prove that smug look wrong. I can cook, and just because my house used to be a twinkie teen delivery vehicle doesn't mean I can't cook properly in it.

"I don't know," he says, checking his ridiculously expensive looking watch. It's Saturday. Where could he possibly have to go, that he couldn't spare another hour for lunch?

"Oh, come on, Sir Frowny. You have to be hungry. I know I am. Let me make you something as a thank you for taking me to the museum and letting me sell my boba at your conference."

Again, he side-eyes my bus exterior, then through the door to what he can see of the interior. From his point of view, he can only see the driver's seat, part of my couch, and if he's paying attention, the side of Fred's cage.

Clearing his throat, he lifts his chin and stands taller, if that's at all possible. The man has perfect posture. Almost like there's a stick so far up his butt, it reaches his neck, keeping his spine ramrod straight.

"Sure. Why not?"

"That's the spirit. Come on in. Mi casa es su casa."

Henry visibly cringes when he enters and sees all the pink girliness that makes up my home. It may be pink, but I believe it's tasteful and elegant. He makes himself somewhat comfortable on my couch, and when he sits, he finally notices Fred in his cage.

"What in the sweet hell is that?"

"*That* is Fred. My ferret."

"Why is it pink?"

"Why not?" Unlatching Fred's cage, I reach in and pull him out.

He scurries up my arm and circles my neck, chittering away as usual.

"Don't take it out. Put it back." Henry's forehead is drawn in a deep scowl, making him look like an angry cartoon character. I laugh at the sight of him afraid of my sweet little Freddy.

Reaching up, I grab Fred and hold him out to Henry. He recoils to avoid contact. The laugh that comes out of me starts abruptly, but from deep in my chest, and I can feel it roll through me and out my mouth. It's hilarious to see a grown man of Henry's size recoil in fear from a little pink ferret.

"Don't touch me with that thing."

"Are you afraid, Henry Bardot? Does the little, tiny ferret scare the big bad man?" I really shouldn't be taunting him, but I can't help it. This is too easy.

Fred dangles from my hand, his tiny pink claws trying to reach out and grab onto Henry. He has to stand and shuffle to the side to avoid him.

"No. I'm not afraid. I just don't like animals. Or rabies."

"Huh!" I scoff in offense for my poor, dear Fred. "Fred doesn't have rabies. How rude." I bring Fred by to my shoulder, where he climbs and starts playing with one of my pig tails.

"Ok, he might not have rabies, but I still don't like animals." His frown is less severe than before, but his lips still pull into a thin line.

"Did you never have a dog as a child?"

"No. The nannies wouldn't let us."

"Nannies?" I know rich people have things like nannies, and really it should have been obvious from the beginning this man was raised by them, but it's still shocking to hear it. No wonder he doesn't know what a healthy relationship looks like if he didn't have his parents around to show him.

Instead of answering my question, he ignores it and changes the subject. "Are you going to make lunch, or are we going to have to eat the rodent to survive?"

I don't let him eat Fred, and just to make him comfortable, I return him to his cage and lock it so he can relax and enjoy his meal. Fred tends to be a little intrusive in personal space anyway, and I have a feeling that won't go over well with Henry.

In the kitchen, I decide to make us chicken salad for lunch with the left-over chicken I had from two nights ago. It's easy and quick, and doesn't have to be cooked. I mix in some fresh vegetables, Dijon mustard, mayonnaise, grapes, eggs, and a few other spices, all under the watchful eye of my surly gargoyle, perched at my tiny peninsula counter.

I can't tell if he's impressed or constipated, but I carry on, not willing to let his frown turn my smile upside down. After toasting some whole grain bread I bought at the farmers market, I make us sandwiches with lettuce and the chicken salad. Sliding the pink plate across to Henry, I watch him inspect it.

"You're not allergic to any of that are you?"

"No. Just surprised you would make something like this."

"What? Something healthy?"

"Well... yes. And not pink. I was half expecting you to feed me a bowl of pink cotton candy with sprinkles."

"I'll have to remember that for next time."

He bites into the sandwich and his eyebrows raise in what I can only hope is approval. When he continues eating, I start in on my own sandwich.

We're almost completely done with our sandwiches when he brings up the topic of the conference. I was waiting for him to bring it up because I figured it would be rude for me to.

"The conference takes place in late June. It will take place at a prestigious hotel, where our company and a handful of other local Realty companies will come together for two days of panels, workshops, and networking gatherings. I'll have my assistant Thomas send you all the details and information. Let him know how much space you will need, and if you'll be bringing help with you. Whatever you need, he'll make sure you have it. And I would suggest bringing more than one person. You and Shay may be able to handle the farmer's market crowd, but it would be wise to have additional help for the conference."

Nodding along, I make a mental note to ask Paloma and Pilar if one or both of them would be willing to help out for that weekend. I'll have to get them branded t-shirts to wear. I'm not sure I can convince either of them to wear pink, but I'll try. "Ok, I can do that."

All I get is a firm, sharp nod in response. We sit in silence for a beat before I need to busy myself and pick up our dishes. I make it to the sink before realizing Henry has followed me.

"Here let me help with that. It's only fair since you made lunch." In the small space of my bus, he's right on top of me, pressed close and reaching around me to remove the plates from my hands.

The heat of his body runs up my spine and I shiver. *That was different.* No man has ever made me shiver just from his presence, or at all really. Making me shiver because he decided to take me on a date ice skating in the snow doesn't count.

I try to sidestep out of his way, but he mirrors my movement. I shift the other direction, and again we collide. Both trying to go around the other, we both end up right back where we started. Only now that we've fumbled around trying to untangle, we've managed to get more tangled. His arm is wrapped around one side, my hip is pressed into his thigh, and I'm flustered, trying to twist around. Now we're pressed front to front, my ass against the sink. His hands remain holding the plates, hovering over the sink, keeping them locked on either side of me.

Right then, my traitorous nipples decide to perk up and pay attention because a sexy man is pressed against them. Great. They're hard, his glare is hard, and it's getting really hot in here. Or is that just me? Probably just me. Or maybe my air conditioner is broken. That has to be it.

This shouldn't be happening. I should not be attracted to this man, no matter how hard his jawline is, or how solid his chest feels. He's a groucho. He hates pink. He's so not my type. My type is spontaneous trips to go strawberry picking, or weekends spent at a nude beach. Not nine a.m. trips to a museum or driving in silence with absolutely no smiling or laughing. But then again, like me, he doesn't want anything serious. He doesn't want a relationship or a girlfriend. There's no pressure or concern for getting in too deep. Because he won't let it. And although his personality isn't my type, his body sure as hell is. Yet, from previous experience, he doesn't seem to approve of my appreciation for his physical form.

But he's not moving. As a matter of fact, it feels like he's pressing closer. Pressure increases against my chest, and I lean back, only to remember I'm trapped against the counter. Dishes clatter in the sink behind me, and one of his hands splays out flat against my back, stopping my involuntary retreat as he leans closer. Those mossy green eyes darken as I feel his hard length press low into my stomach just above my pubic bone.

Jesus fucking Christ.

He is hard and thick, and my air conditioner is most definitely broken. My whole body is flush with heat, and I can barely breathe with him this close.

Something passes in his gaze as it shifts from my eyes to my lips. His other hand has snaked up my neck and his thumb slides along my jaw and down to my collar before sliding back up to circle my throat. He tilts my head up just before he slams his lips into mine. Hard and hungry.

He grinds his dick against my core, using one knee to spread my legs so I can feel exactly what he's working with. And, oh yes. Right there. It feels so good. So much so, it doesn't even compute that it's Henry, the man who never smiles and sneers at all my pink, whom I just met not two weeks ago.

None of that matters when his tongue demands entrance, and I moan into his mouth as it dives in and takes charge. The hand against my throat squeezes ever so slightly, keeping control of my movement, and I do not mind it one bit.

I'm a greedy, horny bitch, and I am not looking a gift horse in the mouth. Arching my back, I press farther into him, my hands slipping under his shirt where I get a brief caress of the hard muscle hidden beneath before I'm roughly disconnected from him. Cold air washes across my heated flesh.

Panting, I regain some semblance of stability and open my eyes to see Henry breathing heavily and standing as far away from me as he can. Which in a bus is only about three feet or less. His hands clench and release at his sides. His impressive erection strains behind his zipper, and I want to reach out and set it free. But the look on his face and the distance between us says otherwise.

Lust and anger, and what looks like disorientation, cloud his handsome face. It's hard to read. He looks like he wants to rip off my clothes as badly as I want to remove his, but also like he's disgusted with what we just did. Not knowing how to react, I just stand there, gawking at him, waiting for him to decide.

He initiated, so he must be the one to decide if we continue or not.

Without uttering a word to me, Henry turns and stomps out of my bus. A moment later, I hear the purr of his Jag, and then the sounds of his engine get quieter the further away he drives.

I don't know if he didn't want to continue or did, and that's why he left. All I know is I'm hot, wet, and need to find a vibrator right now to finish what he started.

16 – Lala

Neon faux fur coats and reenact Elton John's Crocodile Rock

awn offered to take me to one of the flea markets she thinks I could sell my boba at today, and asked me to meet her in the main lobby of her father's realty company. Here I stand, hiding in a corner, hoping Henry doesn't walk by and see me. I can only imagine the displeasure on his face upon seeing me after his abrupt departure the other day.

After he left—and after I took care of my most urgent needs—I hid for the rest of the day, avoiding the twins and fermenting over what could have gone wrong. It must have been something I did or said. The physical attraction was there, but he must have thought better of it when he came to his senses and realized who he was kissing and groping. Maybe he was right. Maybe I wear too much pink and it turns people off.

Could it be the pink? Nah. No one hates a color that much. I can't let Henry and his disagreeable personality make my decisions for me. I am who I am, and others will just have to accept that. If I like all my pink, that's all that matters, just as it always has. No one but me needs to make decisions for me. Other people's preferences and opinions don't guide my life and decisions. I live my life, not them.

Standing a little taller, I stop trying to burrow under the pristine white marble floor of the lobby and remove my back from the corner. Taking up a spot by the windows, I look out at the hustle and bustle of the active downtown street. This is part of what I love about city living. The activity and constant thrum and beat of life. Living in a house on wheels allows me to participate in cities and towns of all types. Large cities that never sleep, everything you could ever want within walking distance, and thousands of people to get lost in. Small towns where everyone knows everyone, where there's only one stoplight, and all Friday night dates are held at the bowling alley with your neighbors. I've fallen asleep to the sounds of sirens and club goers, also babbling brooks, and the wind billowing through trees.

My phone rings, the sounds of Journey pulling me from my trance. It's Fawn.

"Hey Fawn. Where are you? I'm in the lobby now."

"I'm upstairs in my brother's office. Would you mind coming up and meeting me? I have a few things to finish up, and don't want you waiting down there for me."

Oh great. I was hoping to avoid Henry and his frown today—and maybe forever—to save the last bit of dignity I possess. "No, I'm fine. I can wait here. There's even a chair. Take your time, no rush."

"Nonsense. Come on up." Fawn pauses for a beat before continuing. "There's something I want to show you and Henry… about the baby. And I'd like to show you together. Just come up for a quick minute, and then we can leave."

"Ugh." I don't mean to groan in exasperation, but I do. Apparently, my polite decline didn't work. She's not going to give up until

I go upstairs and see whatever it is she has. Fawn can be a bulldog when she makes up her mind. There's no way she'll let it drop until she gets what she wants. As I learned, after my first family dinner, she is capable of making her brothers attend her mandatory meal for fear of repercussions. If she can compel her stubborn brother to attend, I have no doubt that no matter what I do, I'll end up going upstairs to meet her in Henry's office. I might as well get it over with and get out of here. "Fine. I'll be up in just a sec."

"Great. I'll just stay on the phone with you till you find me."

That's a strange request considering I know where Henry's office is. She's the one who gave me directions to it so I could bombard him and drag him to the Bounce Palace.

I step off the elevator onto Henry's floor and instantly look around for either Fawn or Henry. Hoping to find Fawn first, but no such luck.

"Where are you? I don't see you."

"In Henry's office. Just walk back there to meet us."

There's no receptionist at the front desk, so I round it and make my way to the corner office where I found Henry last time. Not as many of the employee's watch me this time. Since I'm not making a scene with Paloma and Pilar, I suppose I'm not as interesting. Also, my pink attire is rather tame today. Since we're just going to a flea market and maybe grab a bite to eat, I went for modest pink and comfort. In light denim ripped jeans and a loose V-neck t-shirt in a pink so pale it's almost white, paired with a few layered gold chain necklaces and bangle bracelets, I suppose I look more normal than before.

Rounding cubicles, I make my way to Henry's office. His door is open, and inside, I instantly spot him sitting behind his desk, all regal handsomeness in another perfectly tailored suit. There's another man in the chair opposite him. Henry looks just as handsome in this suit as he did the other. His closet must be filled with all manner of designer suits. Dark, nautical navy, like the deep cold seas. Soft dove gray of lost feathers on a breeze. Hard, charcoal black, like the burnt remnants of the broken hearts of unrequited love.

The one person I don't see is Fawn.

"I don't see you in Henry's office. Did you step out?"

"Not exactly. I kind of lied before." I can hear the cringe in her words. Why do I feel like I was just caught in one of those hidden camera joke shows? But not as one of the people behind the curtain, laughing at the poor schmuck who just fell for the obvious lie to coerce them into the kill zone. "I'm not in Henry's office. I'm not even in the building."

"What?!" My voice rises high and loud enough to attract the attention of the man I both loathe and lust after, as well as his guest, Samson, his friendly brother. One smiles, while the other does not as they both catch sight of me. In a whisper yell, I try to control my anger at Fawn. "What do you mean you're not here? Then where are you?"

"If you could just put me on speaker so I could talk to you and Henry, that would be great. I'll totally explain."

Samson has stood and is making his way over to me, a sparkling smile in place that says, 'I wouldn't mind making out with you, and definitely wouldn't leave in the middle of it without a word'. His brother's non-smiling face behind him says absolutely nothing. His face is impassive as ever. Neither pleased nor displeased at my presence.

"Hey, Lala. What are you doing here?" Samson greets me at the entrance to the office.

"Not what I thought I was."

"Excuse me?" His grin doesn't fade, but his curiosity piques. As does mine. Whatever Fawn is playing at, I'm not sure I like it.

"Ask your sister." Clicking the speaker button on my phone, I hold it out and take a few steps into the sterile, undecorated office, so they can hear whatever explanation Fawn has for this parent trap moment. "Alright, Fawn. I'm here with Henry and Samson, so please explain why you're not."

"Hey, guys. Sorry to throw this at you last minute, but something came up at work, and I can't take Lala to the flea market as I promised her. I was hoping Henry could take her, but I suppose either of you could. I was just going to be a tour guide to help her find it. Could either of you fill in for me please?"

Samson brightens up immediately. "I would be delighted to show Lala around."

I am both relieved and disappointed. Because apparently, I like tormenting myself. Even though it's been made abundantly clear that Henry wants nothing to do with me, I'm still drawn to him... and his grumpy, sexy energy.

"Oh, I suppose that would be ok. I guess one Bardot is as good as another." I try to play off my confusion and disappointment with humor. I'm usually better at it, but this time, it comes off a little flat.

A huff of obvious indignation comes from Henry, who still sits behind his desk, but is paying full attention to our conversation, and me. As a matter of fact, he hasn't looked away from me once. Every time I glance his way, his gaze burrows inside my gut and makes its way down to my belly, where it sizzles and fizzles and melts into goo. I want to drown in that goo and let it consume me. Let it burn off my clothes and hesitation and fall face first into my lust.

"I would beg to differ with that statement."

"Oh, is that so, big brother? You don't think I'm as good as Fawn?"

"Not even close. Fawn is far better than both of us. But of the three of us, you would be last, below me and Fawn," Henry states plainly.

"So, now you're better than me, too?" Samson jests, obviously unaffected by his brother's comment as he brushes his fingers through his chestnut brown hair.

"Of course, I am." Henry's confidence is both attractive, and infuriating. He doesn't even blink or flinch when he says it.

"Well, I would disagree with that statement." The two brothers stare off with one another. Samson standing tall, facing his brother, who remains sitting in his leather chair, shoulders squared, and fingers loosely laced rest on his desk.

"I don't care if you disagree. It's the truth."

"Just because you believe it to be the truth, doesn't mean it is. What makes me any less qualified to show Lala around than you? You don't even call her by her preferred name."

"I call her by her given name. It's called respect."

"Sure, you're all respect, aren't you?"

Their argument seems to be bleeding from playful brotherly jesting to outright arguing. I'm not sure how to stop it. I don't have siblings, and I was never able to win a conversation with my parents until I moved out. At this point, I can only stand and stare, blinking and trying to follow along.

"Boys, boys!" Fawn calls from my phone I had completely forgotten was still in my hand and still connected on a call with her. "It doesn't matter which one of you shows Lala around as long as *she's* Ok with it. So, why don't you ask her who she wants to take her around, and then decide like grown men?" Fawn huffs a sigh before speaking to me this time. "I'm so sorry, Lala, for ditching you like this and leaving you to the follies of my arrogant brothers. I hope you can forgive me, and possibly not kill them in the process. I really have to get going. I hope you don't hate me."

"Of course, I don't hate you, Fawn. I could never. We'll figure something out, don't worry. You just deal with your work issue, and I'll see you Thursday for Pilates."

"Thanks. I'm so sorry again. I promise I will totally make this up to you."

"It's no problem, Fawn."

"Behave you two, and listen to Lala," she scolds her brothers before disconnecting the call.

Returning my phone to my purse, I turn my attention back to the brothers. Samson stands on the opposite side of Henry's desk, looking down on him, and yet I feel like Henry is still the one holding the higher ground. His head does not tilt up to look at him, his eyes are calm and collected. There is so much held below the surface, trapped behind cold calmness that I want to discover. Whether it be lust, joy, anger, or annoyance. Feelings should not be suppressed. They should be let out into the world to do what they will. Even if those results are less than favorable. I can only imagine what could happen when Henry finally releases whatever it is he keeps inside. Letting it out bit by bit is far more manageable than a giant destructive explosion. Or worse, an implosion.

They continue with their back and forth as if I'm not even here.

"She doesn't want you to take her around, I'm far more fun," Samson starts, flashing a full toothed, panty melting smile. I wonder if Henry's smile would be just as swoon worthy.

"I have more knowledge of the city and her business," Henry counters. Standing he leans in, placing his splayed fingers atop his desk.

"I have a better car."

"I have a better vocabulary."

"I can make her smile."

"I can make her money."

"I'm better looking."

"No, you're not." Smug amusement plays at the edges of his lips, and I almost swear he wants to grin that same way he did at the trampoline park.

"I have more free time." This has Henry briefly pausing to process his retort before his next response.

"Thomas." Two seconds after Henry calls for his assistant, he appears in the doorway, quickly assessing the situation he's stepped into. He gives me a once over with a knowing smirk before turning back to his boss.

"Yes, Mr. Bardot?"

"Clear my schedule for the rest of the day."

With another quick glance at me and then Samson, he nods and grins. "Yes, Sir."

Thomas promptly exits the fighting ring I've somehow found myself in the middle of, leaving me to fend for myself. Although I have a feeling my input is not wanted in this dispute. No matter what I say, they're going to decide for me. And I'm pretty sure I know who's going to win.

Raising his eyebrows, Henry challenges Samson. "Now, so do I." Samson gives his brother a once over and rubs at his jaw.

"Alright then, how about we ask Lala who she wants to take her."

"Not necessary, because I'll be taking her. End of discussion." Rounding his desk, Henry grabs Samson by the shoulders, spinning him towards the exit. "Thanks for stopping by, Samson. Now don't you have a stripper to go woo or something?"

Leading him firmly by the arm, Henry escorts a displeased Samson from his office before shutting the door and locking him out.

"Let me just get my jacket and we can leave. Do you have the address for the flea market?" He doesn't look at me as he removes his jacket from a fancy looking freestanding hanger thing. I think it's called a valet. I watch him slide both powerful arms in and shrug it over his broad shoulders, and I'm too stunned to speak.

Last time I saw him, he was running away from me, scowling after rubbing his cock on me and tasting my tonsils with his tongue. Now, it appears he's back to his cocky, demanding self.

I still haven't spoken by the time he slides his cell phone into his inside jacket pocket and approaches me, hand extended towards the door.

"Well? Shall we?"

"Oh, right. Yes. Sure." *Real eloquent, Lala. You're a genuine intellect. He'll be sure to want to spend naked time with you now.* Opening the door, Henry allows me to exit first, the flat of his palm on my lower back as we leave his office almost as abruptly as I arrived.

I don't really know how I ended up in this position, but it seems Henry is determined to be my guide today. And who am I to say no to him?

The flea market is easy enough to find, though not so easy to find parking. Eventually Henry just chooses the valet of a nearby, no doubt five-star, hotel. I use the term flea market loosely here. It's more of a shabby chic, antique, used to be garbage but now it's treasure type of market. The place where small businesses and artists have bought old furniture and clothing and either repurposed, reinvented, or refurbished them to sell. It's definitely my kind of place, and if I had my tiny pink trailer, it would fit right in. *Le sigh.* Someday.

We don't speak much as we peruse the market. I'm not really here to shop, but to just scope out the joint. See if it's a place I want to be selling. And it most definitely is. I will be emailing the organizers tonight, no doubt.

Henry's small talk game is just as good as it was before, which is atrocious. Samson was right, he would have been more fun. He would have said yes when I asked if he wanted to try on the neon faux fur coats and reenact Elton John's Crocodile Rock (my all-time favorite Elton John song) with me. Alas, Henry sneered and said no. Another opportunity for joviality and fun missed due to Grumplestiltskin. Someday, I'll pay him back for that. And when that day comes, he will wish he sang Crocodile Rock with me in the flea market.

Between the market and the hotel we parked at, is a strip of boutique stores, one of which is a bougie baby store. Seeing as Fawn's baby shower is imminent, I figure it wouldn't hurt to take a gander.

"We should go inside. I want to look for a baby shower gift for Fawn." Pulling him to a stop in front of the window display of tiny baby sized things, I give him my best doe eyed pouty face. It doesn't seem to be working. "Come on, you're going to be an uncle. Don't you want to pick something out for your future niece?"

"Her shower is months away, and I was planning on having my assistant pick something off one of her registries." He is completely serious. He has no intention of picking something out for his first niece. Well that just won't do.

"Nope, na-ah. That is unacceptable. We're going in, and you're picking something out yourself without a registry."

"I don't think—" He doesn't get to finish his refusal because I drag him by the lapels of his ridiculously expensive suit, through the store front door and into the land of the cute and tiny.

Filled with onesies covered in cute puns, mobiles of zoo animals, cribs, bouncy chairs, and all kinds of useful trinkets, ranging from thermometers to booger suckers to pee-pee tents. Since Fawn is having a girl, she won't need those. I take in all the utter cuteness surrounding us.

I've always loved babies. Not sure I'd ever be a good person to have one, but I love doting on and pampering other people's kids. Especially when I get to do it in my favorite color—pink! I know girls can wear colors other than pink, and boys can wear it too—as a matter-of-fact guys look great in coral, salmon, and powder pink—but I tend to default to pink for girls. Ruffle dresses and sparkles galore! Fawn is going to be drowning in it if I have anything to do with it.

Henry looks downright frightened. I doubt he's ever even held a baby. He's going to have a lot to learn before his niece is born.

"All right, let's see what we can find." I circle shelves and displays, eagerly exploring the possibilities, skipping along gleefully and instantly zero in on anything pink I find. Henry crosses his arms and tucks his fingers in close to keep from touching anything, looking as if one brushing graze will contaminate him.

"It's not poisonous, Henry. You can touch it."

"No, thank you."

"Alright, then. I'll pick out things, and you say yes or no."

"No."

"I haven't even started yet."

"I was being proactive." He may not smile at his own joke, but I will, so I smile for us both.

"How about this?" It's a mobile made up of pink butterflies.

"No."

"Ok. How about this?" I hold up a high-end breast pump bra system. Holding it up to my chest I model its full coverage and removable pumps.

"No."

Threading my arms through the straps and securing it in place without hooking the back, I strike a pose. Hands on hips, shoulders thrust forward, I give him my best impression of duck lips. I probably look ridiculous, but that's the point. Henry doesn't even twitch an eye at my antics.

"Come on, you can't tell me this isn't the next big thing in mommy fashion. With its wide supportive straps, easy access front openings, and detachable double pumps, it's the latest and greatest in wearable pump fashion."

I'm full-on runway posing, and even strutting a few steps, pivoting for full effect.

"No. Especially now that I've seen you wearing it."

"Ouch, burn." I shake my hand out like I just touched a hot stove and burned myself, cringe grinning at my own hilarity. He just rolls his eyes.

"Alright, fine. Not this then." Removing the bra pump, I return to its display on the table. "Ooh, this one. This is the one." It's the most adorable onesie with a cartoon drawing of a milk bottle and beer bottle and says *Uncle's drinking partner.* "You have to get this for her. It's adorable."

"I don't drink beer."

"That's what you have against this onesie?" Silence. "You're going to say no to everything aren't you?"

"No. I'll say yes when you suggest we leave."

"Ugh. Well, I'm going to find something for her whether you do or not."

From the moment we walked into the store, the pretty brunette behind the counter has been eyeballing us... well Henry. Now that she sees we're doing more than just browsing, she leaves the counter to approach us.

"Hi there. Is there anything I can help you find today? I saw you trying on our bra pump. It's the best on the market. Made in multiple sizes for every shape of breast." Her smile is cordial and sweet, but something in her eyes glitters when she looks at Henry.

If I didn't know any better, I would think she's trying to check his ring finger for a wedding ring. But since his hands are tucked tight under his arms she can't.

Before Henry can say no, I answer the perky sales clerk. "We're actually looking for something pink."

"Oh. Are you and your husband having a little girl?"

Woooowww. If I weren't in a baby store where this question is probably common, I would see it for the blatant probing question it obviously is.

"We're not married," Henry answers blatantly, unfolding his arms and unintentionally displaying his empty ring finger.

"Oh, I'm so sorry to assume. Boyfriend then?"

Holy shit, this bitch is seriously trying to hit on him in a baby store. I suppose she may not have much opportunity elsewhere, but seriously. Have some class, lady.

"No. We're looking for my sister. She's the one having the baby girl." Either Henry is just being forthright and polite, or he's interested in this woman. Or he's just oblivious, since he is practically ignoring the woman and her inquisition.

"Oh, well, in that case, we have many things in pink over here you might be interested in." She barely acknowledges me after this point, leading Henry by the bicep to the girly pink section, pointing out this and that. He doesn't seem particularly engaged, but he nods and holds a few items she hands to him. He wouldn't even look at the items I suggested, yet he willingly handles the pink things she presses into his hands. *Her* hand lingers on his forearm in glancing touches. You know the kind. The ones women do to signal to a man she's interested. Ones I've never mastered.

I follow along behind them like a baby duck being left by its mother to find its own way. There are very few things or people who can make me feel small and insignificant, but this bubbly brunette somehow manages effortlessly. She introduces herself as Miranda to Henry and offers her "assistance in any way necessary". I may have just thrown up in my mouth a little.

There, hanging on a rack near where *Miranda* is showing Henry a bassinet filled with pink gifts, is the most adorable pink fuzzy jumpsuit with teddy bear ears on the hood. I take it off the rack, feeling its warm, downy exterior. She's going to be born in the fall, so she'll need a winter outfit. This would be perfect. Along with a silky soft pink plush teddy bear to match.

Holding out my choices, I try to grab Henry's attention. "What about these? I think they would be perfect."

Miranda side eyes my picks and completely ignores me, holding out the gaudy gift basket to Henry again. "I think this would be the best choice for your sister. It has a great variety of high-quality products every mother and daughter could need."

Her sickly-sweet smile and come-hither eyes make me want to do something very unlady-like. But it also stirs up feelings I thought long suppressed. The ones that came about every time a boy in school would laugh at me and wrap an arm around the head cheerleader, or every time girls would shun me from their lunch table. Being unique in a small southern town didn't garner me many friends.

My entire pink wardrobe may have been cute and acceptable as a child, but as a pubescent teenager, not so much. Especially when camo was considered acceptable for prom dress material.

My smile falters, and I can feel myself shrinking, receding, folding in on myself just as I did then. When I allowed others to make me feel small and insignificant.

Looking down at the pink, fluffy jumpsuit, I wonder if what I chose was wrong. I know it can't be used on a daily basis, and she'll most likely outgrow it in a few months, as babies are prone to do.

But I still like it. It's cute and sweet, and a chubby pink cheeked little girl would be the sweetest in it.

Large, strong hands reach out and lightly grasp mine around the pink puff suit. Henry's hands. Soft and delicate, yet strong and sure.

When I look up, his face is just as his hands are. Sure and decisive, yet soft. For the second time, he graces me with a semblance of a smile. This one is more than the last, which was just a hint of a smirk. This... this is a full blown, single sided, lip curling grin. Only the left side, but it's enough. Enough to make my heart skip and my breath stutter.

"I think we'll get these ones. Fawn will love them." I'm not sure if his words are for me or for Miranda, and I don't care. When a man like Henry looks at you like he just looked at me, nothing matters.

17 - Henry

You feel like every sin I ever wanted to commit

She got me to smile again. The pink little temptress managed to make me smile again, this time without even trying. I couldn't stand what that saleswoman did. Treating her as if she were insignificant and unimportant. Forcing away her inner light and joy. I may not have that myself, but no one deserves to take it away from her.

I bought the fluffy pink things she had picked out for her gift to Fawn. I have more than enough money, and I gathered from her need to book markets and my conference, she didn't. She objected at first, half-heartedly. In the end, she gave in to me, taking the bag of pink and allowing me to guide her by the waist out the door.

Once again, her and I sit in my Jag as I drive her home to her pink bus. It's odd how quiet she is sitting next to me. When she doesn't reach for the radio, I turn it on for her, to the same station as before, but at a far more reasonable decibel. She's not quite smiling, but the light in her eyes has returned as she watches out the window.

At her pink bus, I park and hop out to round the hood of the car to open her door that is already swinging open. I grab it and open it enough that she can stand, but block her into the wedge of space with my body.

"Are you Ok?"

"What? Of course, I am. Why wouldn't I be?" By the way she tangles her fingers in the ribbon handle of the store bag, I'm not sure she is. I frown at her uncertainty. In the short time I've known her, she's always been so outgoing and confident. Seeing her quiet like this is... weird.

"For one, that woman at the store was extremely rude to you."

"Oh, you mean *Miranda*. Was she? I didn't notice." She shrugs one shoulder, but the playful tone has returned to her voice.

"Never allow others to dampen your smile, Micaela. They're not worth its loss." The words are out of my mouth before I even have time to comprehend the thought. My hand threads through her hair, pulling her lips into mine before I even realize what I'm doing. My body responds to hers, hardening under the attention of her mouth.

Micaela melts into me like butter on hot toast. Seeping into my pores and heating my blood. I'm hard and may actually fuck her against my car. How did this strawberry shortcake washed in pink manage to get under my skin so thoroughly?

Creamy arms snake around my shoulders and lock behind my neck, pulling me down to meet her. Slipping my hands under her perfect round ass, I hoist her up against my chest, her legs wrapping around my hips, and her warm center grinding into me.

I disconnect my lips from hers by a fraction to bite out a curse. "Fuck, Shortcake. You do that again, and I won't wait to get you into that ludicrous pink bus of yours before tearing these absurdly tight jeans off your perfect fucking ass."

"Henry Bardot." She breathes out my name in an attempt to

sound shocked, but the sound of it on her lips, all hot and bothered, just urges me on further. My dick flexes between us, trying to reach through my slacks and thrust a hole through hers. "Did you just call my ass fucking perfect?"

"Yes, I did. I've been staring at it for days, and now that I have my hands on it, I'm going to do unspeakable things to it." I gave said mind-blowing ass a squeeze, emphasizing my point.

"Yeah. Ok."

Her breathy consent has me kicking my car door shut without losing my grip on her hypnotizing body. Reaching her front door in four long strides, and never breaking contact with her lips, I bite gently on her bottom lip to get her attention. She moans into my mouth and rocks her pelvis into mine. I swallow her lust greedily. It's fire fueling my own, fanning and stoking it into an inferno.

"Shit. Keys, Shortcake."

"Uh huh." Her hand fumbles with her purse and she produces a keychain, holding one key I assume unlocks her bus. I take it before she can gouge my eye out with her flailing arm and unlock the door.

Stepping up into the bus, I know where everything is from the last time I was here. There's not much to her house, and I head straight to the back, where I saw her bed before. She's already flinging her purse and the pink filled baby bag on the couch as we pass. Running her hands under the lapels of my suit jacket, she tries to push it off my shoulders. It gets stuck of course, since my arms and hands are occupied holding her.

I want nothing between us. I want to feel her hands on every inch of my body, and my lips on every inch of hers. It's been a torment of unrecognizable fathoms since the moment she first kissed me in the street. I didn't recognize it or acknowledge it then, but her imprint set in on me that day.

From the moment she wrapped her arms around me and forced

her fuckable mouth onto mine, something shifted, sparked to life. I may not have admitted it then, but now, having her wrapped around me like a horny koala, I can't deny it. I've been drawn to her and her pink glow since day one.

I never wanted to be. Being drawn to someone can be dangerous. Allowing someone to sink under my skin can only lead somewhere damaging and unwanted.

Right now, where she's leading me is towards her bed, and premature ejaculation if I don't get her naked soon.

Micaela arches into my kiss, pressing her fuck perfect tits against me. We are still wearing too many clothes. I need her naked and writhing beneath me. She telepathically hears my unspoken need, and when she can't remove my jacket, she strips her own shirt off. Legs still latched around my waist, she reveals her glorious breasts bound in ballerina pink lace. Perky, soft, and extremely lickable.

I want to see every pink part of her, taste it, and find out if it's as sweet as I hope.

My knees bump into her bed, and I drop her onto the pink cloud-like surface. She bounces as her butt makes impact, those pretty pink tits of hers following the movement. My eyes are glued to them as I remove my jacket and tie, tossing them behind me, not focusing on where they land. I don't have time to hang them properly. Not with Micaela looking up at me through long lashes, and leaning back to crawl onto her bed. She kicks off her shoes, and I follow suit.

When I reach for my belt and slacks, Micaela leans forward and takes over. *Impatient little she-demon.* Deftly, she unbuckles and unbuttons, letting my pants fall to the floor, joining my discarded shoes.

The last time I was this impatient to get a woman naked and

under me was in a different life, a different time. A time when I used to smile regularly. When there was one girl who made me. That was then. This is now, and Micaela is nothing like her. Micaela doesn't want a future or a commitment. This is all about pleasure and fulfilling ours. There are no strings attached to her, except for the conference. But as I've clarified before, that's just business. Just like this is a form of business. No matter how carnally inappropriate my thoughts are towards her, we're just two people participating in a transaction. One made of sweat and lips and lust. My second favorite kind of business transaction.

Shimmying out her jeans, she adds them to the growing pile at my feet while I unbutton and remove my shirt. Both of us are now in our underwear, her's pink and sweet, mine black and tight around my dick. She eyes me appreciatively, and I preen under her attention.

Women always look at me with lust and desire, whether it be for my body or my money, and it never affects me. But when Micaela watches me beneath her half hooded, glassy eyes, it feels different... more. I want her to look. I want her to appreciate and partake in whatever dirty fantasy is running through her head.

I take a moment to appreciate Micaela's beauty before me. The sweet feisty temptress that's lured me into her sex bus. Soft curves and lush skin. I want to taste all of her. Spread her out and feast on her sweetness until she comes apart around me.

— Lala —

This is not where I thought my day would end today. But I am so glad it did. Being around Henry and not touching him, not giving into this weird sexual attraction I have for the grumpy guss has been difficult. We're complete opposites, and yet I want him more than I've wanted any man before. I want to touch him and feel him on me. His lips on my flesh, and his extremely hard cock inside me.

I have been so sexually frustrated for months, even before I met Henry. Not even my stockpile of vibrators can satiate my desires. From what I see tenting Henry's boxer briefs, I have no doubt he'll be able to satisfy my needs. Just thinking about him sliding that monster inside me has me squirming in anticipation.

Henry is even more magnificent naked than I imagined him to be. Corded muscle flexes tight across his abdomen and chest, bronzed skin glistening in the fading afternoon light. Soft patches of dark hair curl across his chest and below his navel, traveling to his naughty circus below his waistband. His body is in peak condition, and he even has the coveted Adonis belt V.

My mouth waters.

None of my past partners had it. Honestly, I thought it was a myth only gym rats and photoshopped men had. Seeing it in person within groping distance has my fingers itching to reach out and trace the steep line. Then, promptly follow it into his underwear and claim my pot of gold at the end of his rainbow.

Biting my lip, I watch as he reaches down and squeezes his shaft through the cotton underwear. Giving it one strong stroke. Those beautiful biceps flex with the motion.

"Eyes up here, Shortcake," he growls, tilting my chin with one finger to bring my focus to his face. "I'm going to taste every inch of your sugary sweetness now."

"I'm Ok with that," I manage to breathe out. I am sooo down with that. He can do anything he pleases with me.

Gripping my thighs, he pulls my ass to the edge of the bed, knocking me on my back. Stepping between my spread legs, he places himself at my core, pressing his hard cock into my wet pussy. Only the thin layers of fabric between us, I'm already halfway to orgasm, and feeling him there makes me weak in the knees in a way that makes me happy I'm already on my back.

He maneuvers my legs, hooking them over his elbows, and leans into me. His lips once again find mine as he claims my mouth as his.

God, he feels fucking fantastic. I want to strip away the layers between us and let him claim me, take me, and ravage me. My outsides may seem sweet and innocent, but I am far from innocent. I like my sex life how I like my daily life—exciting and in many positions.

"Henry." His name slips out on a moan as he shifts his lips from my mouth to my neck and nips on the spot behind my ear. I don't know if I'm asking, pleading or chastising.

Either way, he responds.

"You taste like sugar and sin, little Shortcake. You're not as goody two shoes as you appear to be, are you?"

I can't even answer him as his hands slide across my stomach and up over my breasts, pinching one nipple through the pink lace. He removes my bra and panties in swift, effortless movements, leaving me bare and wet, presented for him like a goddamn sacrifice. If the sacrifice is to allow him to punish me with his cock, I will gladly volunteer as tribute.

He groans loudly before dropping to his knees and spreading me out before him.

He doesn't even give me a chance to adjust to our new position before his mouth presses against my pussy. First in an open-mouthed kiss, and then long soft licks before sucking on my clit, then repeating the actions. I'm squirming under his attention as he sends uncontrollable quivers through my body.

"You taste fucking delicious, Shortcake. First, I'm going to make you come on my mouth, and then you're going to come on my dick while screaming my name."

"Uh huh." My brain can't form cohesive thoughts, let alone a full sentence. I'd probably agree to do the macarena in the middle of his office butt naked if he asked right now.

My fingers dig into his hair, that oh so tantalizing hair I've wanted to get my hands on since I first saw him. The stands are thick and silky and just long enough to get a good handful. He hums in approval, as I grip tight, then returns his attention to my throbbing pussy. Slipping his tongue into my wet heat, a tightness clenches my core as he pushes me higher and higher until I'm coming undone, screaming his name just as he predicted. Legs quaking around his shoulders, he laps up my orgasm before extricating himself from my thighs.

"Condoms?" he asks, standing and sliding his underwear down those powerful thighs, giving me my first glimpse of his perfectly beautiful dick, standing tall and thick and long, reaching for me. Yes, beautiful. Cocks can be beautiful. With a glistening, swollen tip, precum leaking from his slit, a thick shaft with pulsing veins, engorging him for me, and a tight, heavy sack that pulls up further the longer I look at it.

I may be partially dead from that orgasm, but I lean up and slide my lips around the head and suck gently. My own personal push-pop.

"Fuck. Really could use that condom now, sweetness." Growling, he grips my hair but doesn't pull me away or push me farther down. There's controlled restraint in his hold. Not forcing me to do something I don't want, and allowing me to guide my actions.

Pulling my mouth from his delicious cock, I lick my lips and see his jaw flexing, heat burning his irises into pools of lava.

"Top drawer." I point to the set of built-in drawers next to the head of my bed.

Opening the drawer, he digs around its contents, pulling out one pink vibrator after another. "Sweet, misleading Micaela. Are these what I think they are?" He raises an approving eyebrow at me while fingering three of my vibrators.

"Well, they're not kids' toys. That's for sure."

"No. They most certainly are not." Putting back my g-spot vibrator, he pulls out a condom, tearing the foil with his teeth and sheathing his length. "Perhaps next time, we can play with some of those."

"I do believe that is the sexiest thing a man has ever said to me."

"Then you've never met a real man."

"You're making that clear to me now."

"Well, I'm about to make a few things even clearer."

I'm still positioned at the edge of my bed, legs dangling, propped up on my elbows as he repositions himself where he had been before. Standing between my thighs, he hooks my knees over his elbows. His tip slips against my wet entrance. Just watching him slide the condom down his length has me wet and ready for him again.

He doesn't thrust into me as I thought he would. Instead, he plays with me. Sliding in just the tip, then pulling out again, sliding his length through my aching pussy, rubbing his stone hard erection against my sensitive clit before sliding back in.

Man sure as hell knows how to use his dick. I was most definitely wrong about the missionary, boring sex. Henry holds secrets of his own that I very much want to discover.

This time, when his head lines up with my entrance, he does thrust deep, seating himself to the hilt.

"Oh fuck, Henry!" I scream. I can't help it. He feels so goddamn good. Thick and hard, filling me and stretching me in a wonderfully aching way. My fingers dig into the blanket beneath me, twisting as I writhe in pleasure from the most amazing dick I've ever had inside me.

"Goddamn it, Shortcake. You feel like every sin I ever wanted to commit."

Henry folds in half over me, pinning my knees to the sides of my ribs as he begins to move and thrust inside me. Sucking one of my nipples into his mouth, he flicks his tongue in a delightfully torturous way.

"Fuck yes, Henry. Harder. I want all of you." He obliges me by pulling out and pistoning his hips back in faster and harder. Giving me what I want. What I need. What we both need. Fulfillment. Deliverance. Release.

His fingers dig into my ass with every pump of his hips. With every heavy breath against my skin, I grow more heated, climbing that peak higher and higher, until I'm so close. My second orgasm is a fraction of an inch away. I can feel it creeping up my spine when he slows, turning his hard thrusts into long languid pulls. My peak of pleasure doesn't subside, but it also doesn't crest. He holds it there, lingering on the precipice, torturing and pleasing me to no end.

I want to live in this limbo forever.

Lips and tongue and teeth taste my body, traveling from breast to nipple to collar bone and settling on my neck. Taking his leisurely time tasting me, just as he said he would. I both love and hate it.

Am I going to interrupt his ministrations? Abso-fucking-lutely not. He can draw this out till the end of the year for all I care.

Time stretches out, and I'm delirious with lust and pleasure coursing through my veins. Henry's mouth isn't just on my body, but my lips, pressing in hard and devouring with his tongue, exploratory and teasing. Nipping at my lips, he sucks on each one gently.

I'm not the only one who tastes of sin and forbidden fruit.

When he's had his fun, his pace increases again, slowly returning to manic pounding. Henry leans back to stand straight. Gripping my foot, he kisses up my leg, starting at my knee and ending at my ankle. He rests them on his shoulders, holding my legs straight against his chest, banding one arm over my shins to hold them in place. *And holy sinner and saints in a locker room.* This new position has my legs shaking and my body on the edge of a razor. One gentle push from a ghost would force me over the edge. I can feel my pussy clench around his steel shaft. A few more thrusts and I'm going to come.

"Not yet, sweet thing, you have to wait for me. I want to feel your tight orgasm milk mine out of me. You come when I say you can. Because your orgasms belong to me now. Isn't that right?"

"Yes," I groan as I shamelessly press my ass to his thighs. The friction and angle in this position is no joke. I may have agreed to wait for him, but I don't know if my body will let me.

"Right there, sweetness. Fuck, yes. Is that sweet pussy of yours going to make me come?" I love it when a man isn't afraid to talk dirty during sex. It makes me so much wetter.

"Yes. Henry, I wanna come. You feel so good. God, you're so fucking hard I can't stand it. Please let me come." I'm rambling now, begging really, just letting the words topple out of my mouth. He has me wound up so tight I can feel my nipples brush against the air they're so hard. Not wanting to neglect the poor girls, I use both hands to pinch them, squeezing my tits and rolling my pink buds just the way I like.

Henry watches me, eyes glazed and hungry. He likes watching, and I like him watching. If this continues past today, I am definitely going to suggest some mutual masturbation time.

Man, I am so goddamned turned on, I don't know how I'm still conscious.

Reaching his big hand down, Henry rocks my fucking world all over again by pressing his thumb against my clit and circling it. He keeps his eyes on mine with a few quick glances down to where we are joined while his hand does wicked things to me.

"Shit... I can't... I'm going to come."

"Yes, you are. Say my name and come on my cock." I do. I'm putty in his hands once more. Literally.

"Henry!"

"Micaela!" He roars my name as he comes, his dick pulsing and throbbing inside me, biting down on my calf as he holds himself balls deep. His chest rises and falls in heavy staccato breaths.

My entire body shakes as the aftershocks of my orgasm ripple through me. I shudder every time Henry shifts his hips where we're still connected.

We remain like this until one of us is able to move, which would be Henry. Sliding his still semi-hard cock from my tender—and very pleased—pussy, he removes the condom and disposes of it in the bathroom. And like a true gentleman who understands the reality of sex, he returns with a damp cloth for me. When I reach out to take it, he surprises me further by batting away my hand and gently cleaning me himself with a tenderness I did not expect. No man has ever cleaned me.

He returns to the bathroom for another moment before he's swaggering back into my room. "Let me help you up the bed. You're about to fall off." Henry lifts me by my hips and slides my body effortlessly onto the mattress. Laying my head on the pillow, he joins me, stretching out on his back. I watch as he makes himself right at home.

Reaching out, he pulls me to his side, nuzzling my hair before draping my comforter over us both.

Pinky Promise

Henry Bardot is an animal in the sack, a grump on the street, and a softy who assists in aftercare and cuddles. This man never ceases to surprise me.

18 - Lala

Two orgasms and a smile. This is my lucky day.

In the past, after sex, I was always the one to get dressed first or roll over and "fall asleep". Cuddling was not something I did. A self-preservation method to keep from getting too attached. To not put down roots when I wasn't ready. Whenever a guy I was dating or seeing would try to pull me close and participate in any after copulation cuddling, I would slip free, roll over, go to the bathroom, or even get dressed to leave. I'm basically the anti-cuddle girlfriend. Which seems to go against everything people would think me to be.

When Henry carried me into Tallulah, kissing the ever-loving crap out of me and squeezing my ass in a way that had me wet before we crossed the threshold, I had no thought in my mind about after sex cuddling. All that was going through my mind was *Holy shit he's a good kisser*, and *Is this really happening?* Not, *I wonder if we're going to cuddle after.*

I was more focused on removing his ridiculously sexy suit to see his ridiculously sexy naked body underneath. Once I managed to get him naked, there really weren't any more thoughts in my mind beyond *yes please.*

Laying here pressed against Henry's side, partially wrapped around his still naked body, listening to his steady heartbeat, somehow, I'm not anxious. The jittery twitches that usually take over, forcing me up and out are nowhere to be seen. My body is relaxed, my mind is at ease, and my heart rate is calm and steady. For once, I don't want to leave. There's no pressure to be more, that it means more. We're just comfortable and relaxed, enjoying the aftereffects of amazing orgasms.

In another action I would have never expected from Henry, his fingers draw lazy shapes along the exposed skin of my shoulder and arm, twirling the ends of my hair in-between.

He's not staring into my eyes lovingly or adoringly. There's no weird shift to lovey dovey or any such thing. Laying on his back, his face is turned up to the ceiling and his gaze is hooded as he stares at nothing really. His face is blank as always, revealing nothing. I have no idea what he could be thinking, but he seems content to remain here. Maybe he's resting up for round two. After a snack and a power nap, I'd be game.

"So, why a bus?" Henry breaks our mutual silence with a question out of left field. Not exactly what I thought he would say, but whatever.

"Because a van was too small." I grin up at him.

"I don't know, you're pretty tiny, Shortcake. You could probably live in a van comfortably enough."

"Was that a joke?" Shifting, I rest my chin on his chest to get a better look at him.

"No. Just an astute observation. Seriously, Micaela, what motivated you to live in a bus?"

To him that may be an innocent enough question, but for me it's loaded with a whole hell of a lot of back story. I struggle to find a place to begin. "I mentioned to you before that it was my aunt that inspired me to get the bus, remember?"

"Yes. You said she was a modern-day hippie who never left the seventies." Of course, he would remember my exact words. He probably has an eidetic memory.

This conversation seems too personal for us and our type of relationship, especially while naked and pressed against one another. If we were talking about this completely clothed and jesting while out somewhere in public, it would be different. But here, stripped bare after multiple orgasms seems too close. To distance myself, if only just a little, I sit up and disconnect from Henry. Wrapping my sheet around my chest, I rest my elbow on my bent knees and look around my small and wonderful home.

"Growing up in a small town where most people married their high school sweetheart to some may seem ideal. But to me—it felt like a life sentence. Like from the moment I was born, a chain was locked around my neck, tethering me to that town. To those people. There is a great wide world out there, with so much to see and experience. I never wanted to stay there. I always had this itch like cabin fever to escape. To go anywhere... everywhere."

It's more than just going anywhere for the sake of going. There are specific things I dreamt of. Waking up Christmas morning in a log cabin to a fresh layer of snow coating the world. Strolling through rust colored falling leaves on a jack-o-lantern lined street on Halloween. Spending a sunny day in the sand and sea, soaking up rays and salt. Ringing in the new year amongst thousands of glittery people in Times Square. Gazing up at the stars and galaxies on a cloudless Arizona desert night. All of which I've done since venturing out on my nomad adventure.

I've experienced and lived and met so many interesting people on my journey. Even with all I've seen and done, I always wanted more, wanted to go and move. To get lost in the world. Now, I fear I've become too lost, swallowed by my own fears. Drowning a little in their wake, trying to find my way back to shore.

I sigh and risk a side glance at Henry. He's sat up, propped against my headboard, patiently watching and waiting. Far more interested in my story than anticipated. So, I continue.

"When Auntie Lulu came to visit—"

"Lulu?" Henry interrupts. "Like Lala? Is that where the nickname came from?"

"Yes, she did give me the nickname. Not sure if it was for altruistic reasons or not, but it is what it is. Anyways, Auntie Lulu came into town when I was in college, and I told her how I wanted to leave Farmington and go anywhere. Possibly travel. We got to talking, and she suggested an RV or travel trailer. To take a year and just travel wherever I could drive. The idea took root, and well, one year led to two, which led to five, and here we are, six years later. I'm still traveling, still on the move. Unable to stay anywhere for very long." Raising my arms, I gesture to the bus around us. The only thing permanent in my life these days. "This is home, and it's all I have."

"You went to college?"

"Really? That's the thing you latch onto out of all of that?" Turning I face him. The shadow of a smirk drifts in his eyes and on his lips.

"The rest of it was expected. Figured there was something about your past life in your hometown that led you to this lifestyle. What I didn't know was that you went to college. Did you graduate?"

"Um…" Shit, I did not think this through before opening my big mouth. "Yes?"

"Is that a question or a statement?"

"Which one gets me out of answering the question?"

"Neither."

"Fine." I grumble. "I did graduate, and I do have a degree."

"What in?"

Oh dear. Ok, here we go. This usually makes people chortle, so maybe, at least I'll get a smile or a laugh out of him. I clear my throat, but the words still come out mumbled. "Animal Husbandry."

A sound as beautiful as Christmas bells on Santa's sleigh rings from Henry's throat. A laugh, almost a bark, bursts out, followed by three short chuckles. Accompanied, of course, by the mandatory smile that cannot be avoided when laughing. His is crooked and rusty, but beautiful and unique. The thing I had set out to force from him is finally mine. Modeling a breast pump bra, singing in the car, and taking him to a trampoline park hadn't done it. If I'd known all I had to do was inform him what my bachelor's degree was in, I would have done it days ago.

He tries to cover it up with his hand, literally trying to smooth down the edges of his mouth. At first, he doesn't succeed, and I lap up every morsel of his smile. I scoot closer to Henry to make sure I get a good long look. Even trying to stifle it, it's dazzling. Before he wrestles it back to the flat frown he normally wears.

"Henry Bardot. Was that a smile *and* a laugh? Well, holy shit. Two orgasms and a smile. This is my lucky day." My own smile is large and wide.

"It is your lucky day indeed. But don't expect another smile out of me. You simply caught me off guard. I expected you to say fine art or nutrition. Not animal husbandry."

"My parents thought I was going to take over the ranch and business. When they realized I wasn't, they sold it and retired to Florida."

Something playful and sultry colors Henry's expression. Leaning forward, he slides one hand under the sheet to run along my bare thigh and butt cheek.

"So, does that mean you are versed in all manner of copulation and mating?"

This teasing side of Henry is new and greatly appreciated. "Perhaps. There were classes on the most effective way for a male and female to... *copulate*."

Our teasing leads to touching, which leads to kissing, and eventually back to fucking. By the time we collapse sweaty and exhausted on my bed, the sun has set and I can barely keep my eyes open.

After Henry's gentlemanly attentions, he tucks us back into bed with my back against his chest. And that's how I fall asleep. I'm oddly comfortable being spooned by Henry, the harumphing grump, after the best sex I didn't see coming. Ok, well, I saw him come twice, but you get what I mean.

19 - Henry

Perfectly matched and fitting effortlessly

Unlike most mornings, I wake slowly and tangled in my sheets. Normally my sheets are smoothly draped over me, cool and crisp, and in the same position as when I fell asleep. Today, I can't seem to straighten them out. They're also warmer, stickier. *Wait, why are they sticky?* Did I spill something in bed before falling asleep?

Cracking open an eye, I'm not surrounded by heigh ceilings and polished cement floors with tasteful, functional furniture in tones of gray and black. Instead, the world is washed in pink, and the walls are practically on top of me. And those sticky sheets? Those are Micaela's arms and legs, and I am not displeased with the position we're in.

Most guys think spending the night means committing to something more than sex, or that cuddling mean you're somehow irrevocably tied to that girl now. It doesn't. One can participate and enjoy, both without the unspoken strings believed to magically appear afterwards. They're just included benefits. Why should I leave when I was perfectly comfortable in Micaela's bed? Why should I not hold her sweet, luscious body close to mine as I sleep off the exhaustion from our… transaction? She didn't refuse.

Her skin is soft and pliable. Not tight and rough like girls who starve themselves to the point of a living skeleton, all sharp edges and sunken flesh. One girl's hip almost pierced my abs with her sharpness. I'm not into blood play. I like my insides on the inside. I like a woman to be shapely, with soft curves and lush flesh I can sink my fingers and teeth into. Speaking of…

Pulling the atrocious pink blanket down off Micaela's naked body, I take a leisurely stroll down her curves. Over her shoulders, down the side of her ribs, cresting her wonderfully full hips and ass, and those generous thighs I plan on having wrapped around my shoulders again, and soon.

For now, I'll settle for a taste. Pressing my lips to the flesh on the side of her thigh and ass cheek, I nip at it gently with my teeth.

A syrupy, satisfied, sleepy moan escapes Micaela, but she doesn't wake.

Salty sweat mixes with her sugary flavor, and I give the area a small lick before rolling over and off the bed, leaving Micaela naked and exposed. She whimpers in her sleep and nestles into her pillow. A vision of pink flesh and sheets laid out before me in offering.

Slipping on my boxer briefs, I find my way the three steps to her bathroom, escaping the silent beckoning to wake her with my face between her thighs. Relieving myself then washing my hands, I decide to take this opportunity of quiet to inspect her bus a little further.

The kitchen is well thought out, with useful and space saving designs. She must have had her pink fridge and convection oven custom made because I've never seen one in such a color in all the kitchen's I've been in. Being a realtor, I've been in a lot, even if I specialize in office complexes.

Above the petite farmhouse sink, jars hang from their lids, filled with varying pink things. One is completely filled with what looks to be pink gummy bears. I could use a little sugar after last night. Unscrewing the jar, I steal two pink bears and pop them in my mouth before returning the jar. The sugar seeps into my taste buds, and a little of my expended energy returns.

There's a desk built into one side, and a couch opposite, all upholstered in pink with white and gold accents. I have to admit, it's not as gaudy as I would have expected.

Fred, her pink ferret, is curled up in a hammock in his cage, twisted like a pink cinnamon roll, fast asleep. Early morning sunshine filters through the gauzy pink curtains, streaming warm, dusky light across the bus.

Reaching the front, I lower myself onto the pink sheepskin covered seat. Hydraulics lift and drop me until they settle under my weight. The front windshield is draped in the same pink curtains, hindering my view, but also hiding me from passersby's. A long, dangling chain of pink crystals hangs from a rear-view mirror that no longer serves its original purpose. Small glimmers of muted light sparkle off each crystal and dance across the walls.

In the silence of the morning, there are things that bombard my thoughts. Things that make me question if I should have stayed last night. If I should even be here at all. Giving in to my urge with Micaela was a weakness. One I probably shouldn't have indulged in. I may have told her about my stance on relationships, but we didn't spell things out before getting intimate. This can only spell disaster.

I always make it very clear before getting in the sack with a woman. The promise of her sweet, pink flesh distracted me to the point of delusion.

I've been vigilant in my sexual conquests, keeping them impersonal and disconnected from the rest of my life. Making sure none had the opportunity to get intertwined. Micaela is definitely intertwined. Close friends with my sister, attending our realty conference as a vendor, sticking my cock in her mouth. I'd say things are—mixed.

I let myself get involved once, when I was young, before I learned the truth. Before it was made clear that if I wanted to be a successful businessman, there was no room for relationships. That the involvement of a woman in my life as anything more than casual would cause disaster. No woman is worth the misery that comes with strings and attachment. Feeding chaos into my life isn't worth the arguments and disagreements, the lies and distrust.

Sex is just sex and nothing more. I may have a strange unforeseen attraction to the pink shortcake, but that's nothing more than lack of stimulation. My paid rendezvous have gotten stagnant and boring. I needed a change, and I got one. I can chalk this all up to tedium, and now that I've broken it, I can move on.

It would be pertinent of me to end this now and sever any personal connection, keeping it strictly professional.

Gripping the bus steering wheel, nearly white knuckling it, I set in my determination and decision to keep it casual and finite. It was a moment of weakness, and now that I've satisfied my hunger, we can move on.

Soft warm hands and a matching voice caress my shoulders and insides, slithering down my spine and circling around to settle in my balls. Apparently, my determination lasts only as long as it takes for Micaela's voice to break my will power.

"Are you adjusting my seat so the next time I drive I won't be able to reach the pedals?"

It's nearly impossible to keep my eyes off of her. She's slipped on an oversized tank top, the neckline so loose and low I can see ample cleavage. Her pert little nipples are like diamonds poking the fabric. Like a spark to flint, my body reacts to hers being so close and so accessible. There's no way I can stop having her just yet.

Reaching around, I slide my hand up the back of her shirt and find her backside still gloriously bare and ready for me.

"I was just adjusting it to make room."

"Room for what?"

I answer by pulling her down across my lap, positioning her legs on either side of my hips, straddling me. She settles easily into the cradle of my hips. Not grinding or pressing or seeking friction, just relaxing comfortably. Perfectly matched and fitting effortlessly. Her center is warm and welcoming, and I could spend all day nestled in her.

One strap falls off a milky shoulder, and I take advantage, pressing my mouth to her collarbone, sucking lightly, then harder.

"Already trying to seduce me again, Mr. Bardot? Didn't have your fill last night?"

"Apparently not." My words are muffled into the crook of her neck. Her hair is wild and messy, but still smells like cotton candy and sex. My musky scent mingles with hers, and the mix is intoxicating.

I'm half hard, and now I'm the one absentmindedly rubbing myself against her. Her sleepy moan of approval encourages me to continue my unhurried exploration. In measured, gradual movements, I remove her shirt, slipping it off, over her head and disposing of it somewhere on the floor.

In this position, her breasts are lifted higher and more accessible, I place one in my mouth and suckle. She responds in kind, arching and scraping her nails against my scalp, tugging on my hair in a way I'm learning I love.

Our clash of dark and light, stoic and peppy works in a way I had not anticipated. Mixing in a deadly concoction.

Micaela pulls my mouth away from her delectable nipple to force my face to align with hers. When I go to take her mouth, she slows me with a quick jerk on my hair. It sends a bolt of electricity down my spine and straight to my dick. Instead of devouring her as I wished, she lowers her lips to mine in deliberately delayed movements.

The press of her lips to mine is soft and drawn-out. Openly exploring. It's different from our heated kissing last night. I want to object, to push back and break the connection. But I can't. Her siren call is too powerful, and like so many sailors lost at sea, I feel myself being drawn under her spell.

Micaela releases me from her spell to hop off my lap, but before I can complain, she returns and replaces herself as if she never left. In her hand, I see she's retrieved a condom.

Maybe I have a siren call of my own.

Shoving my underwear down my thighs, releasing my fully erect cock, Micaela sheathes me to the hilt. Unable to wait, she lifts and places herself down on me, sheathing me once more. This time in the heat of her pussy.

The last monocles of sleep disappear under her movements. We're rocking and shifting with the bounce of the hydraulic chair. Her lips are on mine again, far less gentle than before. Manic in her need. I feel her heel press into my hips as she lifts a leg to a position she approves of.

Obliging my Shortcake's wishes, I thread my arm under her knee and grip her wrist and forearm, locking her in place.

We're a messy tangle of limbs and fingers, tongue and teeth. Finding our rhythm, using the motion of the seat to our advantage. She comes on my dick, her head thrown back and my name on her lips.

I follow right behind her, burying my face in her tits as I pulse out my release inside her.

As this morning has proven, I am not done with Micaela Hart yet. One night and morning will not be enough to satiate my hunger for her sugary sweetness. I'll have to be extra vigilant to make sure to break off anything before it develops into more than what it is. Sex.

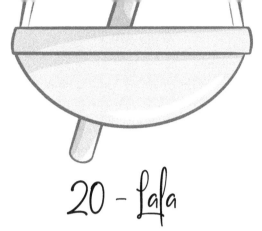

20 - Lala

A grown man with great genetics

ave you ever had that after sex glow? The one that makes you feel light and airy. Having sex with Henry gave me that feeling times a thousand.

The heavy weight of anxiety I felt about finances and booking events is gone in the wake of orgasms provided by Henry. I no longer feel dragged down, and don't fear my phone call with my parents this week. I'm actually looking forward to telling them about the conference. I won't, however, mention the fact that I'm sleeping with... slept with? Still not sure if this should be past or present tense yet. Either way, I'm not mentioning anything about Henry, other than the fact he's Fawn's brother and got me the gig.

If they hear any inkling that Henry is more than a business associate, they will pounce, asking me their possible future son-in-law version of twenty questions. No, thank you.

After our morning romp in my driver's seat, which I will never again sit in and not think about how Henry felt inside me, Henry drove me to pick up my Jeep from the parking garage of his building. That was two days ago, and I haven't heard from him since, but the glow still remains.

Neither of us wants anything serious, so not talking for a few days after sex is nothing to stress about. Because we aren't together. Now, would I like a replay of two days ago? Hell yes, I would. Am I going to force it if it doesn't happen? Not at all. It is what it is, sex. Mind blowing, body numbing sex. With a guy who has the body of a mythical creature and the mouth of a porn star. And I'm not even going to mention his magical dick and panty melting, heart throbbing smile. If he decided to wield that like a weapon, we would all be slaughtered on sight.

This morning I received an email from a ThomasArthur@bardotrealty.com with all the details for the conference, as well as his questions about what I will need. It was all very professional, even after the twins and I bombarded him that first time at Henry's office. Thankfully, he doesn't appear to hold any grudges. I think he actually likes me.

The conference takes place in late June, about two months from now. Still not as soon as I would have hoped, but I'll take it. Gives me plenty of time to prep and order any additional supplies I'll need. I sent Thomas my list of required space and plugs, and he sent me a confirmation. I'll be setting up in ballroom *Sierra* on the day of. It's the designated food and break room.

This information, of course, only adds to my post coital inner glow. Which I hope is not visible externally. I've already been mistaken for a pregnant lady once this week. I don't need it to happen again because someone misreads my glow.

Today is also Pilates day, and I managed to convince Paloma and Pilar to join me and Fawn. We're all in a row on mats at the end of class, stretching when Paloma opens her big mouth. The small talk had been simple and casual through the entire class, and I had high hopes it would stay that way. Paloma, as usual, has trampled those hopes.

"A few days ago, I noticed a sleek black Jag parked outside your bus." She leans over to touch her toes, watching me. Waiting for me to fill in the blanks.

I know she was spying out her window, no doubt watching Henry arrive and enter—carrying me. I had been sucking his face and grinding against him like a cat in heat. My face flashes crimson at the memory and idea that we were being watched.

"Oh yeah… Henry drove me out to a flea market when Fawn had to cancel last minute. That was just him dropping me off."

"Mmhmm. All night? Don't try to lie to me, little Lala. His black Jag was still there in the morning when I went for my run."

"Well…"

Should I deny it? Should I play it off as nothing? Or should I admit what happened? We're all modern-day progressive women. I'm sure they would understand our… situation. Telling his sister about our torrid sexcapades was not on my to do list today, but she seems as intrigued as the twins.

"I didn't know Henry dropped you off at home. Is there something going on between you two?" She wiggles her eyebrows suggestively, in a manner a bit disturbing for a sister talking about her brother. She seems to be all on board for the idea though.

"I don't know about 'something going in between us', but we did have sex," I say tentatively, hoping Fawn doesn't disown me as her friend for sleeping with her brother.

"You know that's the very definition of something happening, right?" Paloma retorts.

"No. Having sex and having something going on are completely different. We have no expectations of one another. As Fawn can attest to, Henry wants nothing to do with relationships, and I don't stay in a city long enough to become permanent."

All three women pause mid-stretch, glaring at me disbelieving-ly. Why is it whenever a man and woman get involved, it has to be "that" kind of *involved*? It's like there's never been a successful fuck buddy relationship in the history of the world. I've had plenty of friends with benefits that I didn't fall in love with. Henry will be no different. Especially since we live on opposite ends of the spectrum, color and otherwise.

"You can glare all you want. It won't change the facts."

"Ok then, Mrs. Robinson, at least tell us how he is in the sack. That boy looked like he had a year's worth of pent-up frustration in him. Was it wildly erotic or was he a dud?" Paloma asks.

"Yes, inquiring minds would like to know. I saw you two when you arrived, and he did not look like the dud type," Pilar adds, wide, sparkling brown eyes inquiring and a wicked knowing grin on her lips.

"Uh...," I croak elegantly. Looking to Fawn for help, knowing she does not want to hear this. "I don't think Fawn really wants to hear about her brothers sex life."

Fawn shrugs one shoulder and attempts to touch her toes. She is unsuccessful since her baby bump gets in the way, and instead pulls her feet together in a butterfly inner thigh stretch. "I've heard just about everything about Samson's sex life. As long as you don't describe his dick in detail, I'm sure I'll survive."

"You sure? I mean, I don't have a brother, but that seems a little weird to me."

"You have no idea how weird a family we are," she quips, shaking her head. But she's smiling, so the memories can't be all bad.

"Ok then, well he's most definitely not a dud. He's kind of the opposite. He's quite the stud," I say, chuckling and absolutely blushing.

The girls hoot and holler their cat calls at me. Paloma bumps my shoulder with hers, and I feel like a teenager at a slumber party. The kind I never attended. Sure, I had a few sleepovers with my BFF, but never in a group setting.

Paloma and Pilar are all girly giggles, and although Fawn isn't cringing or gagging, she's also not hooting her praise.

"And how did this all come about? I thought he was mister grumpy pants?" Pilar asks in all sincerity.

"Oh, he most definitely is. But he's a hot as hell and hung like a..." I catch Fawn's eye, and the look of horror on her face makes me think better of praising Henry's generous package. "Grown man with great genetics, grump," I say instead of the naughty thing I was going to compare his dick to.

"And there's nothing else going on between you two? Romantically?" Fawn asks this in a tone I can't quite decipher. Something along the lines of hopeful optimism. Does she want me to have a romantic, more than just sex, relationship with Henry? She knows that'll never happen.

"Uh, no. We're strictly physical. We're attracted to one another and have chemistry in bed. I have no idea if it'll even happen again. We haven't talked since then, and I'm Ok with that."

And I am. I don't know how long I'll be in Pittsburgh. I could leave in a month. I don't plan to, but that's the reality of the life of a nomad. Entering a city, I never have plans for how long I'm going to stay. Sometimes it's a few months, sometimes a year. It all depends on what happens once I'm there. If I remain on this path and attend the conference and the Anime Con, I could be here another good six months easily.

Will this very gratifying and pleasurable arrangement last that long? Please, God, I hope so. To be getting that kind of sex on a regular basis would be awesome.

"Is that all Henry wants out of it?" Fawn asks.

"Well, we didn't sit down and lay it out or anything, but we discussed our stance on relationships and what we want and don't want out of them. I got a clear picture from him. No strings, no commitments."

"Suuuure," Paloma drawls. "That's what they all say when getting porked by a hottie with a body and a bank account to match. It's just sex, nothing serious, we're never going to fall in love and live happily ever after," she mocks in a high-pitched Disney princess voice. I roll my eyes and stand to get my bag.

"We are not going to fall in love and live happily ever after. That kind of shit only happens in movies and fairytales. Not in reality. I can attest to that. I've had plenty of failed relationships to back it up."

The rest stand, Pilar helping Fawn to her feet. Her baby bump gets bigger with every day and intervenes in such daily activities as tying her shoes and standing from a seated position. But she loves to use it as an excuse to eat whatever she wants, which she is obviously allowed.

Once we're all watered up and outside the studio after Fawn pee's for the fifth time since we arrived, she continues her inquisition. "Are you going to call him?"

"Call who?" I ask knowing full well who she means.

"Henry. Are you going to call him and see him again?"

"I don't know. Maybe. Probably not. I think it's safer to wait to see what he wants. He seems the type to need to be in control."

"That he is." Fawn agrees.

Paloma claps her hands to redirect our attention. "Ok, girls, that's enough dick talk. On to more important things. Where are we going to eat?"

On Friday, my first shift at Wheelies starts with the owners Bloody Dollface and Coco Carnage showing me around. Yes, those are their preferred names. They're really their roller derby names, but they like to go by them instead of their real names. I don't even know their real names.

Bloody Dollface, or just Dollface for short, got her name because by the end of every game, there's always blood on her doll-like face. She looks to be in her late twenties, and like she's been teleported back to the fifties at a pinup photo shoot. Her platinum blonde hair is coiffed and sprayed to within an inch of its life in a style of large cresting waves and victory rolls. Paired with her big blue eyes and perfected killer red lip, I am jealous of her salon level abilities. Mine only reach basic levels of aptitude. Mascara, eye liner, and basic lipstick or lip-gloss. Anything beyond that and I'm lost.

Her partner in business is Coco Carnage, or Carnage for short. I asked why not Coco, and she said it was because it made her sound too sweet. Apparently, her name comes from her beautifully coco skin, and her ability to leave a trail of carnage behind her. Carnage is a chocolatey African American goddess with short, tight Shirley Temple ringlets threaded through with gold highlights. Big sparkly gold hoop earrings I would kill for dangle below her short curls. Gold is an amazing color on her and matches her bright hazel eyes. She looks to be a few years older than Dollface, maybe early thirties, but like a hot thirties. You can only tell she's that old because of the way she carries herself. And because she has an eight-year-old daughter with her partner Asha that she talks about nonstop.

Both women are in excellent shape, physically stronger than most men I know (except for Henry—that man's six pack could cut glass) and carry themselves with an air of confidence that comes with knowing you are one bad bitch.

They show me around the store and backroom, introducing me to two other employees, Jeff and Veronica, before giving me a thirty-minute lesson on the register. Which is one of those fancy new ones that uses a tablet instead of an old POS. Everything is meticulously organized and categorized, making it super easy to learn.

When I interviewed for this job last week, I had informed the owners I may not be here longer than a few months. They were totally cool with that since summer months are far busier than winter ones. They usually cut back on employees and hours when temperatures drop and snow covers the streets. Usually, people don't like to skate on snow... or ice.

Once I'm vaguely familiar with the lay of the land, Carnage takes me to pick out a pair of skates and wheels. I get a fifty percent discount, and if needed, can make payments to cover the skates. I definitely need to make payments. Even at half off, these are the most expensive footwear I've ever purchased. Since they are totally for employee's wearing the products, they don't mind that I can't pay all at once.

I, of course, pick out a pair of pastel pink skates with glittering pink wheels. It's been years since I was on skates, but muscle memory is a magical thing. Within the hour, I'm skating backwards and working on my spins. I'm pretty sure my face is going to cramp from all the smiling and laughing I'm doing today.

Jeff and Veronica turn out to be wicked awesome people. Veronica is in culinary school, and Jeff is working on designing his own video game. Compared to them, I'm kind of a loser.

Dollface and Carnage like to give their employees derby style nicknames. I don't have one yet since I've been here all of four hours. Dollface says the name has to come organically, naturally.

"With a name like Lala, I don't think you'll need a derby name," Thrasher, or Veronica, tells me as she rolls behind the counter. She earned the name Thrasher because when she started, she wasn't very good at skating and would thrash around whenever she lost her balance. But she kept the name because it sounds like she'll thrash anyone who messes with her.

"Yeah, we could just call you Lethal Lala. Then you wouldn't have to learn to respond to a new name. Took me a month to get used to mine," Twitch, or Jeff, says from his place stocking wheels against the wall. They call him Twitch because of all the streaming he does while playing video games. Not truly a full derby name, but it suits him.

"Well, if they don't give me one immediately, I will definitely suggest it." I probably won't though, I'm curious to know what my bad ass bitch derby name would be. Most people in general are not frightened by me. It could be all the pink, or the small stature, but maybe if I had a name that suggests I could eat your insides for breakfast without flinching, they might not underestimate me.

By the end of the day, I have four new friends, a new pair of skates, and a date for my first paycheck deposit. No derby name yet, but there's always tomorrow.

21 - Henry

I can think of a few things a good tight grip can be used for

Am I an asshole for not calling or texting Micaela in the four days since we had sex? It seemed we were on the same page when I dropped her off at her Jeep late the following morning. After she rode me like a prized stallion, nearly making me black out from the massive orgasm she gave me. She didn't ask me to call her or try to cling to me when we separated. She simply smiled, winked, and said to have a nice day. In the same way she had after she kissed me on the street, that suggested more.

It's not that I haven't thought about her, or even thought about calling her, scheduling to see her again. As long as we don't have to go on some ridiculous date that isn't a date. I'm not in the game of placating women so they'll have sex with me. We both want to have sex with one another, so why beat around the bush? Why deny ourselves what we want?

Hell, just thinking about her and the feel of her sitting on my dick has me getting hard in my sweats. Which isn't ideal with how visible every ridge is under the thin material, and my two closest friends standing nearby.

Asking Eddie and Leo would only send us down a rabbit hole I do not want to risk. Even telling them I slept with Micaela could be catastrophic. Eddie would be planning our wedding, and Leo would be so far up my ass about sleeping with Fawn's friends, I'd need to have him surgically removed. For now, it might be best to just not mention it, at least until I speak with Micaela about... us. To make sure she understands the only us there is, will be the one in the bedroom. To reiterate my no relationship rule.

I've had women in the past say they were fine with only being a casual thing, but then would call and text me at work, make lunch plans and show up out of the blue. I even had one crazy try to contact my siblings and invite herself to Christmas dinner. We all had to change our numbers after that one. Making sure we both understand is vital.

It is the reason I haven't had a sexual partner who wasn't paid for the past couple years. Too many complications and feelings. Breaking my own self-imposed rule to sleep with Micaela was something I didn't see coming. I didn't see her coming. Until I made her come on my face.

Micaela coming is a beautiful thing. She's free and unencumbered when she fucks. Open and willing. There's no apprehension or timidness about her body or sexuality. She gives as beautifully as she takes. There's no fake porn star moaning or proclamations of love mid-orgasm. Once this runs its course, and I return to call girls, it won't be the same, or nearly as fun.

Which leads me back to wanting to contact her and have her show up to my condo in a trench coat and a thong and nothing else. Sure, she'd probably wear a pink trench coat and thong, but the pink isn't that horrible. Not when it's wrapped around Micaela's sweet body. I'm growing used to seeing her in it.

The bag I'm holding knocks into the side of my head. I'd gotten lost in my pink sex thoughts of Micaela, and my grip slipped, allowing Eddie's massive right hook to shift the bag enough to knock some sense back in me.

"Watch it, you're going to take out my eye." I know it was probably my fault, but I'm not going to admit I got distracted thinking about fucking Micaela's pretty pink pussy.

"Well, that wouldn't happen if you were paying attention." Eddie slicks back his sweat-soaked brown hair with one hand, while trying to steady the swaying bag with the other.

"I am paying attention."

"Sure, you are. That's why your eyes were glossed over and there was a dumb struck look on your face. What were you thinking about anyway?" Eddie's annoyingly astute observation has me tripping over my words to answer. Something that rarely happens to me. So, I lie.

"Just work. I thought I had this client ready to sign, but he's been stringing me along and won't sign the papers." It's not a lie that I'm getting strung along like a backup plan b date. What I thought was a done deal with the Peterson property has once again turned into a back and forth with no one agreeing on anything. That's just not what was distracting me.

Eddie and Leo each give me appraising looks. They're not falling for my bullshit work excuse.

"Nah, that was not your 'I'm pissed about work' face. There's something else on your mind," Eddie so helpfully suggests.

Leo nods his head in agreement. "Yeah, perhaps like a woman. A curvy pink haired woman who I heard you left work with early on Tuesday to show around a flea market. Then didn't show up till halfway through Wednesday."

Goddamn Fawn and her big mouth having to tell her husband everything. How he found out I showed up late on Wednesday I'm not sure, but using the work excuse isn't going to cut it now. I release the bag and circle to the benches, turning my back on them, killing time and filling the silence with the sounds of Velcro peeling away from my gloves.

"Yes, I showed her around a flea market and drove her home. *Because* Fawn was held up at work. She asked for a favor, and I agreed. That's all." When I turn around, Leo pokes the inside of his cheek with his tongue, a mischievous glint in his eye.

"Uh huh."

"What do you mean, *uh huh*?"

"I mean, I also know why you showed up late on Wednesday. I was waiting for you to bring it up, but apparently that's not going to happen."

Leo shucks his gloves, and we have a silent stare off, each waiting for the other to break first. He's going to be waiting a long time if he thinks I'm going to be the first to break. Crossing my arms over my chest, I flex and straighten, challenging him. He simply cocks an eyebrow at me and grins. Damn it, he does know, and he is really going to make me talk about it.

"Well," he begins triumphantly, as if he wanted to be the one to spill the beans. "When I got home Thursday night, Fawn had a rather intriguingly juicy story to tell me."

Fuck, I totally forgot about her Pilates class with Micaela. I hadn't thought about whether she would tell anyone.

Eddie's eyes brighten and he steps nearly in front of me to face Leo. The ever-attentive pupil. "Really? What kind of juicy? We never get to gossip about boring ole Henry," he says, thrusting his thumb behind him at me. "So, this must be good."

"As I hear it, Henry didn't just drop Lala off at her bus."

"He didn't? What did he do?" Eddie is like a kid at a campfire, playing right into the hands of the storyteller. He knows who "Lala" is because I told him all about her after our first meeting at Fawn's. He almost peed himself laughing.

"He stayed the night."

"Huh. Nooo." The gasp that comes from Eddie is almost comical enough to laugh at. Since they're talking about my recently established sex life with Micaela, I don't find it that funny.

"Yes. He stayed the night and participated in a few extracurricular activities from what I hear."

"Perhaps you should get a hearing aid because I think you heard wrong," I suggest not so helpfully, grinding my teeth to the point of possible lock jaw.

"No, I heard right. Fawn was very clear. She heard it directly from Lala herself. Our boy here is apparently a stud in the sack. According to Lala."

A warm rush thrums through my chest and up my neck making me swallow hard. *Micaela thinks I'm a stud. And she said so to her friends.* I want to preen with idiotic pride that I satisfied her so thoroughly. But I shouldn't, and I shouldn't want to. It doesn't matter because we're just fuck buddies. Friends with benefits. A booty call. A midnight rendezvous.

Then why is my pulse picking up? Why does it seem to mean something to me that she bragged about me to her friends? Granted, one of those friends was my sister, and I inwardly cringe at the thought of them discussing my dick and performance in bed, but not enough to care to stop it.

"I think he's blushing." Eddie turns around to stare and point out the flush in my neck.

"I am not." My arms uncross of their own accord, and my hands drop into fists at my side, taking a fighting stance instinctually to defend myself.

"Oh, you totally are," Leo agrees. "I am so telling Fawn about this tonight over dinner."

"Please do not discuss my sex life with my sister. It's disturbing."

"It's a little late for that."

"Gross."

Both men laugh and punch me in the chest and shoulder at my discomfort. Almost as if they like it. Sickoes.

"Ok that's enough of that. Can we move one now?"

"Fuck no. I need details man. How did it happen? Why did it happen? Is it going to happen again? Is Lala a tiger in the sack?"

My hand shoves at Eddie and he falls back a step under my strength. "That's none of your business," I growl at my best friend of over a decade. I don't like him talking about mine and Micaela's sex life. End of story.

"Woah, easy, big guy. I was just messin' with you. No need to get violent over it."

Eddie is rubbing at his chest where I pushed him. I hadn't meant to hit him that hard. I just reacted. In a way I never have before.

"You don't have to tell us anything you don't want to. We just haven't seen you show interest in a woman for a long time. We think it's a good thing." Leo is talking to me like a madman on a ledge holding a dead man's switch. "We like Lala."

"Yeah," Eddie agrees. "She's a sweet girl, and if she can make you happy, we're all for it."

I ignore their approval of Micaela. It makes that warm electric feeling start up again. For some reason, I like that they approve of her.

"Sorry," I grumble. Turning to face my bag on the bench, I take in a deep centering breath. Nothing like this has ever happened to me before. I never cared about keeping my sex life secret. I've described, in detail, women and my sexual encounters before. Something about Micaela gets under my skin and makes me react.

Not wanting to linger on that thought, I pack up my stuff and sling my bag over my shoulder. When I turn around, Eddie and Leo are still watching me. Not angrily like I thought they would be.

"What?" I ask dumbly.

"So, what exactly is going on between you and Lala? Are you two dating?" Eddie asks tentatively. Keeping a few steps away from me this time, I notice.

"No. It's just casual. She knows I don't date, and she said herself that she doesn't want anything permanent."

"You sure?" Leo asks.

"Positive." At least I will be once I call Micaela and make sure of it. Now I'm going to have to suck it up and contact her. Later—after I get home and shower. When my mind is clear and calm. I don't want to yell at her about it. Then she might not sleep with me again. And that is unacceptable.

"Sure, you are." Eddie's smile is back in place, all angry shoving forgotten.

The guys don't bug me anymore about Micaela as we leave The Left Hook. Leo heads straight for his car, no doubt to drive straight home and tell Fawn about our little talk. I suppose it could be worse. She's obviously not upset with me for sleeping with her friend or she would have stormed over to my condo and berated me for hours if she was. Does this mean she approves of me and Micaela? She's never approved of anyone I've slept with. Usually, she sighs and shakes her head at me. I'm not sure I like her approval.

Eddie continues walking with me towards my building. He parks in my garage sometimes when there isn't any street parking by the gym. The concierge knows he is on my permanent guest list and is always allowed to park in the guest parking. Since I own the building, there's not much he can say about it.

We're in the middle of a conversation about his company's newest build and the issues they're having with permits. Ok, it's not really a conversation, more Eddie yammering on about it while I nod but don't really listen. My mind has turned back to Micaela and the best way to broach the topic with her. I've narrowed it down to just outright blunt clarification, or inviting her over and then bringing it up in a way that makes it appear as if she wanted to talk about it. It's kind of the coward's way out, but I feel being harshly blunt with her might hurt her feelings, and for some reason I don't want to do that.

In the middle of me mentally writing a rehearsed speech to bring up the topic with Micaela, the object of my obsession whirls by in the window next to us.

I stop dead in my tracks.

Did I just see that?

The swirling pink mass rolls back going the opposite direction now. The sign says Wheelies, and I notice all the roller skates and wheels inside the store. Right behind, a swirling roller-skating Micaela in a little pink dress that lifts and twirls every time she spins, briefly flashing me a sliver of pink panties underneath.

What in the holy hell is going on?

"What is it?" Eddie steps up beside where I've plastered myself to the window like a goddamn stalker.

"It's Micaela."

"Who's Micaela?"

I literally growl out a groan. I am so tired of people asking that question. Why can't she just go by her given name? I'm not actually mad that they don't call her Micaela. I'm more irritated because the longer I know her, the more Lala wants to roll off my tongue instead of using her full name. It's much more suited to her, but to call her that now would undermine my own stubbornness. So, for now, I'll stick with Micaela.

"You would know her as Lala."

"Oh right, you mentioned Lala was short for something." He peers around the display of rainbow wheels and catches sight of Micaela dancing on her skates. Another man and woman also putz around behind her, but not nearly as animatedly. No one is as peppy as she is. "Wow. She is way prettier than you made her out to be."

My knuckles crack under the pressure of my fisting hand. I don't like the way he watches her, and I really don't like the way I react to him watching her. *She's not mine, he can look at her however he wants to,* I remind myself like a mantra. It doesn't calm my heating blood though.

"Come on. Let's say hi. I want to meet this girl that has your panties all in a bunch."

"What? My panties aren't in a bunch. I don't even wear panties."

He just laughs at me and circles around to the door and strolls right in, not waiting for me. I jog to catch up to him, catching the tail end of her greeting as I enter.

"...do you for today?" Her smile is so big and bright she's practically sparkling. A flush pink washes her cheeks, and I see it the moment she recognizes me.

I wasn't sure what to expect, polite courtesy, embarrassment, awkward silence, a lude comment perhaps. I get none of those. Instead, her eyes grow wide, and I can see her suck in a breath. It's like she's taken aback by my presence. As if just seeing me increased her heart rate and electrified her nerves. Because that's what her presence does to me.

Her smile shifts from retail clerk friendly to a secretive familiar kind of smile. "Hi."

Her one-word greeting has me almost on my knees. That's a rather strange reaction. I cover it up with just as eloquent a greeting.

"Hi."

"Hi. I'm Eddie, Henry's best friend. Only friend, really." Eddie sticks his hand out to Micaela, breaking our trance. She accepts it, and the heated look she was just giving me is gone as fast as it arrived.

"You are not my only friend."

He laughs and leans into Micaela as if revealing a secret of epic proportions. "Yes, I am. At least, the only one who counts."

Micaela's responding giggle is like windchimes in a gentle breeze. "It's nice to meet you, Eddie. I'm Lala."

"Oh, I know who you are. Henry told me all about the kissing bandit."

"I'm sorry, the what now?" asks the other woman in the store. She remains behind the counter, but Eddie doesn't really have an inside voice.

"Nothing. I'll tell you the story later." Micaela brushes off her coworker's curiosity and turns her attention back to me. "What are you guys doing here?"

"What am I doing here? What are you doing here?" I counter.

"I work here."

"Why? I thought you had your boba booth?"

"I do, but until I book more events, I needed something to supplement my income. I noticed last week they had a help wanted sign and applied for the job. Yesterday was my first day." She adds to clarify. Because she most certainly did not mention this on Tuesday night.

I grunt out some sort of noncommittal noise that she interprets as understanding.

"We were just walking back to Henry's place from the boxing gym. He saw you through the window, and I decided I needed to meet this pink haired girl he's been talking about."

Micaela turns her dazzling aquamarine eyes to me, eyebrows raised in surprise. "He's been talking about me, has he?"

"No." I answer immediately.

"Yes, he has. Recently, I even heard—"

"Why don't you take a look around the store, Eddie?" I grip his shirt and thrust him in the opposite direction of Micaela and me. He only chuckles, but does as I so forcefully suggest.

"I didn't know you could skate." I say in a way of transition. The skates on her feet are pink, as expected, and look rather expensive. Not like those cheap ones you get as a kid that fell apart after two days.

"Oh yeah. It's my useless skill number two hundred and twelve."

"What are numbers one through two hundred and eleven?" The question comes out low and gravely. My mind went straight to the gutter thinking about her *skills.*

"You'll just have to wait and find out," she quips.

"How about tonight?"

"Tonight what?" She acts all innocent, like she doesn't know what I mean, but she does. I can tell by the sultry grin she wears and the way she nibbles lightly on her bottom lip.

Naughty girl.

"Come over to my place when you get off work. Show me some of these useless skills. I'm sure we can find a use for them."

"You know of another use for being able to open any jar lid?"

Our bodies have moved closer together. Not sure if I moved or she did, but we're only inches apart now. Her sugary sweet scent fills my senses, and I can feel it all over me. Again, I have to rain in my thoughts before I pitch a tent right here in the store.

"I can think of a few things a good tight grip can be used for." I lewdly suggest. I have never been this vocal or provoked by a woman before. I don't completely hate it. Mainly because of the way Micaela responds to me. Her neck flushing red and her glorious tits rising and falling in shallow breaths.

"I get off at six."

"Oh, I plan on getting you off, Shortcake."

"Shortcake?" a female voice interrupts our hot and heavily innuendoed conversation, forcing me to take a step back and put unwanted distance between us.

The question came from a woman who looks directly out of a fifties pin up calendar. Skin tight, high waisted jeans, sleeveless white button up with a red scarf tied around her neck, topped with those coke can curls and bright red lips. However, her biceps look like they could crush a weaker man.

"Dollface, this is Henry, my… friend. He likes to call me Shortcake. I don't really know why. He's never explained it."

"Because you remind me of Strawberry Shortcake. The first time we officially met, you wore a pink dress with strawberries on it, and it made me think of her." The explanation is out of my mouth before I can stop it. It's not considered attractive for a man to know a child's cartoon character from the eighties. Not only because it makes me sound old, but also because it's about a girl and her friends who are designed after fruit. Not exactly manly.

"Nice to meet you, Henry. I'm Bloody Dollface, but you can call me Dollface." She winks and reaches out a hand to shake mine. Her grip is firm and tight.

"Bloody Dollface?"

"It's my roller derby name. We all go by them here. That's Thrasher and Twitch, and I think you just gave me an idea for Lala's."

"Is that so?" The corner of my mouth quirks in amusement at Micaela's frown. She does not want them all calling her Shortcake. It was kind of amusing being the only one to do it, but knowing she'll hear it at work and think of me every time someone calls her that is even better.

"Yeah, Death by Shortcake. But we'll just call her Shortcake for short." Dollface is beyond thrilled with her name choice for Micaela. I'm glad I could inspire her derby name. Now she'll hear my voice whenever they call her Shortcake, and that gives me immense pleasure.

"I like it, Shortcake." The girl named Thrasher tests out the name, and Micaela gives her a look of exacerbation. Thrasher seems to appreciate it, and only gets more enjoyment from it.

"Now look at what you've done." Micaela scolds me, but I can see the twitch in her lips and the soft crinkle around her eyes. She's not really mad about it.

"Tonight. I'll text you my address. My building has a concierge. Just tell him your name and he'll send you up."

"So demanding."

"Yes, I am."

She gives me another smile before Eddie inserts himself in the conversation, and I quickly direct us to leave the store before Micaela can convince Eddie to force me to buy roller skates. I can see he's halfway to buying them for me when I push him out the door, calling our goodbyes to Micaela and the others.

Back on the sidewalk outside, Eddie starts in on how cute Micaela is, how sweet and friendly. And how completely opposite of me she is, and how he has no idea why she seems to like me.

When we arrive at my front door, Eddie stops me before heading to his car in the parking garage.

"So, tonight, dinner? Then drinks after?"

"No. I have other plans."

"Since when? You didn't have plans before the gym." Eddie stands casually with his hands in his pockets and a question on his face. He watches me for a brief moment before realization sparks in his eyes. "Ooooooh. You made plans with Lala the Shortcake while we were at the store, didn't you?"

A smirk the size of Texas spreads across his smug handsome face that I instantly want to slap off.

"Yes. I made plans with Micaela to come over after her shift is over." I grind out between gritted teeth.

"Ok, alright. Next weekend, then." He starts to back away towards the garage entrance. "But I want to hear all about this later, understand?"

"Yeah, yeah." I wave him off, and he chuckles over his shoulder all the way to his car no doubt.

22 - Lala

He tastes like wet dreams and ice cream

enry's condo is only a block away from Wheelies, so I leave my Jeep in the small parking lot behind the store and decide to skate to his building. I was more than pleased to see him this afternoon, and even more so when he asked to see me tonight. More demanded really. I like his demanding side. Just like when he claimed all my orgasms were his now. They are, even when he's not present, he's the one in my imagination getting me off.

Rolling to a stop in front of his building, my jaw drops and my head lifts to see the complete height of the tastefully modernized warehouse turned condo building. It's easy to tell that a lot of thought and care went into the design. Preserving the industrial look while smoothing out the harder lines to modernize it to the point of classy. Made with Henry's favorite colors; gray and white.

The lobby is tastefully, but minimally, decorated in dark and light grays with washes of white paired with dark polished wood, and to my surprise, splashes of tastefully accented royal blue. There are even fresh spring flowers in a vase on the entry table. The space isn't too small or too big, just enough for people to sit and wait or pass through without having to squeeze by each other. It's actually more quaint than I would expect from Henry.

The man behind the front desk is dressed in a matching royal blue three-piece suit. The only thing hinting at his position as concierge is a name tag on his left breast that reads Jackson. His smile brightens when he sees me rolling in, in all my pink glory.

"Welcome. How may I assist you today?" Jackson appears to be in his late thirties or early forties, with sandy blonde hair cut short, and clean with warm brown eyes.

"Hi. I'm here to see Henry Bardot."

"Your name?"

"Lala Hart."

Jackson taps on his tablet before furrowing his brow. "I have a Micaela Hart on my list."

"That's me. Lala is short for Micaela." I give the man a sweet smile, shifting on my skates to keep me balanced.

"That's a pretty nickname. Would you mind showing me some ID to confirm?"

"Of course." Reaching into my purse, I shove aside my ballet flats that I shoved in there and produce my driver's license. It's a Kentucky license, but he doesn't even flinch as he compares the picture to me, then hands it back. Since my hair has been pink for so many years, I don't have to explain the color difference from my natural blonde because the photo on my license is also pink haired.

"I was curious who this mystery woman was that Mr. Bardot added to his guest list. I have to admit... you're not what I expected," he says, taking a quick scan of me head to toe. Not in a sexual manner, just cursory.

"I know. I'm better." I flip my pink hair with a cheeky grin that hopefully conveys my humor and not that I'm a self-centered bitch.

"Why would you be so curious about Henry adding a woman on to his guest list?"

"He's never had one that wasn't his sister," Jackson answers plainly, like this is public knowledge.

"Oh. I had no idea. I would have expected him to have many female guests with that handsome face of his." Adding humor into my underhanded inquiry disarms Jackson enough to naturally divulge the information I secretly want. Like how many women have passed through this lobby to Henry's place.

"That may be, but he's never had any female guests that I know of. And I've been here since we opened."

"Huh." I shrug off the information with a fake nonchalance, but am internally doing a weird happy dance. Being the only woman he's invited into his home is oddly satisfying.

"Take the last elevator on the left to get to Mr. Bardot's."

"What floor do I get off on?" I ask as I begin to slowly skate backwards towards the bank of elevators.

"That elevator only goes to one floor." His grin widens, and I see pearly white straight teeth. "The penthouse."

Of course, it does.

The back wall of the elevator is mirrored, the others are paneled in the same smooth dark wood and polished nickel hardware as the lobby. Just as Jackson had said, there are only two buttons; one with a P, the other with an L. Penthouse and Lobby. I chuckle and smile while firmly pressing the P. Since there's no floors to watch ding off as I pass, all I have to listen to is the smooth jazzy elevator music.

When the doors open, they reveal Henry's penthouse. No hallway or front door, just direct access into his place. Jackson must have some secret button that unlocks and locks the elevator to guests. Fancy.

I call out for Henry as I skate on to his polished concrete floor penthouse. "Henry. You home?"

Noises come from the only door in the condo. "I'll be right out." Comes Henry's voice from within.

I take this opportunity to snoop around his place like I caught him doing on my bus the morning after our first night of mind-blowing sex. There's not much to see, especially since it's all in one large open concept space.

To my right is a shiny state-of-the-art kitchen with stainless steel appliances and dark black cabinets. Very few items clutter the white countertops. I notice a coffee maker, toaster, and weirdly, a bread box. *Do people still use those?* I thought they were just used in the fifties.

The rest of his space is filled with a desk and computer in one corner, surrounded by bookshelves filled to the brim. A leather wingback chair sits next to a small table and mini bar. There's a dining room table made of glass and silver, and a plush gray leather couch facing a TV half the size of the wall. With lots of open empty space in between it all.

To my left, along the white walls is something that truly surprises me. A watercolor painting. Made with the most beautiful array of every color possible. I stop and stare at it, backing up to see it in its entirety. Swirling masses of organic pinks, purples, and turquoise make up a sky at sunset over a rippling lake. It's serene and breathtaking.

I'm not sure how long I stand there staring at the painting, but a large warm hand on my upper arm breaks the art's hold on me. Henry's warm body steps in close to my back, his heat radiating against me. His warm breath tickles my neck as he leans in to speak into my ear.

"What was it you said about people's choice in color? It says a lot about them. What does this say about me?"

A shiver slivers down my spine and courses through my body, making my nipples pucker and harden. His soft lips brush against the curve of my neck in a gentle kiss.

"I think it says you secretly have a soft heart, a beautiful smile, and passion hidden under all your layers of discontent and grumpiness. You hide it to protect yourself. Bottle it up and store it in this painting. So that every day you look at it, it reminds you that it's there and it's safe."

"You got all that from a painting?" Henry's lips disengage from my neck as he looks up at the painting with new eyes. With new understanding. He couldn't see or understand why he had this painting. That's clear from the wonder in his eyes as he tries to see what I see.

I didn't just see all that from the painting, but from the time I've spent with him. I can tell he hides himself under layers of protection he believes he needs. I don't know when or who broke his heart, but someone did, and since then, he's barricaded his emotions and love so deep inside, he's forgotten he even has them.

I think I'd like to help remind him. At least remind him that he's allowed to feel and be happy and enjoy the wonderful things life has to give him. I may not be the one to mend his broken heart or make him love again, but I can make him smile. And if I'm lucky, make him laugh again.

"Sort of." I don't know how to confess to him that I know all too well why he hides himself. I may not hide my colors, and tend to be on the loud side, but I, like him, have unintentionally blocked my heart from feeling real love. Stopped myself from getting in too deep and investing with one man to allow him to fully claim my heart.

We're opposites in a way. I'm all color and frivolity, hiding away the dark sad parts of me for no one to find. Keeping a smile on my face, even when I want to cry. Henry wears his discontent and disdain on his sleeve with pride, using it as a weapon to fight off anyone who tries to get too close to his technicolor center. Forcing a frown instead of allowing his light to shine through.

I watch Henry in profile, still in the cradle of his body. His hand, which started on my arm, has slid down to rest across my hips, keeping me from rolling away from him on my skates I still haven't removed. Mom would be furious if she knew my lack of polite etiquette, claiming I was raised better. If she were facing the deadly attractive man I am, she would forget to take off her shoes too.

His eyes shift back and forth, and the smooth lines of his face harden back into their permafrown. So close. Maybe, at least, he'll look at this painting differently from now on. Slowly allowing some of it to bleed into his daily life.

Tight fingers dig into my hip before releasing. "It's just a painting. Done by a renowned artist I sold an art studio to once. That's all. That's why I have it. He gifted it to me. I didn't pick it out."

Henry steps away from my body, leaving me cold and a little sad. In true Lala fashion, I plaster on a smile and soldier on.

"Either way, it's beautiful. So why did you want me to come over tonight?" I try shifting the conversation to distract him from my unscheduled color therapy session.

"I... enjoyed our night together and thought you did too." Henry takes a few steps backwards, leaning against the kitchen island as I roll around on my wheels to face him.

"And you wanted to repeat it?" I suggest, gliding closer to him and running a finger down his t-shirt clad chest. This one is pure white over well-worn denim jeans that hug his thighs sensually.

"Yes," he admits unabashedly. "Very much so." I can see his fingers gripping tightly around the edge of the granite countertop, and I wonder if he's trying to restrain himself from touching me.

"Ok. Well, if we're going to be doing *that* again, I'm going to need to eat first. I haven't had anything since lunch and I'm starving. If you expect me to be your booty call, you're going to have to feed me first."

I'm joking, obviously. I don't expect anything from him. Except maybe more mind melting orgasms if that's what he's into. But I find joking to be a great distraction and messing with Henry is fast becoming my favorite pastime.

"There's this new Indian restaurant I passed on my way to work that just opened down the street. I would kill for some naan and curry right about now."

"I don't eat Indian food. Too many spices." His tone is completely serious. Not surprising. Wait, is he actually going to buy me food? Score. I bite back my shock and hold in the happy dance I want to let loose, and go for something more chill.

"Well, you're missing out. Lentil curry is delicious." I sing song. "And if I'm going to perform to the best of my ability, I need curry."

This is too easy. I'm going to get a free meal, and get to partake in Henry's perfect dick again.

"We could go to the restaurant and eat, then come back here and get comfortable. Maybe put something on that giant TV of yours." I suggest.

He huffs out a long breath. "I'm really not in the mood to go out anywhere, Micaela. I was hoping we could stay in. I could order you some Italian food from Bella Italia across the street, have it delivered. You can watch whatever you like on the TV."

"Hmm." Tapping my chin, I casually ponder his offer. "Maybe. Or we order in curry and watch Crazy, Rich Asians. Then I'll allow you to have your way with me. If you're really nice, I won't even wait till the movie's over."

Leaning back, Henry watches me with a great deal of confusion and delight. "Fine. We can order curry, *but* we are not watching some ridiculous romcom. We will watch a movie of my choosing."

A spark ignites in Henry's eye, challenging me to argue more, delighted in the prospect of negotiating our terms for the evening's proceedings.

I take my time leisurely skating in circles, twirling my hair around the ends of my fingers. Pursing my lips, I pretend to pout my disapproval. Although, I have nothing to disapprove of. Naan and curry, and a movie with Henry, followed by sex? Yeah, not much to disagree with there.

Exhaling loudly in an overly dramatic way, I stop right in front of him, using the toe stopper to keep from rolling, and place both my hands on his chest. "Fine. I suppose I can agree to those terms."

Pulling me by the hem of my skirt, there's no resistance as the wheels on my skates roll with the movement, bringing me flush against Henry's front. His hands grip my ass and thrust my pelvis into his. The hardening bulge of his erection is obvious in the lack of space between us.

"Pinky promise?" he whispers against my parted lips. My lady bits quiver under his touch, and his words. He's playing with me just as I play with him. Using my beloved pinky promise to get me to submit. I will gladly submit to his man if he wants to feed me, then bed me.

Unclenching my left hand that's trying to permanently attach itself to Henry's shirt, I extend my pinky in the small space between us. Begrudgingly, Henry releases one ass cheek to take my pinky in his, pressing his lips into mine while our fingers are still intertwined.

He tastes like wet dreams and ice cream, and I want to lick up every drop of him. The kiss goes from soft to possessive. Sealing our promise. Henry's hold on me is more than sexual. It's possessive and protective as he releases my pinky and wraps his arm around my back. Holding me firm, but not to the point of discomfort.

It's more that he wants to ensure I don't roll away. That I stay right where I am. Right where he wants me, and where I want to be. Every time I'm in his presence, my ability to maintain a normal heartbeat is thwarted. He stirs me up on the inside, making me utter mush. I'm getting mushy over Henry, and if I'm not careful in restraining my emotions, that'll lead me straight over a cliff I can't recover from. Falling fast and hard for the straight-faced Henry Bardot.

He is the one to break our kiss and pull back enough to look me in the eyes. There's a playful upturn to his lips that, for once, I didn't have to force from him. The smile is small, but easy, comfortable... happy. I want to rip off every stitch of clothing right now and jump ahead to the end of our night at the sight of it. My stomach has other ideas as it growls loudly, interrupting our moment. But it doesn't deter Henry's grin. Instead, he widens it and raises an eyebrow at me.

"Perhaps I should get you that food now, before you wither away."

"That would be preferable."

An hour later, we have a spread of the most delectable smelling naan and curry and spiced meats on Henry's coffee table. I waste no time digging in while Henry queue's up whatever movie he's deemed better than Crazy, Rich Asians. Spoiler alert, whatever it is, isn't.

"Schindler's List?" He can't be serious. "You want us to watch the most unsexy movie in the history of movies?"

"I wouldn't categorize it as the most unsexy movie. Have you seen any Nicholas Cage movie ever? This is a classic with historic significance and substance."

I roll my neck to side eye him. "You expect me to want to jump your bones after watching the persecution and murder of innocents in the greatest tragedy of recent history?"

The glare he sends my way seems to be trying to discern if that is actually possible.

"I'll be crying like a baby by the end. Not really a sexy time kind of movie. Pick another less depressing movie please."

He groans, but relents, scrolling through his digital library before clicking on Indiana Jones and the Raiders of the Lost Ark.

"I would never have pegged you as an Indiana Jones fan."

"Why not? It's a classic. Everyone loves Indiana Jones."

"That is true, but it's still surprising." I watch him thoughtfully from my place on the couch opposite him. He's far more relaxed here in his space watching Indiana Jones than I've ever seen him. It's… nice.

"What?"

I realize I was staring and quickly avert my gaze to the screen where the movie has already started and Indie is already crawling through spiderwebs as thick as gauze in a hidden, previously unknown, temple.

"Nothing."

Eating some of the best Indian food I've had in a long time and watching Indiana Jones with Henry, haha irony. Henry. Henry Jones Junior. Anyway, as I was saying, it's been heaven burrowed deep in his surprisingly comfy couch, stuffing my face with naan. To my immense pleasure and shock, Henry actually chuckles at a few of the jokes in the movie. It must be a favorite of his. When he tried to get me to watch Schindler's List, even though it is an amazing movie, I didn't think it appropriate for our evening plans of debauchery.

This is much better.

Now I get to watch two hot Henrys sweat tonight. Harrison

Ford was a handsome man in his day. He's a bit old for my taste these days, but him in the eighties, yowza.

We don't cuddle on the couch, but we sit close enough that our thighs touch. Every time his heat washes over me, it sends a tingle up my leg. By the time Indie and Marion are trapped in the cave of snakes, I'm eying his trouser snake for movement. My head is facing forward as if still watching the movie, but my eyes are locked on to his groin.

It's hard to tell from this angle, but I'm pretty sure it's getting bigger. Or that could be my wishful thinking.

Nope. Definitely getting bigger.

"You keep looking at it like that and we're going to miss the end of the movie." Henry's gravelly voice reverberates across my neck and makes its way all the way down between my legs.

"Is that a threat or a promise?" Raising my eyes, I see him watching me under a hooded gaze. He runs his tongue along the corner of his mouth. Enticing me to reciprocate the gesture. Without thought, I suck my bottom lip into my mouth and slowly release it. It draws his attention as he leans over and runs a hand up my skirt.

The tip of his nose traces the line of my jaw as his fingertips trace the edge of my panties, seeking the heat of my core he's created there. He brushes up against the rapidly dampening center of my panties, rubbing fidget inducing circles at the apex of my thighs and tracing my slit through the wet cotton as far as his finger will reach.

"That's a promise, Shortcake." His warm breath heats my neck as he speaks. Using my nickname that now sends floods of wetness to my pussy. Which clenches in response begging for him to do more than light touching and heavy breathing.

To do just that my legs spread invitingly. Henry's responding chuckle doesn't make me want his hands on me any less.

Henry moves his mouth from my throat to my ear, nibbling on the lobe. "Do you want me to bend you over this couch, Micaela? Flip up this teasing little skirt and plow into you from behind? I bet you'd like that, wouldn't you?"

"That sounds agreeable." I manage between moaning whimpers.

This man turns me into a sack of jelly around him. The warmth he spreads through me is not just skin deep. It's bone deep. My desire to have him has only grown as of late. Desire to be near him, to see him and his rare smile. To hear his rough voice growl out his customary no's and demands.

From day one, on that street, I've been drawn to him. Seeking him out for some unknown reason. After our non-date-date, the dinner and movie tonight, I only want more.

Henry cuts off all cognitive thought with his mouth on mine. Demanding my attention and tongue. Swallowing my gasp of pleasure and devouring it.

His hand, now under my panties, slips through my wetness, finding my entrance, and thrusting one finger, then two inside me. My back arches and I shamelessly grind into his hand seeking more, always more. My breasts brush against his chest as he leans over me.

"Take me any way you want me, because there's no way I don't want you."

23 - Henry

I was wrong. She can.

The last ounce of my self-control snaps at Micaela's words. I've been half hard since she arrived. I fulfilled her desire for dinner and a movie. Really, it wasn't that hard of a request to agree to. Just having her near me has settled the anxious energy I've felt the past week. I hadn't even noticed it was there till it was gone. Washed away in her sweetness and wetness.

My dick swells as soon as I make contact with her wet pussy. It's where I've wanted to be for the past two hours, and to finally sink my fingers inside her sends a quaking ripple through my body, that both hardens and softens parts of me at the same time.

Micaela shudders under me, her skin smooth and yielding under my touch. When my thumb makes contact with her clit, she grips my arm and cries out in indecent gratification.

"That's my pretty little Shortcake." I mumble against her throat as I suck and bite and try to devour her whole.

My balls are so blue at this point, if she even touches my dick I'll probably come all over her before I can even get her naked. Not wanting that to happen, I shift our position. Standing, and unfortunately, removing my hand from her holy land.

I remove my shirt and unbuckle my belt before lifting Micaela from the couch. Digging my hand into her ass, I peel away her damp panties while claiming her mouth in a kiss that says she's mine, and I dare any one to say otherwise.

As soon as her panties hit the floor, I spin her around and place her back on the couch on her knees. She braces herself against the back, already arching her back and presenting her perfect ass and pussy for the taking.

Then I do exactly as I told her I would. Lifting her skirt and pushing it up her waist, revealing my new favorite artwork, two pink ribbon bows with crescent moons at their center knot. We didn't get to this position last time, and it was a true shame.

My hands shake with an uncontrollable want for this girl clad in all pink and dripping with desire for me. There's nowhere I would rather be tonight than here on my couch with Micaela. *Lala*. Whether it's eating far too spicy Indian food—that I'll most likely be paying for tomorrow—watching my favorite movie franchise or plowing my cock into her sweet heat. No matter how much I fight her on things, I want her.

Before, I thought there was nothing that could make me smile. I was wrong. She can.

With Micaela facing the opposite direction, she can't see the boyish grin I feel forming on my face. It quickly morphs into a wicked grin as I drop my jeans, grabbing the condom from the back pocket I had placed there when she arrived. I knew I would need it. I just didn't know when.

Kicking away my pants, I slide my dick between her wet folds, covering it in her juices before slipping it between her ass cheeks. Sliding along her crack and nudging slightly, just enough to let her know I'm there. She moans in response. Of its own accord, my hand smacks her ass, letting out a ringing echo of my palm connecting with her plush, round bottom.

Fuck, I've wanted to do that since I first saw those damn tattoos. Just because I can—and she seems to like it—I slap the other cheek, marring it with a matching pink handprint. One more pink thing to add to her body. Possibly my favorite pink thing after her pussy. I've even started to appreciate her pink hair. It falls in haphazard waves around her shoulders as her head lolls forward.

I guide the head of my cock back to her entrance and rub against her slit, then up to her clit and back. My cock twitches and throbs in my hand. I squeeze the base to keep from nutting all over her. *Not until after I get inside her tight pussy.* I tell myself. Then I can spread my cum all over her pretty pink skin.

"Henry, you better stick your dick inside me right now, or I might actually die of sexual frustration."

"Yes, ma'am."

I quickly sheath my cock in the condom and do as the lady demands, lining my head up with her dripping pussy and slamming into her with a guttural roar between clenched teeth. Her body shifts forward under the force of it, and she grips the back of the couch tighter.

"Jesus Fuck!" she cries as I seat myself to the hilt and hold for a brief moment, enjoying the way her pussy pulses and squeezes my shaft.

I'm still standing while she's kneeling on the couch, knees spread and head thrown back. I pump into her, loving the feel of her around me. Loving how right it feels to be connected with her. I want more, need more. We're too far apart. I can remedy that.

Guiding her forward, I shift Micaela so she's almost pressed completely against the couch, and I join her. Knocking her knees together, I place each of mine on either side of her legs, which are now firmly pressed together. In this position, the pressure on my dick intensifies, gripping me and rubbing against her inner walls in a way that makes her roll her hips into me with a soft whimper.

Her little sounds of approval and unintentional grinding against me sends my heart into a buzzing frenzy. She's not forcing it or faking it for my benefit. She wants this as much as I do, and that only adds to the heightening sensations growing between us.

Now that I can press my chest to her back, I want to feel only skin on skin, so I remove her dress over her head. Much to my delight, she's not wearing a bra again.

"Naughty little Shortcake not wearing a bra. Just begging me to play with your beautiful tits."

"That wasn't the idea when I got dressed this morning, but I'm sure as fuck glad I did."

I chuckle into her neck, wrapping one arm around her to cup and knead at her breast. Burying my face in her hair and scent, letting it settle into my senses and overtake me. I keep one hand braced on the couch to keep us steady. Micaela straightens and leans back into me. Our bodies are still connected with my cock deep inside her.

She does some sort of wave motion with her body that oscillates her hips as she tries to top me from the bottom. Wrapping her arms around my neck, holding me tight to her. This position is both extremely hot and oddly intimate. Her movements are slow and methodical, her fingers in my hair light and sensual.

I want to lay for hours with just her fingers running through my hair.

Brushing her hair away from her neck, I place soft kisses starting at her ear all the way along her exposed shoulder. I want to breathe her name into her skin, whisper it against her bare flesh.

Lala, Lala, Lala. My lips ache to form the two syllables sitting on my tongue, but they don't. They can't.

Being far gentler than I ever have been with a woman, I lean into her, my firm grip on her breast loosens, running the pads of my fingers over her sensitive nipple. It pebbles under my touch. My soft caress continues around her breast to the center of her chest, drawing a straight line down between her cleavage and I don't stop till I reach her belly button. Rounding it and diverting to her hip.

My kisses never relent on her skin until one of her hands lifts my chin and directs me to her lips. What I feel when they meet, I can't even explain. I can't hear the movie playing behind me, or the traffic passing by outside. I can't see the gray concrete of my floors, or the watercolor painting Micaela dissected earlier.

I only feel. Feel her, her lips, her hands and skin. My world has been narrowed down to only Micaela. The sensation of her world-shattering gentle kiss, and of my dick still inside her. I should focus on that, not the fluttering in my chest, or the fact that I feel punch drunk from her kiss.

Trying to break whatever magic she's cast over us, I slowly begin to thrust inside her, until my thrusts become hard enough to sever our kiss. Forcing Micaela to put both her hands on the couch to steady herself. Good. This is far safer than whatever the hell it was we were just doing.

Gripping her hips, I find my rhythm, punishing her pussy with deep thrusts. Reaching my cock so far inside her, she shakes around me. After a few minutes, my head has finally cleared of the fog from earlier and I am focused on my goal. Making her come on my dick and then coming on her back. I want to mark her with my seed and scent.

I feel her legs shake and her inner walls begin to clench moments before she speaks. "Fuck, Henry, I'm going to come. Yes, right there. Don't pull out, stay deep. Oh, yes."

I press all the way inside her and rock my hips to press my head against her g-spot without pulling out an inch.

"Right there, baby. God, I can feel your orgasm in my balls." And I can as she screams and falls apart, coming so hard on my dick it feels like she's strangling it. I squeeze my eyes shut, holding my own orgasm at bay while I pump every last drop of hers from her pussy.

When I know I can't hold mine off any longer, I pound into her sensitive pussy hard a couple more times before pulling out and ripping the condom off my cock. Gripping my dick, I give it a few long, tight strokes before my orgasm shoots through my spine, up my balls, and I come so fucking hard, shooting my cum all over Micaela's heaving back. I'm still stroking myself and growling out the last drops of my release twenty seconds later. If it weren't for my one hand on the couch, I would fall right the fuck over. I'm light-headed, and the amount of cum on Micaela's ivory skin is bordering on obscene.

"Don't move, I'll get a towel. I may have made a mess all over you."

"No problem. I'll just be here, trying to find the soul that just left my body." I chuckle and pat the non-cum covered part of her butt gently as I go to get a towel to clean us up.

Later, when we're dressed, the movie long over, and all the food containers are cleaned up, Micaela starts to put on her shoes and gather her belongings.

"Where are you going?" I ask.

"Home. It's late. I figured you would want to get to bed soon. I figured you would want me out of your hair." she says shyly. By her tone, it doesn't sound like she wants to leave. And I don't want her to leave.

"Do you have a market tomorrow morning?"

Her brow furrows in cute confusion. "Uh, no. There were a few Sundays that were already fully booked when I signed up, so I don't have the farmer's market tomorrow."

"Ok, then. Stay." My offer isn't demanding or questioning, it's just a statement. And Micaela fiddles with her purse as she watches me. Probably trying to interpret my offer. Good luck. I don't even know what it means. I just know I want her here, in my bed next to me. Pressed against me like she was when I slept at her bus. I haven't slept so soundly in forever, and I want to do it again.

"You sure?"

"Absolutely." After another moment's pause, she relents with a small smile.

"Ok." Then I'm the one smiling.

24 - Lala

Nothing is sexier than a man that cooks

I don't argue when Henry asks me to stay the night. It's what I wanted anyway, but I didn't know if me staying the night at his place was the same as him staying the night at mine. Guys can be fickle like that. What's Ok for them isn't Ok for us. I'm glad to discover this sleepover aspect of our... whatever we are... goes both ways.

Henry gives me one of his shirts to sleep in, and like before, when we climb into his bed, he pulls me close to him. Like I'm not allowed to sleep without touching him. Before we had spooned, him wrapping around me from behind. Now, I'm facing him, our legs tangled together in an intimate embrace. My one free arm is wrapped around his waist. Henry sleeps topless in nothing but boxer briefs, and his skin is warm to the touch.

My head rests upon his bicep, and my face is nuzzled against his chest. The dark hairs there tickle my nose when he inhales. The strong arm wrapped around my shoulders is comforting in its protective, even loving embrace.

He says he doesn't want anything more than a sexual relationship, but the way he holds me when we sleep suggests otherwise. I can't let it get to me. *Cuddling does not mean anything.* There are people who are professional cuddlers, who charge strangers to lie in bed with them, just so they can feel the comfort of another human body against theirs. This is no different, except he paid me in food and sex. Not that I'm complaining. Both were phenomenal.

This is how we both fall asleep. Satiated and warm, wrapped around one another.

I wake up in quite a different position. I'm alone in Henry's bed. His side is cool to the touch, which means he got up some time ago. Hazy, warm sunshine filters in through the window letting me know it's morning. The smell of freshly frying bacon wafts in through the partially open bedroom door. My stomach growls.

"Guess that means it's time to get up."

Stretching my arms and legs, I roll out of his huge king size bed, tossing the black comforter and gray sheets to the side. He really should buy things in more than one color. There is so much gray in his home, it's like I'm living in a black and white movie.

Searching for my dress that I left on the chair in the corner next to the dresser, I can't find it or my underwear. I went to bed without them since they were damp from my arousal. I figured they could air dry overnight to be more comfortable to wear home today. But I can't find either pink pieces of clothing. I even check under the bed just in case.

Giving up on my search and giving in to my growing hunger, I head out of the bedroom towards the kitchen to find Henry. Maybe he knows where my clothes went. The cement floor is cold beneath my feet, and I tip toe quickly across to the beckoning warmth of the kitchen.

I was not prepared for a shirtless Henry in soft gray lounge pants standing at the stove scrambling eggs and flipping bacon.

Nothing is sexier than a man that cooks.

Ask anyone. They'll agree with me.

"Good morning."

Henry turns to find me leaning against the end of the counter watching him. "Good morning. You must have been tired. You barely noticed when I got out of bed earlier."

"Well, *someone* who shall remain nameless, fucked me senseless last night, and I needed to recoup my energy."

One corner of Henry's mouth quirks in a grin. He seems to be doing that a lot more frequently than when we first met. I return his smile. It's not hard to when faced with his billboard worthy grin.

Stepping away from the stove, Henry wraps one hand around the back of my neck and pulls me in for a firm toe-curling kiss that ends far too quickly.

"Are you hungry?" he asks, returning to his pan and pulling perfectly crispy bacon from it. I don't know how he can cook bacon shirtless. I wear long sleeves and still somehow manage to burn myself with grease splatters. It's like those little fuckers can seek out the tiniest sliver of skin like a heat seeking missile.

"Starving."

"Good. Breakfast is almost done. Take a seat and I'll make you a plate." He gestures to the island barstools and the two place settings he's set. One already with a glass of orange juice waiting.

"Is the orange juice for me?"

"Yes. I also have coffee, but I didn't know how you took it."

"Three sugars and a heavy pour of hazelnut creamer. If you have it." I briskly hop over to the barstools to avoid too much contact with the cold floor and hop on to the thankfully padded stool.

"No creamer, only milk." He pours me a mug and places a sugar bowl in front of me before turning to the fridge to get the milk.

"Why were you hopping around on your toes?" Henry places

the milk on the counter and leans on it with both hands as I scoop sugar into my coffee.

"The floor is really cold on bare feet. I don't know how you can stand walking around on it all the time."

"I wear slippers." Sticking one foot out from behind the cabinets, he shows off his loafer style black slippers. Little tufts of furry lining poke out around the edges. They look warm and comfy. I frown.

"Well, I don't have any slippers." I stick out my bare foot and wiggle my toes accusingly.

"That's not my fault." The pan behind him begins to sizzle and he returns to it, removing the bacon and eggs. Plating them onto two plates that he places on the mats, one in front of me and one at my side.

"Yes it is. I'm a guest, and since I did not bring an overnight bag or get advance warning of ice tundra flooring, you should provide me with proper footwear to survive your house."

He scoffs. "I don't ever have overnight guests, so there's no need to have a spare pair of slippers lying around just waiting to be used."

"Well then, you should consider buying a few area rugs. That way, you won't have to have slippers for guests, and I won't lose a toe to frostbite walking on your ridiculous flooring."

"I'll take that into consideration."

The eye roll he gives me doesn't compel me to believe he actually will. He sits down next to me with his own cup of far darker coffee than mine and slips off his enviously warm slippers, shuffling them under me.

"Here. Wear mine so you won't lose any precious toes."

"Thank you." I slip my feet in the far too large house shoes, but they're warm from his feet being in them, and I perk up in my seat a little at the added warmth.

We eat our breakfast in a weirdly comfortable silence. The bacon and eggs with toast is delectable, and I scarf it down with all the grace of a hippo.

As soon as I finish my last bite, Henry is picking up my empty plate and taking it to the sink. For such a grumpy Gus, he sure is a clean one.

From somewhere in the depths of the condo, my phone rings, blaring out the lyrics to *September* by Earth, Wind and Fire. My mom's ringtone. Shoot. Jumping off the stool, I run to dig my phone out of my purse where it hangs on a coat hook by the door.

"Hello." I hold the phone close to my face so she can't see what I'm wearing or where I am.

"Oh, hey, honey, are you still at the market?" Mom asks, her head shifting as if she could see around me through the small phone screen.

"Uh, no, not this week. It was fully booked. So, I'm not at the market." I manically brush my fingers through my hair when I notice it's still a bird's nest from sleep... and sex. I have sex hair while facetiming my mother. Great.

"Where are you then?" Dang it, why is she being so inquisitive today?

"Oh, uh... just..." Shit, my brain is not awake enough yet to come up with a believable answer. While I'm stumbling over my words and trying to cover it up by rubbing away the sleep still lingering around my eyes, I don't pay attention to my phone and what's in view of the camera.

"Who's that?" My mother's question removes the last lingering dregs of sleep, and my head pops up to see Henry's shirtless form exiting the edge of my screen as he enters his bedroom.

Instantly, I turn my back to the wall so she can't see anything else besides me and my purse hanging on the hook behind me.

"Oh uh, nobody. Just a friend. I'm at a friend's house today, hanging out. Since I have the day off." I'm a rambling idiot.

"That was a half-naked man, Lala. Are you seein' someone?" The utter glee that spreads across her face is beautiful and unfortunately misplaced.

"No. He just spilled coffee on his shirt and is going to get a new one." The lie rolls out of my mouth so quickly I'm afraid she won't believe it. Panicking, I do the only thing I can. Quickly say goodbye and hang up on her.

"Ok, well, gotta go, Ma, talk to you later. Lots of love to Dad."

"Wait, Lala. I'm not done yet."

"Okthenbyyyye." I rattle off the words so quickly they're more like one continuous word as I hit the red end button before she can argue with me. "Ugh," I groan, hitting myself in the forehead with my phone. She is going to be on me from now until the Armageddon trying to find out anything and everything about my male shirtless friend.

Already my phone is vibrating with texts. I ignore them and put my phone on silent and slide it right back in my purse. I'll deal with that later. That's an issue for future Lala. Monday Lala. Today is Sunday Lala, and she doesn't want to deal with her nosey mother and answering her ten million questions.

"Done with your phone call?" Henry asks when he reenters the room, this time wearing a shirt. *Sad face.* I was enjoying the view watching his muscles flex and contract every time he reached up to place something in a cupboard.

"Uh, yeah. My mom likes to call on Sundays and talk about her week."

"That's nice. I don't think I've spoken to my mother directly in years. I'm pretty sure the last time she called me on a non-work-related matter was to find out if Fawn would be having Dom Pérignon or Laurent-Perrier champagne at her wedding. Because some socialite posted about how Dom is no longer the "it" champagne, and she wanted to make sure Fawn didn't embarrass herself by having the wrong brand of champagne for her toast."

Stunned, I blink at Henry, who delivered his little speech with very little feeling, completely serious. He actually had this conversation with his mother. She sounds like a piece of work.

"Wow. Your mom sounds like... a gem."

"If she's a gem, then she's one made of pure black, buried beneath a volcano that has never been discovered before."

I can't hold in my laugh, and it bursts out of my throat. I try to stifle it with a hand over my mouth, trying not to be rude. I guess he doesn't have the kind of relationship me and my mom have.

"Was that a joke? You're getting pretty good at those." I tease. His lips twitch as he pulls me close by the slack of his oversized shirt I'm wearing. It rides up, revealing a flash of naked skin that he eyes hungrily.

"You know what's not a joke?" he asks, flashing me a quick smirk.

"What?"

"How fucking sexy you look wearing my shirt." One hand slips below the hem of said shirt and palms one of my butt cheeks. "I like this no underwear thing. Makes for easy access."

"Speaking of underwear, have you seen mine? And my dress? I swear I put them on the chair in your room, but I can't find them."

His answer is muffled in the crook of my neck as he sucks on my throat, causing me to shiver and smother an approving groan.

"I put them in the wash this morning. Figured you would want clean clothes to wear, since, as you pointed out, you didn't bring an overnight bag. They're in the dryer now. Should be done shortly."

I'm a little speechless for once. Henry is just full of surpris-es. That grumpy, disagreeable attitude he portrays to the world doesn't seem to filter over into his home life. Or his manners. He's so polite and thoughtful. Nothing like I would have guessed him to be when I saw him at Fawn's wearing that uptight suit to a weekend family dinner.

There are so many things about Henry that I still don't know, and I have a feeling I may never know. But I like getting to discover the real him underneath all the frowns and boring gray.

Pulling away from Henry, I disconnect his lips from my neck so I can look him in the eye. "That's really thoughtful, Henry. Thank you."

"You're welcome. Now as for payment for my laundering ser-vices, I believe a quickie in the shower will suffice."

He lifts me, and I can't hold in the shriek of laughter when Hen-ry wraps my legs around his waist and walks us into his luxurious bathroom through his bedroom.

Our time in the shower is not quick. He takes his time lathering me with soap and touching every part of my body before taking me up against the white tile wall.

Playful, thoughtful, and foul-mouthed Henry is a great way to spend my Sunday morning.

After we finish our shower and Henry retrieves my clothes, I make my way to the elevator doors to head home. It's already noon, and I need to check on Fred and send out more email inqui-ries for fairs, as well as order a few more boxes of branded cups for the conference. According to Thomas, there will be a few hundred people in attendance, and I want to make sure I have plenty of sup-plies.

As I reach for my purse, strong arms wrap around my waist and tighten as Henry kisses the side of my neck. I'm starting to realize he really likes doing that. Burying his face in the crook between my throat and shoulder. Either nuzzling, kissing, or even just inhaling me. I don't even think he realizes he does it so often. Or even why. Or that it's extremely intimate.

There are things I don't think Henry realizes about himself or us. From the sounds of it, he hasn't had a girlfriend, or even a serious relationship in a long time. So, I doubt he realizes his behavior mimics that of a boyfriend. I just have to keep reminding myself of that. *He's just doing it because he wants to and it feels good. Nothing more. There is no meaning behind his actions beyond surface level.*

Since I'm not trying to marry the man—hell, I don't even know how long I'll be in Pittsburgh—I'm going to enjoy all the affection and touching ,and yes, sex, I can.

"When can I see you again?" come his muffled words.

"Um, I have a shift at Wheelies on Tuesday. I could come over after, or Thursday after Pilates."

Henry legitimately growls in my ear. "Thursday is too long. Come over Tuesday. Or, even better, I could swing by your bus tomorrow."

I chuckle lightly at his persistence. I know the sex is good, but we shouldn't be seeing each other every day. "I need a day to recover from your massive cock. I'm a little sore, and I think you'll live if you wait till Tuesday." Turning in his arms, I break his embrace to face him, looping my purse strap over my shoulders and picking up my skates.

"Uuugh," he sighs. His head falls back like a toddler pouting. It's adorable. "Fine. Tuesday. What time are you off?"

"Um…" I mentally pull up my schedule and try to recall Tuesday's shift. "I have the opening shift, so I'll be done by four. Is that too early? I can wait and come over later—"

"No." he interjects. "Four is fine. By the way, I know you walked, or rather skated here. You don't have to do that. You can park your Jeep in the guest parking in the garage. I'll make sure Jackson has you on the list."

"Oh, Ok. Thanks." I'm pretty sure his workday doesn't end by four, and I have a feeling he's leaving work early just to meet me. "Are you sure four isn't too early? I don't want to upset your schedule."

"Don't worry about it. I make my own schedule. I'll see you at four." Leaning down, he whispers in my ear, "Don't wear panties. And don't bring an overnight bag. I like seeing you in my clothes." He places a soft kiss on my jaw before withdrawing.

"You know, I can bring an overnight bag and still wear your clothes? I'll just bring toiletries and a change of clothes, so I don't have to do the walk of shame in the prior day's outfit."

"If you must."

With one last domineering kiss that almost has me pulling my panties off again, we say our goodbyes and I head home to Fred. Who will no doubt be very upset at me for not being home for nightly cuddles.

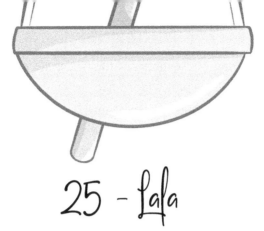

25 - Lala

Pink is now my new favorite color

For the next two weeks, Henry and I meet up a few times a week. By a few times, I mean practically every other day. The man is insatiable. His sexual stamina is awe inspiring. Most of the time, we go to his place, since he lives so close to Wheelies and the Pilates studio. On weekends, when I have the farmer's market, we stay at my bus. Henry helps me load up my Jeep on Sunday morning, and then we go our separate ways. He doesn't come to the farmer's market with me. He knows I have Shay to help, so he doesn't want to impose. We don't go on anymore "dates", but we do have meals together. Sometimes out, but mostly in.

Getting Henry to smile is far easier to do these days. I don't need to revert to fun filled outings or impromptu fashion shows in baby stores. Now, whenever he first sees me, he smiles. When I strip naked and prove to him I'm not wearing panties, he grins. When I devour more food than him at every meal, he chuckles and smirks at me, knowing my excuse is that he works out all the carbs during sex.

I'm not wrong. I burn more calories having sex with Henry than I do at Pilates. We've pretty much had sex on every surface of his condo and my bus. There are days he can't wait to get me to a bed or the couch and takes me up against whatever surface is closest. I think those days are the ones when things don't go as he planned at work. When he needs to relieve a little excess stress.

Sometimes we talk about work. But mostly we don't. We talk about movies, food, art, places I've lived, buildings he owns, his weird obsession with not trying anything new. He tells me about his brother and sister, and I tell him about my parents. He doesn't tell me anything about his parents other than their professions. It's very clear they have never been close and aren't included in anything "family" related. To Henry, family means Samson, Fawn, and Leo. Sometimes even his friend Eddie, who I met before at Wheelies.

If I work on Saturday, they always make sure to stop in and say hello. Leo came with them once, but only stayed a few short minutes, claiming he needed to get back home to Fawn. I love how devoted they are to one another. The only way I'll stop traveling in my bus is if I find a man as loving and devoted as Leo is to Fawn. Anything less isn't worth it.

There are times when I feel like this thing with Henry could be growing, could be more. But since nothing in our lives overlaps, it's hard to tell. He doesn't hold my hand when we walk down the street or make out with me on park benches. He does pull out my chair at restaurants and place a protective hand on my back when leading me through crowded spaces. There's also the fact that when we are alone, it's like he can't not touch me.

Before, when we would sit on the couch, we would sit side by side, maybe our thighs touching. Now if we watch TV, he pulls me onto his lap, practically wearing me like a snuggie. He's far more affectionate than he believes himself to be, or he's just a very private person and doesn't share that side of him in public. Possibly both.

Tonight, we decided to eat out, and on our way back to Henry's place I force him to stop in at the ice cream shop I've been eyeing for weeks to get dessert.

He picks vanilla ice cream with nuts on top—gross—and I choose strawberry ice cream with marshmallows. I'm making fun of his boring ice cream choices as we're leaving, when a familiar voice catches our attention.

"Henry. Lala!"

We both turn to find Eddie and a beautiful Asian woman with sleek black hair that ends just above her shoulders, approaching us on the sidewalk.

"Eddie. What are you doing here?" Henry asks. He doesn't look upset to see Eddie, but he also doesn't look pleased. So, it's kind of how he looks most of the time. Unreadable. The only time I can read his feelings is when we are alone and naked. And they're usually of the horny variety.

"Just out on a date. Ana, this is Henry, my good friend. Henry, this is Ana." Ana reaches out a hand and Henry accepts it, shaking briefly before Eddie turns to introduce me. "And this is Lala, Henry's—"

"Friend." Henry supplies. I suppose it would be weird to introduce me as a fuck buddy. Still, the word stings a bit. We are far more than friends. Friends don't know your secret tickle spot under your left butt cheek, or that you like your nipples licked when you orgasm. That's the kind of thing girlfriends know, or at least people who are more than just friends.

Damn it. I should not be upset by this. I knew it was possible that we could run into people we know and have to act like there aren't passion filled sex marathons followed by weirdly comfortable cuddling and sleep overs. I just didn't think it would be this difficult to do.

"Hi, it's nice to meet you." I say to Ana as I shake her hand and smile at the couple. Eddie slings an arm around her shoulders and gently squeezes her bicep in a move that is both natural and easy.

Henry does not do the same to me.

Instead, he shoves his free hand into his jeans pocket, his boring vanilla ice cream slowly melting and dripping into the napkin wrapped around the cone in the other.

"So, what are you two doing out here?" Eddie wiggles his eyebrows and looks between us hopefully. "Are you guys on a date too?"

"No." Henry answers immediately. "We were just having some ice cream after dinner. That's all."

"Kind of sounds like a date to me."

"Everything sounds like a date to you. Is it a date every time we go to dinner together?" Henry retorts.

Wow, he really doesn't want Eddie to think we're out on a date. His words aren't harsh, but they are blunt.

"No. I suppose not."

"Ok, then."

The two men stare at each other, communicating something between them that neither Ana nor I can interpret. I look between the two, then to Ana, who is as confused as I am.

"Mmhmm," Eddie mumbles thoughtfully, pursing his lips and squinting his eyes at Henry, as if that will reveal all his or our secrets.

I'm pretty sure Eddie knows we're sleeping together. Fawn knows because I tell her, and she tells Leo, who probably tells Eddie. So, I'm not sure why this whole charade is taking place outside the ice cream shop on the sidewalk.

Like a child watching a cartoon, I lick my ice cream and watch, waiting to see what happens next. What does happen next is Eddie grinning like the cat who ate the canary, and Henry scowling. It's quite hilarious.

"So, are we still *not* doing anything for your birthday next week?"

"What?! It's your birthday next week and you didn't tell me?" Turning to Henry, I smack him on the arm with the hand not holding my ice cream. He doesn't even flinch.

He lets out a deep sigh, giving Eddie the stink eye. Eddie just smiles wide with all his teeth. He knows he just gave away something Henry didn't want known. By just me, or by everyone, I'm not sure.

"Thanks for that, Eddie. Yes, my birthday is next week, and *no,* we aren't doing anything, like always."

My jaw drops, and I can't believe what I'm hearing. Who doesn't celebrate their birthday? Henry Bardot, apparently.

"Why?" I ask dumbfounded.

Eddie answers instead of Henry. "You see, Lala, Henry dislikes anything having to do with parties, cake, and the simple pleasures in life."

I see Henry shift his eyes to me, "Not all pleasures in life." His words are quiet, but firm, sending flutters through my stomach. Henry's eyes return to Eddie, not lingering on me for long. But everywhere they touch feels like a caress made with those fingers I have become so familiar with.

"Well, that's a shame. I'll have to try and convince Lala here to get you to at least come to dinner with us. Maybe Leo and Fawn, too," he suggests. I am instantly nodding my head in agreement. Henry is doing the opposite.

"And why do you think Micaela is going to be the one to convince me to celebrate my birthday when none of you have been able to for the past five years?"

"I just have a feeling."

"A feeling?"

"Yes, a feeling. Normal humans have them." Ana elbows Eddie in the ribs and scolds him without words. I like her already. "Right. Well, we'll let you get back to your non-date ice cream. Lala, I'm depending on you to persuade this stubborn ass to let us take him out for his birthday."

I mock salute Eddie in acceptance of his challenge. I will most definitely be making sure we do something for Henry's birthday. Fawn will be most delighted to conspire with me, no doubt.

Eddie and Ana say goodnight and continue on their way down the street, still holding on to one another like a normal couple on a date. A wistful feeling passes through me watching them. Something that makes me feel dizzy with longing, and a little empty knowing I don't have it. Then it shifts because maybe I do have it, we just haven't figured it out yet.

The heat from Henry's palm warms my back as he makes the first contact with my body since we ran into Eddie. Steering me to resume our walk back to his penthouse. Its welcome presence gone when he removes it far too quickly.

"I'm sorry about that," Henry says quietly, shuffling his feet awkwardly like a boy on a school yard.

"Don't worry about it. Eddie can be a handful, but he's a sweet guy."

"No. I mean about how I acted. I wasn't sure what to say, and I kind of panicked. I've never really had someone like you." Even in the low light, I can see the slight reddening in his cheeks. He's blushing.

"Oh."

I have no idea what to say. I've had friends with benefits before, but Henry feels like something more. Something deeper. Something I don't have a name for yet. Something I probably shouldn't be feeling with a man who is against relationships in every form of the word. The smart thing to do would be to disengage and keep it platonic. But I don't want platonic. I want Henry, and I'm going to have him because... why not?

"You better eat your ice cream before it melts." Before I can do as he instructs, he holds my hand and ice cream cone in his free hand and licks the dripping pink right before it reaches my fingers. "Mm, not bad."

"I thought you didn't like pink things?" I tease, taking a hearty lick of my ice cream. I think I'm being seductive, but it's hard to tell. Henry has a very good poker face. I haven't played poker with him yet, but I'm sure I would lose. I have a horrible poker face.

"I've changed my mind. Pink is now my new favorite color. I think I may change everything I own to pink." We turn and continue to stroll down the street side by side, eating our ice creams, but still not holding hands.

"Yeah, I don't believe that. But it's nice to know you aren't repulsed by my entire wardrobe anymore."

Henry stops and turns me by my hip to face him, a small frown creasing his brow. "I could never be repulsed by you, Micaela." Reaching up, he brushes a strand of pink hair back from my face and tucks it behind my ear. "You are far too beautiful to be repulsed by. Just looking at you sometimes catches me by surprise at how much I don't want to look away."

"Why don't you like to celebrate your birthday?"

Henry and I are back in his penthouse, curled on the couch, far more familiar and unguarded with one another. His hand rests languidly around my waist, keeping me tucked under his arm, pressed against his side in a way that is far more than friendly.

"I just don't."

"Ok, I know getting older sucks. But why? It's an excuse to eat cake and get presents and celebrate being alive with the people closest to you. Why wouldn't you want to do that?"

"Because I didn't have birthday parties or presents when I was a kid. My parents didn't believe in giving a gift to a child for them bringing me into the world." Henry's voice is flat and stoic. As if what he's saying means nothing to him anymore than taking out the trash.

"I'm sorry. That's so sad. My birthdays were always so overboard and extravagant. My parents were always so grateful I was there, and they took every opportunity to celebrate and make me feel loved and wanted." I watch Henry for his reaction to see if it makes him uncomfortable to hear me talking about my overly loving parents. It doesn't seem to affect him. His eyes shift from my face to the movie playing on the TV.

"My parents were… different. They had children because it's what was expected of them. They're not really the family type."

I want to ask more questions, to force him to tell me all about his childhood and call his parents horrible names, but I don't. I remain quiet and patient, something I admit I'm not the best at. Having to pinch my lips shut and bite down just to keep the words from spilling out of my mouth. Luckily my patience is rewarded.

"My parents each came from well off, prominent families, raised with unrealistic expectations, far too much money, and far too little supervision. So, when it came to their own children, it was much the same. They didn't know any better. To them, it was normal. Hire nannies, delegate responsibility to others, keep your distance, and check it every so often to make sure we were doing what they perceived to be important. Grades were high enough, appearances were polished and high end, girlfriends or boyfriends were of acceptable families." He pauses and takes in a slow breath before releasing it to continue.

"We didn't celebrate Christmas sitting around a personally decorated tree in matching pajamas and ripping open hand wrapped presents. No, we wore suits and dresses and went to brunch at the club. Presents came in the form of money transfers into our personal bank accounts. Birthdays were even less so. The day would be acknowledged, my father would congratulate me on living another year without being arrested or caught snorting blow off a stripper's ass.

"Mind you, it wasn't the fact that I could have done that, it was about not being caught doing it. My parents didn't care what we did with our time as long as it stayed quiet and out of the papers." I can hear his anger and frustration with his parents growing along with the deepening crease between his brows.

Rubbing my happy childhood and loving relationship with my parents in his face isn't going to help. And I don't want to. He doesn't need to hear about my many birthday parties and arts and crafts presents. What he needs to hear is that he has a right to be hurt and upset with his parents.

Reaching up, I run the pads of my fingers along his smooth jaw line and brush my thumb across the apple of his cheek, cupping it softly. Making sure he's looking directly at me when I speak.

"You are worthy of appreciation and celebration. You are loved by your brother and sister, and even Eddie and Leo. You are a good man and deserve a day once a year to spotlight your life and accomplishments. Even if that's only having lived another year."

Leaning in, I place a soft and unhurried kiss on his lips. Hopefully conveying my adoration. Adoration his parents should have given him, but I am more than happy to make up for now.

I break the kiss, even though his hand has found its way under my pink crewneck sweater, inching its way higher towards the curve of my breast. Trying my damndest to ignore it long enough to finish what I started.

"We're celebrating your birthday this year, and you will not argue with me, Henry." He opens his mouth to do just that, and I halt his words with my finger on his lips. "You will allow your friends and family to take you out to dinner and give you presents and sing you happy birthday *with* a cake."

"And if I don't? What motivation do I have to attend this involuntary birthday dinner?"

"Beyond the cake and presents?"

"Yes."

I can't believe that's not enough motivation. Anyone says cake and presents and I'm there. I don't care what we're celebrating. Exhaling a huff of frustration at his inability to enjoy and participate in life in general, I take another course to convince him.

"Fine. I pinky promise that I will allow you to choose the restaurant and cake flavor, if you attend and accept everyone's presents and affection *without* argument." Extending out my pinky in a manner he is now familiar with, I offer him my ironclad promise.

"No presents."

"Not a chance. I already know what I'm getting you."

"Fine, no cake."

"I don't think so. It's not a birthday without a cake."

With a growl of defeat, he links his pinky with mine. "Fine."

"YAY! Ok, so now, what day is your birthday?"

Dropping his head to the back of the couch with a thud, he grunts and shuts his eyes. "I regret this already."

His words don't match his hand that has resumed its journey to my breast, caressing my under-boob before cupping and squeezing gently.

"No, you don't."

"Yes, I do. Ugh. My birthday is May twentieth."

Swinging my leg over his lap, I straddle him in hopes of distracting him from trying to back out of this deal now.

"And how old will you be?"

"Thirty-one. Speaking of, how old are you? You've never told me."

"You never asked." I give him a cheeky grin and play with the collar of his t-shirt.

"Now I'm asking, smartass. Now tell me, Shortcake, before I start thinking I'm robbing the cradle here."

"I'm twenty-seven. And in case you're wondering, my birthday is September eighth."

Henry raises his head and watches my hands roaming his chest, efficiently distracted, just as I planned. I can already feel his erection growing harder underneath me. This conversation isn't going to last much longer from the feel of it.

"And why would I need to know your birthday?" He sits forward a fraction, tilting his head and watching my mouth.

"So, you can buy me presents and cake." I inch forward, mirroring his movements, taunting him as he does me.

"Is that so?" His lips are a fraction of an inch from mine, breathing his words into my mouth.

"That's so," I confirm, pressing my mouth into his.

For the next hour, we worship each other's bodies, and there's no way my heart could not be in it. Not after what he told me about his parents and their lack of love for their own son. There's no way he can't feel it in the way I kiss him, and in the way he holds me. But we don't say it. We don't verbalize our emotions. Instead, we convey them through physical attention. The only way Henry knows how.

26 - Henry

What the hell is happening with your face?

The past few weeks have been... different. In a positive way. Spending my nights and weekends with Micaela has made me feel far more relaxed, and dare I say, happier than I have been in years. She's like Xanax without the medical side effects. Relieving my anxiety and boosting my serotonin without a single pill. They should bottle up her energy and smile and sell it in little pink bottles with the cutest cartoon hearts in existence on it. With zero side effects, she could very well put Xanax out of business.

But I'm a greedy motherfucker, and I'm keeping her all for myself. Not that I want to keep her. *Do I? Fuck, maybe I do. That can't be right.* I don't need a woman in my life to make me happy. I have my job and my properties and my money. Although, to be honest, none of that is what finally made me smile after years of scowling. After years of listening to my sister and Eddie criticize me for the choices I made, for cutting out even the possibility of a relationship or marriage.

I didn't want it. I *don't* want it.

What I do want is Micaela. In her pink clothing and pink hair with her pink ferret named Fred. She's the only thing that makes me happy. The only one who can make me smile just by entering a room. The things she said after I told her about my parents and the lack of a love filled homelife, warmed something inside me. There were things I wanted to say that I've never considered telling a woman before. Being with her has me thinking things. Things I shouldn't be. Like what ifs. And what ifs are bad. They lead to questions, to answers, to commitments. Things I don't have room for in my life.

Things are getting muddled in my brain, and thinking about it too long just makes it worse. Best to not dwell on it and just move on with my day. Instead of worrying about what it means that I can't wait to see Micaela tonight, and not just fuck her but talk to her, hear her laugh, and make *her* smile, I'm just going to think about what strange food she's going to force me to eat. Focus on what movie we might watch, or which one of my shirts she'll wear to bed.

She's forming quite a collection of her favorites. There's my Columbia t-shirt, a gray V-neck with a ripped collar that I was going to throw away—she demanded I keep it just for her—then, there's my favorite, the white long sleeve button down. Yes, it's cliché. I know that, but I never had a woman wear mine before. I never allowed them. It was too personal.

I like seeing Micaela in it. I may have even snuck a few pictures for my own personal reasons. Not spank bank photos...ok, they kind of are spank bank photos, but that's not why I took them.

My mind is split between thoughts of Micaela in my shirt and the counter offer I'm drafting for a client in the middle of a bidding war for a piece of commercial real estate. She wants to open her second restaurant after the success of her first, and the current owner is giving her the runaround, thinking he can swindle her because she's still new to the world of commercial property ownership.

Now, I may be a ruthless, heartless real estate mogul, but even I wouldn't cheat a businesswoman into overpaying just because I could. I will gladly gauge extra zeroes out of another mogul who has the money to spare, but never an up-and-coming restaurateur. Who, by the way, serves the best seared ahi tuna in the city, and I would like to be welcome in her restaurant, not banned for life.

Maybe I'll take Micaela to the restaurant when it opens.

"Ok, Boss, you have a conference call at—woah." Thomas enters my office carrying his ever-present tablet that serves as his secondary brain, and freezes, hand hovering over the touch screen. "What are you wearing?"

"What?" I ask, sitting back in my chair, trying not to grin. Plastering on the most indifferent expression manageable. "You don't like it? Of all people, I would have assumed you would appreciate my divergence in attire. You're always saying how I don't try new things."

"Yeah, but I didn't expect you to take it to this level." Thomas gestures to my attire. "You're wearing pink for god's sake."

The pink he is referring to would be my new pastel pink dress shirt. I paired it with my dove gray Brioni. I think I look rather dashing in pink actually. And I did promise Micaela I would wear pink to work one day. And I never go back on my word. I even made sure to send her a photo this morning to prove it. Doing one of those horrid douchey reflection photos in my full-length mirror. The smirk I wore was the one I give her when I catch her watching me.

"Do you not like my choice in color?" I ask in all seriousness.

Thomas chuckles. "I would like any color you choose to wear, as long as it's not gray."

Wow. Do I really wear that much gray? Looking around my office, I realize just how gray and dull my world is. Light gray walls, black chairs, silver metal frames holding black and white architectural photos of the city, brushed nickel desk frame and glass top. There isn't one inch of color in the whole office. Except now for my pink shirt.

For the first time since I moved into this office years ago, I feel the desire to change. Change the décor in my office, change all the gray that I wear, change the way people see me. It's not something I ever cared about in the past. Not that I want to change to appease them, but to appease myself. Looking in from the outside, I'm starting to see why my friends always pester me.

I have been hiding behind all the gray and stoicism. This is all Micaela's fault, no doubt. Her pink is bleeding over into my monotone gray world, washing it in a prism of color. Almost as if I put on those ridiculous pink lens glasses she wears. Seeing everything from a new perspective.

I shake off the slightly world altering realization and focus on Thomas. "Well, it's nice to know I can pull off pink. I hear it's not for everyone."

"Not every man, no. It suits you." Thomas eyes me curiously, tilting his head to the side. "Does this mean you're going to be wearing *other* colors too?"

"Like what?"

"Blue, green, yellow, purple. I think you would look great in purple." Making his way deeper into my office, he gives me an encouraging smile.

"I'll take that into consideration." I give him a small smirk. Something I rarely ever do in public, and haven't done in the presence of anyone but Micaela recently.

"There's definitely something different about you. Beyond the obvious pink shirt."

"No there's not," I lie. There is something different about me. I can feel it shifting, altering. What that is, I try not to focus on. Giving it attention will only make it grow, give it life. I'm not ready for that yet.

"Yes, there is. You can deny it all you want, but it's there."

"Whatever," I grumble. I don't have time to argue. There are contracts to draw up and offers to send out. Not to mention, I'm supposed to check in on one of my properties this afternoon, and this particular manager is always a pain in my ass.

"Sure," he chuckles and returns his attention to his tablet, waking the screen and pulling up my calendar. "Ok then, back to the grind. You have a conference call at eleven, and then a late lunch with your brother before heading to meet with the manager at North Penn Plaza."

I almost forgot about my lunch with Samson. He's been around more than usual, and I think he's bored and looking for something to do. His usual flings aren't enough to entertain him, and his party friends are out on some yacht in the Caribbean. Claiming he missed home and wanted to see us more is his excuse for not joining them. I can't tell how true that is or not.

"Fine. Put the call through at eleven, confirm the reservation for lunch, and make sure that good for nothing manager Jimmy is going to be there when I arrive. Last time, he made me wait for over an hour."

I really should replace Jimmy. He never answers my calls, smells like a dirty sneaker, and does the bare minimum required.

"Sure thing, Boss."

Thomas knocks his knuckles on my desk before turning to leave my office. Before he does, I call to stop him.

"Wait, Thomas." He stops and turns to face me, hand tucked in his pocket. "The Charity Gala. Am I still able to get an additional ticket?"

"Now you want to bring a date?"

"Maybe."

"Well, it's too late. Tickets are sold out, bookings are closed. Everything's full. I told you when I asked you weeks ago that it was then or never. Remember?"

I do remember. I told him it was never. Because at the time, I had no intention of taking a date. Now things have changed. I want Micaela on my arm when I enter the Gala. I want her at my side, sipping pink champagne and diverting boring conversations with boring people into something tolerable. I want to see what kind of pink dress she'll wear. Looks like none of that is going to happen now.

"I can check with Debra just to make sure if you like. If available, what name should I put on the ticket?"

"Micaela. Micaela Hart."

For the next hour, I research and order new furniture and décor for my office. A mustard yellow vase, tufted teal chairs, and new watercolor paintings from the artist that painted the one in my home that Micaela liked so much. One a rendering of the three Sister Bridges, the yellow of their arches complimented by the rainbow of colors reflecting off the water, the other a solitary pink peony sitting in a jar on a windowsill.

Lunch with Samson isn't as bad as I thought it would be. We sit in a booth by the window of the café, Samson biting into his gourmet burger, while I stab a forkful of niçoise salad.

"What are you doing to occupy yourself these days?" I ask before filling my mouth with a bite of cherry tomato, kalamata olive, and grilled chicken.

Like the gentlemen Samson sometimes pretends to be, he wipes a smudge of sauce from the corner of his mouth with his cloth napkin. "A little bit of this and a little bit of that. Whatever I can find."

"You mean whomever," I suggest.

"That too. You know what they say, the best way to get over a woman is to get under a new one."

Laughing, I let the smile break across my face. Normally, I would ignore his crass jokes, but today, after my colorful shopping spree, I'm feeling more at ease, less tense. As such, I can more easily appreciate his humor.

Silverware clatters on the tabletop and I look up to see Samson gawking at me. "Holy fucking shit! What the hell is happening with your face?" One accusatory finger points at me. "Are you... smiling? What is happening? How? Why?"

"Who, actually."

"Who," he echoes. "Like a person. Like a woman?" he guesses. All ideas of eating are forgotten as he watches me, eagerly awaiting my response. Leaning forward, he crowds the table.

"Yes, a woman."

Samson's back thuds against the padded booth, his arms slacking to his sides in disbelief.

"I was just guessing. I didn't really think... wait. It's Lala, isn't it?"

Micaela. If I can't call her Lala, neither should he. "Damn. I'm going to have to buy her a present to thank her. I never thought you would smile again."

"Don't you fucking dare. If anyone is going to buy her a present, it's going to be me. Understand?" snapping at him, I lean forward on my elbows, death gripping my fork and knife. The last thing I will tolerate is him buying Micaela presents. It's not his place to do so.

"Fuck, chill, man. I get it. But why all the possessive growling? You two have something going on?" His corresponding grin is devious, and I know he's aching for the dirty details. Samson and I haven't talked about Micaela much, and I haven't told him that we're casually fucking every other day and twice on Saturdays. He would only make it weird if he knew.

"Why all the fucking questions?"

"Just curious." Eyeing me suspiciously, Samson picks up a golden salted fry and pops it in his mouth, chewing slowly. "You've never been like this with a woman."

"And how is that?" Stabbing another fork of food, I try to distract him or myself from the question and its answer.

Another denial is already forming on my lips. He will no doubt call me out on my bullshit, and I will inevitably deny it. That's what I do; deny, deny, deny. Anything and everything. Deny every woman who's ever wanted more. Deny my siblings a brother who enjoys their time together. Deny my own desires. Deny my feelings.

"Like… a boyfriend. You've been taking afternoons off, spending the weekends busy, doing God knows what. You're wearing pink and smiling for fucks sake. It seems like she means something more serious to you than the casual trysts you usually have."

The denial is on the tip of my tongue, waiting to be spoken. It gets caught in my throat, the lie choking me, keeping me from denying the truth. I tap my fingers on the table, agitated at my inability to form the words I want to. Unable to speak, I simply grunt at my brother, who is still watching me carefully from across the table.

Diverting the conversation away from whatever this is, I distract him with another piece of news that will be more unbelievable than me smiling. "Speaking of presents, I'm having a dinner for my birthday this Saturday."

"What the hell is going on? Are you serious?"

"Yes. I'll send you the time and address."

The news of my birthday dinner is enough to keep him talking about gifting me a pet rock, and finding those candles that you can't blow out, and making the restaurant staff sing happy birthday to me in the most embarrassing manner possible. I don't doubt he'll end up doing all of those things.

As long as he doesn't ask me who's planning it and what kind of relationship we have.

27 - Lala

I'm really going to have to buy some sanitizing spray before I return these

There wasn't much time to plan what I wanted to get Henry for his birthday, but there was one party rental store that had what I needed. I only get it for two days, but it's better than nothing. You know that age old question of what do you get someone who has everything? You get them an experience. You get them a ball pit.

That's right, I rented an inflatable ball pit for Henry's birthday, and they even had the option for all pink balls.

Fawn and I made a reservation at this swanky restaurant that belongs to one of Henry's clients for later tonight. The one Henry picked out, as was our promise. Right now, he's at the boxing gym with the boys, and I'm taking the opportunity to have the ball pit set up in his penthouse.

Jackson, my co-conspirator, lets me and the two party rental employees into the penthouse elevator, and when we enter his place, it looks as it always does, immaculate and shiny. Thankfully, the two young men carrying bags of pink balls don't react to setting up a ball pit in a penthouse obviously belonging to a single man.

I direct, and they obey. Unlike Henry, who argues with me on everything. I grin thinking about our arguing, and how it inevitably leads to kissing and then sex. Rubbing my thighs together at the growing ache between them, I wonder if my present will instigate one such argument. I hope it does.

When the two guys are done, and there's about a thousand shiny pink plastic balls inside an inflatable kiddie pool looking thing, I have about twenty minutes before Henry is due to arrive home. I thank the party employees and send them on their way down the elevator.

Standing at the edge of the ball pit, the square shape reaches mid-thigh on me, and I cannot stop myself from testing it out. Slipping off my pink chucks, I thrust myself forward, diving into the balls and sinking into the pink wonderland.

Man, I wish I had room for this in my bus. I would use it every day. Since I don't, I'm going to take full advantage of having it here now. I spend the next few minutes swimming through the balls as if they were water and laughing at myself. If you can't laugh at yourself, what can you laugh at? Right?

I hear the elevator begin its ascent, and I know Henry will be here soon. Climbing out of the pit, I make my way to what would be considered his front door and wait, very impatiently bouncing on the balls of my feet. The elevator pings and the doors begin to slide open.

Once there's enough room for me to slip in, I pounce, and I do mean that literally. Jumping on Henry so he stumbles backwards, my hand pressing over his eyes.

"What the hell?"

"It's me, don't freak out." The tense muscles under my arms relax and he blindly hugs his arms around my torso, squeezing me close.

"Well hello, Shortcake." A smile pulls at the corner of his lips, and I press a quick kiss to them. "To what do I owe this pleasure?"

"Happy Birthday. I have a present for you."

"A present? I hope it involves something pink and lacey that I can rip off with my teeth." Teasing Henry is one of my favorites, but that will have to wait till later. Because I do have something pink and lacey to wear under my dress for dinner that he is more than welcome to remove with his teeth.

I didn't have the money to buy a new dress to wear to dinner, but when I told Dollface where we were going, she let me raid her closet for something to wear. Ironically, I found a form fitting vintage gray dress with decorative buttons down the front. Since Henry likes gray so much, I thought I would wear it for a change. I'm pairing it with my pink Mary-Jane pumps, belt, purse, and jewelry of course. Can't be completely devoid of pink.

"You'll have to keep your eyes closed to find out." Lifting my hand, I peek under to make sure his eyes are closed. They are. Guiding him out of the elevator, I take his gym bag and drop it by the door while walking backwards towards the ball pit.

This is definitely a surprise he will not be expecting, and will most likely not really enjoy at first, but I'll show him how much fun they can be.

Positioning him at the end right in front of it, I step back so I can get a good look at his face. I strike my best Vana White pose before announcing, "Ok, open your eyes."

The grin he was wearing falls as he opens his eyes and looks down in confusion. "What is this?"

"It's a ball pit. Watch." Demonstrating my flawless ball pit dive, I splash down in the pink plastic balls. I can hear a few of them escaping their prison pit and bouncing away across his concrete floor. Hopefully not rolling under the couch where they will be lost forever until he finally decides to move to a real house. Which could be an eternity.

"Aren't these for like, kid's parties?"

"And adults who love to embrace their inner child."

"That sounds like a felony."

I fling a pink ball at his head. It smacks him right in the chin. "Stop complaining and get in. Take off your shoes first, though. It's a rental."

Henry stands perfectly still, scowling at the giant kiddie pool full of pink balls in the middle of his living room. Specifically, *not* removing his shoes and jumping in.

"You better get in here, Mister Grumpasaurus, or you won't get that pink lace surprise later."

Heated green eyes find mine in challenge and warning. *That's right. I will withhold sex if you don't cooperate.* He gets my telepathic message and jerkily removes his shoes, and surprisingly his shirt as well. Leaving him in only his black basketball shorts.

He doesn't dive in like I did. No, he gracefully steps in like a gazelle wading through the pink to get to me. Plopping down somewhat ungracefully on the unstable ground, which makes me smile.

"And why is this my present?" he asks, tentatively tossing balls with his fingertips.

"Because I wanted to give you something I knew you would never buy yourself. I wanted to give you the experience." As steadily as I can, I crawl into Henry's lap and straddle his waist, pushing balls out from between us so we're skin to shirt. As if this is the most natural position for us, he locks his arms around my waist, holding me with strong hands.

"You give me a new experience every time I see you," he quips, licking his lower lip in invitation.

"True, but this one is more fun."

"I beg to differ."

A squeak escapes my lips as he crushes our bodies together, and in a move opposite of his abrupt embrace, he kisses me with long, tender presses against my lips. My hands linger on his skin, feeling their way across his shoulders and around his neck and arms. Moving in unhurried exploration of places I already know by heart. The dip of his collar bone, the rounding of his bicep, and the slight day-old stubble on his jaw that will no doubt be gone by the time we leave for dinner.

It's all familiar and still mysterious. Every day and night we spend together, I learn a little more about Henry, seeing him piece by piece. I also learn more about myself, what I want in life, and who I want to be. The growing emptiness in my chest is slowly filling. Filling with love for Pittsburgh, love for my new friends at the skate shop, love for Fawn and Leo and their future daughter, love for my Pilates classes with the girls, love for our brunches. Love for this neighborhood, and Henry's penthouse. Love for Henry.

Oh shit. I think I've fallen in love with Henry. Fallen for his grumpiness that only I can turn into laughter. For his stubbornness in not trying new things, for how we argue over what type of movie to watch, and where to get dinner. For the way the corner of his mouth quirks when he's thinking something pervy when he teases and jokes with me. Fallen for the way he looks at me. With such intensity, I'm not sure if I should melt into a puddle on the floor or run away.

This wasn't supposed to happen. I wasn't supposed to allow him and his gray life into my pink one. He's permanent, cemented in place, not only in this city, but in his life. He has no room or want for a significant other. Literally. His penthouse has one room and one bathroom. This isn't the home of a man who wants to build a future with someone. He's even said as much.

Yet my heart picks up at the thought of spending all my time with him. Of waking up every morning and going to bed every night with him. To celebrating holidays and birthdays like today with him. Taking a trip down to Florida for him to meet my parents, and then taking him to Disney World, where I would force him to meet and greets and take pictures of him glowering at the camera with Tinkerbelle at his side. And the one thing I never thought I would ever want, staying in Pittsburgh and living in a brick-and-mortar home built with a foundation and everything. Planting roots, just like mom wanted. And I guess now what I want. But first... I have to convince Henry.

That task may be a grand one, but unlike when I first met him, I no longer think it impossible. Difficult, yes. But not impossible. Not anymore.

Our kiss breaks and Henry runs his nose up the column of my throat. I know where he's headed just as he presses a kiss and soft bite in the crook of my neck.

"Should we add ball pit to our growing list of places we've had sex in my condo?"

The life altering realization of my love for Henry is smothered under his dedicated attention and lips. Our bodies begin the practiced dance we both know so well. Stripping clothes from flesh, surrounded by pink plastic balls that I really hope they wash and sanitize before allowing small children to play in them after us.

Henry moves us to the side of the ball pit and uses it to prop himself up, leaning his back against it, getting quite comfortable. Even surrounded by a child's play set, our sex is not rushed or impatient. It's not wild or unhinged. Instead, it's a leisurely discovery of small movements and light touches. Heightening every sensation in delicious delay. I remain straddling his hips, and when our bodies shift and roll in perfect harmonization, we do something we have yet to do.

We make love.

We do not fuck or have sex. Something's changed. I don't know when or who changed first, but here we are. In the middle of a pink ball pit, making love. Discovering each other in new ways before unknown. When we come, we come together in heavy breaths and quiet moans. Our previously vocal and loud sex has converted to something quiet, yet still immensely intense. Both our bodies vibrate with our release, my sweat mixing with his, coating the plastic balls in a light sheen.

I'm really going to have to buy some sanitizing spray before I return these.

I ignore the questionable sanitation to enjoy our serene embrace. Resting my forehead against his, I can taste his hot breath on my tongue when he exhales. He's the one to press our bodies flush, not caring about the sticky sweat pooling between us. My breasts squish against him, and I love the way it feels to be like this with him. Quiet, close, exposed.

"You are... unexpected, Micaela Hart. I never saw you coming."

I would make a joke about how he just saw me come if it weren't for the thoughtful seriousness in his eyes and the relaxed muscles in his face that are not tense or playful. He is completely calm and earnest. His words don't seem meant for me, but rather himself. So, I say nothing. Letting him ponder, and brush damp hair away from my face, and run his fingers along my jaw.

Hours later, we're just finishing getting ready for dinner when Henry exits the bathroom and sees me in the gray vintage nineteen fifties dress I borrowed.

"Wow. You look... stunning."

"Do you like the color?" I ask, spinning in a slow circle so he can get the full view. "I picked it just for you." I realize as I say this that he's wearing a pink dress shirt under his gray vest.

"And I wore pink. Just for you," he chuckles, and I can't stop staring at him as he saunters over to me. All cocky swagger and predatory smile, teeth and all.

When he reaches me, he places a possessive hand on my ass. "I think you look sexy as hell, but don't change your color just for me. I like you in all your pink just as much as I'd like you in any other color."

Then he leans down and presses a hard heated kiss on my lips, ruining the pink lipstick I just applied. Barbie pink is smeared across his lips when he pulls away.

"You might want to clean that off before we leave," I suggest with a haughty tone. One finger reaches up and dabs at his lips, and he pulls it away seeing the pink there.

"Hmm. Wouldn't want them thinking we did anything inappropriate now, would we?"

Most of the people attending this dinner know about us, but not all, and he still doesn't kiss or touch me in public. Inwardly, I sulk a little at the answer that echoes through my mind. *No, no. He wouldn't want them knowing we do inappropriate things to each other.*

At the restaurant, we meet Fawn and Leo, Eddie and Ana, his date from the night we ran into him on the street, Samson, and his date, some brunette named Candy? Caramel? I don't remember. We also invited Henry's assistant, Thomas and his boyfriend, Paul.

Technically everyone is in a couple, except for me and Henry.

Because that's not part of whatever we are... yet. It's strange to be his date, but not be his date. I don't like it. I want to be with him in public as we are when we are alone.

Ok, not entirely. Minus all the naked stuff. All the joking, and teasing, and affectionate touching, and closeness. The lack of propriety and limits of what he wants us to be versus what we really are.

Watching the waitress flirt with him and touch his bicep all sultry like when she wishes him a happy birthday makes me want to break every delicately painted finger on her hand. It's not her fault though. It's mine and Henry's. Mostly Henry's. Let's face it. At this point, if he asked me to be his girlfriend, I would totally agree, no hesitancy.

But he doesn't. So, I keep my hands in my lap and my mouth shut. My eyes though, I can't stop them. They can glare and judge and stare daggers as much as they want.

To his credit, Henry doesn't seem to notice or reciprocate the attention, and when she leaves, he doesn't even glance at her ass once as she walks away. That's a good omen, I suppose.

We all sit on either side of a long rectangular table, Henry at my left, Eddie and Ana to my right, with Fawn, Leo, Thomas, and Paul opposite us. It's been a long time since I sat at a table with so many people I would call my friends, all gathered to celebrate one of their own with smiles and drinks. Fawn gives me an appreciative smile and a mouthed thank you when Henry outright laughs at one of Leo's horrible dad jokes.

I can't take all the credit. Henry always had it inside him. I just gave him an easy avenue to let it out. I'm deep in my own thoughts, watching Samson trying to impress his date when a large warm hand runs up my thigh. Resting comfortably without expectation of more. Just remaining there for no other purpose than to be.

Henry leans in and speaks quietly into my ear. "You were right. Thank you for forcing me to come tonight. I don't know why I've avoided this for so long."

Turning, and trying not to brush my lips against his in the process, I give him my easy half smile. "Probably because you didn't want to admit you were getting old."

His chuckle is quiet and deep in his throat. "You're probably right. I hate to admit it, but you usually are."

"Remember this day, Henry Bardot. Because I will be quoting you on that."

"I don't know if I'll ever forget this day."

Our eyes remain locked for a long-charged moment that is only broken when interrupted by Eddie nudging my elbow.

"Lala, tell Ana about your bus, and how you travel around the country in it."

I get this request a lot from pretty much everyone who knows me, and it's easy to fall into the practiced speech of my bus and how it is to live in a Skoolie—a converted school bus—and all the states and cities I've lived in. At some point in my explanation, Henry's hand slips free of my thigh and the space feels empty and cold in its absence.

"Where were you before here?" Ana asks, her voice a sultry tone that I have no doubt would make for a great phone sex operator. *Do they still have those?* I feel like with the invention of the internet, they've kind of gone the way of the dodo.

"I was in Savannah, Georgia before here. I came here because my friends Paloma and Pilar were here and invited me to come join them. Figured a summer here was far more mild than the humidity of the south and thought, why not?"

"That's amazing. You've probably seen so many interesting places."

"I have."

"And you don't stay any longer than a year in one place?"

"I haven't yet, no. Nowhere felt like home. Felt like a place I wanted to stay." Until now. But I don't say that. Things like that just scare off guys like Henry, and he is attentively listening, even if he tries to act like he isn't. I see his eyes shift over to look at me every so often. You can't hide from me, Henry Bardot. I see right through you.

"And where do you think you will go after Pittsburgh?"

No one stops eating or talking, but I can feel a few pairs of eyes shift to me for my response. I can't tell who without looking around, and that would feel suspicious, so I don't. Even though I hadn't once thought about where I would go after Pittsburgh, since every day I spend here, I want more and more to stay. I suppose it wouldn't hurt to consider where I might go were I to leave.

"Um, probably farther north. Towards the Midwest. I haven't been to Montana in a few years. I wouldn't mind seeing the mountains and snow again."

Montana is where I found Fred in an exotic pet store. The peace of the snow-covered mountains is something that can't be imitated. If I were to leave Pittsburgh, I no doubt would need somewhere like Montana to recover from the heartache of losing this city and the people I would be leaving behind here.

"That sounds beautiful. I've never been anywhere farther west than Chicago. And that was just for a work trip."

"What is it you do again?" It's a surprise I hadn't asked her earlier. I must seem so egotistical talking about myself so much.

"I'm an insurance adjuster. I deal mainly in home and life policies."

Dinner passes and we move on to cake and presents. Samson bribes the waitress with a hundred-dollar bill to get a few other servers to come over and sing with us to really embarrass Henry. We are rather loud, but it doesn't seem to affect him. He watches on in quiet amusement. Although his features are soft, and he continues to smile, occasionally he seems distant in a way that wasn't there earlier.

Henry tries to blow out his candles, but they just continue flickering in the low mood light of the restaurant's private room we're in. Samson is laughing his ass off, thoroughly amused with himself for finding them. Henry flips him off and plucks the candles out of the chocolate cake—his choice; I would have never pegged him for a chocolate cake kinda guy—and drops them in a half-drunk glass of water.

Everyone brought a present, much to Henry's dismay. Fawn and Leo give him a "World's Greatest Uncle" coffee mug they insist he has to use at work. Eddie gives him an ice cream maker, and winks at me when I realize what the contraption is. Thomas and Paul give him a rich eggplant purple colored dress shirt that Henry chuckles at. Some sort of inside joke by the looks of it. And lastly, Samson gives him a giant black dildo that is at least a foot and a half long. Henry chucks it at his head. There's also a Costco size box of condoms, and a bottle of strawberry flavored lube. He also looks at me and winks.

Does every fucking person at this table know we're having sex, but not verbally acknowledging how Henry acts like we are nothing more than platonic friends?

Uuuugggghhh! This is annoyingly infuriating. When they all ask where my present is, I tell them about the ball pit I had set up in Henry's penthouse. Pretty much everyone there doesn't believe when I tell them I got him to actually get in it.

On our way out, after everyone besides Fawn is thoroughly inebriated and full of chocolate cake. I stand in the foyer, waiting for

Henry to get our coats when Samson approaches.

"This was great fun, Lala. Thank you for forcing him out."

"It was my pleasure. I think he enjoyed it more than he thought he would."

"It's not just that." He steps closer and speaks a little quieter, looking over his shoulder to make sure no one approaches.

"Look, I've never seen Henry like this with someone. Not since college. It's been a long time since I've seen him happy. And I know how he can be about relationships." He pauses again, giving me a small genuine smile. "Don't let him push you away. He'll regret it for the rest of his life if he does."

Before I have a chance to formulate a response, Henry appears behind Samson, holding our coats and handing me mine.

"Are you ready to go?" he asks before shifting his gaze, which hardens slightly on his brother. "Samson."

"Henry." Samson's reply is far more playful, and it seems to confuse Henry. He shakes it off before placing his hand on my lower back and guiding me out into the night, where we make our way to his Jag, and then to his place. We repeat our love making from earlier, but this time in his bed, and it is far more heartbreaking the second time.

28 - Lala

Damn him and his hypnotic penis

The past few days since Henry's birthday have been strange. Not like sounds coming from inside the walls strange, but just... off. It's as if he's become reluctant of us again. We took one step forward, and now he's taking two steps back. Still moving forward, but hesitantly. As if something is gnawing at his insides that makes him unwilling to allow himself that which he truly desires.

It doesn't stop him from inviting me over, or stripping me naked and indulging in our mutual physical satisfaction. Nothing is quite like how it was when we made love on his birthday. He's reverted back to physical gratification and closing off his heart from the actions. But I know it's still there, simmering below the surface, and once he takes that step forward again, it will overflow. I just have to convince him to keep moving forward.

Relationship phobes like Henry have to make the realization on their own, otherwise they'll scare right back into their hidey hole. There's no reason to rush. I myself am still getting used to the idea.

Familiar with the acceptance that I might love him and want to remain in Pittsburgh.

I can only hope to convince Henry of the same. He might claim to hate and despise relationships and marriage, but his actions speak otherwise. And I can only believe that actions speak louder than words. If not, my heart won't handle the fall out. So, I put on a brave face and ignore the tickling unease in my chest. Henry will be here soon, and I'm trying not to scare him away.

It's nearly six when he finally knocks on my bus door. I baked my mother's meatloaf for dinner, and it sits warming in the oven, two place settings laid out on the counter. Fred is securely in his cage. Even though Henry's gotten more comfortable with him, he's still a bit skittish, especially when eating. Henry, not Fred. Fred likes to steal food off people's plates, and Henry doesn't like to share.

Answering the door, I let Henry in. He's still wearing his suit from work, sans jacket and tie. Already partially unwinding from his day. I like it when he loosens up, unbuttons his shirt, and rolls up his sleeves. But I also love him, all serious and terse. It's the most fun to tease him when he's like that. Trying to keep his professional composure while I skate circles around him and teasingly brush my hands across places I shouldn't while in public.

"Oh, I didn't know you were making dinner."

"Why wouldn't I?"

"No reason."

Again, with the strange behavior. We always eat when we're together. The calories are needed for our activities. Henry strolls past Fred's cage, ignoring my little ferret, even when he stares up at him with wide hopeful eyes. Fred still isn't his favorite, but Henry has gotten more familiar with him, so much so, he usually sticks a finger through the cage and gives his head a little scratch in greeting. Tonight, he doesn't even acknowledge him. Poor little Fred looks so dejected.

I go over to his cage and give him a reassuring scratch. It puts him enough at ease to crawl into his little hammock and relax.

Sitting at the counter, Henry waits, stoic and quiet.

"You, Ok? You seem distracted." Standing behind him, I rub at his shoulders and neck. The muscles are tight and tense, and I can feel them loosening the longer I massage.

"Yeah, just a long day is all. Sorry." Turning, he places me between his knees and buries his face in my cleavage with a deep sigh. His breath is warm on my skin, and I can't help but hold him close, running my fingers through his hair and scratching lightly.

His arms remain loose around my legs, idle fingers making nonsensical patterns on the back of my exposed thigh. We stay here for a few minutes, doing nothing more than soothing caresses. Only the sound of his deep breathing fills my small home.

Without a word, he disengages and turns back to the place setting. We eat mostly in comfortable silence, with a little bit of small talk.

"I can't see you on Thursday after your Pilates class this week."

"Why not?"

"I have a gallery opening to attend for a client."

"Oh. Is it a big thing?" My voice is small and uneven, and I don't fully know why. I can't seem to control it.

"Kind of. It's a pair of artists actually, and they're well known throughout the city. Their work is getting more notoriety. I think a journalist will be at the showing to write about them in some extremely exclusive art publication."

"Wow that sounds... important." Standing, I take our empty plates to the sink and begin to rinse them.

"It is to them. I'm only going because it's good business to appease your clients. Their needs may change, and they could require a new, larger space or even a second gallery. I, of course, will want them to come to me if that should happen." Henry stands and leans against the counter behind me. I can feel his gaze roaming over me. A mix of cold and hot chills takes over and I suppress it.

"And you're going alone to this event?" I don't turn around because I don't want him to see how important his answer is to me as I hold my breath and wait.

"Yes. I usually do. But there will be people there I know. Business acquaintances and such."

A relieved exhale deflates my lungs just as a longing wave of dejection washes over me for the briefest of moments. He's going alone, as usual. Nothing different, as if nothing has changed. Attending events like this stag, just like he would have before meeting me. *I am not important enough to bring as a date to a work event.*

I clear my throat and plaster on a smile, turning around to face him. He's not smiling or scowling, but watching me with that intense gaze that could melt iron. Like a stalking predator, he crosses the short distance between us in long, stretching steps, knocking the sense right out of me with a kiss that empties my head of all thoughts.

His kiss is demanding and needy, hungry and starving for me. One hand is knotted in my hair as the other curls around my ass and lifts me in one fluid motion, sitting me on the countertop next to the sink.

Then there are no thoughts of galleries and dates. Just touching and need. Lust courses through me, pulsing in my blood. I can't help it. As soon as Henry's lips make contact with mine, I get instantly horny. Maybe there's a hormone in his saliva that makes me all sex crazed.

Maybe it's just Henry.

With swift and precise movements, he is removing my shirt

and unbuttoning his, revealing toned golden skin underneath. He doesn't remove his shirt completely, and he is all the more hot because of it. I quickly release his buckle and unzip his pants. His cock is hard and ready for me. I reach in and grab it through his boxer briefs, and he groans into my mouth.

In a move worthy of superman, he lifts my ass off the counter, just enough to slide my cotton lounge shorts and panties right off me. I never release my hold on his dick. It feels too right in my palm.

We shuck off his pants and underwear, and Henry has himself sheathed in a condom in moments. I didn't even see him open the wrapper. His lips find mine again as his tongue demands entrance. He lines the head of his cock up with my pussy, rubbing through my wet folds, spreading my desire to ready me for him.

I gasp into his open mouth as he presses inside me, swallowing my moan as my pussy swallows his cock.

He takes me hard and fast on my kitchen counter, and I hold onto his open shirt for the ride of my life. He makes me come in minutes, but doesn't finish himself until he carries me to my bed and makes me scream a few more times in ecstasy. All thoughts of Thursday are forgotten in the fog of our sex.

When Thursday rolls around, I've almost forgotten about not seeing Henry tonight. Almost. It still stings that he didn't ask me to attend with him. I know I'm not his girlfriend per se, but that's the sort of event you take a date to, even if she is "just a friend." Friends take friends as work event dates all the time, right? So why is this any different? I could have been his buffer to people he didn't want to talk to, his entertainment when he got bored of socializing and staring at red dots on yellow canvases. If anything, I could have been there just to keep him company. But he didn't ask, and I didn't argue.

Now I kind of wished I'd argued. Since when was I a pushover? Since when did I sulk and pout because a guy didn't ask me out? That's not me. That's not who I am. If I want something, I go for it. I don't let others decide for me. Normally I would have pushed and demanded to either be his date, or for a good reason as to why I couldn't be.

Instead, I sulk like a teenager. Damn him and his hypnotic penis for distracting me so thoroughly after telling me. I never even had a chance to argue. I was half asleep and boneless when he kissed my cheek and went home that night.

Inwardly, I groan in frustration. Outwardly, I grunt in exertion in the middle of our Pilates class. Fawn has gotten to the point where she has to modify her workouts because of the pregnancy, and doesn't do anything that requires her to lay flat on her back or stomach, obviously. She sits and uses a TheraBand around her foot to flex and extend her ankle, while I grunt away doing frog squats with my feet in the straps of the reformer I lie on.

Sweating is good, pushing myself to distraction is good.

When class is over, we decide to get smoothies. We're sitting at our customary table, waiting for our names to be called and enjoying the after workout burn.

"Remember how I said I would make it up to you when I pawned you off on my brother a few weeks back to take you to that flea market?"

How could I forget? That was the day of the infamous baby store adventure, and the first time Henry and I had sex. Definitely not a forgetful day.

"Yes, I remember."

"Well, I think I can finally make it up to you."

"How?" The girl behind the counter calls our names, and I retrieve our smoothies, returning to my seat and greedily sucking mine down.

"Well," Fawn continues, "turns out Leo can't attend a charity Gala we were scheduled to attend next week. The ticket is already paid for, so I figured you could come in his place."

"Wow. That sounds amazing. I've never been to a Gala before."

"They're usually pretty boring, but there is great food and silent auctions. Sometimes there's a live band and dancing. This one is to benefit the public-school teachers in the city. To help fund their classroom supplies and such."

Teachers are so underappreciated, and it's nice to know they're getting financial support from those who can afford to help. I won't be able to make any kind of donation, as I don't make much from Wheelies and the few markets I've been attending. The anime con I was hoping to land fell through, and now I don't even have that to make up for the lack of events. At least there's still Henry's conference.

Speaking of funds, a Gala sounds fancy. Like black-tie fancy. I don't own a single thing that would pass as Gala worthy, and I have no money to buy anything new. Perhaps Dollface has another vintage piece hidden in her massive closet that would suffice? I could ask.

"Um… is it a black-tie affair kind of Gala?" I ask tentatively. Fawn smiles brightly at me.

"Oh, yes. Everyone gets dolled up and glamorous. It's really the only reason I go. To have an excuse to wear something sparkly and long. Well, and the food." She doesn't realize at first why I'm asking. When she looks up, straw in mouth, and sees that I'm not excitedly jumping up and down in my seat at the prospect of wearing some-thing sparkly—no matter how much I really want to wear a gown like a princess—her face falls.

"Oh, my goodness. I didn't even think, Lala. How incredibly thoughtless of me. I swear this pregnancy brain is going to kill me."

"It's fine, Fawn. I just don't have anything to wear, and can't afford to buy something new. I appreciate the offer, but I don't think I can go." My shoulders slump, and I stare down at my smoothie. I *really* wanted to go. The last time I wore anything even close to an evening gown was senior prom in high school.

I may treat every day as a reason to dress up, but ball gowns aren't exactly proper attire for a skate shop or farmer's market.

"No."

"No?"

"You heard me, no. You are going, and I'm going to take you shopping to buy you a new dress, and you are not going to argue with me." She holds up a finger like a scolding mother when I try to do just that.

"I want to do this for you, Lala. You are a wonderful person and a great friend. Not to mention, you've done the impossible with my brother. He smiles and laughs more now like he used to. None of that would have happened without you. And don't you try to tell me otherwise."

That one I'll have to give her. It didn't seem like Henry was on the path to rediscovering his humorous side when I met him. And although I don't want to take all the credit, I have to admit I did help a lot. Even if he didn't ask me to be his date to his stupid work art gallery thingamajig tonight. Speaking of Henry...

"Will Henry be attending the Gala as well?" I try to sound all nonchalant, but it must be obvious that I care because Fawn grins wide at me.

"Yup. We always go together, sit at the same table even." She rubs her belly and drinks her smoothie, all while watching me with a knowing look. I'm about to say yes, and she knows it. I really need to work on my poker face.

"Ok. I'll go. But only because you're pregnant, and no one can argue with a pregnant woman."

"Woohoo! Yes! We are so going shopping on Saturday. I had a dress picked out, but I think it'll be too tight on my belly. I've grown more than I expected since I bought it."

Now I am smiling and laughing. I've always paid my own way, and supported myself without handouts, but I suppose a gift in repayment is acceptable. Along with a free ticket to a Gala. It was supposed to be Leo's, but since he can't use it, it'll just go to waste if I don't. And we can't have that. Someone might as well take his place and enjoy the night with Fawn... and Henry.

The thought of Henry in a tux has me all hot and bothered. Should I tell him I'm going or leave it a surprise? Not sure. I'll have to discuss that with Fawn. Especially since I just realized that Henry again has an event that requires a date and previous planning that he did not mention to me or ask me to be his date for. Maybe I shouldn't tell him. Just to punish him.

We finish our smoothies and head for the exit. Since I'm not going to Henry's, I have the evening free with nothing to do. I haven't hung out with Paloma and Pilar in a while. I should give them a call.

"Are you heading over to Henry's?" Fawn's question has me stumbling. I didn't realize she knew I went over there on Thursdays. Am I that obvious?

"Oh um... not tonight. He has a work thing."

"A work thing?" She scrunches her nose at me in confusion.

"Yeah, an art gallery opening for one of his clients."

"And he didn't take you as his date?" Her outrage is heartwarming that she would be mad at her own brother for not considering me. My own heart swells even more for her.

"No." My word comes out livid on a low growl.

"That asshat. I thought he was getting better. Looks like we'll just have to show him what he's missing." She elbows my arm and winks at me. What is she planning?

"What are you talking about?"

"The Gala. We're going to doll you up to the point every man at that Gala is going to drool when they see you, and he's going to realize how stupid he's been."

Surprising Fawn and forcing her to stop in the middle of the sidewalk, I grab her and squeeze her in as tight a hug as I can with her baby belly between us. "I love you, Fawn. You're the best."

She returns my embrace, chuckling. "I know."

29 - Henry

Ok, Ok calm your tits

This show is immensely boring. The art is—well, it's art—supposedly. Not really my style. All splatters and brush strokes and indiscernible shapes meant to be interpreted through multiple theoretical lenses. Seems like a lot of work for paint on canvas. I want to know what I'm looking at in my art. Even if it's a depiction of a man's hairy ass crack, at least then I know what I'm looking at.

I've worked my way through two glasses of wine and circled the gallery more times than I would care to. Since I haven't had a chance to speak with the artists, Arturo and Sandra yet, I don't want to leave until I make my presence known.

I should have brought Micaela. I could tell when I told her about the show that she was expecting me to ask her to be my date. It's what most guys in my position would have done, but not me. No, I had to be the jackass that insisted I go alone. I don't need a date. Not even a friend to pass the time with.

I'm a fucking fool.

In my attempts to try and maintain our friends with benefits status, I pushed her away. Bringing her as my date would only have blurred the lines further than they already are. I can't let that happen. I'm already far too close and attached to her than I should be. At my birthday dinner, I was reminded that she's not staying. Any day she could just decide to up and leave. Leave Pittsburgh, leave Pennsylvania, leave me. She doesn't do permanent. I can't allow myself to get in too deep with her. I never wanted to in the first place. I have to remind myself this is all for physical pleasure and enjoyment, not emotional attachment and love.

Love. I cannot let my feelings become that. I will control them, not the other way around. Because my feelings don't control me, I made sure to keep Micaela at arm's length, at least in public. In private, I don't tolerate her being more than grabbing distance away from me.

So, here I stand, sequestering myself in a corner of the room, waiting for my opening to speak with the artists so I can get the fuck out of here.

Checking my watch, it's only a quarter to eight. Still early enough to see Micaela if she'll let me. Perhaps make up for not bringing her tonight. In the long run, it was probably the right choice to make, but at this moment, I regret it. Mainly because I have to stand here alone, looking like a creeper watching everyone with derision in my eyes. Little do they know, it's mostly directed at myself.

I sip on my second glass of wine in hopes it will make time move faster. It doesn't. But it does make me hallucinate. Because that's the only reason I am watching my brother stroll towards me right now. I look down at my wine and sniff it just to make sure no one spiked it. Smells like Malbec.

"Hey there, bro. Fancy meeting you here."

"What the hell are you doing here, Samson? And how did you even get in?"

"I had Thomas share your calendar with me, so I knew you would be here tonight. When I found myself bored sitting on my couch, I decided to crash. As for getting in, I just gave them the name Bardot and they let me right in."

Of course, because that's what all sane people do. Stalk their brother's calendar, and then pretend to be him to get into exclusive art gallery events.

"What is with you lately? You're always showing up and being a pest. Don't you have friends and parties to attend?"

Samson grabs a glass of champagne from a passing server and checks out her ass as she walks away.

"Yeah, I have friends, but they're rather repetitive these days. I've been looking for new sources of amusement. Broadening my horizons." He gestures with his wine glass to the surrounding art show. Considering what he's done in the past, I would think an art showing would be low on his list of things that would interest him.

"By attending an art show uninvited and invading my life?" I give him a firm scowl to emphasize my displeasure in his continued infiltration in my life. I love my brother, but this is more time than we've spent together in years. I like my privacy and solitude—other than Micaela—and I'd like to keep it that way.

"Your life has become far more interesting in the past months, and I find myself intrigued by the recent direction of events."

I give up sipping my wine and down the rest of the glass in one swallow. He is apparently here to stay, and I'm going to need alcohol to endure his antics.

"Just don't intervene or speak to anyone." The last thing I need is him ruining a deal because he opens his big mouth and propositions the wrong person.

"No promises."

Nothing less than what I would expect from Samson. He does

well keeping his hands to himself and his conversation to polite chit chat. There was rarely a time when we were young that Samson actually listened to me, and I'm surprised he is now.

In between polite socializing, I can hear Samsons phone buzzing in his pocket. It has been for most of the hour he's been here. He may be taking time away from his friends and that lifestyle, but it seems they aren't. He pulls out his phone to check the dozens of notifications filling his screen. When he clears the push notifications, I can see his wallpaper clear as day. Fucking Micaela's "spank bank" photo of her in her work out leggings that he sent himself from my phone.

"What the hell is that?" My voice raises, and a few people standing nearby eye us curiously. I try to rein in my temper, but it festers, causing my fingers to curl into fists.

"Oh, yeah. Forgot I had that on there. Honestly, I don't even notice it." He says this like it's a stock photo of some unknown woman on his phone.

"Then change it," I grit out between clenched teeth, trying to play it cool and utterly failing.

"Why? You didn't seem to care when I took the picture off your phone. Why do you care now?"

"I don't. It's just inconsiderate. Use a different photo." I punctuate every word with clear annunciation to make myself perfectly understood. Even through the clenched jaw.

Samson side eyes me, and I glare without blinking. "Ok, Ok, calm your tits." I watch as he changes his wallpaper to a shot of a tropical beach near the ocean with, of course, a half-naked woman lying in the sand sunbathing. Correction, a completely naked woman lying in the sand sunbathing. And he thinks following me around on my obligatory art gallery show is amusing?

My anger subsides, minutely. "I would delete that photo if I were you." My tone allows for no miscomprehension. He knows which photo and why.

"Why isn't Lala here with you?"

"Why would she be?" I bristle at his tone. It's calm and condescending. And his change of subject is unsettling.

"Because you two are a thing now. Isn't this the type of event a guy in a relationship would normally bring his girl to?"

"We're not in a relationship, and she's not my girl." I spit out the words like poison. They're true, but also false. She is mine. I just can't keep her. I don't need to keep her.

"Not from where I'm standing."

I scoff. "And where would that be exactly?"

"Across from you every time Lala's name is mentioned. And the look in your eyes does not say fuck buddy. It says girlfriend."

"You must be getting cataracts, because my eyes never say girlfriend."

"Don't worry," he adds, interrupting my dismissal of his incorrect observation. "She looks at you with boyfriend eyes."

"Wait," I stutter, "she does?" Why does this excite me? I should not be excited about a woman wanting to be my girlfriend. I don't want a girlfriend. Yet, somehow, those words are losing their significance. They don't sound as finite as they used to. The reason for their presence fading away under Micaela's smiles.

"And that right there is exactly why you have become more interesting." Samson points at my face, and I realize it's because I'm smiling. Thinking about Micaela being my girlfriend made me smile. The good feeling is squashed under the weight of the truth. After Pittsburgh she's going to Montana, sufficiently smothering my smile back into a straight line.

In all the times past that I've heard a woman agree to nothing serious and only casual sex, just to turn around and beg me to meet her parents and attend a family vacation, I had wished for someone like Micaela. No strings, unattached, and completely in line with my desires. Now I hate that she is exactly what I had wanted. I wished for a tolerable woman to sate my sexual needs and nothing more. I hate that my wish was granted.

When Arturo and Sandra finally find their way to us, I give them the standard compliments. Things look great, what a wonderful turn out, congratulations, I wish you the best of luck in your endeavors. Etcetera, etcetera, etcetera. Same old meaningless bullshit. Sometimes it gets tiring. What I'd really like to tell them is that their art makes no sense to me, and I get more enjoyment watching the old lady in the park feed the pigeons. But thanks to having to be politically correct, I'm not allowed to voice my true opinions. Not if I ever want their business again.

Once the obligatory pleasantries are over, I discard my empty wine glass on a nearby table and make my way to the exit.

"What, we're leaving already?"

"I'm leaving. I don't care what you do." My words are short and terse. I've already been here longer than I wanted. It's now after nine thirty, and I'm not sure if this time of night is considered a booty call or not. Every time I've met with Micaela in the past, it was right after work or her Pilates class. We've always scheduled ahead of time or made arrangements. It's never been a late-night text to just show up for sex. Which is strange, considering that's all our relationship is.

Or is it?

"Come on, Henry. Stay out with me. Have a few more drinks and we can hang out like we used to."

Samson follows my brisk pace as we exit the gallery and I hand my ticket over to the valet. I ignore him and mentally compose a text message to send to Micaela. So far I have; Hi. Is it too late to come over? Cringing at my own bad and obvious propositioning sext, I mentally erase it and start over.

"Henry. Henry, come on."

"Why are you so adamant about spending time with me?"

"I don't know, maybe I missed my brother, and lately you've actually been tolerable to be around."

Ouch. Turning to face him, I realize he's being sincere. Which for him, is as rare as seeing Halley's comet. Weighing my choices, I have to decide between maybe seeing Micaela—which is not assured, since I did leave her behind instead of bringing her tonight—or hanging out with my brother, who seems to be trying rather relentlessly to spend more time with me.

I would so much rather spend the night naked in Micaela's pink bed, but I realize I should spend some time with my brother. He seems to need it for some reason.

"Fine. But we are not going to some raging techno club with music so loud my ears bleed."

Samson grins wide, and his eyes light up at my acceptance. "Yes! That's the Henry I know and love. Let's go!"

Tonight is full of regrets, starting with not inviting Micaela, and ending with me agreeing to go out with my brother. We don't go to a club so loud my ears bleed, but we do go to a club and drink far too much. So much so, I actually have a hangover the next day. Even with the headache, and aversion to loud noises and bright lights, it made Samson happy, and I can't completely hate the night.

30 - Lala

Now this is a stopping traffic kind of dress

"I look like a beached whale," Fawn laments as she is again unable to zip up a dress. This would be dress number five. We had hoped the empire waist would make it easier to accommodate her budding baby belly. Oh, it drapes around her belly just fine, however, her overly full boobs are smooshed together and nearly touch her chin as we try to zip it around her lush cleavage.

"I didn't think about how much my boobs have grown along with my stomach. Damn it." Fresh tears well in her eyes, shining like tiny glittering stars.

"Don't cry. We'll find something. They have plenty more dresses to choose from. We just need something with more stretch."

Now fighting to unzip the dress, I try to give her my most supportive smile in the mirror. Her arms drop in defeat, and her lip quivers while her breasts look like cantaloupes in compression socks on her chest.

Finally freeing her from the dress, she strips it off, dejected, and I can tell she's losing her shopping high the longer we go without finding something that fits… and doesn't look like a moo-moo on her. She slides her arms through the silk robe the store gave us to wear between gowns and sighs. This has to be the fanciest store I have ever been in, in my entire life. There are crystal chandeliers, mirrors lacking child size fingerprints, tufted suede white couches and free champagne. Well, champagne for me, and sparkling water for Fawn.

We're in a private—yes, *private*—fitting room with a few curtained cubicles for changing, and a central area with the white couch—thank goodness they gave me champagne and not red wine—and mirrors like the inside of a ballerina's music box. Everything is sparkly and white and gold and expensive as shit. I nearly had a heart attack when I looked at one of the price tags. After my adamant insistence to leave and go somewhere cheaper, Fawn made sure the sales associate removed any price tags before bringing them to us to try on.

I've had about as much luck as Fawn picking a gown for the Gala. Not because they don't fit, well other than needing massive hemming, but because all the ones in pink are hideous, and I dislike any of the other colors she's brought me.

Turning my attention back to my pregnant, and almost bawling friend, I call the sales associate woman over. "Would you happen to have something made with a stretchier material?"

"We may have something. I'll pick a few more items and bring them to you."

"Thank you."

While I wait for the associate to bring more choices, I slip into one of the dresses I have hanging in my changing room. It's silver and sparkles from head to toe with thin spaghetti straps and a slit almost to my coochie.

Standing on the raised platform in the semi-circle of mirrors I feel a little like a disco ball, shining and reflecting light in every direction. The dress fits like a second skin and shows off all my curves.

"You look gorgeous." Fawn sighs dreamily and with a little jealousy at me in the mirror. "I love being pregnant, and being able to eat whatever I want, but I can't wait till I can wear normal clothes again."

I say nothing. I don't want to make her cry again. Watching my silver shining reflection in the mirror, I try to picture entering the Gala in this dress, and what Henry would think of it. With the amount of skin showing, I have a feeling I would be getting a lot of unwanted attention in addition to the one whose attention I desire. I want to look beautiful and cause Henry to stumble, not slutty with the perceived title of paid escort.

"I think this one's a little too much."

"Or too little." We both snicker at the flimsy dress.

After I remove the sultry silver number, I return to the couch in the center, wearing a matching robe to Fawn's and sip some more champagne, wary that we're going to find anything in this store.

Before I completely give up hope, the sales associate in her all-black ensemble appears with a rolling rack and at least a dozen more options.

"I found a few more pieces I think might be suitable." Pulling a deep purple satin gown from the rack, she holds it up for Fawn's inspection. "I believe this one might have the proper amount of stretch, Mrs. Ashwood."

Fawn tentatively takes the gown and inspects it, pulling at its sides to test its elasticity. To her surprise, it pulls farther than either of us expected. A spark of bright hope reignites in her at the possibility that it might fit.

"I also found a few more pink pieces in the back that are new and hadn't been put on the floor yet for you, Miss Hart."

There, on the rack, hangs three more pink gowns, and from here, they don't look as horrible as the previous choices. Fawn isn't the only hopeful one with these new dresses. Fingering through the rack, I try to get a better look at my new pink options. One is a deep magenta with embroidery accenting a corseted bodice. Another is Barbie pink with puffy peasant style sleeves and a short hem. The third option is a pale pink closest in hue to my pastel hair, strapless and fitted throughout, with a slight flare at the bottom into a mermaid skirt.

Choosing the simplest one, to my disbelief, I take it to the changing room and emerge a minute later, zipped into a dress that feels perfectly tailored to my body. The hem still drags on the ground, but just enough that if I pair it with a decent height heel, it would barely dust along the floor. Returning to my previous position on the mirrored pedestal, I'm shocked by what I see.

Elegant long lines stretch from neck to floor with absolutely no adornments or sparkle. The material is smooth with no shine, and yet stands out in its pink allure, hugging my breasts and ass, creating the perfect silhouetted outline of my body.

Now this is a traffic stopping kind of dress.

"It's perfect," I whisper to no one in particular.

"This is the one. And don't you dare try to ask the price. This is the one you're getting. No arguments." I couldn't argue with her, even if I wanted to, because there are no words in my brain, and my vocal cords have forgotten how to function.

Fawn comes to stand at my side, watching me in the mirror. Her tears are gone, and the deep purple gown is now on her instead of the hanger. It takes me a moment to notice she was able to get the dress on without my help, and it also seems to fit perfectly. "Fawn, you look beautiful. I told you we would find one for you."

Stepping down, I let Fawn take my place to better see her pick.

She's radiant in all her pregnant, glowing beauty. The dress is fitted through the torso, stretching around her full breasts and rounded belly, then flaring out just below her hips, swishing around her ankles. Just short enough that she can wear flats and not trip on it. Delicate beadwork lines the scoop neckline and small cap sleeves, catching the light when she shifts. It's a shame Leo won't be at the Gala to see her like this. I'm sure he'll enjoy her and her gown when she gets home afterward though. No man in love as much as Leo is, would be able to refuse Fawn in this dress.

"I suppose you were right," she admits with a small smile.

"I'm always right. I don't know why you don't believe me."

"Yeah, yeah, yeah. Alright let's get this off me, and get these dresses bagged up before my belly grows anymore and rips it open." Her smile is far lighter than before, and her small laugh is music to my ears.

Fawn turns, and I help her step down the two steps from the platform with a hand on her arm.

"Ok, now we need to find shoes."

"Shoes?" I ask. She never mentioned anything about shoes. I figured I would just use a pair I already own.

"Yes, shoes. My feet have ballooned to the size of Clydesdale hooves. None of my regular choices will work. Especially since they all have heels, and I'm going to need flats for this."

"Oh, Ok. Makes sense."

Fawn waddles over to the dressing room, and just before she closes the curtain, she turns to call back over her shoulder. "Oh, and a new pair for you too. You didn't think I was going to let you get away with wearing some old worn-out things with that dress, did you? If we're going to knock some sense into my dense brother, we're going to do it right."

Then, she closes the curtain before I can protest. She has a point. Not that I think Henry is going to pay any attention to my footwear, but completing the look would be nice. Since I know there's no way I'm going to win an argument against an attorney, I just yell back at her, "Fine, but nothing over a hundred dollars."

We spend more than a hundred dollars.

Since it's Saturday, once I'm done shopping with Fawn, Henry meets me at my place. Just like we have for the last three Saturdays. Only, this is the first time I've seen him since Tuesday, since he was busy on our customary Thursday night get together. Going to an art gallery show without me. Then, according to Fawn, he went out with Samson to some club. Where he did who the fuck knows what. Danced, drank, groped, kissed, fucked. The possibilities are endless. I'm ashamed to say I got extremely jealous and somewhat angry when I heard he'd gone out. Which, of course, is ridiculous because he's not my boyfriend.

It still felt like a bee sting to my heart. *God damnit!* Why did I have to put myself in this position? I just had to have a little self-control. That's all I needed. Will power to say no. To *not* kiss Henry. Too late for that now, I suppose.

I am so confused. Fawn and the girls tell me he looks at me like more than a casual fling, but then he keeps me at arm's length. Except when we're boning, because if he could, that would mean he has the longest schlong in all of history, and I would cower before it.

Fawn says he just needs a little convincing to realize how good we are together. For someone who hasn't been in a relationship outside the bedroom for the last decade, it may take more than a *little* convincing.

When Henry arrives, I try to be chill and act as if he didn't ditch me on Thursday to party at a club. I'm not sure if I should show how hurt I feel or pretend nothing happened.

I don't get a choice. As soon as he closes the door behind him, he pounces on me, locking his lips to mine in a kiss that requires no explanation, leaving me gasping, trying to catch my breath. Because he knocked it right out of me. I latch onto him, and he takes me directly to my bed, strips me down and fucks me in a fevered frenzy. I haven't seen him like this since we started this whole casual fucking thing. As if he can't get me naked and inside me fast enough. As if I might disappear at any moment.

The sex is bus rocking good, and I don't even care if Paloma and Pilar can hear my screams of ecstasy next door. Henry is ravenous, and there's no stopping him once he starts.

We lay naked, and still slightly sweaty, in my bed after he melts my world with his outrageous fucking.

"You're awfully quiet tonight." he comments, his fingers combing through my tangled pink locks as I try to regain my ability to move while lying on his bare chest.

"Hmm. Am I?"

"Well, beyond the screaming orgasms, yeah. Usually, you're talking my ear off about what happened at Wheelies this week, how many boba's you sold at the market, or something absurd my sister said."

"Oh." I hadn't realized he actually listened when I rambled on about my day and conversations me and Fawn had.

"Is there something wrong? Did something happen today with Fawn?" He raises his head off my pillow and looks down at me with concern etched in his features. A flutter spins through my stomach at his attentiveness.

"No, nothing happened today. I just don't feel very talkative is all."

His brow furrows in adorable skepticism. There's rarely been a day when I didn't feel like talking. Now that there's quiet silence between us, I don't know what to say. It was so much easier to talk to him before my emotions got involved, when this was nothing but good old fashioned naked time fun. With my heart pounding and becoming jealous of imaginary girls at bars, it's become less simple.

Laying here naked and damp, staring up into his soft jade eyes that look at me with such openness, I decide I don't want simple. I want messy and tangled and intertwined. I want the right to be angry and jealous if he goes out without me. And I'm tired of denying it and worrying about what could happen if he doesn't feel the same. Because it's obvious he feels something. More than what he admits with his words.

Pressed against him, I shift higher, so I can reach his lips with mine. Kissing him gently, I seal my promise to myself that I will no longer fear us. I will not run from him like I have all the others. If he'll have me, I'll stay. I'll make no plans to go to Montana, or anywhere else. I'll make Pittsburgh my home. For once in all these years the weight lifts from my shoulders, the ever-present compression of the expected gone.

Henry is not what I expected when I moved here almost five months ago. I was not looking for him, and he wasn't looking for me, yet somehow, we still found each other. Two magnets pulled together against our will, opposites in all manners. None of that matters now. All that matters is how my heart thuds beneath my breastbone, fiercely approving of my choice.

Henry's eyes flutter open when I pull away, his breathing rough.

"What was that for?"

"Everything."

"Everything?" I nod and he grins, shaking his head side to side, chuckling softly at me. "Sometimes I do not understand you. Shortcake."

"You're not meant to. If all men understood women, what fun would that be?" Cuddling in closer to him, I tuck my chin into his chest and nestle against his neck. He rests his chin atop my head, and I can feel him release a deep breath, relaxing into our embrace.

He may not know it yet, but he too wants this. Wants us. I can feel it in the way he holds me, the way he kisses me, and mostly in the way he smiles at me.

"Oh... um... there's something I need to tell you." His tone is despondent, but I don't let it affect the warm glow sitting in my chest. I make a light questioning noise, signaling for him to continue.

"Well, there's this event next weekend. A Charity Gala actually. Most of my family goes to it every year. Even my parents. Even if they sit at a different table than Fawn and me. But I wanted to tell you because I'm going, but I don't have a plus one ticket. If I did, I would ask you to go with me. I even tried to buy one last week, but they were sold out."

He tried to buy a ticket so he could bring me? My heart leaps into my throat, but I act calm, cool, and not at all super stoked that he wants to take me as his date to a Gala. This is a big step for him. Even if it's just admitting he wants to take me. When we first met, he said he doesn't do dates. By my count, we've been on at least a dozen if you count all the dinners we've gone out to eat.

"Oh?" is about all that I can manage without squealing like a little girl and spilling my secret about taking Leo's place at the Gala. Both Fawn and I decided it would be way more fun to surprise Henry and see the look on his face.

"Yeah," he says, his fingers fiddling anxiously on my back where his hand rests. "I just wanted you to know that if I could take you, I would, but I can't. No matter how much money I offered to donate." He grumbles the last bit, and I can hear the displeasure in his voice at being unable to procure me a ticket.

"That's real sweet of you, Henry." Leaning up so I can look him in the eye, I rest my chin on his chest. "If you did ask me to go, I would absolutely say yes."

He sighs in relief. "So, you're not upset?"

"How can I be upset about something that can't be controlled? What's important is that you tried." I want to add that there will be a next time, and he can ask me then, but again, I don't want to scare him off with too much future relationship type talk. Plus, he's going to get a great surprise when he sees me walking into the Gala with Fawn in that pink dress.

31 - Lala

You look like a cotton candy wet dream that I don't want to wake up from

There is more makeup on my face right now than there has been in the past twenty years combined. I don't mind it though, because the makeup artist Fawn hired—another expense I'll have to someday figure out how to pay her back for—has made me look like a cover model. With smokey pink eyes, complete with glitter, soft rosy cheeks, and bright pink lips to set off all the soft tones, I look like Persephone in springtime according to Lore Olympus. All I need is pink skin, which I'm pretty close to naturally anyway, so I count that too.

Fawn tried to convince me to wear my hair up to show off my shoulders and negligée, but I dismissed the idea, instead styling my hair in big soft waves that fall and crest over my shoulders like pink cotton candy. Henry likes to play with my hair, and I want to entice him to reach out and touch me. Also, it's far more comfortable wearing it down than up. Bobby pins are my personal form of hell.

I wear a simple white gold chain with a teardrop pink gemstone, and a matching bracelet, with small pink stud earrings. My hair covers my ears most of the time anyway, so why bother with anything more. My phone vibrates on the counter of Fawn's gigantic master bathroom where we're putting on our finishing touches.

> **Mr. Grumpasaurus:** *I'm leaving for the Gala now. If I can manage it, I'll leave right after dinner. I could be at your place around say, ten? Would that be Ok?*

I giggle to myself as I type out a response. Keeping this from him all week has been the best. Whenever he brought it up, he suggested not going and staying in with me instead. I, of course, had to convince him it was totally fine, and he should go. After all, I couldn't let his sweetness get in the way of my surprise.

> **Lala:** *That sounds great. Text me when you're on your way.*
> **Mr. Grumpasaurus:** *I may text sooner. These things tend to be tedious and boring.*
> **Lala:** *You can text me all you like.*

He doesn't text again till we're in the town car heading for the Gala.

> **Mr. Grumpasaurus:** *What are you wearing?*

I can't very well tell him what I'm really wearing. That would create too many questions. Instead, I let my dirty mind answer for me.

> **Lala:** *A vibrator and a smile.*
> **Mr. Grumpasaurus:** *Not fair.*
> **Lala:** *I think it is since I don't get to go to the Gala.*
> **Mr. Grumpasaurus:** *I told you I would have stayed in with you instead.*
> **Lala:** *And I told you it would be wrong to back out of your promise to attend.*

Mr. Grumpasaurus: *Then help make it better.*
Lala: *How?*
Mr. Grumpasaurus: *Tell me how you're touching yourself.*
Then send pictures.

Well, holy shit. My panties are getting damp reading his texts, and I squirm in my seat next to Fawn, angling my phone away so she can't see me sexting with her brother.

Lala: *I think you'll just have to wait till later.*
Mr. Grumpasaurus: *I can't, my dick is so hard now I'm going to have to go to the men's room and jerk off just to get through the night.*
Lala: *Send photos, I'll use them to get myself off thinking of you.*

Another minute passes without a text, then a picture comes through. It's from his point of view looking down at his rock-hard cock jutting out of his undone pants, his hand wrapped around the base, squeezing. It's obvious by the background that he's in a bathroom stall. I can't believe he's actually jerking off in a public restroom because he was thinking about me touching myself.

I quickly minimize the photo and put my phone in my clutch. If I keep looking at it, this is going to be a really awkward car ride. Even without looking at it, I think about what he's doing right now. That only makes me wetter. Fuck.

We arrive at the Gala ten minutes later. There's a red carpet rolled out to walk into the event, and a few paparazzi linger near the door. Fawn told me a lot of the top socialites in the city attend this Gala, and they're here for them. A few turn to inspect us to ascertain if we're anyone important. Some take a few quick snaps, but Fawn doesn't slow down or stop, so I follow along at her side, keeping my stride steady. If they don't know who we are, they'll learn real quick I am nobody, and they're not going to get any use out of those pictures.

"Ok, Henry said he's by the bar, and I should meet him there," Fawn informs me as we enter the grand room.

There are tables scattered throughout the massive space, surrounding a shiny white dance floor that already has a few couples moving around it. A stage is set up with a full band that plays covers of oldies songs that I appreciate. Along the right wall of the room, tables are set up with displays of varying items next to clipboards that people are writing on. Some sort of silent auction by the looks of it. To the left, we find the massive white bar with glowing color changing LED lights all along the underside of the bar top.

There are hundreds of people here, and we don't spot Henry right away. We're almost all the way to the bar before I spot him leaning on one elbow, glass in hand filled with clear liquid. It stops halfway to his mouth as his gaze makes its way over the crowd and snags on me.

My spine straightens and my chin lifts along with the corners of my pink painted lips as he watches stone still, except for his rapidly blinking eyes.

Henry looks as handsome as he ever does in a suit. Only this time, it's not a suit. It's a tux. And he looks exquisite. No more gray, but all black, crisp ebony so dark I can almost see the stars trying to shine through it. His shirt is the polar opposite of the purest white. One the presence of all color, the other the absence of all color. The bowtie at his neck is perfectly tied, and the urge to pull at the tail and undo him is so great, I have to consciously hold my hand still at my side.

"I see he's spotted you," Fawn giggles in my ear. "I'll leave you to it then." She winks at me and gracefully shuffles away, cradling her belly, making sure no one elbows her as she passes.

Henry slowly sets down his glass, almost as if he's completely forgotten it's in his hand. His eyes are half hooded now as those apple greens lazily crawl over every inch of me, starting at the top, working their way down and then up again. As he does, I begin my calculated saunter towards him, swaying my hips just a little bit more than what's natural, angling my chin down to look up at him through my lashes. Enticing him to come closer, but he's frozen. Dumb struck in place.

I feel like the goddess Persephone taking Hades down to his knees before her. I could really get used to this.

My approach to Henry is abruptly cut off, and I almost stumble into the man who's interrupted my goddess moment.

He looks to be around forty with a few gray hairs around his temples, with dark blonde hair, and blue eyes that are sharp and focused directly on me... and my cleavage. His smile is slimy, and I have a feeling he does this a lot to women far younger than him.

"Hi there. Can I buy you a drink?"

"No," Henry booms from behind the man before I can even open my mouth to reject him. "She's with me."

"Is that so? I don't see your name on her." Wow, this guy is a douche.

"That's because she'd have to walk around, flashing her ass to show everyone. And I don't like to share."

The obviously wealthy, but unsophisticated man scoffs. I ignore him and round to Henry's side, pressing my breasts up against his side and slipping on arm around his shoulder. In response, he places a possessive hand on my back so close to my ass that a millimeter more and he would just be out right groping me. The man gets the message and turns on his heel in search of another poor girl to horrify.

I turn, smiling to face Henry and laugh at the ridiculousness of some people, but he's not smiling. He is completely serious and dead focused on me. His hand tightens around me, bringing me so close I feel like I'm practically riding his thigh. I don't mind it at all. I bite the corner of my lip the longer he stares at me.

Running the back of his knuckles along my jaw, he fingers a curl of pink hair and follows it down to where it rests on the swell of my breast. Which is being held up and offered like a present to this man. His fingers brush against the sensitive skin across the top and he licks his lips.

"You look like a pink cotton candy wet dream that I don't want to wake up from."

I giggle like a schoolgirl with a crush. "Oh, Henry Bardot, you say the sweetest things."

Because I can and I want to, my hand not wrapped around his shoulders slides up the front of his dress shirt, and I playfully finger his bowtie. I want to untie it, but I'll wait till later.

"What are you doing here?"

"Leo couldn't make it, so Fawn asked me to come instead. We thought it would be a fun surprise for you."

"It was a surprise alright."

"I can see that. Your face when you first saw me will be etched into my brain forever. As will that photo you sent me earlier." I may rub myself against him a little harder to feel the friction it causes. That picture left me wet and horny.

"Uuuhhh," he groans between his teeth, turning his body to press front to front with mine. "I literally just jerked off not ten minutes ago in the bathroom, and already you've got me hard again."

To emphasize his point, he gently grinds his pelvis against mine, his hardening erection obvious against my lower stomach. With these heels on, his dick is far closer to my happy zone now, and it's torturous. At least he got to relieve some of his arousal. I'm still wound up and only getting tighter.

"Dance with me." It's not a question or a command, just a statement. He knows I will say yes, so there's no need.

Henry leads me to the dance floor as the music changes to something slow with measured beats that allow for a soft sway and close embrace. He keeps one hand on my hip, and the other holds my hand close to this chest. We don't speak as the music guides us, stepping in some patterned moves that I don't comprehend, but Henry seems to know by heart. Using the beat of the music to time our movement, we circle the dance floor twice like this. Silent and lost in the music.

Pulling me close, Henry nips at my ear. "Would you like me to ease that ache between your thighs? I imagine since you weren't pleasuring yourself earlier, you must be aching for my touch."

My traitorous pussy clenches in response. It would like that very much, as would I. "Yes, please."

"Good girl." His deep tenor rumbles through my veins, making my nipples harden beneath my dress. I have no idea what he has planned, but I will agree to anything if it involves any part of him between my legs.

Henry leads me by the hand off the dance floor, through the crowd, and down a side hall.

"Where are we going Henry?" Pulling me to a stop, Henry places one finger over my lips, silencing me.

"If you're a good girl and keep quiet, you'll find out."

Well, hello, Zaddy Henry, welcome to the party.

Before he can pull his finger away, I open my mouth and draw it in, sliding my lips to the base and sucking. He groans in appreciation, and I want to make him do it again, but I can't. Because he pulls his finger from my mouth and replaces it with his tongue.

Devouring me with his lips, his tongue plays with me in the way he knows drives me mad. Now I'm the one groaning. He swallows the sound eagerly, fingers doing just as I hoped, burying themselves in my loose hair as he holds my face still so he can do with me as he pleases. When he pulls away, my pale pink lipstick has stained his swollen lips.

"Naughty girl. For that you shall be punished."

"Please punish me, Zaddy."

"I have no idea what a Zaddy is, but if it has anything to do with me pounding into you, I will gladly fulfill that role."

Without allowing me to say another word, Henry pulls me by the hand through a door labeled "Employee's Only". Obviously not giving a rat's ass about not being an employee, we step through and enter what appears to be a linen storage and washing space. There are a few washers and dryers against the wall, and shelf upon shelf of white linens.

Henry locks the deadbolt behind us and promptly seals his lips to mine, pushing me up against a table filled with unfolded towels.

"I want to see if you taste as sweet as you look, Shortcake."

"By all means, taste away," I encourage.

Kneeling on one knee at my feet, Henry slowly curls the edge of my hem in his hands, placing them on my shins as soon as he gets underneath, sliding hot palms up my legs till he reaches the apex of my thighs. His fingers brush across the damp center of my panties, and I whimper. I need a hell of a lot more than a brushing tease.

"Oh, Shortcake, what a naughty girl entering the Gala so wet for me. Is this where you need me?" With barely any pressure, he presses a kiss to my pussy through my dress. It's just hard enough for me to feel it, but not enough to satisfy and I whimper again.

"Yes."

"Are you going to ask nicely?"

"No."

"No?"

"I don't beg for sex. I demand it."

"And I obey."

Done with the chit chat, Henry slips his head under my dress and pulls my panties to the side running his tongue from my entrance up to my clit and sucks. I almost come with that alone, he has me so tightly wound.

"Again," I demand. And he obeys.

Henry eats my pussy with a feverish hunger that has me digging my nails into the wood of the table I cling to. If it weren't for his strong hands banded around my thighs, I may have fallen over long ago. And because Henry is the master at tasting my pussy, he hitches one of my legs over his shoulder, opening me up farther for him. His tongue slides inside me, fucking me as if it were his cock.

Thank fuck for the sounds of the washing machine to drown out my moans and muffled screams. When I come, I nearly fold in half over Henry, gripping his head through the pink material of my dress.

"Holy fucking, Zaddy." I can barely breath as I shake and try to regain my composure. "We are going to have to do that again."

"Mmm," Henry hums as he licks up my orgasm before removing himself from under my skirt.

"So, what's the verdict? Do I taste as sweet as I look?"

"Even sweeter." He emphasizes by licking his lips before placing a soft kiss to my lips. I don't know that I would call my taste sweet, but if he thinks so, I'm not going to correct him.

"We should probably get back before Fawn comes looking for us," I say once I have enough equilibrium to stand without swaying. Henry wraps arms around me, holding me between him and the table. His bowtie is not even one millimeter out of place after eating me out in a laundry room.

"Do we have to?"

"Yes. I've never been to a Gala, and I would like to know what all the fuss is about. Plus, I was told there would be food, and I'm starving."

I can feel his chuckle rumble through his chest, and the accompanying smile is wide and beautiful. I love that he smiles more now. He was handsome before, but when he smiles, he's breathtaking.

"Very well my pink princess. Your Zaddy shall fulfill your every need. Whatever a Zaddy is."

"You are when you call me a good girl." I give him a little wink and grope his still hard dick through his slacks. "And what are we going to do about this?" I ask.

"That will wait till later because I want to take my time with you. Peeling every single stitch of pink off you and licking the skin beneath."

I shudder uncontrollably. "Ok."

He chuckles again before unlocking the door and guiding me back out to the main floor to find Fawn and our table.

32 - Lala

Well, that clears things up perfectly

alas are awesome. Just saying. There's live music and dancing, an open bar, all the food I could eat, and good company. If I were a rich hoity toity person like most of those in attendance tonight, I would totally go to these things all the time. I see now why people like them. Dressing to the nines and feeling like royalty is *the best.*

I eat far too much and indulge in one of their signature drinks for the night called the Pop Quiz. Everything is themed to education and schooling since this is a fundraiser for public school teachers. The straws look like number two pencils, and some of the drinks are even served in glasses the shape of tiny milk cartons. They put a lot of effort and thought into the ambiance, and I love it.

Henry, Fawn, and I peruse the silent auction tables, where there are items ranging from footballs signed by some of the Steelers, to spa weekends and archery lessons. Fawn takes a particular interest in the mommy and me basket of goodies. Henry doesn't seem particularly interested in any of it. I suppose, if he wanted any of these things, he has the money to buy them outright. Me, on the other hand, I can't afford any of it. Not even in a silent auction. I'm pretty sure most of the bids are higher than the actual cost of the item. It is a fundraiser after all.

The one thing I do linger at, even though I know I can't bid, is a custom perfume. I'm not the biggest fan of overly strong and pungent perfumes, or things that smell like fruits and vegetables. I would love to design a scent that's soft and light with hints of floral and sugar. Not sure that would smell very good, but you never know till you try.

I'm pretty sure I saw Henry bid on both the custom perfume and the mommy and me basket after Fawn and I had expressed our interest and walked away. It's super sweet of him not only to bid on something for his sister, but for me as well. If he weren't filthy rich, I would probably care more. But if he wants to buy me things, I'm not going to stop him.

It's almost ten by the time we run into Henry's parents. Separately of course, since I now know they rarely speak to one another. First, it's his mother, Lucielle Cartwright. She's not as tall as her children, but her hair, makeup, dress, and everything else is perfectly paired and applied with precision. Not a mahogany-colored hair out of place. Not a single gray marring her lush locks. I can't decide if she dyes it or is just lucky like that. Her posture is hard, and even though her hands rest loosely together in front of her, I can tell every muscle is taut and ready to strike if need be. She kind of reminds me of Henry when I first met him. That stick up his butt must have been hereditary, because his mother has a matching one.

Her nose is sharp to match her green eyes, which take me in with little actual interest, but she's polite. At least as polite as is required in public. She doesn't gush over Fawn and her pregnancy, only politely inquiring as to the gender and how far along she is. Making sure both are healthy, and that's about it.

Sheesh. Henry was not joking when he said they were not the family type. It's a wonder their children have any sort of emotional balance at all. I suppose that could be thanks to their nannies.

We only speak with Ms. Cartwright, as she asked me to call her—no casual Lucielle here. I'm not important enough for that— for about ten minutes before she excuses herself and waves to greet someone else.

Not long after I'm introduced to his father. A tall man with a head of salt and pepper hair and a wide smile. Although he's smiling, I feel there's just as much distaste behind the civility as with their mother. They both disapprove of me and that... kind of sucks. Even knowing they aren't close, every girl wants to be accepted by the family and parents of the person she's seeing. Fawn, Leo, and Samson like me though, and that's what matters.

Malcom Bardot turns out to be quite a ladies' man. He winks and flirts with servers, and the date he has draped on his arm looks younger than me. *Gross.* She's blonde and perky, and looks a little bit dumb. Or incredibly clever, depending on your point of view. Malcom is a wealthy man who isn't completely unfortunate looking at his age. She could be using him as much as he is her. If that's the case, more power to ya, honey. She remains silent and uninterested in our conversation.

Malcom is far more entertaining to speak with than uptight Lucielle, but only as long as it takes him to start discussing some of the "tactics" he uses to close a deal with female clients. And on that note...

"I have to use the restroom," I announce, not really interested in partaking in this particular conversation. Henry gives me an apologetic look and tight smile, knowing exactly why I feel the need to relieve myself at this very moment.

"So do I. Pregnancy bladder and all." Fawn shrugs and holds her belly as we turn and briskly walk towards the restrooms.

When we're far enough out of ear shot, Fawn sighs and turns to me as we continue walking. "I am so sorry about him. He's kind of a lecher. Not much we can do about it since the girls are of age and willing."

"Yeah, doesn't look by much though. Pretty sure his date isn't old enough to drink."

"You're probably right. Younger women were always father's favorite. It's what ultimately led to the divorce."

We find the restroom and Fawn does pee, while I check my hair and makeup in the mirror before washing my hands and reluctantly returning to the Gala. If we stay away too long, poor Henry will not be happy, and he's already grumpy enough as it is. I want him smiling and playful when we leave tonight. Because I will be leaving with him, even if I arrived with Fawn.

"I'm going to go back to the table and sit for a while. All this walking has my feet barking."

"Ok, I'll go find Henry and try to save him from his father."

Fawn and I part, and I slowly make my way back to the bar area where I left Henry and his father. When I spot them, Malcom's date is nowhere to be seen. Both men are sipping from plain glass tumblers, their backs to the crowd behind them. Henry is wearing a blank expression, and I'm not really sure I want to rejoin them just yet. Whatever conversation they're having, it does not look like an opportune time for me to interject. It may be a welcome interruption for Henry, but his father looks less than inclined to agree.

I know I said it didn't matter what his father thought of me, but it does. And interrupting a private serious conversation, by the looks of it, will not help to bolster me in his eyes.

Instead, I quietly slink behind an inflated crayon a few feet from where they stand, just out of their line of sight. I order water from the bartender as I don't want to be sloppy drunk tonight when I ravage Henry in the car on the way home. From my hidden vantage point, I can just hear their conversation over the low buzz of people and music in the hall.

"So, what's going on with this girl? You never bring dates to these kinds of things," Malcom asks.

"Nothing is going on Dad. She's just my date."

"Doesn't appear to be just a date. If she was, you wouldn't have bothered introducing her. Plus, she looks close with Fawn." Malcom pauses for a moment, probably sipping his drink, and I hope he chokes on it. Sadly, he doesn't. "You know how a pretty face and good pussy can distract a man from his work. Don't let her pull you in like your mother did me. Get your fill of her and drop her. She'll only be an issue the longer you string her along."

I want to gouge out his eyes. But I stand still, gripping my glass. There's no way Henry will allow him to speak like that about me. So, I wait to bask in the fury that is pissed off and protective Henry. When he does speak, my blood runs cold, not only at the tone of his voice, flat and bored, but at his words.

"Don't get yourself all worked up. We're fuck buddies and nothing more. She doesn't even live here permanently. She moves from city to city, never staying more than a year. There's no concern to be had with her overstaying her welcome. If anything, she'll move on of her own accord. Probably in the next six months."

What the fuck is he saying? It's partially true. I do move around a lot, but I have never once said I would be leaving. Is this how he thinks of me? As just a temporary plaything? Here for the time being but gone before it gets serious. I thought we had something between us. I thought we were moving past fuck buddies into something more. He just had his face between my legs not two hours ago telling me how I tasted.

But I suppose that's all he wants from me.

Sex.

A hole to stick it in. A *pretty face and good pussy* to pass the time.

Hot tears well in my eyes, and I try to hold them in, tilting my head back and blinking furiously. One still manages to escape, and I quickly swipe at it before it can leave a trail down my cheek. Evidence of my stupid heart thinking Henry cared for me as much as I him.

Just when I had decided to let go of my fears and allow him to possess every inch of my heart, he has to go and turn back into his callous unfeeling self. I had hoped was a front, but apparently it holds more weight than I gave it credit.

"Good. It doesn't matter how great she fucks. No woman is worth it in the end. Remember that."

"Right," Henry agrees and another piece of my heart shatters.

I was so fucking stupid. Stupid, stupid girl with her stupid feeling heart and naivety. I can hear that infuriating dark voice inside my head snickering and saying, "I told you so." I can't take it anymore. I can't hear whatever else it is they are going to say about me. I need to leave. I have to get out of here.

The space is too small, and I feel like I'm being suffocated by all the bodies and smiling faces. I don't think. I just go. Taking strides so large I'm nearly running. Pushing my way through the crowd, I bump and shove people out of my way when I can't get past fast enough.

I think I hear my name being called behind me, but I can't be sure. The rushing blood in my ears is too loud to hear much of anything. More tears want to fall, but I don't let them. I suck them in and bite my lip to keep from sobbing out loud.

I just need to get out into the fresh air. Free of gowns and tuxes, and the intoxicating smell of Henry's cologne that still lingers on my dress. If I wouldn't be standing here naked in my underwear, I would tear it off just to separate myself from the smell.

"Micaela!" comes my name again in a deep masculine voice.

Henry.

Shit.

I manage to muscle my way through the ballroom door and out into the cool night air. My lungs suck in large gulps of cold air, but my legs don't stop moving. Out in the open, Henry catches up with me easily since he's not wearing four-inch stilettos.

"Micaela, wait." His hand grabs my elbow and forces me to stop, spinning me to face him. "What is going on? Where are you going?"

"What am I to you Henry?" I spit out the words before I lose the nerve to confront him. Or perhaps before I barf all over his far too sexy tux.

"What... what do you mean?"

"What am I to you? What is this?" I gesture wildly between us.

"This..." His words are choked off like he's not sure if he should speak them or not. After a moment, he does though. "This is what it is."

"Well, that clears things up perfectly," I bite out, letting my anger take over. A sob catches in my throat. "And what would that be, pray tell?"

"Sex," he says plainly. Like it's that obvious.

"Just sex?"

"I thought you understood what this was? I told you a relationship isn't possible. It never was and it never will be." He says this with a determined finality that creases his brow. He does not have the right to be angry in this situation. I am the one who was used and cast aside like old dirty underwear. "If you can't accept that then..."

His words trail off, insinuating but not spelling it out, just like the coward he is.

"If you were any other man, Henry Bardot, but you're not. It may have started casual, but I can't only have a part of you. It won't be enough." The words are as much of an admission of my love for him as I can muster through my choked back tears. I can't use the actual words. To not hear him reciprocate would crush me and the tiny shard that remains of my heart.

"I can't give you all of me." The words appear to pain him to say, but he does say them.

"Then you can't have any of me."

A heart-rendering silence falls between us. The stubborn tears I attempted to hold at bay begin to fall from my eyes, and I won't let him see me fall to pieces for him. I won't give him the satisfaction of watching me crumble under his scrutiny. He doesn't deserve my tears, but they don't know that and fall all the same, hot and acidic, burning tracks along my cheeks and jaw before dripping onto the most beautiful dress I've ever worn.

When he says nothing more, I turn and walk away.

Henry doesn't follow.

33 - Lala

Now I sit in the burning ashes of my own creation

I can't breathe. My lungs have decided to quit working, and I'm going to suffocate to death in the back of this Uber. Thank God I was carrying my clutch with me when I decided to run from the Gala like Cinder-fucking-ella. There was no way I was going to slink back in and steal it off our table while trying not to break down crying or be caught by Henry or Fawn.

Fawn. I should probably text her and make up some excuse. Violent diarrhea or something equally horrifying. Except the truth. That would be too much to admit to her right now. How fucking wrong I was about her asshole brother. How wrong she was. He didn't need time to accept us. He'd already come to his conclusion, and it appears nothing I do or say will change that.

Thankfully the driver is silent and understanding of my mental breakdown happening in his backseat. Like my mother, he has a box of tissues in the back seat, and I take full advantage, not giving two fucks that I'm ruining the beautiful makeup so artfully applied. It's no more than a Van Gogh painting at this point. Somewhat reminiscent of what was once a human face but is now just smears and swirls of paint. Blurred by ridiculous optimism.

My mind blinded to the truth I knew was there, my heart choosing to ignore it. All of that congealing into tonight, a hard awakening and eye-opening recognition of reality.

Henry doesn't love me. He never will.

I love Henry, and I shouldn't have allowed myself to. Because now I'm paying the price for it. I've become one of the many women he had warned me about. The ones who act like casual is easy and they're totally fine with it, just to eventually fall for the stupid asshat and get their heart crushed when he doesn't reciprocate.

How foolish of me to think I would be any different. To think I would be the one to change him. To open his eyes to see how wrong he was about swearing off relationships.

In the past, I was never concerned about being the one to get hurt in a relationship. I was the one pushing him away and keeping my distance. I was the one to end things and leave shattered dreams and unfinished business in my path. It never occurred to me that I could be the one left picking up the pieces that would never truly fit back together again. There was always an escape pod ready and waiting for me to jettison out of a relationship at any moment. Not this time.

With Henry, I allowed myself to settle in, to let the escape pod be ignored to the point of disuse. Incapable of launching or supporting life outside the burning ship. Now I sit in the burning ashes of my own creation, unable to stop the flames from consuming me whole.

So, I don't. I let them crawl over my skin and melt into my bones. This is what I deserve. What I *need* to remind me that there will never be a place for me. Whether it's due to my own inability to acclimate, or the fact that there is nowhere I fit. The jagged pieces of my puzzle have long lost their ability to click into place.

Maybe Pittsburgh doesn't have the answers. This is not going to be my forever home. No matter how much it was beginning to feel like such.

Perhaps once all my obligations are fulfilled, I will return to Montana. Seek refuge in the snowy mountains where there aren't any real estate moguls or Pilates classes or skate shops with roller derby nicknames.

Shit. The first time anyone at Wheelies calls me Shortcake, I'm going to have another mental breakdown I don't think I'll be able to handle. I'll just have to explain to Dollface and Carnage the situation and ask to just be called Lala. Henry never once called me Lala, so at least there's that. I'd have to change my name completely if he had. Hearing his voice in my mind growling out Micaela will already be ingrained in my memories for all eternity. It would be too much if it had been Lala instead.

The Uber stops at my Skoolie, and I exit just as silently as I entered, giving the poor driver a five-star rating just for putting up with my blubbering ass. Along with an additional tip that I probably can't afford, but what does it matter anyway? Upside to living in a Skoolie, you can never truly be homeless. There are plenty of places I can park without paying or being arrested.

Unlocking my home and stepping in, I don't even bother turning on a light as I remove the most beautiful gown ever made and hang it gingerly in my small closet, not wanting to ruin it, even though my night was ruined. Slipping into the largest and coziest sweats and sweatshirt I can find, I scoop up Fred from his cage and curl into my bed with him.

The place that was once my haven, my escape and retreat from the world, is now riddled with unwanted memories of Henry. His naked body in my bed, in my shower, sitting at my kitchen counter drinking coffee and eye balling Fred.

I should have never let him in here. I may have to burn everything and start over now.

I sigh, because I'm far too broke for that. And some of the things he touched are custom made and bolted to the floor.

Fuck. My. Life.

The first chance I get, I'm getting the hell out of Pittsburgh. Out of Pennsylvania.

There's nothing here for me anymore.

34 - Henry

Yup, definitely a heart attack

icaela just ran away from me. Ran from the Gala like it was on fire. Then she was crying and confronting me, and I had no god damn idea what to do or say. Watching the tears roll down her cheek was the most painful thing I've ever experienced. There was so much of me that wanted to reach out and wipe them away, pull her close and keep her there forever.

But I didn't... couldn't.

Something inside me wouldn't allow it. It gripped my insides with fear and pain remembering the gut-wrenching torment that occurred the last time I was emotionally intimate with a woman. She demanded submission, for me to give up on all that I was and worked for just for her. I tried to give her what she wanted and what she needed, but I lost myself in the process. We grew angry and bitter with one another, saying cruel things and doing even crueler ones. In the end, when I didn't give in, she did. When the stress became too much, and our worlds were about to implode, she cut our ties, and I felt a freedom so satisfying it's what led to my outlook on relationships ever since then.

Getting tangled deep in another's life isn't worth it. One always has to give, and when the bough breaks, we *all* fall. My one and only serious relationship caused riffs with my friends, my work, my mental stability, and my health. The reward for the price wasn't equal. I got less than I gave, and I didn't like my books being out of balance. So, I vowed to never let it happen again. Watching my parents, I should have known better. Unless I wanted a mail order bride to bear my seed, there was no need for marriage, or *love*.

Love makes you weak and brittle. I would not be weak again.

In this moment, staring at my fourth—or is it fifth?—scotch I've forced down my throat, however, I feel weak. Broken. Like I'm missing a vital piece. And I'm pretty sure it left with Micaela.

Shaking my head, I try to clear the thoughts that won't stop crowding in. Replaying the words I spoke to her. Telling her exactly what I was supposed to. The same thing I've told every woman since that first epic mistake. The words that usually made me feel better, that relieved me of guilt and responsibility. Shucking off the expectations and commitment. They didn't make me feel better this time. In fact, I think they had the opposite effect. Instead of the relief and calm it usually brings, I feel turmoil churning my gut. Or that could be the self-loathing for being a total and utter dick to Micaela. Yeah, that's probably it.

I don't know what to do now, other than ordering another scotch. I can't even feel the burn anymore as it slips down my throat and likely corrodes away my liver. I need it to numb away this horrid sensation that makes me feel like human fecal matter.

I did what needed to be done. I reminded her what we really are. That's good. Right? Yes.

"There you are." My sister's voice breaks through the mush in my brain and I turn to face her. She looks worried or constipated. Not sure, the scotch is starting to impact my vision, so it could be either.

"Here I am," I agree with a slight slur.

"What the hell is wrong with you? How many of those have you had?" Like a good sister, she's more concerned than angry at my drinking in excess. Probably because I haven't drunk myself into a stupor since I was twenty-four.

"Not enough," I answer bitterly, signaling the bartender for another. He doesn't look like he wants to give me one, but I pull a twenty out of my wallet and shove it in the tip jar and he obliges. Well, I think it was a twenty, could have been a fifty. *Whatever.*

"I don't have time for your indignant attitude right now. Where's Lala? I can't find her."

"Gone."

"Gone?"

"That's what I said." My scotch appears, and I sip this one. Things are starting to get spinny, and it's probably because of the booze.

"Why?" Fawn asks, completely uncaring that she's now standing at a forty-five-degree angle.

"Ask her. She's the one who ran out crying and yelling at me."

"What?! You made her cry?"

"Pfft. No." I pause and try to remember what she said and if it was me that made her cry. *Was is? Fuck.* "Well, maybe," I admit.

"Henry Bardot," Fawn screeches my name, slamming a hand over the rim of my glass, and I almost drop it. Thankfully, it and my hand land on the bar top held down by Fawn's stern grip.

"The fuck, Fawn."

"What did you say to her? What utter stupidity did you spew this time?"

"This time?"

"Yes. You know, like last time, when you told the blonde accountant she wasn't worth your time. Or when you told that lovely preschool teacher you could never marry her because her teeth were too big."

"They were like horse teeth. Could you imagine our children? No, thank you." Not my finest moment, but who the fuck cares at this point.

"My point is, you tell women cruel things that make them cry, and whatever the hell you told Lala, I'm sure she did not deserve it."

That we can agree on. Micaela is far too sweet and perfect to deserve anything I've said to her. She doesn't deserve my unwilling participation and blunt dismissal. She deserves a man who wants to eat spicy foreign foods and jump into surprise birthday ball pits. Not a grump like me who wants nothing to do with any of it. Which is why I don't deserve her. Which is why it's better this way. Stop it now before we get too deep. I fear I may have already.

"Well?" Oh right, Fawn, my beautifully pregnant sister is glowering at me like I'm Satan himself. Not completely wrong. She's so good. I don't know how she turned out so well adjusted.

I gurgle out a sigh and have to think really hard to remember words, rubbing at my temple, trying to ease the throb there. "Something about our relationship only being about sex and nothing more, I think."

"You think?" Now she's getting angry. I scrub a hand down my face, trying to wipe away some of the drunkenness and think straight enough to answer her.

"Yeah. I don't recall the exact words, per se. It wasn't a long conversation. As a matter of fact, it kind of came out of nowhere." I have no idea what led to her running from the Gala, or the subsequent confrontation. I barely had enough time to register her tears or her words to figure it out.

"Jesus Christ, Henry. You couldn't, for once, just not be an ass-hole, and maybe try to have feelings for someone other than your-self?" She's asking a question, but I get the feeling she doesn't real-ly want me to answer, so I don't.

Slipping my glass out from under her hand, I down the amber liquid before she can stop me.

"That's it, Henry. Let's go." She pulls at my arm, and I stand from the stool, instantly losing my balance and falling into the bar.

"Jesus, you're wasted."

"Mmhmm. Seems so." I try to stand straight again, slowly this time. Fawn reaches out to steady me by my elbow.

I don't see the people we pass, or remember getting in a car, but I'm in one. Fawn is sitting at my side, worrying her lip between her teeth as she looks down at her phone, probably trying to con-tact Micaela. My heart leaps at the prospect of hearing her voice and immediately drops when I realize she will have nothing sweet to say to me. There will be no sultry or teasing smile in her tone and only ugly words that are all true.

"You've really done it this time, Henry."

I don't ask her what she means. I know. I know what I've done. Leaning my head against the window, I let its cool bite sting the al-cohol induced heat from my skin. I think I hear Fawn talking again, and I'm not sure if it's to me, the driver, or if she managed to get Micaela on the phone. Doesn't matter.

Closing my eyes, I drift off to the smooth lulling noises of the tires on the road until I'm abruptly awoken by a hard smack on my shoulder. Opening my eyes, I see the front door to my building just outside the car.

"Get out. You can carry your own drunk stupid ass into your building."

Fawn is going to be mad at me for a long time because of this.

And I don't mean the drunken exit from the Gala. She could care less about our public image. Of the three of us, I think I'm the only stupid one to actually care about my appearance to others. To care what is said and written. Just like my fucking parents. I wish I was more like Samson, not caring about anything, and just diving head-first into life. Or like Fawn, who pours her entire soul into helping others without a care for herself.

But nope. I'm just me. Walking in the tainted bitter footsteps of my parents. Working in the same profession, caring more about my portfolio than my personal life. Growing my bank account to obscene digits, but with nothing to spend it on.

I liked spending it on Micaela... Lala... Shortcake. My sweet sugary pink Shortcake. Not mine anymore. I've thoroughly fucked that up.

Stumbling from the car, I manage to make it to my elevator, waving inelegantly at Jackson as I pass, returning his pleasant greeting with a grunt.

In my penthouse, I stare at the empty cold gray expanse. It's unwelcoming and dull, just like me. Except for that one piece of colorful art hanging on my wall. According to Micaela, it's the part of me I keep hidden from everyone, or some such nonsense. It hurts my head to think too much, and when I flip on the light, it burns my eyes and I turn it back off.

Stumbling through my home—no not home. This isn't a home, it's just a place I live. There's nothing homey or comforting about this place. And I never seemed to notice it before. Until Micaela made it so painfully obvious with her warm smiles and affectionate kisses.

Pain lances through my chest, and I must be having a heart attack. Yup, definitely a heart attack. Because to call the ache in my chest anything else would be admitting I miss her. Admitting she altered something I thought unchangeable.

Ignoring the possible heart attack, I unsteadily make my way to my bedroom and manage to strip off my tux before face planting on the bed in my underwear.

I just need sleep. When I wake up, I'll be back to normal, and nothing will have changed. I'll still be single and entirely against the concept of marriage and love. My chest won't hurt, and Micaela's tears won't make me feel like tearing down the world to get to her and make them stop.

I barely get off the couch all of Sunday. The pounding in my head and unease in my gut doesn't allow me to do much more than sip tea and slurp some brothy soup. I haven't had to deal with a hangover of this caliber in years, and my thirty-one-year-old body is not having it anymore.

By Monday, the lingering aftereffects of my scotch splurge on Saturday at the Gala have worn off, but the bleak feeling consuming me has not.

I don't smile or nod or even say good morning to the receptionist as I enter my office, ignoring all other attempts at civility with little less than a passing glance.

By lunch, it's apparent that news of my foul mood has spread through the office because when I make my way to the filing room, every person in my path steps out of my way as if I were a passing train about to run them over. In a way, I am. I have little to no patience for people today, and Thomas, my assistant, is no exception.

"Ok, what is going on with you today? You're acting like, well like you did before you met Lala."

"Excuse me?" The words come out on a growl. I don't want to hear her name. Even the ridiculously adorable nickname I refused to call her. In the beginning, I said it was because it sounded like I was talking to a kindergartener. Really, it's because it was far too familiar, too intimate to call her that. Lala suits her far more than Micaela. I've wanted to call her Lala for a while now but felt it would be weird after calling her Micaela for so long. I'd done it out of stubbornness. Now I regret missing my opportunity.

"You heard me. You're all grumpy and sour faced again."

"I'm not anything. This is how I always am."

"No, not when she's around."

Fucking hell. Is this how it's going to be now? People telling me what a better man I was with her around? Saying how much more I smiled and happier I was? Because if they think I don't know that, they're wrong. Of course, I know that. Which is why it was a good thing it ended. We were getting in too deep and I needed to end it.

Grinding my teeth so hard I'm amazed I don't chip a tooth, I white knuckle the arms of my chair, trying not to throw the stupid decorative blue paperweight I bought when I decided my office needed more color, at his annoying face.

"Well, get used to it because I doubt she'll be around anymore."

"What? You guys broke up? What did you do?"

"Why do you assume I did anything? Maybe it was her who ended it. And we can't break up because we were never dating," I tack on at the end, more for my sake than his.

"Because Lala is the sweetest, nicest, most wonderful girl you've ever gone out with, and there's no way she did this. This has your name written all over it."

"And how would you know that? You're my assistant, not my life coach. How about you do your job before you don't have one."

Thomas snaps his mouth shut, eyes pinching in hurt. I wouldn't ever fire him, but this conversation and every future conversation on this topic needs to end now before they start. Any talk of Lala and what I did to fuck it up doesn't need to be had in my office. And if I can avoid it, anywhere else.

"Fine, Sir. Sorry to be human and care about your feelings. It won't happen again."

"See that it doesn't."

Thomas leaves in a huff, and I return to my work, drowning myself in emails and offers and contracts. Silencing the growing discomfort left from Thomas's astute observation of my personality shift. For the rest of the day and the following ones, Thomas communicates through email and memos, avoiding speaking with me. He even stops bringing me my afternoon coffee. I let him keep his distance because I don't want to be around anyone anyway. I don't want anyone to see the cracks forming in the façade that is Henry Bardot.

I keep to myself and mortar over the cracks, sealing them as best I can with stubborn determination.

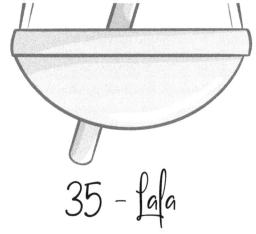

35 - Lala

Not sure if he's into pony play

Time is a snail on the driveway of my life. It literally passes by at a glacial pace, and I want to gouge my eyes out with a paperclip. Minutes feel like days, hours feel like months, and a week feels like a whole fucking year.

The past seven days have been utter torture in their unending eternity. I don't know what to do with myself anymore outside of work. Pilates with Fawn was… awkward, but eventually we got to a point of bearable solace. She knows everything about what happened at the Gala, and I know Henry drank himself into a stupor. Which made me feel miniuculy better, but only for a brief moment.

I've also received a few emails from Thomas, first consoling me on the "break up" that he agreed was completely Henry's fault. Secondly, sending me the final arrangements for the conference, which is in two weeks.

I suppose I should be happy it isn't any sooner. That gives me time to pull my shit together into some semblance of a functioning adult. My extra inventory and supplies have all arrived and are stacked neatly in the under-storage area of my bus. Five hundred fresh new Lala Boba cups, lids, pink straws, packages of napkins, business cards, bobas, and tea.

It's bittersweet now thinking of the conference and the income it's going to rake in. If I didn't need the money so badly, I would back out, not wanting to see or speak with Henry ever again. As it is, I'm too broke to cancel now, especially after buying all the supplies. I'll just have to bite the bullet, put on my big girl panties, and deal with it.

The fact that Henry hasn't even tried to reach out or contact me only makes it that much worse. The sting of his words turning into deep cuts that fester.

Fawn says she's been berating him every chance she gets, but that hasn't been many. Since she does have a full-time job, a pregnancy, and her own life to live. As well as the fact that he's apparently also dodging her as best he can. But she doesn't give up so easily. She wasn't the one hurt. I think her pregnancy hormones are amping up her anger and irritation because she's told me some of the things she's said to him, and they make me cringe.

It's only Saturday, but for some reason, my mom is calling now instead of tomorrow. Not sure why. Today is not a good day for me to talk to her. She'll take one look at my unsmiling dark shadowed face and know something is wrong, and she won't drop it till I tell her. I'm not ready for that. Especially since she didn't even know I was *involved* with someone. Because apparently, we were never *dating*.

I ignore her call and send her a text, using the excuse of being in a loud place and I can't talk right now. Putting my phone on silent, I slide it in the pocket of my oversized cardigan and trudge out of my bus and over to Pilar and Paloma's. Fred is happily sitting on my shoulder, excited to be going to see friends.

Knocking on the door to their double decker bus, I wait till it opens. Pilar stands there as cute as ever in a pale-yellow crop sweater and whitewash jeans. Her yellow-blonde hair is tied up in a high pony that sways from one side to the other when she sees me.

"Lala, how nice to see you. Come in." She gestures and steps aside allowing me entry.

"Thanks. Is Paloma here too?" I ask.

"Oh yeah, she's upstairs. Paloma," she calls up the spiral staircase to her sister. "Lala's here, get your ass down here."

There's a few soft thuds, then feet appear on the stairs. Their bus is the coolest conversion I've ever seen. There's a kitchen, living room, and full bathroom downstairs, with two small separate bedrooms, and a small studio space where they record their social media videos upstairs. It makes me wish I had considered a double decker when I built my Skoolie, but it's just me and Fred. We don't need that much space.

"Lala, it's so good to see you. What brings you to our humble abode?" Paloma engulfs me in a warm and tight hug that I didn't realize I needed till this very moment. Fred gets in on the action and scurries around our shoulders in a circle, seeking space between our necks to wiggle his way in. I bask in the warmth of the hug and hold on a little tighter before pulling back.

"I was wondering if you guys would be available two weekends from now."

"For what?" Pilar asks, guiding us to the couch, and we all sit. Fred jumps from me, making himself at home, running around their living room and searching for small things to steal and hide.

"I have that realtor's conference. There's supposed to be a few hundred people, and I was hoping you would be able to help me run my booth. I would pay you, of course."

"No, you will not," Paloma rebuffs, almost offended that I offered. "We have plenty of money, and we know it's been tight for you lately. We will absolutely help you out, but we will not take a penny of your earnings."

"No, that's not fair. I couldn't—"

"You could, you can, and you will." Pilar nods finitely along with her sister. Sometimes It's creepy when they do the whole twin synchronicity thing.

Their pure friendship and support make tears sting the back of my eyes. Pretty much everything makes me cry these days. Maybe I should check to make sure I'm not pregnant with how wild my mood swings have been lately. Although, they're mostly one directional. Sad and depressed. Plus, I just started my period, so it's not likely.

"Thank you, guys, that means a lot to me." Pulling my hands inside the long sleeves of the cardigan, I fiddle with a loose thread and really try not to cry. After all the tears I've shed the past week, I thought I would be running low. Apparently not.

"Don't cry," Pilar coos. "We didn't mean to make you cry."

"It's not you, trust me. This is all me and my own doing."

"No, it's that butthead Henry's doing." Paloma scowls like he's in the room and she could burn through him with her glare. They, of course, know all about Henry and the infamous Gala.

"She's right. This is not your fault, Lala."

But it is partially. I let this happen. I let it get to this point where it would hurt so much. I don't tell them that though. Arguing with the twins always ends with me agreeing with them one way or another anyway. So, I just skip over the back and forth and nod silently.

"Ok, so I'll send you the information about the conference, and I have shirts for you to wear as well. I'll bring them over later."

"How about you come over tonight and we'll make dinner, open a bottle of wine or two, and we can either bad talk Henry or watch a few movies till we're too drunk to see straight. Sound good?"

"Or we could place a fifty-pizza order and have it delivered to Henry's apartment, along with a box of not so subtly packaged sex toys. Like the really weird freaky ones that are so bizarre you have no idea what they do or where they go." Paloma's suggestions are always far more juvenile, but more enjoyable than her twins. I'm kind of partial to both ideas.

"Can we do both. Eat and drink till we can't see straight, then order the non-discreet sex toys?"

"Yes," they say in unison. And the prospect of doing something that makes Henry even a little bit more unhappy, uncomfortable or embarrassed has me quirking a tiny half smile. Making Henry more of a grump than normal is always satisfying.

Later, I return to the twin's bus with t-shirts in hand, and we eat and drink at least three bottles of wine. When we are good and sloshed, we find the dirtiest sex toys we can find online, mark them as urgent overnight delivery, and make sure they don't have discreet shipping.

Paloma picks out a full body sensory deprivation suit. It has a full hood that covers the eyes, ears and mouth, with a hose at the nose for breathing. Paired with a black latex body suit that looks part straight jacket and part body bag.

Pilar chooses a pink and turquoise monster themed flesh light that looks like the kraken's tentacle and salt-n-seaweed scented lube. Girl's got a secret kinky side I decide because she was really excited about finding it. Not gonna lie, the monster themed dildos aren't looking too bad. I take a photo of the screen and website so I can find it later. There's no way in hell I'm going to remember it in my inebriated state, and I want to check these out when I'm sober.

I find a rather stunning butt plug with a rainbow-colored horse tail and pink riding crop, which I decide to pair with a full leather horse eared bridle and ball gag. Not sure if he's into pony play, but now his whole building will think he is.

All three of these kinky sex packages put together make for a disturbingly inappropriate image for his fancy neighbors. I can only hope his name is clearly written on the box for all to see as it sits in the Lobby waiting for him to pick it up.

I have nothing against these types of toys and accessories. To each their own. But I know it will mortify the prim and proper boring Henry Bardot to have people thinking he likes the kinky and weird.

The twins splurge on the sex paraphernalia as a feel better soon gift to me, and for the first time in a week, I smile and laugh and feel like maybe things can get better. Maybe not better than they were when I was with Henry, but back to a semblance of what life used to be before him.

I swear off men and Indiana Jones movies for the foreseeable future before stumbling back to my Skoolie and passing out on my bed.

It's not that I haven't contemplated drinking myself unconscious since the Gala. I just haven't been able to bring myself to spend the money to do so.

Passing out into a dreamless sleep, I'm questioning my decision not to have done this sooner. If three bottles of wine is all it takes to dull the pain of the ache Henry Bardot left in me, I should have done it sooner. And might have to do it again tomorrow.

36 - Henry

Monster cocks to get off your monster rocks

pparently now that I'm no longer sleeping with Lala—yes Lala, because why fight my desire to call her such anymore—I'm even more unpleasant to be around than before. Thomas has started talking to me in clipped short words, but it's better than nothing. It's hard to get work done when my own assistant won't speak to me. Others in the office, however, steer clear of me whenever they can. My patience is nonexistent, and I bark out orders to people in terse sharp words.

The only upside to all this is that people leave me alone. No one tries to stop by and have a friendly chat, and my office remains blissfully quiet while I work.

The quiet, however, begins to grate on my nerves when once again I get an email rebutting my offer for the Peterson Plaza office complex. This deal should have been done and signed months ago, and I have had it with this greedy asshole and his back and forth.

"Thomas."

A moment later, Thomas appears in my office, face stoic and hands folded neatly in front of him. No quippy "yeah boss" or friendly greeting these days. Whatever, he'll get over it.

"Yes, Mr. Bardot."

I inwardly cringe at his tone. I don't have many friends, and honestly, Thomas and his boyfriend, Paul are the closest thing to friends beyond Eddie. The fact he's still pissed with me hurts inside, but I don't let it show. Because I am Henry Bardot, the heartless, unsmiling real estate mogul.

"Call Mr. Peterson and tell him if he doesn't accept our current offer with the conditions listed, we will be pulling our offer and going elsewhere. He will also never receive another offer from us in the future for any property, and we will never manage any of his properties again if he does not accept. I'm tired of his bullshit, and if this is how he handles business, I don't want to work with him again."

Thomas nods and leaves my office without a word. Normally he would have argued with me, made me soften my threat to something less finite. Now, I'm not even worth his ire.

I always thought the silent treatment was a ridiculous way to punish someone. Getting in an argument and then having the other person stop yelling at you and leave you in peace sounds like heaven to me. Until now. Until I'm on the receiving end of it. I guess it holds more weight when you're actually invested and close to the person who's mad at you. Although, these days, it seems everyone is mad at me.

Fawn calls me every day to leave snide angry voicemails, because after the first five calls I stopped answering. Leo doesn't show up for boxing because Fawn won't let him, and although Eddie is still around, he gives me this weird pity filled look. And then, there's Thomas, of course. Even Samson scowls and shakes his head at me when I see him. Which, thankfully, is less now that he's not popping in every other day to have lunch or sit and watch me work for no reason at all. The only person who doesn't seem to notice the change or care is my father.

My calm was already at the end of its rope today, and after the Peterson bullshit, I'm done. I'm not going to get any more work done today and decide to take off early. I'm sure everyone in the office will appreciate my absence.

Grabbing my jacket and briefcase, I head for the door. Might as well go home and drink. Seems to be all I'm capable of doing these days.

"I'm leaving early," I say as I stroll past Thomas's office, not waiting for a response. I do hear him mumble under his breath though.

"Good. We could use a break from your brooding."

I ignore it as I have all the comments I've heard whispered behind hands about me. I could care less what they think of me.

Stepping into the lobby of my building, I nod at Jackson, noticing the strange green and purple box sitting on the front desk. With what looks like tentacles drawn all over it.

"Mr. Bardot. Sir. There's a package for you."

A package? I didn't order anything. As a matter of fact, I hate ordering things online, and always either pick it up in store or have it hand delivered, after ordering it in store. You never know what you're getting with online crap.

"I didn't order anything."

"Well, you have a box. A couple of them actually." Jackson looks from me to the small tentacle box on the desk and back again, an unreadable look on his face. Like he's trying to remain passive but can't. A thread of curiosity slips through, along with what looks like disbelief.

"I had the other boxes taken up to your penthouse. They were causing quite a bit of... chatter amongst the other tenants."

Now I really have no idea what he's talking about. Even if I did manage to order something while drunk, which occurs more often than not these days, I have no idea what I could have ordered that would cause gossip.

Jackson nods to the tentacle box warily. "This one just arrived, and I hadn't had the opportunity to take it up yet."

Curious, I walk over to the desk and check the box. Sure enough, it has my name right there in bold letters on the outside. I pick up the box to inspect it further and read the label.

Monster cocks to get off your monster rocks.

What the fuck? Upon closer inspection, it appears to be some sort of sex toy dildo company that makes monster themed products.

"I did not order this," I balk, dropping the box on his desk as if it were hot coal. Trying to wipe the touch off on my slacks. "This is not mine."

"Well, it has your name on it, Sir."

"Doesn't matter. I don't want it. I didn't order it. Send it back." I bet this is Samson's doing. He loves to pull crap like this all the time.

"Sorry, Sir. I can't do that. You'll have to handle it with the company if you want to return the...items."

Oh, fucking hell. Now everyone in the building is going to think I'm into monster porn.

"Wait. You said there were more boxes?"

"Yes, Sir. They were... larger and of the same nature." Jackson is trying to be nice about it, but there's no way to sugar coat it. Someone sent me multiple boxes of weird kinky sex toys. And apparently opted out of discreet shipping.

I sigh. "Great."

Picking up the tentacle monster cock box, I hold it with as few fingers as possible like it could contaminate me. Which of course it can't, but still.

"Thanks, Jackson. Please let me know immediately if any more packages show up. So, I can return them." I make sure to say, so he knows these are not things I ordered nor want.

The entire ride up the elevator, I dread finding out what's inside the other boxes. And inside the one in my hand. I have a pretty good idea, but even with how horrified I am at its arrival, my fucking curiosity has me wondering what exactly it is.

Inside my penthouse, two additional boxes sit on my kitchen island. I place the monster cock box next to them and read their labels.

One is from the Latex Palace, 'your place for pleasure and pain'. The other... Jesus fucking Christ. I rub a hand down my face staring at the pastel rainbow box that proudly states, Pleasure Stables for all your pony play dreams. There's even a picture on the side—of a person's ass from the back, a tail sticking out from between the crack.

I really don't want to open the boxes, but I need to find a packing slip, and maybe an explanation of who sent them. First, I need a drink.

Only once I've changed into lounge pants and cotton crew neck, large scotch in hand, do I return to the boxes and crack them open.

The latex box is filled with a black latex suit with a lot of buckles and a weird mask that does not look comfortable. The pony play box has one of those butt plugs sporting a rainbow horse tail. It came with a matching harness and bit made with a ball gag. The only thing inside that I would even consider using is the pink riding crop. Spanking is always an option.

The smallest and last box, thank fuck, Monster Cocks is thankfully not a dildo but a strange silicone tube or sleeve of some kind. It looks like a tentacle with little round suckers inside and out in a mix of pink and turquoise. I'm guessing the idea is to stick your dick inside and fuck it. People are really into this stuff? There's also a bottle of lube that smells like sea water when I open it and take a whiff.

The only information I find in the boxes are the standard packing slips telling me all items are included. At the bottom of the monster cock box, I find a small bifold card that reads:

A little monster for the monster dick (and not the one in your pants)

Still doesn't answer who sent it. At this point in time, that could be from anyone. Pretty much everyone thinks I'm a dick these days.

Shoving all the items into the largest box, I shove the whole thing to the back of my closet. Maybe I can use them in the future as gag gifts for Samson, Eddie, or Leo. I'm sure it has to be one of them that sent these anyway. Considering there's three boxes, it wouldn't surprise me if all three of them sent one.

37 - Lala

Stop being so Goddamn attractive

Three weeks. It's been three weeks since the Gala. Three weeks since I've seen or heard from Henry. Three weeks of total and complete heartbreak. I've tried to stay busy, but when your job isn't a nine to five, five days a week, you end up having far too much free time.

However, I have been using my free time to plan my route to Montana and reserve a spot at an RV park halfway up a mountain, where there's little to no people. I came to the decision about a week and a half ago while spending my sixth consecutive hour lying in bed watching Ancient Aliens. It is time to move on. After Fawn's baby shower next week, I'm leaving.

I've canceled all my reservations with farmer's and flea markets, only staying to work the conference for the money it will make me, give Fawn her baby gift, and then I'm gone.

Out of here, and hundreds of miles away from Henry and anything that reminds me of him.

I just have to make it through this conference first. Pilar and

Paloma are here with me in their Lala Boba shirts, working away and organizing the supplies, making sure everything is prepped and ready. The first break of the conference is going to start in ten minutes.

Thankfully, I haven't had to deal with Henry, only Thomas, throughout this whole ordeal. If I'm lucky, I won't even see him today. Let's face it though, I'm not lucky, and I am one hundred percent sure he's going to be here, and it's going to be majorly weird and unpleasant. As long as I don't cry, I'll consider it a win.

The first few people trickle into the ballroom we're set up in with the few other food and drink vendors. Soon, they're coming in a constant flow of customers. My stall gets a line and all three of us get to work. Pilar takes orders because, of the three of us, she's the friendliest, and Paloma and I make the drinks.

We've found a decent rhythm, and the twins make sure I only have to interact briefly with customers. My bedside manner is not so great these days. Not that I'm rude. I just don't want to talk to anyone. I don't want to plaster on a fake smile and act interested in what they have to say. I just want to get their money, make their drinks, and leave.

I'm in the middle of mixing a drink when a familiar and unwanted voice breaks my concentration and practiced zoned-out state of being.

"Well, hello again. It's Micaela, right?"

At first, I think it's Henry. He's the only one who calls me Micaela but when I look up it's someone I loathe more than Henry. His father. Malcom Bardot. The man who instructed his son to get his fill of me then drop me, if I remember correctly.

"Lala, actually."

"Oh, alright then. But you are the Micaela that Henry took to the Gala, aren't you?"

"Yes. That was me."

"I thought so. I only recognized you because of the pink hair. Not easy to forget."

"No, I suppose not." I don't smile, nor do I make eye contact. I try to engage as little as possible. But since it is his company putting on the conference, I can't very well ignore him completely.

I don't stop making drinks, hoping he'll get the hint that I'm busy. Sadly, he does not and keeps talking.

"Henry hasn't mentioned you since the Gala. Are you two still seeing each other?"

Wow, what an ass. Gritting my teeth, I manage a mangled response that sounds strangled out of me. "No. Not anymore."

"Shame. You're far prettier than the women he usually *dates.*" He emphasizes the word dates like we both know that's not what he does. And he's right. I know he doesn't date. That's just the most P.C. term to use in current company.

"Am I? I wouldn't know. Haven't met any of them."

"Oh, yes, you are far more attractive." His eyes roam down the length of me behind the table, and he leans to one side to get a better angle. What a fucking perv. "More girl next door. He usually goes for the vixen, sex kitten type. It seems he's diversifying his tastes along with his portfolio."

Gag me now and drown me in the river. This is the most disgustingly disturbing and hurtful conversation I've ever had.

Passing him his drink. I smile a tight-lipped semblance of a friendly smile that hopefully conveys how many shits I give about this conversation.

"Here's your boba. Enjoy." I dismiss him without another word, but he still doesn't move. Others are moving around him, not in the least hindered by his blockade of my booth. They just ignore him, take their drink, and move on.

"If you and Henry aren't *together* anymore, perhaps you might consider spending time with someone a little more dignified and diversified."

Huuuaa. I have to consciously stop myself from gagging out loud. If he's insinuating he is experienced with women of my age and who aren't prostitutes, that's going to be a hard pass.

"Sorry, but no. I don't think that would be proper after *dating* Henry." His name is like gravel in my mouth, and it hurts to speak it. "I hope you understand."

"Can't say I'm surprised, but I am a little disappointed. You wouldn't regret it, I promise. There are things that not even Henry is proficient at." He winks at me—actually winks. Who does that?

Again—barf. This man is older than my father. There has to be at least a forty-year age gap. I'm supportive of daddies and zaddies, but this is like granddaddy territory, and I do not want to enter.

"No, thanks. Besides, I'll be moving to Montana in just over a week." I try to say this as politely as possible because I do not want to make a scene while I have a line of paying customers. I *really* need their money. Especially if I'm just going to hide out in the mountains in Montana and not work for a while. Take some time to find my center, as Pilar says.

"Very well." He sighs like I've just missed out on the best thing of my life. And I have. It just wasn't him.

I would love to tear into him and tell him what a horrible father and person he is. To shame him for his adultering ways and under-age preferences, but I don't. I bite my tongue and return to mixing and blending drinks. He finally gets the hint and leaves, sauntering away like nothing happened. Like he didn't just proposition his son's ex... whatever I am.

The encounter leaves me feeling slimy and gross, and when the line thins out, I step away to wash off the feel of his words. Leaving my booth in the capable hands of the twins, I go to the bathroom to freshen up.

I wash my hands and face with cold water, and take a moment to collect myself, giving myself a little pep talk that only partially makes me feel better before leaving the shiny polished bathroom. Crashing directly into a large body upon my hasty exit.

"Oh, sorry," I stutter, not looking up and trying to sidestep the person.

"Lala."

The voice that haunts my dreams and warms and chills my heart at the same time. The voice that causes my nerves to vibrate speaks my name low and soft. Coaxing me to stop and look up. I don't want to. I even tell my body not to. Still, it moves against my will. Bringing me to face him.

"Henry." His name is a soft exhale of sound, barely forming on my lips before passing them.

For a moment, he just stares at me, unblinking in his shock. He's not the only one. I have no idea what to say, how to act. Should I just turn and walk away? Am I supposed to be civil and hold polite conversation, as if I don't know what the feel of his lips against my inner thigh feels like? Because I can't.

"How are you?" he asks. I almost balk at the sheer idiocy of the question. I do let out a low humorless chuckle.

"How am I?" I ask a little hysterically. I may be losing my shit in about three seconds, and I'm not going to stop it. "How am I?" I repeat, a little more heated now.

"Let's see..." Ticking them off on my fingers, I count the many ways I am NOT Ok. "I got dumped by the guy I was seeing and possibly had real feelings for, even though he didn't consider us dating. Overheard his father instructing him to hit it and quit it because no pussy is worth it, to which he oddly agreed." Henry's brow furrows deep between his eyes, and the edges of his lips turn down, but I don't let that slow my roll. "Then, after dumping, not dumping me, he ghosted me with absolutely no explanation or apology and now, I'm having to work at his work conference. Where his pervy disgusting father hit on me and tried to convince me he's better in bed than his son."

Taking in a stabilizing lung full of air, I try to come down from my high at finally letting loose on Henry. "So, to answer your question, I'm fan-fucking-tastic. Never better actually. Life is grand." I say, a little too hysterically to be serious.

Henry looks as if he's about to grind through his teeth with how hard he's clenching his jaw. "My father did what?"

"Out of all that, all you care about is your horrid father hitting on me? You and he are far more alike than I realized. Selfish, egotistical bastards who care more about their image than the feelings of others."

The anger in his jaw subsides a little at my words. As if I've just slapped him across the face, he blanches slightly.

"Lala, that's not it at all. I just... this is weird for me too, Ok. I don't know what to do here," he admits. A stupid piece of me softens a little. Seeing the hurt and confusion flashing through his seafoam gaze soothes like a balm over the cuts inside, if only briefly.

"Well... you could... I don't know... stop being so goddamn attractive for one. That would help."

His laugh is muffled, and the grin only reaches one side of his mouth, but it's there. And the sight of it, along with the divine sound of his laughter, is almost enough to undo all the anger knotted up inside me. It pulls at the ends of my tangled heart string, wanting to twine them around his fingers and let him be my undoing. I so want to let him, but that would only hurt me more. Because the moment I expose my heart to him, he will only cut those strings and burn the remnants to ash. He doesn't want my strings no matter how much I want to cord them around his insides and squeeze.

"Stop." The command comes out on an exhale. It has no strength or heat, but it hits him as if it were screamed through a megaphone. His grin falls, and the playful glint growing in his gaze fades to shadows.

"It wasn't my intention to hurt—"

"Stop," I say again, cutting off whatever he was going to confess. I don't want to hear it. "It's done. It's over. Just let me move on."

He nods slowly only once. His lips pinch into a thin line to hold back the words he so desperately wants to speak, allowing the silence to stretch long and heavy between us.

"Are you going to Fawn's baby shower?"

The question surprises me, but I suppose it's neutral grounds to speak on. "Yes. And then I'll be leaving."

"Leaving? Where are you going?" I can see his fingers stretching out as if he wants to reach for my hand, but thankfully, they stay at his side.

My voice wavers slightly as I confess, I'm running away. Running from him and everything he makes me feel. "Montana."

"Oh. I didn't know."

"How would you?" I don't intend for the words to be cruel, but I see the flinch he can't completely hide at my response. I almost apologize and then swallow the words. He doesn't deserve them. There's no reason I should be apologizing. I'm nobody to him, as he's made fervently clear.

"I suppose I deserve that."

"And more."

"Right." His despondent down-turned eyes hurt my insides, but he deserves every bit of my indignation. He brought it upon himself. "I guess I'll leave you alone then."

With a hand running through his hair and frown lines forming on his brow, Henry side steps me and walks away without another word.

There. I saw him, we spoke, it was bad, but it's over now. I can return to my life and move on. No matter how badly I want to chase after him and demand he confess how he truly feels for me. To stop lying to us both and tell the truth. Even if it's not what I want to hear, I know what he said at the Gala wasn't the truth. And I need to know the truth.

My feet remain firmly planted in place, digging roots into the cement and stilling me firm. The first time I've ever been rooted anywhere, and it had to be out of fear of hearing another rejection from Henry's perfect lips.

38 - Henry

Fuck, I love Lala

My father is a dead man. I am going to choke him to death with my own two hands and bury his body so no one can ever find him. How dare he make a move on Lala. Not only is that insulting to us both, but inconsiderate and heartless. What kind of father tries to get with his son's ex? Mine, that's who. Malcom Bardot has no morals or conscience. Lala was right about one thing, he does only think about himself. She was wrong about me though. I do think of others—well, one other in particular. And it's her I'm thinking about as I tromp through the hotel halls, searching for my father so I can break both his legs.

I find him standing with a small group of men outside one of the ball rooms converted to a meeting room for the conference. Without faltering or slowing, I break through their small group and thrust my father against the wall, my forearm pressing against his throat. I can tell I'm cutting off his air by the way he sputters and gasps. Good.

"What the hell did you say to Lala?"

"What?" He gasps and claws at my arm with his nails ineffectively. It does nothing through the sleeve of my suit, and it only enrages me further. So, I press a little harder, sneering at the man who supposedly helped birth me.

"Lala. I just spoke with her, and she said you propositioned her. Is that true?" He gasps again, opening and shutting his mouth like a dying fish. I lessen the hold just enough for him to speak.

"I simply asked if she was interested. What is your problem?"

"My problem is you and your inability to keep it in your pants." My jaw hurts from how hard I'm grinding my teeth, and I'm sure people are watching. I don't give a shit. He's about to learn something he probably should have learned a long time ago.

"You will never speak to her again. You won't even look at her. If I find out you did, I will come for you. And don't for one moment think because you were the sperm donor to half my DNA that'll stop me from ending you. Am I understood?" My voice is booming in the hall, and I'm sure everyone can hear. Let them.

My father sputters but doesn't answer, so I ask again. "Am I understood?"

"Yes, Ok. Just back off."

I do, but slowly, keeping my control over him for as long as possible. He's no longer smiling, and his face has gone purple.

Stepping into his space once more, I keep my tone low but do not touch him again. "Remember this, Father. Because I will."

With that, I leave. I leave him gasping for breath and stumbling for excuses as to why his son just nearly strangled him in the hall. I answer to no one as I leave the conference. If I stay any longer, I'll lose it more than I already have.

Lala is leaving. I've missed my chance. She's going to be gone, and I'll never see her again, and the thought has my heart trying to escape my chest. I can't let her leave. I have to make this right. But I don't know how.

I thought I could just move on from her if I stayed away long enough. I see now that's not an option. I can't stay away from her any more than the world can stop spinning.

She is everything. Everything in my life that makes me happy. As has been proven by the weeks of miserable nights spent alone in my penthouse at the bottom of a scotch bottle. I haven't smiled since she left and ran away from me crying. Not until I saw her again. Even in the depth of my self loathing and her insults, she still managed to make me smile.

It makes more sense now what happened at the Gala. She overheard my asinine father telling me to drop her. To get what I want and move on. As I always have, I gave him my robotic response so he would move on and stop talking about it. I didn't actually mean any of it. I just wanted him off my case. With him, there's no rationalizing feelings and relationships. He's long lost his ability to feel anything beyond greed and self-satisfaction.

In reality, it burned my tongue to say those words to him. They were partially true, but I desperately wanted them not to be. I don't want her to move on and leave. I want Pittsburgh to be her home. I want to be worthy of her. Because she is so far beyond my deserving that I thought her incapable of wanting me as more. I thought myself incapable of having what Fawn and Leo have. A functioning love-filled relationship. Lacking all the spite and distrust our parents had in theirs.

Even if she hates me and doesn't want me, I have to try. Try before it's too late, and the only woman I've ever loved slips through my fingers.

Fuck... I love Lala. I should have admitted it long ago. So many things would have been different. For one, I would have punched my father at the Gala when he suggested Lala wasn't worth my time. I wouldn't have made her cry. I could have saved us both from the last three weeks of tormented agony.

I may not know what to do, but I know someone who does. Sliding into the driver's seat of my Jag, I pull out my phone and dial the one person I know will help me, and who will know exactly how to fix my fuck up. I press the phone to my ear and hope she answers, because if she doesn't, I may lose Lala forever.

"Hello?"

"Hi, Fawn."

"Are you calling to grovel and beg my forgiveness? Because that's the only way I'm not hanging up on you." I chuckle at my sister. She knew a long time ago that Lala was meant for me. I should have listened. Well, I'm listening now. I just hope it's not too late.

"Yes, actually I am."

"Wait. Really?"

"Yes, really." With those two words, I've managed to silence the unsilenceable Fawn Ashwood, attorney at law.

"Well... Ok, then. Please continue."

"I'm sorry, Fawn. You were right."

"I'm sorry. I didn't hear that. Come again?"

The smile that makes its way across my lips has the ache in my heart easing. Fawn will help me make this right.

"You were right. I was an ass to Lala, and I need you to tell me what to do to fix it," I admit.

"Ohhh," she drawls. "So, it's Lala now?"

I laugh. Damn it feels good to do that again. My chest feels a hundred pounds lighter. "Are you going to help me or not?"

"Oh, I'm going to help you. I just hope you didn't wait too long. She's been really sad, Henry. You broke her heart."

Hearing it out loud has the joy slowly building in me faltering. "I know, Fawn. I never meant to. But I can't lose her. She's... she's everything I never expected."

Pinky Promise

"I could have told you that. As a matter of fact, I think I did. But you were too pig-headed to listen." She scolds me as if she were the older sibling.

"Probably. Tell me what to do now and I'll do it. No matter what it is." I grip the steering wheel, hoping she has a plan, because I don't. I'm not used to begging for forgiveness and admitting I was wrong. But I'll do it because she's worth it. Always has been. I was just too stupid and blind to see it.

"Ok, but it's going to take your complete dedication. Can you do that?"

"Yes."

351

39 - Lala

The scent of my Hart

Today is my last day in Pittsburgh. Tomorrow, I leave for Montana. Dollface, Carnage, Thrasher, and Twitch gave me a short farewell party. Nothing big. Just a small cake and going away presents. A pair of light up pink wheels from Dollface and Carnage, a recipe book from Thrasher, and Twitch gave me a pink graphic tee that saves "Livin' the Skoolie Life." I cried, of course.

The twins got me well and drunk a few nights ago, berating me for leaving without them. They still have obligations in Pittsburgh and aren't able to leave for a few more months. Otherwise, I have no doubt they would be pulling out right behind me, headed for Montana.

Today, I'm trying hard not to cry as I pull up to Fawn's house for her baby shower. Fawn knows I'm leaving but hasn't insisted on doing anything or trying to stop me. She just quietly accepted my decision. Even though a few tears were shed, they were brief.

At least if I do cry today, I can blame it on all the cuteness and happiness for Fawn and her baby.

The decorations around the house are a mixture of pink, white, and mint green. Balloons, streamers, and a flag banner spells out "It's a girl" hanging across one of the archways. People, both male and female, peruse the house, eating snacks and leaving their gifts on a table in the living room near the wet bar. Everyone is smiling and happy and enjoying themselves. Everyone but me.

I'm the raincloud on everyone's parade. I try to smile and make small talk, but I don't know any of these people, and I'm not interested in getting to know them.

As I'm sitting at the bar nursing a very spiked punch, someone I do know sits next to me. Samson leans on the bar, and I manage a smile when I see him. He's friendly and funny, albeit rather flirty, but he's harmless. His own smile is bright and happy to see me, unlike others who have been privy to my company today. It's hard to be happy when you're leaving in less than twelve hours, running away from heartbreak.

"Hey there, sweet Lala. Haven't seen you in a while. How ya holding up?"

Of course, he knows about me and Henry. If there's one thing I love about their tight-knit group, it's that they actually communicate with each other. Right now, however, it might be less embarrassing if they didn't.

"Yikes. Where's that beautiful smile you always wear? You look like a pink rain cloud."

I try and fail to laugh. "I'm hanging in there. What about you?"

"Oh, you know me. Nothing new. Fawn tells me you're leaving Pittsburgh. Is that true? Please tell me it's not because of my idiot brother." He looks truly bummed that I might be leaving. That's sweet.

"Yes, I'm going to Montana. Time to move on to the next town."

"Are you sure you don't want to stick around? Henry was so much more tolerable with you around. Now he's all brooding and unpleasant again."

"Sorry to disappoint you, Samson, but I don't think that'll be happening. Your brother made it very clear what he wanted, as did I. And those two things didn't match. I just need to be somewhere new. Away from… all this." I sigh, and he nods. I down the rest of my vodka spiked punch, then Samson takes my empty glass and circles the bar.

"Here, let me make you one of my famous old fashioneds. I think you and I both could use a good drink right about now. All this baby talk has women preening to have their own."

"Not your scene, huh?"

"Not even remotely. I'm only here for Fawn. I promised her two hours, then I'm out. There's only so much I can handle."

I feel the same way. I love Fawn and had intended on staying through till the end to get as much time with her as possible, but I don't know if I'll be able to make it through opening presents.

Samson mixes the drink with a flourish, and I wonder if he's ever been a bartender. I suppose he wouldn't have to considering all the money he has. From what Henry told me, he has no need to ever work. Never has. He hands me the drink, and I sip. It's good. Of course, it is. At least I don't have to be sober through the cutest baby shower in all history.

"So, is your brother coming today?" I try to keep my voice calm and uninterested, but my shifting eyes and twitching fingers give me away.

"Henry? Pretty sure he said he was. Promised Fawn at our last monthly dinner. Haven't seen him yet though." He eyes me with soft apprehension. "Would you like me to warn you if I see him?"

His offer is unexpected, but welcome. I nod. "Yeah, that would be nice."

"I know how it can be when you run into an ex you don't want to see. Happens way too often to me. It's like they're stalking me or something."

"Maybe they are. Maybe you're just that enigmatic, they can't resist your charms."

"That is true. But I really wish they wouldn't."

Joking with Samson has me relaxing a fraction, just enough to take a deep breath. It's nice having him here to distract me from everything else, and I let him. We stay close to the bar, and I have a second drink. When my buzz is warm, I stop because I still have to drive home, and then again tomorrow, and I don't need a hangover while driving my bus.

Another hour passes in relative ease before Fawn announces she's going to start opening presents. I still haven't seen Henry, thankfully. Maybe he won't be coming after all, and I can finish up this party without a confrontation. Although, secretly I am wishing to see him just one more time before I leave. I hate myself for it, but that's the truth. No matter how many times I remind myself what he said, my stupid heart just won't listen. It's really fucking annoying to have to argue with yourself. I never win.

Leo and Samson rearrange the chairs and seats around a fluffy armchair where Fawn carefully lowers herself. Her belly is the size of a basketball, and she's tied a large pink ribbon around it. She's absolutely radiant. We all sit or stand facing Fawn and Leo, who stands by, ready to hand her presents from the overflowing table.

I scooch my stool closer, but stay to the back, still able to see clearly, but not in the middle so as not to taint the happiness with my gloom. Not even my customary outfit of all pink, not just in honor of Fawn's baby girl, can boost my mood.

Women coo and men chatter amongst themselves where they

stand lining the back of the room as Fawn opens one box after the other of the tiniest clothing and all the necessities a new mom could want.

"This one is from Henry," Leo announces, checking the card before handing it to Fawn. The package is large and swathed in pink, tied like a sack with a frilly ribbon.

Fawn doesn't even question where Henry is or look around to find him in the crowd. Which only confirms my suspicions that he isn't here and didn't plan on attending.

Unlacing the ribbon, the pink wrapping falls away, and inside is the extremely expensive gift basket she was eyeing at the Gala. I guess that means he won the silent auction. Fawn begins to pull out one item after another. There's a baby grooming kit, towels with hoods, the fanciest burp clothes I've ever seen, a baby monitor with a camera, a mobile, and more. Near the bottom of the basket, which is made of braided pink rope and can double as a storage basket, she pulls out a small pink box with a ribbon and paper tag tied to it.

"Oh, this one isn't for me." Fawn doesn't sound surprised, but pleased. "It's for Lala."

Excuse me, what? Did she just say Lala? That can't be right. I must be hallucinating. But people are looking around, a few staring right at me, including Fawn, who has a giant smile plastered on her face. *Why is she smiling? And why is it making me nervous?*

A gentle elbow nudges me from my side. I jump at the contact, shaken out of my mortified shock. Samson is watching me curiously. He's not the only one.

"Well, are you going to get your present?"

"Um..." I shake my head, trying to clear the fog as I look to Fawn and then Samson. When it doesn't appear I'll be moving, Samson steps forward to take the box from his sister and brings it to me.

356

He sets it in my hands gently, probably worried I'll drop it since I seem to be unresponsive. It's about the size of a tissue box, and the pink isn't wrapping paper but the box itself. All I would need to do is pull on the end of the ribbon and lift the lid to see what's inside. But the small, folded piece of paper on top has me frozen again. As much as I would love to think this is from Fawn, there's only one person who could have done this.

Knowing the name I'll find on the card, I can't bring myself to open it.

"Aren't you going to open it?" I look up to see Fawn and Leo watching me, and they're not the only ones. Since she's not opening any more presents, and appears to be waiting on me, so is everybody else.

"Uh, I don't think—"

"Nonsense. Open it," Fawn presses.

"Ok."

Pulling out the folded paper, I gingerly open it to find what I knew I would.

You are my Hart.
-Henry

Intentionally misspelling heart to match my last name. Tears sting the back of my eyes and… Goddamn it. I WILL NOT CRY.

Lifting the lid of the box, nestled in pink tissue paper inside, rests a crystal pink heart shaped perfume bottle. A short hose and squeeze pump dangling from the top. Pulling it out, I see name "Lala" engraved in beautiful calligraphy on the front.

"That's beautiful. Who is it from?" I don't look up to see who asked the question. It could have been anybody. All my attention is focused on the perfume bottle.

"It's from Henry."

"Henry Bardot?" the same female voice asks, obviously disbelieving. "Why would Fawn's older brother be giving *her* a present at his sister's baby shower?" The woman obviously has no idea who I am and Samson shushes her, much to my delight.

Ignoring the world around me, I read the tiny tag hanging on the bottle. The logo for the perfumery that had the custom perfume on auction at the Gala is embossed in gold on the suede paper. On the backside it reads: *The scent of my Hart. An intoxicating blend of sugary sweetness and a morning breeze through a field of wildflowers.*

Spritzing it, I smell exactly that. Somehow, they managed to mix a scent that is purely me.

"That smells delectable," Samson whispers, and I almost jump out of my skin, having forgotten all about the room full of people around me.

I can feel wetness staining my cheeks, and the weight of dozens of pairs of eyes watching me. With the pink box and perfume in hand, I stand from my stool and scurry from the room, making my way to the rear of the house and the family room, where I can be alone with my misery and have the ugly cry breakdown I know is about to happen.

How fucking dare he. How dare he give me something like this on today of all days. Sneaking it into Fawn's gift and putting me on the spot in front of everyone. Not that I particularly care about the people in that room, but still.

My legs buckle under me, and my knees hit the carpeted floor with a dull thud. I'm sucking in quivering lung fulls of breath while trying to calm my racing heart.

This means nothing. This changes nothing. Men always do this. Buy gifts to make up for doing something stupid, then do it all over again after you've forgiven them. It won't work. But it is working. The lingering smell of the perfume he had made... that he picked out. Without even asking me. Fuck him.

The pink box tumbles from my hand while I cradle the heart shaped bottle to my chest. The tissue paper and another white card fall to the floor. Picking it up, this one reads: *Meet me outside.*

Outside? He's outside?

For a moment, I sit frozen on the ground, staring at the card. Trying to understand what the hell is happening.

"Lala?" Fawn's soft voice and warm hand has me looking up reflexively. "He's waiting for you."

"How did you...?" Of course, she knew. She had to be the one to help set this up.

She just smiles softly and looks down at me. "Here. Let's wipe away those tears. Henry doesn't know how to react to tears. They'll only scare him, and he's already a bit skittish."

She pulls out a tissue from a box on an end table nearby and gently brushes away the smears under my eyes. No doubt I was getting close to racoon status.

"None of your guests are going to be there, right? I don't know that I could handle an audience for... whatever this is."

"No, don't worry. I won't let any of the gawkers follow you. It'll be just you and Henry."

"Why is he here? What is this about?"

"You'll have to go outside and find out." A knowing smirk quirks the corner of her lips and her eyes glitter. She definitely knows what is going on here but won't tell me.

"Do I have to?" I sound like a despondent teenager. I both want and don't want to go outside. I want to know why he's here, what he has to say. But I also fear the pain he could cause with his words. Either way, tears are inevitable. I don't know why Fawn is bothering to clean me up now. They're only going to return as soon as I see him.

"You don't have to, but I think you want to." Lifting me by my elbow, she helps me to stand, which is ridiculous because she's the massively pregnant one. Belatedly, I assist her. "Just give him a chance. Ok?"

"Yeah. Ok."

She knows I don't want to argue. She knows I'm going to go to him either way.

We don't go back out through the front of the house. Instead, we turn to go out the back door, exiting onto the deck and circling the side of the house to the long driveway that stretches the length of the house, leading us to a detached four car garage painted to match the main house. There, in the driveway, paces Henry, wringing his hands and rubbing them through his hair, tousling it to beyond messy. As if he's been doing it for hours, then squeezing the back of his neck in a nervous gesture.

Nervous. He's nervous. But why?

Fawn releases my arm, and I think she walks back into the house. I don't really know. I'm not watching her. I'm watching Henry. He's stopped pacing and now faces me, a hopeful wonder in his eyes. A few short strides brings us face to face. This is the first time I've seen him since the conference, and all the butterflies in the world decide to take up residence in my stomach at this moment. I'm so nervous, I'm shaking. But I shouldn't be. This is Henry. I have nothing to fear from him, at least not physically. Emotionally, he's the wrecking ball that came swinging into my life, punching holes in my already fragile walls.

"Hi," he says.

"Hi." We're full of eloquence today it seems.

"I..." He clears his throat before continuing. "I wanted to see you before you left. I had to tell you, what you heard at the Gala—"

"Henry, don't—"

"No, I have to say this. Please, just listen." He waits for me to nod. I shut my mouth and brace for whatever it is he has to say about the Gala, and his conversation with his pervy father.

"What you heard at the Gala is not how I truly feel. I lied to my father. He always tells me the same thing every time I bring a woman to an event. It's partially why I stopped bringing dates. He's a selfish, heartless, dirty old man, and his beliefs are not mine.

"I think you're worth it. You are not insignificant to me, and even though you've made up your mind to go to Montana, I'm hoping I can convince you to stay. I don't want you to leave. And I want you to be more than a fuck buddy. You were never just a fuck buddy.

"There was always more between us. I was just afraid to admit it. What I feel for you is frightening to me. I've never felt it before, and I didn't know how to react."

He pauses in his speech to take a deep breath and reach out to take my hands. Hands which are slightly trembling. I haven't started crying yet, so that's a good thing. But emotions clog my throat, and I say nothing. Only allowing him to take my hands and lace his fingers through mine.

"I... I think I love you, Lala."

Lala. The sound of it cracks my shell of false bravado, and I let out a surprising laugh. It seems to surprise Henry as much as myself.

"You called me Lala."

His responding smile is as bright as the sun shining down on us. Blinding and beautiful, creasing the corners of his eyes and softening the pinch in his brow. "Yeah, I've kind of wanted to call you that for a while now, but I'm a stubborn ass."

"That you are."

He laughs, and the sound eases the tension in my heart strings while tying them up in intricate knots only Henry knows how to undo. His face softens, but his smile doesn't drop as he continues.

"I love you, Lala. And I don't want this to be casual or temporary. I want you. In my life, in my bed, in my heart. It's all I've wanted since the first day you kissed me. It just took me a while to realize it."

Bringing our bodies nearly flush, he squeezes my hands against his chest and presses a soft kiss to my knuckles. "Well?" he asks.

"Well, what?"

"Don't you have anything to say to me? I'm getting a little worried here. I'm spilling my heart out to you, and you're silent."

"Are you asking if I love you, Henry Bardot?"

"I guess I am."

"Hmm, I'm not sure. You were kind of an ass and have a lot to make up for."

"I can do that." Henry leans in so his breath tickles the tiny hairs framing my face.

"Can you?" My words are breathy, and his nearness is causing my body to heat.

"Yes." Closing the distance between us, he presses his lips to mine, and the kiss is meltingly soft and tender. Still filled with just as much desire as he's always had but delivered with all of his love imbued into it. "If you don't believe me, I brought you another present."

"Another one? Henry, the perfume is more than enough. I don't need anything else from you."

"No, it isn't. It'll never be enough. No gift will ever be able to convey what I feel for you. But that isn't going to stop me from trying."

Untangling his fingers from mine, he steps back to approach a giant white canvas covering something I hadn't even noticed before. Or if I had, I had assumed it was something of Fawn and Leo's. He reaches out and snags the end of the canvas, pulling it off in one swift motion to reveal the one thing I never expected.

My tiny trailer. The one I've always wanted for my boba booth. Shaped like a giant teardrop and painted the exact shade of pink to match my hair. A striped tiny pink and white awning extends out from the service window at the press of a button. Lala Boba is painted next to the window in the same font as my logo.

How did he know this was what I wanted?

"It's... I... how did you?"

"Fawn told me. Said you talked about it nonstop. I didn't know how you wanted it set up inside, so it's a blank slate. Ready for you to personalize to your heart's content."

The tears have dried up, taken over by pure joy and love. I can't stop smiling, and my cheeks hurt from the strain of it. Not bothering to check the inside or get a closer look, I run the few feet to Henry standing at the side of my new trailer, and leap into his arms. I wrap my legs around his waist as he locks his strong arms around me. Not letting me fall. I doubt he'll ever let me fall.

"I love you too, Henry Bardot. And not because you buy me nice things, but because you're a good man with a beautiful heart. No matter how you try to hide it from me. I can see it."

Locking my lips to his, I kiss him harder than he did me, forcing all of my feelings behind the kiss to prove to him my words are more than just that. They hold truth behind them.

"Can I take you home now?" he asks between kisses. Kisses on my chin, neck, behind my ear. I can feel him getting hard against my core, and my body shamelessly grinds into him. I've missed him and his body the past month and am starved for his touch.

"Yes please. I've missed you so much," I admit.

"I've missed you, too. And I am never letting you go again."

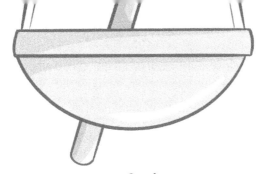

Epilogue – Henry

I'll let you use the plug if you let me use the tentacle

She's trying to kill me. Lala has discovered edging, and she unfortunately or fortunately—I'm still not sure—has perfected it. I've been on the edge of coming for what feels like an eternity. It's more likely five minutes, but the elongated stimulation is maddening. My balls are so tight in the cock ring she insisted on, has me seeing stars. It's so fucking good, I can't stand it.

"Lala, please. Let me come now. I can't stand it anymore." My breathing is labored, and it takes great concentration to speak.

My heart, my Lala, is on her knees between my spread thighs, kneeling before me as if I were her own personal God and she's paying penance. I had started propped on my elbows at the edge of the bed, but I've long lost the battle with gravity and am flat on my back, panting.

Lala pops my dick out of her mouth, and I groan. "No."

"Naughty boy. Now don't you dare touch yourself. I have a surprise."

"Uuuh. Shortcake, you're killin' me."

"Not even close. Don't worry. I'll let you do whatever you want with me after."

"Mmm, I'd be careful promising me such things."

"I highly doubt I won't enjoy it."

She's not wrong. She will most definitely enjoy it, as will I. But first, I have to not die from delayed ejaculation.

Lala stands, still clad in her pink lacy bra and panties, and saunters into my walk-in closet, over a plush blue area rug I purchased just so her feet won't get cold on my floors. Along with a fuzzy pink pair of slippers that live tucked under her side of the bed, so when she gets up in the mornings, they're right there waiting for her. I have no idea what she could be getting in there. I cleared out half my closet for her, so she no longer has to bring an overnight bag when she stays over. Which is often.

It's been six months since I convinced her to stay with my grand gesture, thanks to Fawn's priceless advice and input. She had her baby, by the way, named her Ella. She's a sweet little bundle of wrinkly skin with lungs like an opera singer. She somehow stole the small part of my heart not owned by Lala and made it her own. We have matching shirts. They're pink and awesome. I wear a lot more color these days, thanks to Lala.

Lala's new tiny trailer is fully remodeled now, and she is in boba heaven every time she takes it out to a market. Which, even though I make enough money for both of us, is still every weekend. She even went back to working part time at Wheelies. She loved it there so much. I will gladly pay for anything she desires, but she likes to work, just as I like to work, and I'm not going to take that away from her.

I haven't been able to convince her to move in with me full time yet because she says my penthouse is still too gray, and "one room does not a home make." Even though her bus has only one room. She doesn't seem to see the irony, and I learned pointing this out to her only ends with me in the doghouse. Little does she know, I put an offer in on a house not far from Fawn's. She'll be living with me more permanently in a very short time. She just doesn't know it yet. I plan on surprising her once it closes, which should be any day as I am paying in cash.

I hear Lala shuffling things around and I grunt. My dick is as hard as granite and standing tall and proud, leaking precum like a champ, waiting for his favorite person to return and finish him off. I think of golfing and sweaty fat men in saunas farting to try and minimize the throbbing in my dick. It helps, a little. Just enough I can calm my breathing until Lala returns.

Which she does.

With a silicone suction cupped tentacle dick sleeve in her pretty little hands.

"Where the hell did you find that?" Pressing up from the bed, I manage to get into a sitting position without falling over.

She grins maniacally. "Found it last week and was just waiting for the right opportunity to use it." She rolls it in her palms, thumbing the suckers of pink and teal. The colors remind me of her pink hair and aquamarine eyes. I wonder why it never occurred to me before.

"It's not mine. The guys sent it as a gag gift. They won't admit it, but I know they did it."

"Did they?" Her head cocks to the side, soft pink locks falling over one shoulder, and her grin curls at the edges. She looks like the grinch who knows a secret none of the other Whos can see. "Are you sure about that?"

"Not anymore, I'm not. Why do you look like you already knew I had this?"

"Because the twins and I may have gone on a drunken sex toy

shopping spree and sent you the kinkiest things we could find." Holding up the tentacle, she jiggles it in the air. "This one was Pilar's pick. Mine was the pony play butt plug and riding crop. Which by the way, you have my permission to use. At will."

My dick twitches and thumps angrily between my legs. "Fucking hell. Just the crop, or the plug too?"

"Would you like to use the plug?" She steps closer, painfully slowly, crossing her legs and stepping silently on bare feet. I want to lick her from top to bottom and spank that teasing little ass of hers with that crop. But I sit still... well, as still as possible. My dick won't stop pulsing and twitching with each step that brings her closer.

"Maybe."

"I'll let you use the plug if you let me use the tentacle." She licks her lips and another bead of precum drips from my tip.

"Pinky promise?" Her grin nearly doubles at my use of her favorite type of contract.

Bending at the waist and teasing me with her cleavage, she extends out her pinky and wiggles it at me. "Pinky promise."

I accept her offer, and her giggle is sweet and high pitched, and in my heightened state of arousal goes straight to my balls, and my heart. Her smile and laugh always stick me right in my chest. I think I would actually die if I didn't get to see it every day. Right now, she's giving me her "I knew you would give in" smile. I totally am.

She lathers up the tentacle with lube before kneeling before me again. This time though, the pink and teal monster tentacle in hand. She slips my tip in, and the sensation of the suckers rubbing against my hard length is, I hate to admit this, fucking amazing. She doesn't relent and inch by inch slides my dick inside the monster tentacle. And fuck me, it actually is pleasurable.

My fingers grip the comforter under me, and Lala slides the tentacle up and down my shaft, the tip prodding up against the narrow end of the tentacle. My head drops back against my shoulders, and it only takes a dozen or so strokes and I'm coming. HARD. All the edging and delay has me so aroused, I nearly black out. My dick pulses and thumps against the silicone sleeve in Lala's hand as I keep coming.

A guttural growl escapes my chest, and the pressure that's been plaguing me the last twenty God damn minutes is finally relieved, as I spill and spill into the silicone sex toy.

Lala's lips press against the inside of my leg, mere inches from my balls, and I shiver.

"Good boy," she coos against my groin.

"Isn't that supposed to be my line?"

She laughs against my shaft still semi hard in the sleeve and fuck me if it doesn't start making me hard all over again. How is that even possible after the orgasm I just had?

Gently gripping her wrist that holds the tentacle, I slip it, and her hand, from my cock. She drops it to the floor, and I don't even care if my cum drips onto my floor. That's what Clorox is for. Slipping my hands under her arms, I lift her to the bed and toss her down on her back. Covering her body with mine, I press a kiss between her breasts.

"My turn."

The End

Acknowledgements

First, to my mother for being the weird mom and making up gummy bear orgies in the first place. Who knew it would lead to this one day? Certainly not me. Also, if you read this book, just keep it to yourself. Because now you know how much of a perv I am, and there's no need to discuss it further.

To my BETA's who pointed out when Lala went to the bathroom and didn't wash her hands and let me know they really wanted Henry to buy Lala slippers.

To Natalie aka Speckled Plum for the beautiful artwork that brings this series to life. These are the cutest gummy bears ever!

Finally, to my husband for all his continued support and for never reading my books. He'd probably choke on his own spit if he knew what I really wrote.

For more information on Rebecca's books please visit her
website at
www.rebeccarennickauthor.com

There will be more to come in the Gummy Bear Orgy Series

About the Author

Rebecca Rennick, known to her friends as Becca was born in California but has since converted into a Floridian. Along with her husband, two dogs and a cat. With love for both horror films and the Hallmark Channel, she can be a little dark and creepy while wearing all pastel pink. Growing up in the theater led to her studying fashion in San Francisco where she received a BFA in fashion design. Which only added to her overly massive collection of clothing. She has many obsessions such as tattoos on herself and others. As well as an unhealthy desire to see the entire world. Her only other true passion is eating. She loves to try everything at least once, no matter if she knows what it is or not. You only have one life and you might as well try it all. Except meth, don't try meth.

Lightning Source UK Ltd.
Milton Keynes UK
UKHW010652090223
416681UK00007B/1990